AND NOW TO-MORROW

By Rachel Field
ALL THIS, AND HEAVEN TOO

By Rachel Field and Arthur Pederson
TO SEE OURSELVES

AND
NOW TO-MORROW

by

RACHEL FIELD

And, when the stream
Which overflowed the soul was passed away,
A consciousness remained that it had left,
Deposited upon the silent shore
Of memory, images and precious thoughts
That shall not die, and cannot be destroyed.
WORDSWORTH.

COLLINS
48 PALL MALL LONDON
1943

THIS BOOK IS SET IN FONTANA, A NEW TYPE FACE DESIGNED
FOR THE EXCLUSIVE USE OF THE HOUSE OF COLLINS, AND
PRINTED BY THEM IN GREAT BRITAIN

First Impression	-	-	-	-	January, 1943
Second „	-	-	-	-	March, 1943

COLLINS CLEAR-TYPE PRESS : LONDON AND GLASGOW

TO
ROSALIE STEWART
WHOSE FRIENDSHIP BEGAN
"AT THE JUNCTION"

AUTHOR'S NOTE

The place, action, and characters of this book are purely fictional. There is no Vance method of treatment to restore hearing, nor is the theory based on any actual medical findings.

CHAPTER ONE

IT WAS years since I had set foot in the ell storeroom. But yesterday Aunt Em sent me there on an errand, and the souvenirs I came upon have disturbed me ever since, teasing my mind with memories that persist like fragments of old tunes.

There is a fascination in places that hold our past in safe keeping. We are drawn to them, often against our will. For the past is a shadow grown greater than its substance, and shadows have power to mock and betray us to the end of our days. I knew it yesterday in that hour I spent in the storeroom's dusty chillness, half-dreading, half-courting the pangs which each well-remembered object brought.

So we sigh, perhaps, at the mute and stringless guitar with its knot of yellow ribbon bleached pale as a dandelion gone to seed. So we smile at the tarnished medal that set the heart pounding under the dress folds where it was once pinned. So we tremble or flush again at the flimsy favours and dance programmes with their little dangling pencils and scribbled names.

"Now *who* was he?" we ask ourselves, puzzling over some illegible name. "I must have liked him very much to save him the first and the last dance."

And the old photographs in albums and boxes! It takes fortitude to meet the direct gaze of a child whose face is one's own in innocent embryo. It is hard to believe that the shy young woman with the sealskin muff is one's mother at nineteen beside a thin, merry-eyed young man whose features bear a faint resemblance to one's father. Their youth and gaiety are caught fast on this bit of cardboard all these years after that winter day when they sat for their pictures at the Junction photographer's. Here am I, a child of two between them, and here again at four with my arms about year-old Janice and the clipped French poodle Bon-bon pressing close to my knees. That was the summer I first

7

remember the big lawns and trees and high-ceilinged rooms of Peace-Pipe and all the curious New England relatives who peered at us. They asked questions that must be answered politely in English, not the French which Bon-Bon and I understood most easily. He and I still look bewildered in the picture, but Janice is completely at ease in her embroidered Paris dress and bonnet. Yes, there we are—Bon-Bon who has been still for years now under the thorn-tree at the foot of the garden; Janice whose round baby eyes give no hint of the defiance I was to see there at our last meeting, and I, who will never again fit into those slippers with crossed straps or face a camera or the world with so steadfast a look.

Once when I was a child Father told me of a great scientist who could take a single bone in his hands and from that reconstruct the whole skeleton of the animal to which it had belonged. I wondered, standing alone in that jumble of possessions, among dangling clothes, old books, and discarded furniture, whether there might be any one wise enough to reconstruct from these remnants the likeness of a family. Yet perhaps out of such very clutter some pattern does emerge if one has the insight to ferret out the faults and virtues, the hopes and shortcomings, the loves and loyalties of one such household. Merek Vance would have the wisdom and patience to do that if any one could. But Merek Vance is three thousand miles away and busy with research of a very different sort. Besides, he would only smile and shrug in the way I know so well, and say that the ell storeroom and its contents are my problem.

He knows that I do not like problems, that I have sometimes lacked courage to accept the challenge of those that belong peculiarly to me. I shunned problems whether they took the form of choosing between a sleigh-ride party and a trip to Boston, or happened to be inside an arithmetic book and concerned men papering imaginary rooms or digging wells that required an exact knowledge of yards and feet and fractions. The same inner panic seized me yesterday when I opened a worn algebra and met those dread spectres of my schooldays, *a* and *b* and their mysterious companion *x* that for me always remained an unknown quantity. Well, I know now that this unknown quantity is something to be reckoned with outside the covers of an algebra. I have learned that it can rise up out of nowhere to change the sum total of our lives.

There were plenty of old schoolbooks on the storeroom shelves, books with Janice's name and mine on thumb-marked fly-leaves. In one I had written in a prim vertical hand the familiar jargon:

> Emily Blair is my name,
> America my nation,
> Blairstown, Mass., my dwelling place,
> And heaven my destination.
>
> *September 19th, 1921.*

I must have been fourteen when I penned that, barely a dozen years ago. Yet "heaven" is a word I seldom write or take for granted nowadays. In this year 1933 I am not so confident of my dwelling-place or my destination.

Another book that bore my name was a Latin grammar, with pencilled jottings on margins and exercises on folded sheets of paper. I used to be rather good at Latin, though it never occurred to me then that truth or meaning might lie behind the phrases I laboured to translate. But as I pored over the pages again they began to take on life and significance. Once, I realised, people had used this tongue to speak to one another, to write words warm with affection or heavy with despair. A phrase held me as I turned the pages: "Forsan et haec olim meminisse juvabit." My lips repeated the words. I wrestled with their meaning as one struggles to move the key in some rusty lock. At last I had it: "Perhaps it will be pleasant to remember even these things." I knew then that it was not some whim of chance that had sent me to the storeroom, that had guided my hand to that book and my eye to that particular phrase.

In the life of each of us, I told myself, there comes a time when we must pause to look back and see by what straight or twisting ways we have arrived at the place where we find ourselves. Instinct is not enough, and even hope is not enough. We must have eyes to see where we missed this turn or that, and where we struggled through dark thickets that threatened to confound us. I know that I have arrived at such a time.

Some day, it may be, I shall tie a handkerchief round my hair and take a broom and duster and set to work clearing out the storeroom. But I must take stock of myself before I am ready for that. I rebelled against returning to this house and the querulous wants of a tired old woman and a middle-aged man with time heavy on their hands. But I am rebellious no longer. Old times, old feelings, old hurts, old loves, and old losses must be sorted and weighed and put in order as well as outworn mementoes. We cannot simply close the door upon them and forget what lies behind it. We cannot let bitterness gather there like a layer of dust.

I fumble awkwardly for words as I sit here at this desk where I have so often dashed off schoolgirl essays full of glib phrases; where I have penned letters marred with self-pity and despair. I am done with all that now. Once I considered myself a very important person in my own world. Now I know that I matter less perhaps in the scheme of things than the tireless, pollen-dusted bee ; than the mole, delving in darkness; than the inchworm that measures its infinitesimal length on a grass-blade.

I don't pretend to know what I believe beyond this— that nothing which lives and breathes and has its appointed course under the sun can be altogether insignificant. Some trace remains of what we have been, of what we tried to be, even as the star-shaped petals of the apple blossom lie hidden at its core; even as the seed a bird scatters in flight may grow into the tree which shall later shelter other birds. And so, those whose names I write here—Aunt Em, Uncle Wallace, Janice, Harry, Old Jo and young Jo Kelly, Maggie, Dr. Weeks, Merek Vance, and I—all of us are changed in some measure, each because of the others. Our flesh and blood, our nerves and veins and senses have responded under this old roof to forces and currents that we shall never be able to explain. We are scattered now, and what we did and what we said will be forgotten soon. It will fade into the unreality of old photographs, like those I stared at yesterday in the storeroom.

I shall begin with the river because without it there would have been no busy Blairstown, with its bridges above and below the falls; there would have been no mills and no bleacheries, no pulsing machinery, no smoking chimneys gaunt against the winter sky or thrusting their darkened tops through summer's dominant green. There would be no reason for trains between Boston and Portland to stop at the brick station with its black-lettered sign above the familiar trademark of the Indian War Bonnet and Pipe and the words that encircle them: "Peace-Pipe Industries."

No one thought it an ironical name until lately. Four generations of American households have known the pipe and feathers and the legend they carry on sheets and pillow-cases and towels the country over: "Peace-Pipe for Quality." It was Great-grandfather Blair who made famous those four words and the product of his mill. But it was a hundred years before his time that the first Blair had made his peace with the Wawickett Indians. Their name alone has survived them in the bright, rushing waters of the river where they fished and paddled their canoes.

More than anything else in Blairstown; more even than this big stone house that rose on the foundations of the first unpretentious family farm, the river is bound up with my childhood. I cannot remember my first sight of it, for I was less than two when Father and Mother brought me back from France to be displayed to my New England relatives. Father used to swear that even then the river had a queer power over me. He would stand on the bridges and lift me up in his arms, and I would stare, spellbound, at the torrent of shining water that fell endlessly, and at the fierce steaming, churning whiteness of the rapids below. In other summers when we returned and Janice was the baby to be held aloft, I would stand peering through gaps in the stonework, never tiring of the liquid drama that went on without beginning or end.

Father was amused and tolerant of my passion for the river, and Aunt Em openly gloated over my preference, but Mother did not seem altogether pleased. She died before I was seven, and so she must always remain for me a dim figure in rustling skirts, with a voice that kept unpredictable accents and cadences because she had learned to speak first in Polish. If we children happened to be with her when we crossed the bridges, she always hurried us over, ignoring my pleas for "just one more little look." Only once I remember prevailing upon her to pause there, and I have never forgotten the occasion. She stayed so quiet at my side that her silence at last made me curious. Though I was young to notice such things, I was struck by the expression of her face as I peered up into it. She was not looking either at me or at the seething water. Instead she stayed still as stone staring over at the mills and the chimneys and the small brick and wood houses where the millhands and their families lived. Her eyes had grown dark in the soft, pale oval of her face. They held a remoteness that chilled me.

"Mamma!" I tugged at her hand. "Don't look over there at the ugly side."

My words brought her eyes back to me, and she answered in her slow, rich voice that blurred softly where words met.

"So you feel shame for that already, my little Emily! But don't worry. You are safe on your side of the river. You're all Blair."

I was to hear that last remark many times afterwards. But as often as it has been said, I can never hear it without thinking of that day on the bridge when my early complacency met its first shock. There we stood together, hand in hand, yet we had hurt each other. The river, shining in the summer sun, and the smoky bulk of the mills with those small crowded houses and yards full of washing, were somehow all part of what had come between us.

Often and often I think of it, until sometimes the Wawickett River becomes more than a hurrying stream that has furnished the power for Peace-Pipe Industries and brought prosperity to our family. It has become a symbol to me, as it must have been to my mother that day. For in spite of its bridges the river did then and does now mark the boundary between secure and precarious living ; between the humble and the proud. Some may cross from one side to the other as my mother did; as young Jo Kelly was to do years after. And there are a few, like me, who stand on the span of its bridges, knowing that we belong to both— troubled and uncertain because we cannot renounce all of one side for all of the other.

CHAPTER TWO

"ALWAYS do what's expected of you, Emily," Father used to say, watching me with eyes narrowed in a habit acquired by years of painting. "I never learned the trick, but it saves a lot of trouble in the end."

No, Father never did what was expected of him, but perhaps it wasn't altogether his fault. Every one expected almost too much of Father, and he was born wanting to please every one he met. He made people happy too easily; and by the same token he disappointed them, because no one can please everybody all the time. He was the oldest of those three Blairs, the handsome, clever one of the family. Aunt Em came next to him—tall, and serious and distinguished-looking even before she was full-grown. She had inherited the Blair shrewdness for business, along with the Blair stubborn streak and the Blair energy. It's a pity that her passion for activity couldn't have been directed as successfully as the Wawickett River's forces had been harnessed into power for the mills. Uncle Wallace came last in order of age and importance, a position he has maintained ever since.

Always he has been referred to as "the other Blair brother." He has never seemed to resent this. I think it's all he ever wanted to be. A pleasant, uncommunicative

man, contented with the mill routine, occasional business
trips, his golf, and his collection of stamps, Uncle Wallace
has fitted himself into the scheme of life to which he was
born better than any of us. He hasn't Aunt Em's will
to fight against the current. He asked little of life and has
paid the penalty of those who ask that; for even that little
has been taken away from him.

But with Father it was different always. His good looks
and gifts marked him from boyhood. Yet he managed,
miraculously, not to be spoiled, and he was never taken
in by himself. Therein lay his salvation. It was also the
reason why he never became a first-rate artist. Tolerant
of others' work, he was ruthless when it came to judging
his own. And so his vigour and friendship poured out in all
directions, enriching those whose genius bore the fruit he
was often the first to recognise. In the memoirs of his con-
temporaries, painters, writers, and musicians living in those
more leisurely years of the early 1900's, Father's name
slips in and out like some comforting and casual tune. I like
to come upon it and know that he mattered more than the
canvases that bear his name in the corner and that will
never bring a price worth mentioning.

"Want to come in the studio and play being a model?"

Those were words I loved to hear, and I always sprang
to answer the invitation. Father had a flair for catching
likeness. The best things he painted are portraits of Mother
and of us as children. I never tired of sitting for him in
the high, littered studios he made so completely his own,
whether he inhabited them for a year or a month. I can
see his big left thumb hooked into the hole of the palette
where he had squeezed brilliant daubs of vermilion and
cobalt and burnt sienna. His right hand held the long
brushes with a strength and delicacy I shall never forget.
He seldom talked when he painted, but he used to hum
in deep, contented monotony like bees in an apple orchard
in May. That pleasant rumble is bound up in my mind
with Father and his studio. It will always be part of the
smell of turpentine and linseed oil and the tobacco in the

pipe he smoked; part of the image of a tall man with eyes as blue as his paint-spattered smock.

Janice can barely recall the studio days, though she says she remembers the afternoon receptions and evening gatherings when we would be carried from bed in our nightgowns to be displayed to the guests. I was never the success that Janice used to be on these occasions, though I was much more dependable when plates of refreshments were entrusted to our passing. Janice needed no encouragement to dance in her white nightgown and red slippers. She was always applauded; and no wonder, for she was a captivating sprite with her fair hair tumbled on her shoulders and falling into her eyes that shone as dark and bright as blackberries. She was the despair of those who tried to catch her on canvas, for she was changeable as quicksilver. I was considered quaint and paintable with my solemn blue eyes and brown straight bangs.

"That one," people would remark, "is her grandfather Blair all over again. Too bad she couldn't have been a boy to carry on the family name as well as the family features."

Once again Father had failed in what was expected of him. Having married a Polish girl worker in the mills and having abandoned the family business, at least he might have provided a son instead of two daughters. But he didn't seem to mind, and from the day I was brought back to wear the Blair christening robe and be called by her name, Aunt Em accepted the marriage and Mother.

"You couldn't wonder he fell for her," Maggie told me once when I questioned her about that match which had been the talk of the country. "When a Polack girl's beautiful she puts the come-hither on a man once and for all."

"The come-hither, Maggie?" I persisted, for I was still very young and curious. "What's that?"

"You'll know right enough some day."

That was all I could ever get out of Maggie on the subject, but I know now how it must have been that day when my father saw my mother sliding down a long patch of ice by the mill gates. The story has taken on the quality of a

legend all these years afterwards. It was closing time, and
the workers were thronging out in the November dusk,
chattering and jostling one another as I have seen them so
often at that hour, a human torrent of youth and animal
high spirits. Skirts were longer in those days, and there
were shawls and braids and thick coils of hair instead of
berets and bright scarfs over permanently waved, bobbed
heads. But the effect must have been much the same then as
now. Father had been out of college for several years, and
the mill routine had been growing more and more irksome.
His heart wasn't in the business. Besides, he was already set
on his painting. In the mill workers he saw living models
that he longed to put on canvas. I don't mean that he was
indifferent to some Polish or Lithuanian girl's good looks,
any more than the other men in the office. But he had an
artist's eye for line and colour as well as masculine apprecia-
tion of a curved body, full lips, or trim ankles.

It was fate, or destiny, or just plain good luck that
singled Mother out from the rest that winter day. The
closing whistle had blown, and Father stood by a window
watching the girls hurrying through the millyard. Ice had
formed round one of the exhaust pipes. There was a smooth
frozen stretch below it. Suddenly a girl broke away from
the rest and took it in one long, graceful slide. It was the
most simple, spontaneous response that he had ever seen,
he said afterward. Though he couldn't see her face for the
gathering twilight, he couldn't forget the free sure motion
of her body, with arms held out to keep the balance true, or
the way her warm breath streamed out in the chillness
under a red knitted shawl that wrapped her head like the
crest on a woodpecker.

That was how it began—strange and improbable enough
to be the climax of some old-fashioned romance in paper
covers. Father must have been born a romantic, but he
must have had his share of the Blair persistence to carry
the courtship through. Certainly Mother gave him very
small encouragement. She had scruples against accepting
attentions from the millowner's obviously admiring son.

Lots of girls had set their caps for Father, and he was well aware of that. It made him cautious at picnics and dances and house parties. Perhaps it made him all the more vulnerable to this girl with her foreign name and speech and her self-guarded beauty. Even more than the heavy coils of light brown hair, the soft oval face and wide-set dark eyes, it was this quality of personal dignity in her that must have stirred and held him.

Well, in love there's no choosing, and Father and Mother were ready for love and each other. I shall never know when they first answered the summons; when they first guessed what had taken possession of their separate lives, drawing them so surely and inexorably together. I shall never be able to conjure up what passed between them during the months when each struggled to keep an impossible freedom. But I can picture how it may have been as they met, day after day, while the building vibrated about them and the mill machinery throbbed like a gigantic pulse. It must have seemed almost a magnified echo of their own pulses and the beating of their two quickened hearts. Yes, that is how I like to think it may have been—shuttles weaving, bobbins twisting, threads like millions of humming harp strings, fine-spun about them. And so they became part of the pattern of life, which may not vary its design, though the two who give themselves to its making are always new.

Afterwards, when Aunt Em had accepted the marriage, she made rather a point of stressing Mother's background. Polish, yes, but far from the ordinary run of millgirls. Helena Jeretska came of good stock. Her father had been a music teacher, and her mother had had a fair education. Both had died in a typhoid epidemic shortly after landing in Boston, and another immigrant family of quite a different type had taken the child and brought her up with their own. Somehow they had drifted to Blairstown and the mills. Mother had gone to work there at seventeen.

"Oh, yes," I can almost hear Aunt Em saying, "she's quite pretty, almost beautiful in a different sort of way. I

think Elliott expects to spend his life painting her. Well,
naturally, it's hard to have him go so far away, but Paris
is the place for artists. It's not as if the business had ever
been congenial to him, and Wallace and I can do our part.
Peace-Pipe Mills have always been family-run, and I trust
they always will be."

It never took Aunt Em long to recover from any shock.
I wasn't born till two years after she met that one, but I've
seen her take a good many since. I know the set of her
head and lips and the old rallying phrases she summons for
times of need. Only lately have I known her to admit defeat,
and she has never accepted it. Even now with her once
active body stiff and restricted of motion, I can tell that she
believes in the power of her own will to accomplish the
inevitable. I am reminded of a picture in an old history
book—King Canute sitting in state with salt waves breaking
about his feet, commanding the tide to turn back.

Aunt Em will resist the encroaching tides of change right
up to her last breath, and I love her for it. For all the
difference in our ages she is younger than I in some respects.
She has not learned what I am only just now beginning to
understand—that no matter how hard and faithfully we
may try we can never compensate another for some lack
in his or her life.

In my own case this sense of obligation came about
naturally through the circumstances that followed Mother's
tragic death the summer I was seven. She had been fatally
injured in a motor accident that spring in Paris, and Father
moved in a daze of despair during those days when doctors
and nurses fought hopelessly to keep her alive. Father was
like a stranger to Janice and me for a long time. His new
black coat didn't smell comfortingly of paint and tobacco,
and we were glad when men came to crate the canvases
and pack furniture and when our things were put in trunks
and sent to the ship that would take us back to America.
We missed Mamma, but our minds were full of the thought
of Peace-Pipe. We longed to see how our big brown poodle,
Bon-Bon, looked after a winter without us. We wanted

to be back before the lilacs were past blooming and in plenty of time to pick wild strawberries in the meadows on the outskirts of town. Father seemed to care little for important things like that, though he was very indulgent of us on the crossing.

One occasion on the voyage I recall with peculiar distinctness. It was the night of the captain's dinner, and Father had promised that I might sit up later than my usual bedtime to watch the people in evening dress go down to the dining-saloon. I was ready long before the dinner hour, and to quiet my impatience Father took me on deck. We sat very close together watching the last fiery shreds of cloud dim as the steamer throbbed on tirelessly through darkening water. It was exciting as if Father and I had escaped to some far and secret place. The tones of his deep voice when he spoke to me out of the dimness were all part of that night, giving emphasis to his words.

He had been speaking of Peace-Pipe and Aunt Em when suddenly his tone changed.

"This summer won't be like the others," he said. "You and Janice are going to be Aunt Em's little girls from now on."

I must have trembled or crept closer, for he added quickly:

"Of course you'll always belong most to me, but you mustn't ever let Aunt Em think that. She needs you, and you'll try hard to make her happy, won't you?"

So I promised, filled with a pleasant glow of responsibility. Yet it seemed a queer thing to me then, as it does to me now, that any one should have to try hard for happiness.

CHAPTER THREE

THERE is one day I recollect most clearly from that summer of our return, because it was my seventh birthday and because it was my first meeting with Harry Collins.

From its start the early August day was mine. I ran out barefoot into a world of dew and opening flowers; of robins making little watery calls and splashing at the rim of the lily pool. I measured my seven-year-old height against the vigorous green of hollyhocks by the fence; but, stretch as I might, I could not reach the lowest pink rosette. By the side door a huge old snowball bush bent double under its load of green and white. I crept beneath and felt the cool shock of dew upon me from shaken branches. Myriads of bees were filling it with sound. As I crouched there in the morning stillness they seemed louder and more insistent than I have ever heard them since. That tireless sound made me think of the water going over the Falls; like the throbbing mill machinery when it came distantly from across the river.

Butterflies and birds were everywhere as well as bees. Droning or darting or drifting, they passed me on invisible currents of air. I was aware of them wherever I moved. There was an intensity to their busyness that made me a little in awe of them. They went about their work as if the world were coming to an end at sunset. I think something of the fierce urgency of their frail bodies must have been imparted to my young self that day to make me remember the shape and colour and sound of each moment as I do these years afterward.

The trumpet vine that covered the side porch is gone now, but I can still see the miraculous spinning of a hummingbird above it. I knew that its wings were a rainbow whirl because they revolved so fast, yet they gave an illusion of stillness, and the long bill seemed held fast to the magnet of a trumpet flower. I stood there, elated and alone, with my bare feet rooted to wet earth. Some vigorous, sweet essence of summer and sun flowed through me in that moment of breathless watching.

"Happy birthday, Em'ly," Janice called down from an upper window, and the spell was shattered.

Then breakfast, with waffles and honey and packages to open, claimed me. Father had gone to Boston, but he had promised to be back on an afternoon train in time for my party. I knew there would be more presents in his arms, and meantime there were plenty to keep me busy— a new doll and carriage and a boat with sails that could really put to sea in the waters of the lily pool. I much preferred it to the blue enamel locket that had belonged to Aunt Em when she was a little girl, but, remembering my promise to Father, I tried to let her think that was my favourite present.

Uncle Wallace let us walk to the bridge with him, and when we returned old Jo Kelly and young Jo, his grandson, were waiting to wish me happy birthday. They lived in quarters over the stable. Old Jo had been gardener on the place as long as Father could remember. He had a bouquet of flowers for me, and young Jo had brought three alley marbles and a tin soldier.

"You can play he's captain," he suggested when he saw the new boat. "He don't stand very good alone, but you can lash him to the mast."

We wanted young Jo to play with the new boat, but he went off to help his grandfather haul fertiliser. They worked side by side, those two, the best of cronies for all the sixty-odd years' difference between them. Young Jo's parents had died when he was a baby, and he had always lived with his grandfather.

Even then there was something to be reckoned with about young Jo Kelly. Gay and good-natured though he was for the most part, he could summon up furies that were terrifying to behold. I have seen his blue eyes darken and his lips turn white when he pleaded with his grandfather not to set traps for the moles that were ruining our lawns.

His hands were clever at unfastening traps. If rabbits or squirrels or mice could have given testimonials, then young Jo Kelly's name would surely have been blessed. Aunt Em, I remember, once had a long conversation with him on the subject of ridding the place of English sparrows. He listened quietly through her explanation that they were noisy, dirty pests who drove the songbirds away. But her arguments left him unconvinced.

"Sparrows are just as human as any other kind of bird," he told her firmly, and for once Aunt Em had no answer.

My party began on the stroke of four when the Parker twins, Nancy and Joan, appeared, bringing their cousin who had arrived that morning. His name was Harry Collins, and he was older than the rest of us by several years. I can see him now as he looked coming up our drive in his white sailor suit with a twin on either side in pink and blue dresses. The sun made his sandy hair look redder than it really was, and he walked easily with an air of being on very good terms with the world. The twins carried gifts, conspicuously displayed, but he came empty-handed.

"Hallo," he called when they were within hailing distance, and I saw that his eyes were hazel with gold flecks that matched the freckles on his nose. "How old are you?" he demanded pleasantly.

"Seven to-day," I explained.

"Seven's nice," he encouraged me. "Wait till you get to be ten."

"Are you ten?" I ventured.

"Well, practically," he amended.

"Not till after Christmas," the twins chorused. "You only have a right to say you're *going-on* ten."

"'Practically' means the same thing," he insisted, and once more he smiled at me.

When Harry Collins smiled one seldom questioned his statements. He turned a not very expert handspring on the grass while we four little girls watched admiringly. If he made a mistake he somehow convinced you that it had been intentional, merely a delightful variation from the usual pattern.

We were joined just then by Jim and Lolly Wood from across the Square, and by the time I had opened their presents young Jo Kelly had appeared from the back garden, more scrubbed and combed than I had ever seen him.

"Who's the kid?" Harry Collins eyed young Jo critically.

I felt uncertain just how to explain him. Young Jo Kelly we had always taken for granted without classification. Yet I knew that he did not usually rate parties.

"Oh, he lives down there," I answered evasively, pointing vaguely in the direction of the garden.

I was glad that Maggie and Aunt Em appeared just then to supervise a hunt for presents hidden in the shrubbery. After that we played hide-and-seek, and it was then that I found the injured chipmunk under the big hemlock.

Bon-Bon, our French poodle, really made the discovery. I heard his excited barks, and by the time I reached him the tawny ball of fur with dark and light stripes was electric with fright. My first impulse was to pick it up, but Bon-Bon's behaviour made me hesitate. I seized him by the collar instead, and it took all my strength to hold him back. The others ran up, attracted by the barkings and my cries. Harry Collins reached us first and bent over the chipmunk, which had begun to make terrified chitterings and to bare sharp little teeth.

"Gee, look at it spit!" he cried. "Get him in a box quick, and then we'll have a pet squirrel."

But Harry had reckoned without young Jo Kelly.

"You leave that chipmunk be," he ordered. "Can't you see it's hurt?"

"Then it'll be all the better in a box. We can crack nuts for it, and——"

Young Jo pulled him away.

"Don't you touch him," he said. "They always die if you shut 'em up."

"He'll die if the dog gets him."

"Sure." Jo was growing exasperated. "We've got to get him back up there."

He pointed to the hemlock, but just then Bon-Bon made another lunge, and I all but lost my grip on his collar. When I looked up again I saw a brown fist double and strike out. It thudded against Harry Collins's face, and though he was so much bigger than young Jo, the sudden surprise of the blow made him stagger back. The next moment Jo stooped down, stuffed the chipmunk into the front of his shirt and made for the lower branches of the hemlock. Up and up he went, hand over hand, while we all watched from below and I still clung to Bon-Bon.

"He hit Harry," the twins kept saying. "He hit him right in the face, at a party too."

"Jo Kelly's got no business coming to parties, anyhow," I heard Lolly Wood protesting. "His grandfather's just your gardener, isn't he?"

The dog's barking gave me an excuse not to answer, and Aunt Em was calling as she hurried to us across the lawn: "Children, children, what on earth is all the racket about? Leave that dog, Emily, and come here."

But I hung on. I wasn't going to let Bon-Bon leap against the tree while young Jo was balanced precariously up there among the spiked boughs. He had climbed to a place where he could brace his feet between two branches and while he held on with one hand I saw him fumbling in his shirt with the other. I saw him take something out and reach up and up with the branch he clung to sagging under his hold. Suddenly he gave a sharp cry and then he was slipping and clutching frantically to keep his hold. Before any of us could move or cry out he came crashing through a shower of twigs and green needles to lie in a heap at our feet.

Every one began to cry and run after that. I let Bon-Bon go free and dashed off to hunt for old Jo Kelly. By the time I had found him and we reached the hemlock-tree again Maggie had taken charge with wet cloths and spirits of ammonia.

My birthday party ended with less festivity than it had begun. We were hustled off to the arbour to eat our ice cream and cake with strict orders to keep out of the house and not to ask questions.

"Send them home as soon as you can, Maggie," we heard Aunt Em say. "Mr. Elliott's just back and I've sent him after Dr. Wells."

We gulped great spoonfuls of ice cream and talked in excited whispers. Later we stood at the gate in a subdued little group.

"Good-bye," the twins said politely. "It was a nice party, and we had a lovely time."

"You asked us from four to six, and it's only a quarter to," Lolly Wood said reproachfully as they turned to go.

"So long, kid," Harry Collins laughed through the fence at me. "I'll be seeing you."

"My birthday'll be next," Janice was saying beside me. "You won't have another for a whole year."

"Mine's not over yet," I reminded her.

But I felt low-spirited because the party had been spoiled before it was over and because young Jo had been hurt. The sun had slipped to the level of the lawns, lighting them to a strange clear green, deeper than the emerald in Aunt Em's ring. The frogs had begun to grunt in their deep guttural under the lily pads in the pool, and birds made sleepy-sounding calls that filled me with a sadness I could not explain or share. Morning with its shimmering promise seemed years ago. I did not care when Janice pounced on a forgotten package and claimed it for her own.

Upstairs in the room where they had carried young Jo I could hear the murmur of voices and sometimes a long, whimpering cry. Then it grew suddenly quieter and a queer, sweetish smell drifted down to us.

"Emily! Janice! Where are you?" Aunt Em was calling us as she followed Dr. Weeks out to his car. We ran to her with questions, and she comforted us.

"Young Jo's going to be all right," she explained. "The

doctor has just been setting his leg where he broke it. No, it didn't jurt Jo much—he had a whiff of chloroform, and he slept till the splints were on. We'll keep him in the spare room till he's able to be up and about."

We were allowed to say good-night to young Jo later, conversing through the door. He looked no bigger than a chipmunk himself in the middle of the big carved walnut bed. His voice came faintly from between the pillows.

"He bit me," young Jo explained. "I reached to put him in that hole and he up and bit my thumb."

"That was mean," I said, "when you were only trying to save him."

"Oh, he didn't mean no harm." Jo would never let a word be spoken against anything in fur or feathers. "Chipmunks just get rattled."

Maggie was unusually short when she put Janice and me to bed that night. Her temper had been tried by the afternoon, between the extra work of the party and caring for an unexpected invalid. She seemed inclined to blame me for being the cause of the catastrophe, and she made few responses to our chatter, hurrying us through baths and prayers.

"Now, then, no more mischief," she warned us sternly. "There's been plenty for one day."

"What's mischief, Maggie?" Janice demanded from her bed.

She looked so pretty with her yellow hair shaken round her ruffled gown and her eyes dark and shining in her flushed face that Maggie couldn't stay altogether grim.

"Now, Miss Janice," she remonstrated, "you know what I mean, so you needn't put on the innocent airs. You just remember the mother of mischief's no bigger than a midge's wing."

Janice fell asleep before darkness filled the room. But I watched it creep over the familiar pieces of furniture. I hid my head under the covers when it took my clothes draped over a chair and turned them into terrifying shapes. Outside, the frogs sounded very loud and insistent. Suddenly

I wanted Father to come and tell me that everything was all right. I remembered in that moment that Father had not appeared at my party according to his promise. In the excitement I had forgotten that. Surely he must be back by now. I began to feel very sorry for myself lying awake up there in the darkness. I slipped from bed and felt my way across the room. The doorknob eluded me. I fumbled for it in panic, and tears overwhelmed me before my hands felt the reassuring cold brass.

Downstairs lights were bright, and I could hear voices coming from the back parlour. My bare feet made no noise, and although I was breathing hard I managed to smother my sobs. When I reached the portieres I paused, fearing that there might be visitors. I knew Aunt Em would be mortified to have me burst in on guests, so I listened though I knew that that, too, was strictly against rules.

"But what if there is a war over there?" Uncle Wallace was saying. "That's no reason for you to get mixed up in it."

"Thank your lucky stars you're here with the children, not caught over in the midst of it," Aunt Em's voice broke in.

"Besides"—it was Uncle Wallace speaking again—"they all say it can't possibly last more than three or four weeks."

I heard Father give an impatient grunt before he spoke.

"Believe what you want to," he answered. "I happen to know what France and now England too have got ahead. Every one talked war last year, but no one thought it would come so soon. It's happened, and I know where I belong."

"But, Elliott"—Aunt Em's voice sounded as if she were trying hard not to cry—"you can't really mean what you're saying. There's nothing to take you there and everything to keep you here: your work, your children, and——"

"And Peace-Pipe!" Father gave a short laugh that had no fun in it. "No, Em, the mills will go on, the way they always have. And the children will grow the way children always do, whether I'm here or not. As for my work which you so kindly mention, you know as well as I do that I'm no great shakes of a painter, and ever since I lost Helena——"

He stopped, and there was a sudden silence.

I decided that the time for my entrance had arrived.

"Father!" I cried, and burst through the portieres. "It's my birthday, and you forgot to come up and wish me many happy returns."

CHAPTER FOUR

OCTOBER took over New England with a fierce brightness I had never known before. After those first frosty nights the hills round Blairstown were a riot of colour. It seemed to me that the orange and red and yellow and russet trees stood out in the strong fall sunshine like the bright daubs of wet paint Father used to squeeze on his palette. But whenever I looked across the river the brilliance was subdued by a haze of smoke from Peace-Pipe chimneys.

It was then that I first noticed how swiftly night comes to New England mill towns. Even before the sun drops its fiery red ball, the smoke has settled down to make a mock twilight of its own. It seemed to me then, as it does still, that night came less from the sky than from those great chimneys across the river. It was as if the great throbbing presence, breathing out smoke and steam, had power to hasten night and shorten day. If Father had stayed with us I might have talked to him of this, and then the fancy would have taken less hold upon my imagination. But Father had left for France soon after my birthday, and we were full of the importance of his going. People listened with a flattering attention not usually given to children when we explained his absence.

"My father's a poilu," Janice would announce to every one we met. "He's a soldier in the war."

"But not exactly a soldier," a year or so later I was to supplement out of my fund of information. "He's an artist, and he paints ships and guns and airplanes so they won't get hit. He's in the camouflage division."

I felt superior, knowing such a difficult word and what it meant. I took pride in using it at school when teachers called on me to recite for visitors. It was a private school, not the public primary school young Jo Kelly attended.

He had spent a month in our guest room and those weeks had made him part of the family. He and I were always full of secret projects, and when he returned to the rooms above the stable I missed him. Aunt Em had grown very fond of the little boy with his unpredictable ways and quaint manner of speech. I heard her tell Maggie that she would have kept him there for good except that old Jo would have been too lonely without him.

There's a proverb that says "every house is a world," and so it was with ours. It kept pace in its smaller way with the world that was rocking and reeling overseas. Horror and shock and fear came with the newspaper that lay each morning and evening on the doorstep. "Boche," "Hun," "atrocities," "dugouts," "bombardment"—these and other words lost their strangeness, we heard them discussed so often. Aunt Em organised committees that fall, and each had something to do with the war. There were evening meetings when men and women filled our parlours on either side of the hall and overflowed into the dining-room and back study. Speakers came to talk about relief work in France and Belgium and Poland. Janice and I crouched in our nightclothes on the landing to hear snatches of the talk. The German army, we learned, had marched through Belgium and France, almost as far as Paris, and they had blown up whole towns and shelled cathedrals and done things which must be terrible because of the queer, hushed way people spoke of "atrocities" and because they evaded definite explanations of the word. We gathered little by little that it was all the fault of the Kaiser with his fierce upturned moustache. He had started the war, and so we were allowed to scratch his picture with pins whenever we came across it in the newspapers. Gradually we grew used to Father's absence, though his soft felt hat still hung on the hall-rack, and his paints and brushes and canvases were not disturbed in the third-floor studio. Thanksgiving was hardly over and the last of the mammoth turkey making its exit in hash before snow fell and we began to practise Christmas carols.

Janice, young Jo, and I wavered in eager, ill-matched chorus as we played in the winter-shrouded garden or poured pails of water on a slope behind the house to turn it into a glassy, frozen slide. We sang "O little town of Bethlehem, how still we see thee lie," and "It came upon the midnight clear" and my favourite "O Tannenbaum." Father always used to wake us with that one on Christmas morning. Only now the German words had been banished. But I knew the new ones by heart:

> O hemlock-tree! O hemlock-tree! how faithful are thy
>   branches!
>   Green not alone in summer-time,
>   But in the winter's frost and rime!
> O hemlock-tree! O hemlock-tree! how faithful are thy
>   branches!

I loved those words because I could understand them. Standing there under our snowy hemlock where young Jo had fallen on my birthday, I felt almost that I had made the words up myself. They seemed so true and right as I stared up through branches darkly green against the clear, December skies. All the maples and beeches and elms were swept bare of leaves, and the old apple-trees behind the garden looked more twisted than ever in their wintry nakedness. But the hemlock was richly alive in every needle. It was good that this should be so, and that there was a song to fit it.

Young Jo Kelly and I were united by a tremendous secret. We knew that there wasn't any Santa Claus.

Janice still believed that he came with his reindeer and squeezed down chimneys. We were hardened realists and knew better. But we also knew that to the adult world our faith in the legend was appealing. Older people thought they deceived us with their sly references to the jovial Saint and their hurried hiding of presents when we appeared. Young Jo and I discussed it seriously and decided not to disillusion them even though it required constant watchfulness to keep up our end of the fantasy.

"I've known for a whole year," he boasted when I dared to voice my suspicions. "I kind of thought Gran'pa was fooling me, so I fixed a way to find out for sure; and I did all right."

"How, Jo?"

"Oh, I hung up one stocking same's he said to. Then I hung the other one where Gran'pa didn't know. I figured if there really was a Santa Claus he could find it anywhere."

"Well," I persisted, "and was it empty in the morning?"

"You bet it was."

"You two stop whispering," Janice complained when we compared notes in scepticism. "'Tisn't polite to whisper in front of people, and I'll tell Maggie and Aunt Em on you."

"All right. Go ahead and tell them," I urged her. "And then I'll tell who dropped the silver spoon they can't find down the hall register."

Two days before Christmas Aunt Em and I walked home through the winter twilight after the exercises at my school. There had been Christmas carols and a tree, and I had recited a French poem without faltering once. Aunt Em said she was proud that I remembered every word, and that I could be heard to the back row of chairs. She said it was a pity when children were shy and mumbled their words. I can remember exactly how she looked that afternoon, tall and straight in her sealskin coat. In spite of the cold air her long face stayed the colour of my white coral beads and her smooth brown hair exactly matched the fur of her collar and the small toque she wore. She seemed years older than the other children's mothers, yet she must have been only thirty-five. Our school exercises had taken

on importance simply by her presence. I noticed that the
teachers looked to her for approval when each carol or
poem had been safely accomplished. Used to her as I was,
I had had a sense that day of her place in the community.
She did not need to wear bright colours or stylish clothes
to be the most distinguished visitor.

"There will be another Christmas-tree for you to see to-
morrow," Aunt Em told me as we turned in at our gate.
"It's going to be over at the mills, and you can go with me
if you'd like to."

"Across the river?" I was instantly curious.

Janice had run out to meet us.

"Doesn't Santa Claus cross the bridges?" she wanted to
know.

"Of course, dear," Aunt Em explained. "But so many
more people live over there that we must try to help him."

"But," Janice broke in, "he remembers every one except
the bad children. Are there more bad ones over there?"

"Certainly not!" Aunt Em answered hurriedly. "Now
run upstairs, both of you, and get ready for supper."

That other Christmas-tree across the river, I shall remember as long as I recall anything out of those years.

It stood on a wooden platform that had been raised in
the centre of the millyard with the long brick buildings
on all four sides. On that day before Christmas the closing
whistle had blown at four-thirty instead of six o'clock.
When Aunt Em, Uncle Wallace and I reached the gates
all the machinery was silent, and the great open space was
already teeming with workers and their families. I found
myself peering into old faces wrinkled as walnuts under
shawls or shapeless caps. There were women with babies in
their arms and children of all sizes pressing at their skirts,
and trooping from the buildings where machinery loomed
gigantic against lighted windows, came the millhands,
men, women, and young girls. Although the workers
chattered together in languages I could not understand,
they smiled at me and stepped back to make room for us
to reach the platform.

"This is Elliott's older daughter," Aunt Em introduced me to the group of men on the platform. I made my curtsy and stood quietly beside her, secretly glad that Janice had been considered too young to take part in such an occasion. I tried to stand as straight as Aunt Em in my blue broadcloth coat with the squirrel fur and the round muff that kept my hands warm.

A band with banners that bore the familiar Indian's head and Peace-Pipe name had begun to play a march, and over the deep rhythm of the drums I asked Uncle Wallace when the tree would be lighted.

"Pretty soon now. Want to turn on the switch?"

I nodded eagerly, and he lifted me on a chair and put the electric button attached to a long cord in my hand. I wasn't to press it, he cautioned, till he gave me the signal. I suppose that wait could not have lasted more than ten minutes, but it seemed hours to me perched high above the close-packed crowd, hoping that nothing would go wrong in my part of the ceremonies. First the Catholic priest rose and made a prayer in Latin, and then our minister followed him with another that had to do with Bethlehem and with Peace-Pipe and the Blair family. After that the mill band played "Adeste Fideles," and then it was my turn to make those green and fragrant branches come to life.

As I pressed the button a deep murmur rose in admiration, and heads were lifted to the tree. All the faces were touched by the light from that glowing pyramid of quivering tinsel and coloured bulbs like miraculous fruit. I tilted my head back till I could see the topmost star, set so high that it cleared the smoke that still hung low over the yard and mill buildings.

"Now for the presents," I heard Aunt Em say to Mr. Parker, who was the twins' father and also the mill manager. "I must say I'll be glad when they've been distributed."

"Don't worry, Miss Blair," he promised. "We've got more than enough, and everything's well in hand."

Just then a big red-coated Santa Claus appeared, jingling bells and shouting to invisible reindeer that were supposed

C

to have been left outside the gates. He carried a pack on his shoulders, and his white beard waggled unsteadily with every word he spoke.

"Merry Christmas, one and all!" he began. "This here tree's not big enough to hold what I've brought for the folks at Peace-Pipe. So you'll have to line up and come and get your presents. No pushing, *if* you please. Plenty for all, and keep your places in line. Strike up, boys." And he waved to the band-leader.

He took his place just below the platform, and though I could not see much of his face there was a familiar ring to his voice that puzzled me till I recognised it as belonging to Mr. Dolan, the big Irish night watchman. The band was playing another march, and the distribution of gifts had begun. The hand trucks that wheeled cotton from the storehouse had been loaded with filled baskets and hundreds of red mesh stockings that each contained an orange and an apple, a bag of chocolates, a sugar Santa Claus, and a striped peppermint candy cane. Baskets, with chicken legs and celery tops protruding, as well as each red stocking, were identical as pins in a paper. I turned to Aunt Em with shocked surprise.

"But where are the presents?" I asked under cover of the music and the noise of marshalling the long lines into military order.

"Why, right here," she whispered, and then turned back to her place. She was bowing and smiling as the long line moved forward below the platform.

I stared dizzily down at the hands that reached out for the baskets and the stockings, moving along in an endless stream. I felt cold and disappointed and hollow under my coat.

All the magical glow of Christmas had slipped away into monotony. It might have been a grocery store, I thought, except for the lighted tree that every one seemed to have forgotten except me.

"Aren't there going to be any *real* presents?" I tried once more to distract Aunt Em.

Mr. Parker heard me, and they exchanged an amused look.

"What's the matter with these, Emily?" He bent down and pinched my cold cheek. "A chicken dinner and plenty of candy looks pretty good to me. How about you? Want me to get you one of those stockings?"

But I shook my head. My feet had turned to chill clods, and my eyes swam with weariness. Even if I closed them I could still see the stockings and baskets being handed out. The band had paused to rest, and only the drum thumped on to keep feet moving in time. I drew closer to Aunt Em and plucked at her sleeve. She turned to speak to me, and as she did so a sudden commotion began below us.

There was a break in the slow-moving, orderly line. Then something thudded against the platform. More thuds and ripping sounds followed. One of the candy-filled stockings came hurtling and spilled open at my feet. I saw a man's arms gesturing darkly above the crowd. His voice came hoarse and shrill above the drumbeats.

"Merry Christmas—yah—I rather have job back, not this——"

I could see the man who spoke. He was dark and thick-set, and his black hair had fallen across his eyes. Beside him stood a woman tugging at his waving arms and a little girl and boy. The girl's face was buried in the woman's skirt, but the boy did not turn his face away. His lips were pressed together in a thin line, and his eyes looked directly at me from below the platform. Something about his un-flinching look terrified me more than the man's strange, wild voice crying out again in broken, accusing words.

"You give charitee for Christmas—no want—I rather work——" For a moment the voice was muffled, then it broke out again. "No eat your dinner—we starve first. Chicken an' candy—yah—an' other time you throw me out an' no care!"

They overpowered him at last.

"What you care so long your mill run an' your damn whistle blow?" he shouted back as they dragged him away.

"Merry Christmas—sure—I got hell of Merry Christmas—"

The band struck up loudly and drowned out the rest of his words. Aunt Em's hand tightened on mine. I could feel its cold tenseness through her gloves. Below us the line had closed in again as if nothing had interrupted the ceremonies. But the red candy stocking was still lying where it had fallen at my feet with bits of broken candy like splinters of glass. The shouted words still rang in my ears. They made me shiver and feel afraid.

"What was the matter with that man?" I asked Aunt Em when all the baskets had been given out and we were following Uncle Wallace into his office.

"Try not to think about it," she answered me. "He wasn't—well, he wasn't quite himself."

I was not satisfied.

"He didn't like us," I persisted. "Why didn't he? And why did he throw the things away?"

I heard Aunt Em put in a question and Mr. Parker answer her.

"Vancovitch is the name—good worker, but a crank. Never know when something'll set him off. Had to drop him a couple of months ago, but the wife was sick and there's a family. We thought, seeing it was Christmas, we'd let them in for the distribution. Well, we'll have to tighten up on rules next year. Too bad, but you see where sentiment gets us."

I was very quiet all the way home. The lights and the river and the Christmas wreaths had lost something of their wonder. My happy confidence in gifts and carols and the spirit of good will had been shaken.

"What's a crank, Aunt Em?" I broke silence at last.

We had taken our places at the supper table, and I saw her lay down her spoon and hesitate before she answered.

"Oh"—her eyes met Uncle Wallace's across the table— "it's—well—bad feelings about things that get the better of people sometimes. Go on with your soup, dear."

"That man over at the mill," I persisted, "someone said that's what he is."

"I know, but never mind."

"Now, Em," Uncle Wallace unexpectedly took my part in the discussion, "you can't put the child off like that. She was there and she heard it all, so you'd better answer her questions."

Aunt Em frowned and sighed before she spoke.

"Well, then, if you have to remember what happened at the mill party this afternoon, just say to yourself that sometimes people get all twisted up in their minds about other people——"

"About us? He acted as if he hated us, and he meant me too."

A hurt look came into her eyes, but she went on quietly.

"We can't expect to be praised and liked all the time, no matter if we try to do what seems right to us. You'll find that out, Emily, the older you grow. Sometimes people can't see our side, and sometimes, I suppose, they think we can't see theirs."

Long after I had hung up my stocking beside Janice's by the fireplace, I lay awake in bed remembering another stocking of flimsy red mesh, seeing the shadow of waving arms, hearing a voice that shouted accusing words, the more frightening because they had been half-understood. I have heard others like them since then, but I have never learned to be indifferent to hatred and bitterness, on whichever side of the river they may have been spoken.

CHAPTER FIVE

JANICE and I grew into long-legged schoolgirls in those war-shadowed years. But there was little jubilation in our household when Armistice Day came, for Father had died of pneumonia at a base hospital in France two years earlier. Already his name appeared in memorials at the mill and the church; and the bronze tablet above our pew bore the inscription:

> To the glory of God, and the memory of Elliott Blair, who served in war in order that peace might be preserved, and who died in France, March 12, 1916.
> "There is a way which seemeth right to a man, but the ends thereof are the ways of death."

Somehow I could never connect this father who had become a hero with the humorous, easy-going one of the old studio days. His personality grew dim and brittle like the twisted tubes of paint and the dried colours on the palette he would never hold again.

The years were long and separate then, one from another, though now they blur and mingle in my mind. They have run together the way raindrops will on a pane of window glass.

It is strange to remember how Janice and I lived through them side by side, and yet how surely we grew farther and farther apart with each one that passed. We shared the same room till we had reached our teens. We read the same books, practised at the same piano and went to school and parties together. But always our thoughts and feelings moved in separate paths.

It disturbed Aunt Em's faith in family ties that we two sisters should have so little in common. There had been a deep and close relationship always between herself and her brothers. We were happy, though, in our different ways with trips to Boston for concerts and plays and shopping, and dancing and painting and music lessons besides our school work. I managed to keep at the head of my class, and Janice slipped along in hers.

"It's really a shame to keep Emily in a school like this," I overheard a teacher say to Aunt Em once. I was in the next room sketching a medieval castle on the blackboard to illustrate to-morrow's lesson. "She needs more competition. Have you ever thought of sending her to Blairstown High School?"

"To public school?" I caught a note of shocked surprise in Aunt Em's response.

"I ought not to suggest your changing." The teacher was new at school and evidently worried at what she had said. "I'd probably lose my job to-morrow if you quoted me, but I've watched Emily, and—well, if you're from the best family in a town like this, you get to taking a good deal for granted, to lose initiative. I'd like to see Emily have to exert herself, and she would if she had to hold her own with some of those Polish and Russian and Irish youngsters that are trying to be something better than millhands."

"I can think of worse things they could be." I knew from Aunt Em's voice how her back must have stiffened. "Certainly you won't find many mills as progressive as ours——"

Other voices broke in just then, and I heard no more. But I have always been grateful to that teacher whose name I have forgotten. The next September I was allowed to enter Blairstown High School in the face of disapproval from most of our relatives. Cousin Eunice Blair was particularly vehement on the subject when she came to attend the fall directors' meeting.

"You know it doesn't look right, Em, a girl in her position going to public school. People will think you're either poor or peculiar. If you had any sense you'd be sending her to boarding school this year to make good social contacts."

"I like high school," I repeated stubbornly. "If I can

make geometry and Latin up by June I can graduate with the class of 1925."

"That's the year you ought to ' come out,'" Cousin Eunice reminded me. "You're sixteen now and not bad-looking if Em had any sense about dressing you. I was planning to give a dance for you in Boston this Christmas if Em and Wallace felt like sharing expenses."

"I'd rather be in the Christmas play," I told her. "We're doing *Everyman* and I'm trying for the lead though there's a girl named Angeletta Rossi who may get the most votes because she's almost as good as a real actress. She's planning to be one some day."

"I suppose boys are going to take part in this play too?" Cousin Eunice eyed me sharply across the table.

"Oh, yes! Young Jo Kelly's been selected already for the prologue."

"Well," Cousin Eunice turned to Aunt Em with raised eyebrows, "Elliott had plenty of queer ideas, but at least he kept his wife out of the mills once he married her. You seem to be doing your best to put his daughter back there. I suppose you'll go to see this play, Em, and enjoy watching some Pole or Lithuanian boy making love to your niece?"

"She can't," I protested. "It isn't that kind of play. It's an old English morality——"

"Call it what you want to, facts are facts, aren't they, Wallace?"

Uncle Wallace, when directly appealed to, took my side.

"It never did me any harm to rub up against the workers' families when I was a boy. Makes it easier for me to deal with the men now because we went to school together. Plenty of them still call me by my first name."

"A man can afford that kind of thing," Cousin Eunice reminded him, "but it cheapens a girl. And they didn't take advantage of it then, the way they do now. There's too much of this ' I'm as good and better than you are ' spirit, and that's what leads to trouble, like the kind they're having at Fenwick and Low's plant."

"I certainly don't like the sound of that," Uncle Wallace

put in. "And this big strike they've called at Fall River doesn't look as if it could be staved off."

"You'd better keep a firm hand if you don't want one starting here——"

"Oh, not at Peace-Pipe," Aunt Em protested. "We're not like those big impersonal plants where they've lost touch with the workers as individuals. There's a different spirit here."

I was grateful that the conversation had taken this turn, and that I no longer need be the target for criticism.

"Spirit's all right," Cousin Eunice was going on, "but what matters is profit. A mill that's going full tilt and making money doesn't have to worry about trouble with its hands. If the war could just have lasted a few months longer the way we expected it to," Cousin Eunice sighed, "then we wouldn't have been left with all that surplus stock to get rid of."

"Yes," Uncle Wallace agreed as he lighted his cigar. "We ought not to have put in that extra equipment and laid in so much cotton at skyrocket prices. It was against my better judgment, but with those Army contracts it seemed all right."

"Oh, please——" Aunt Em's voice shook. "I can't bear to think of the war that way—in profit and losses. It seems like betraying Elliott. Surely things must get back to normal soon?"

I left them discussing mill problems round the fire, for Maggie had come to tell me that young Jo Kelly was waiting for me. We climbed the stairs to the room that had been Father's studio and was now my study. The easel had been pushed into a corner, and all the unframed canvases were stacked face against the wall like children in disgrace. We spread our books and papers under the lamp on the old flat-topped table, and Jo helped me with my geometry and I checked his outline of Burke's "Speech on Conciliation." Then we heard each other recite speeches from *Everyman*. Jo knew his lines, but he kept making careless mistakes. I could tell that something was on his mind.

"Jo," I said at last, "what makes you frown like that? You haven't walked to school with me for nearly a week now. Is anything wrong?"

His eyes avoided mine.

"Well, no." He shifted in his chair and began to sort out his books and papers. "I got a lot of things to do, that's all."

But it was more than that, and we both knew it. I leaned across the table and made him face me.

"Would you be sorry if I got the part in *Everyman* instead of Angeletta?" I asked.

He flushed.

"I think Angie's better," he said finally. "I'd rather see her act it even if she can't get as good a costume as you could. It's just fun to you, but she really cares."

There was a long, uncomfortable silence between us, broken only by the big maple-tree outside tapping its twigs at the dark window-pane.

"It's got nothing to do with Angie," he went on. "I like you better when it comes to that, only——"

"Only you wish I'd stayed at private school," I interrupted. "And you wish you didn't have to live over here on our side of the river, don't you?"

"Maybe I do and maybe I don't. I guess you just have to find out some time where you belong."

He gathered up his books and turned to go.

"Listen, Jo," I begged. "If you think Angeletta wants the part so much, I could always pretend I've got a cold and not try out for the play."

He turned on me harshly.

"She doesn't want you to *give* her the part."

"How would she know?"

"You couldn't fool her. No, you've got to see a thing through once you start it."

After his footsteps had clattered into silence on the un-carpeted back stairs I sat a long while over the open books. But I couldn't go on studying. Janice had begun to play the piano downstairs, and the music came up to me thinned and saddened by distance and my own inner hurt. Jo had only made more clear what I had felt for some weeks past. It was all very well for me to go to high school, but when the doors closed I walked alone in my direction while the rest streamed back across the bridges to a world into which I could not follow them, any more than they could follow me into mine.

CHAPTER SIX

IT WAS the spring of 1928, a few months before my twenty-first birthday, that I fell in love. I had returned from a winter in Boston with Cousin Eunice Blair, going to art school by day and to dances by night. I knew that I was a disappointment to Cousin Eunice because I could not centre my interest upon any one in particular.

"You can't go on this way indefinitely," she used to warn me. "I was married to your cousin John Blair before I was your age."

"Oh, I'm not in any hurry," I would tell her. "There's nobody special yet."

"Well, there ought to be," she would lament. "That comes of an old maid like Em bringing you up. Not that Em isn't a remarkable woman, but then what woman wants to be remarkable? She'll make an old maid of you yet. Heaven knows she'll never do that to Janice. No, it wouldn't surprise me if Janice married and settled down ahead of you. She's a handful now, I'll admit. But when I was young they used to say wanton kittens make sober cats."

At eighteen Janice was certainly soft and pretty as a kitten and as gay. She liked men and made no effort to conceal the fact. Her irresponsibility drove Aunt Em and Maggie distracted, but it was difficult to stay annoyed with her for long. I had been born with a strong sense of possessiveness, and Aunt Em's methodical training had only intensified my respect for personal property. But nothing was sacred to Janice. She had a genius for losing whatever she borrowed, and she borrowed every article I owned. In those years I was always finding myself left with one earring, or a dress minus its belt, or a glove or stocking without its mate. So it was with a certain relief that I looked forward to that summer when she would be in Europe with the Parker twins. It would be a pleasant change to come back to a room where for the next six months my belongings would stay as I placed them; where I could count on the clothes I expected to wear being in closet and drawers, not on a sister's back.

"I hope you won't find it too quiet here after Boston," Aunt Em said that night of my return while the house was recovering from the flurry of Janice's departure. "You'll have the little car," Aunt Em went on. "It's been put in order for you, and most of the dents Janice put in it have been taken out. That and your painting ought to keep you fairly busy."

"By the way," Uncle Wallace suggested, "they tell me they want to start an evening class in designing over in the new Recreation Building. Maybe Emily'd like to take it over and pass on some of the things she's been learning?"

Aunt Em became enthusiastic immediately. The Recreation Centre where millworkers could take up weaving and pottery and dressmaking, and where certain evenings were devoted to games and dancing, was her pet project. She had fought for it against the criticism of certain directors and townspeople who felt it was unnecessary. Millworkers, they claimed, were not what they had been before the war, and shorter hours and higher wages ate up a large share of the profits. Still prosperity was in the air. A brief, false boom dominated all industry again, and the stock market rose higher and higher. The figures on the ticker tape made older men like Uncle Wallace and Mr. Parker shake their heads and wonder where it would end, and younger men plunge heavily into buying on margin. There was no more talk of Peace-Pipe dividends being passed. If quarterly profits didn't quite come up to expectations company stock holdings could easily be shifted to meet obligations. I hardly realised this at the time, for the talk of the mills was involved with the coming presidential election. If Mr. Hoover were elected it appeared that business and industry must continue to prosper.

But such matters were far from uppermost in my mind that spring night as I strolled down to the Recreation Centre after supper. Aunt Em had a group of committee-women in the parlour, Uncle Wallace was busy in his study, and suddenly the evening stretched long before me.

Outside, the earthy April darkness made me feel lonely and restless. Buds showed on the beech-trees where the street lights struck them, and I could smell the damp sweetness of the flowers old Jo Kelly had under the cold frames behind the house. I saw a flashlight moving round the grape arbour and knew that he must be prowling about on his nightly rounds. In the uncertain light he looked more stooped and knotty than I remembered. I noticed as he came nearer that he moved stiffly as if he were some antiquated member of the mole family with whom I had always associated him.

"Nice night, Miss Emily," he answered my greeting. "Not the kind to walk alone."

"Well, you're alone, too," I reminded him.

"Oh, me! That's been my way so long I don't look for any other, but it's not the right pattern to follow, all the same. Two by two, it was meant to be since the animals went into the Ark. It's a queer thing," old Jo went on, "to raise a family and lose them all one way or another."

"Except young Jo," I reminded him. "What's he up to, these days?"

"To no good, Miss Emily. That's one sure thing."

I had asked the question casually, and the sharpness of his answer startled me. Before I could put another question to him he was going on.

"I had to turn the boy out, and it comes hard to do that to your own grandson, but I couldn't let him go on biting the hand that's fed us all these years. He's down there now." He turned and pointed in the direction of the mill chimneys, dark across the river. "Making trouble. He got these views, you see, very mistaken views."

"Oh, well," I tried to comfort him, "Jo maybe thinks differently from you about a lot of things, but he couldn't ever be bad or wild."

"No, Jo's a good boy, that's the pity of it. I'd rather see him dead and buried like Mollie and the rest than going the way he's going. I tell you, Miss Emily, there's bad things brewing down there, and Jo's at the core of it all because he can't see straight."

"What sort of things?" I persisted.

"All this talk—organise, organise, that's all he and those cronies of his can think about, and unions and wages and closed shop and walk-outs and strikes. I know where it's going to end when all the talk turns into fists and bricks and blackjacks."

"Oh," I refused to take his dire predictions seriously, "what's a little talk? Besides there's never been any trouble at our mills."

"Well, I hope you're right. I'm too old to understand such things, but Jo's got the gift of talk, like my father that was killed in the Dublin riots. It's a dangerous gift. You'd swear black was white if he wanted you should think so. I can't sleep nights for thinking my Jo's there in Peace-Pipe Mills with a squint in his mind that no spectacles can cure."

"Don't worry." I was growing impatient at his talk, and the night was too fine to hear an old voice croaking beside me. "After young Jo's been working in the mills awhile he'll think differently about a lot of things."

"There's no getting round facts," he went on as I opened the gate. "The world's the same's it's always been and there's just two kinds of people in it—the haves and the have-nots. Mix 'em up, and they'll start right in all over again and be the same."

I was glad to be out of the sound of old Jo's voice, which had a rusty insistence, like a cricket's plaint. Yet he had roused my curiosity about his grandson. It must have been a serious difference to cause a break like that between them.

Dr. Weeks was leaving his house when I passed. I hailed him as he opened the door of his car and threw in his familiar bag of instruments. Any car that belonged to the doctor took on his look of shabby, dogged activity, no matter how spruce and factory-finished it had appeared a few weeks before. I smiled at the mud-spattered wheels and hood, the fenders whose scars of battle he had been too busy to have repaired. Off in the outlying country, people used to swear that they knew the sound of Dr. Weeks' engine coming over rough roads at night to answer some urgent summons. I have no doubt they did, for certainly there was some nervous, quick response between that machine and the man who guided it.

"Yes," he answered me after we had exchanged greetings, "I've got a busy night over on the mill side of town. Pneumonia case that looks bad, and a baby due before morning."

"You have got a lot on your hands," I said. "It'll be to-morrow when you get back."

"Well," he agreed, "always plenty doing over there. Someone coming or someone going, that's the way it is."

"Aunt Em says you ought to have an assistant now your practice has grown so."

"Now I'm not so young as I was," he corrected me. "That's what she really means. Well, maybe I will if I can find the right youngster. I've got my eye on a couple of interns right now. Good to see you back again, Emily. Hope you're planning to take the summer easy. You're a bit on the thin side, and it wouldn't do you any harm to take on a few more pounds. Not that you'll follow that piece of advice, I suppose?"

I laughed and shook my head as he studied me intently.

"You grow more like your father and Em every time I see you," he was going on. "Yes, you're Em all over again in modern dress. She wasn't much older than you the year

I came to practise in Blairstown, and I thought—Oh, well, never mind what I thought——"

He gave an apologetic laugh that ended in a sigh as he got in and started the engine. Something about the way he spoke made me remember certain remarks I had heard about how Dr. Weeks had wanted to marry Aunt Em years ago. I wondered if the rumour were true, and why nothing had ever come of it. There he was driving off to his round of night visits, alone and past middle-age, and there was Aunt Em surrounded by a ladies' committee discussing some good work or other. Somehow spring nights are apt to make the waste of human capacity for love and fulfilment seem more poignant then than at other seasons of the year. Or perhaps it only came of my being back in the limits of a smaller community. One felt somehow more aware of human relationships.

"A little town is like a lantern," Maggie Flynn used to say with a shrewd pursing of her lips. "Nothing's hid away from sight."

It may have been some intimate quality of the night, or my own heightened senses that made me unusually receptive to my surroundings. Each familiar house and yard I passed, each tree and fence and postbox arrested me as if I were marking them for the first and last time. Perhaps the river mist had something to do with what I felt; perhaps it was only a sudden sense of place such as all of us have experienced at some time or other. I only know that all this was part of that night in April which must forever punctuate my life, as an exclamation point stands out boldly on the page of a book.

The Wawickett River was swollen with spring rains. I could hear the noise of its waters going over the dam long before I set foot on the upper bridge, as if it were a human presence hailing me. I could not see the torrent rushing under me. But I felt the power that charged it, that seemed stronger than the span of bridge that ordinarily rose so high above it, and that was so bound to me from childhood. My cheeks and hair grew damp with misty spray. A chill wildness was in the atmosphere, so strong and fresh and full of vigour that even the smell of chemicals and machinery and factory smoke could not overpower it. •

In that misty stretch between the two sides, I felt that time did not count. It was as if the bridge had become a sort of no man's land where the past and present might meet and mingle as they do sometimes in our dreams. It would not have surprised me to find my own father swinging towards me with his long, easy strides, or my mother leaning at the rail with a child pressed against her skirts. Now I know that the future was there, too, that every step I took brought me nearer to it.

The clamour of the rushing water had taken all other sounds. I heard no footsteps, my own or those that must have been coming behind me. So I was startled when a man passed by me, then stopped and hesitated as if uncertain whether to speak or not.

When he did I realised that he was not the millhand I had taken him to be.

"Are you Emily Blair?" His voice was young and pleasant. •

"Why, yes." I stopped short. "Yes, I'm Emily Blair, but I don't know who you are?"

"We met at a party." He laughed. "You were seven years old and it lasted from four to six."

"Wait a minute." My mind raced back as I tried to catch at a name that eluded me. "Then you must be the Parker twins' cousin. I've forgotten your name, but I remember you didn't bring me any present."

This time we both laughed.

"Harry Collins—do you remember now? I've been working in your mills since January. Stopped to see you just now, and they said I'd find you if I walked this way. I guess your uncle forgot to tell you I was coming over after dinner. Do you really have to go over to the Recreation Building?"

"No, it was just something to do."

"Let's go back then." We turned and fell into step

D

together. "We'll sit in your parlour and look at the family photograph album."

"Oh"—I shook my head and drops of mist ran off my hair—"we can't do that because Aunt Em and her committee are there, and besides there isn't any family album."

That wasn't a funny remark, and yet it made us laugh. I know now that we laughed because we had both been lonely on a spring night.

CHAPTER SEVEN

How can I tell of that summer except to say that I shall never meet its like again? There may be others more fair, others more busy and full of contentment, but never one so charged with the warm swift current of love when first it takes over an untried heart. The response in me was unpredictable. Sometimes I was restless as the dragonflies that hovered over our lily pool, their wings a shimmer of impatience. On others I was wary and withdrawn as one of our garden moles guarding his secret ways. But whatever the mood I no longer slept or woke or went about my business with the old self-sufficiency. It was Harry Collins this, and Harry Collins that, day in and day out. Nothing made sense without him, and I didn't care who knew it.

To love and be wise, they say, is impossible. They say, too, that if you love you are the slave, and if you are loved you are the master. It was like that with Harry Collins and me from the first night of my return. He had only to beckon and up I sprang, one leap ahead of myself. Foolish —of course it was, but past my power to have it otherwise. Maggie Flynn used to shake her head when she saw me hurrying downstairs to meet him, or dressing for the country-club dances as if my very life depended on being ready an hour before it was time to start.

"Come now, Miss Emily, have patience," she would say "There's all the time in the world and some left over."

And when her words failed to halt me she would add slyly, "Ah, well, the feet go to the place where the heart is."

I was always making some excuse to drive by the mills, hoping for a glimpse of Harry's head bent over a desk, or his familiar figure striding across the millyard. Even when I stayed on our side of the river I would look over a dozen times an hour wondering if he were thinking of me at that precise moment. I was in love, no doubt of that.

There is an old sketchbook of mine in the ell storeroom that always brings back that summer, especially a certain water colour which I pass over quickly. Some time perhaps I shall be able to look impersonally at the painted shape of a tilted thorn-tree in a field with the outline of a low hill beyond. I shall look and not feel memory stirring too sharp for me to bear. For though the sketch is only half-finished it still keeps something of the magic of an afternoon in midsummer. There in the corner the brush strokes end abruptly because I looked up and caught Harry's eyes, and after that—no more reaching for paint and brushes, nothing to do or say but to be aware each of the other.

On summer Saturdays the mills closed at noon, and often Harry and I would drive with a picnic basket over to a place on the outskirts of town. It has changed since then. Only the river is the way it used to be, tranquil and broad after its plunge over Peace-Pipe dam. It flowed there quiet and free of barriers and factory grime, between marshy meadows that spread out below Blairstown. Those marshes are drained now of their cat-tails and their shallow pools that used to make sunsets more fiery in the irregular small patches they reflected. Gone are the thorn-trees and alder thickets, cleared to make room for a parkway and real estate development. Cheap bungalows like rows of painted boxes multiply where field larks used to rise singing from sunburnt grass that was just the colour of Harry Collins's hair.

But I, too, am changed. For I have been drained of a certain bright assurance that love can stay secure; cleared of old hopes and confidences by the ruthlessness of experience. But on one July Saturday not a doubt clouded my mind or heart.

I was waiting in the car for Harry by the mill gates when the noon whistle blew. It was sweet to my ears that day, for all its shrillness, and I heard it as wives and sweethearts of millhands must have heard it, knowing it meant a man's step at the door and a precious half-day to be shared in sunshine and warmth together. He climbed in beside me, so good to see in the heather mixture sweater that was my favourite because it duplicated the little flecks of brown and green in his hazel eyes. We drove for a few miles on the main turnpike and then turned the car into a dusty, unfrequented road that narrowed to a pair of overgrown wheel ruts that ended by clumps of firewood and the cellar of a burned-out house. Here on the flat, sunny doorstep we sat and ate the sandwiches and cookies I had brought, and drank some sour, red wine that Harry had wheedled one of the Italian millhands into selling him.

"It's supposed to be Chianti," Harry explained. "Pretty poor imitation, but beggars can't be choosers in Prohibition times. Roselli didn't want to let me have this for fear it would get out he was making it in his woodshed. It's a farce, this Eighteenth Amendment."

"I know," I agreed, trying not to pucker my lips over the wine. "Last winter in Boston all the men carried hip flasks to dances, and some of the girls brought bottles, too."

"Women don't understand about drinking." Harry leaned back and lit a cigarette. "Oh, not this mild sort of thing." He waved at the wine disguised in a catsup bottle, and went on, "Not that I've been drunk often, but just enough to know."

"How does it make you feel?"

"Oh, sort of equal to anything. It's as if nothing were hard or impossible any more. Kind of like a god until you pass out."

"I've only had enough to feel like giggling a lot," I told

him. "And once, in the middle of a party last winter, I wanted to cry and cry about nothing in particular."

Harry laughed.

"You're funny, Emmy," he said, and I loved the way that nickname sounded on his lips. "Funny, but I like you."

"You're funny, too," I told him, "and I like you."

"I can read you like a book," he went on. "You're really a very pleasant and easy book to read, though no girl likes to be told that for some strange reason." He yawned and put out his cigarette. "And now, with your permission, I'll take my after-luncheon nap and you can paint a picture, but not of me."

He turned over on the grass, his face buried in his folded arms to keep the flies away.

I set out my water colours and opened my sketchbook to a fresh page, and my fingers began marking out the scene before me, the tilted thorn-tree and the tawny patch of field, the familiar hump of hill beyond. My hands worked surely with pencil and brushes and paints, yet my eyes would keep turning to where Harry lay stretched, long-legged and strong of body, in the sun. So still and relaxed he lay, yet so full of vigour and life, that I could almost mark the swift stir of blood in the veins of his freckled hands and arms where the fine hairs were yellower than on his sandy head. Under the white cotton material of his shirt his chest rose and fell, rose and fell, with unbroken regularity. I paused in my painting, and my cheeks began to burn with something far more potent than that home-brewed wine.

"What are you thinking about, Emily?"

He turned over suddenly on his back and studied me through sleep-narrowed eyes.

"Oh, nothing," I hedged, and tried not to give myself away. Then as he still stared and smiled through the slanting sunshine I broke down and confessed. "Well, us, then—if you must know."

"Of course I must——"

He spoke casually, but he broke off and the look in his

eyes turned me suddenly shy and confused, though it was what I had hoped I might see in them some time. Day after day I had searched them for that look. Now there was no doubt, and the age-old instinct to flee was upon me. I sprang up, scattering my book and paints and brushes in every direction. I might have been Daphne in flight, my feet suddenly taking root, hair turning into laurel leaves before the onrush of the pursuer.

"Hey, wait." There was nothing of ancient Greece in his words, but I would not have exchanged them for all the sonnets in creation. "You know—it's funny, I was thinking about us, too—especially you."

His arms were strong and hard and warm about me. His breath was warm, too, on my cheek, and the smell of sunburnt grass was all about him and will always overwhelm me with the memory of that moment.

I had been kissed before. What girl of my age hasn't? But this was different. Whatever I can think of him now—and I have thought plenty, both good and bad, since that day—I can never forget the strength and sweetness of his lips.

He held me close—how long, I shall never know, for time was our friend that day and there was no mill whistle to sound and only a kindly, gradual setting in of twilight after the pink went out of the sky, and the marshy pools lost their reflected fire.

"Harry," I remember, I faltered at last, "does it mean that you and I—that we——"

He nodded and held me closer.

"And we can tell them—to-night?"

"If you want to. But I'd just as soon we kept it to ourselves a little longer."

"They'll know, whether we say a word or not. They'll see it on my face. Oh, Harry, I didn't know, I wasn't sure—about you, I mean. I was always sure about me."

CHAPTER EIGHT

WE moved through those first few weeks of our engagement, Harry and I, like swimmers carried effortlessly by a current that was stronger than we. I say "we," but I can speak only for myself. It is all a warm daze to me now, pricked with moments of awareness that I recall, as if I had not lived them but had read them in the pages of some book.

So I tell myself that the tall girl in the grey organdie with the coral trimmings was really I, and that it was indeed my own quick breathing that made the lace quiver as I pinned it down with the pearl circlet Aunt Em had given me for my twenty-first birthday and engagement present. There were heliotrope and mignonette and a moss rose in a vase, I remember. Their fragrance was almost stifling as my sleeve brushed them when I leaned across the bureau to take a last look at myself before going down for the garden party which was to announce my great news as well as my coming of age.

The dress had arrived that morning from Boston, and I hoped that I looked my best in it. But would Harry like it? Would he be proud of me in the soft grey clinging folds and notice that the coral bands and sash brought brighter colour to my cheeks? If approval did not immediately show in his eyes, then it would not matter who else might praise me. I touched the ring on my left hand for reassurance before I went downstairs. Harry had bought it for me the day before with apologies for the smallness of the stone. He would be paying for it from his salary envelope for months to come, and I knew he couldn't afford it. Even a very little diamond cost far too much for a young man just starting in any business. I had tried to scold him for his extravagance, but my protests had been lost in happiness.

All the guests at my birthday party that afternoon would see it on my finger. They would hear that Harry

Collins and I were engaged to be married, and our love would be a secret thing no longer. That made me feel shy and serious. But I wanted them all to know. I wanted to hear their congratulations and see the curious, searching look in the eyes that watched us. Already I knew that look. I had seen it in Aunt Em's eyes and Maggie's, and even in Uncle Wallace's. I had stared at engaged couples in the same way myself. Curiosity and envy mingled in that look—the older eyes might be tired and practical, but there was a certain envy and approval there, as if they would like to be young and in love all over again; and younger eyes were awed and shy in their appraisal, hoping that the miracle would not be denied them. So Harry and I became symbols to those friends and neighbours who gathered in the garden or moved about the lawns under the maple and beech-trees. I felt that we were, and the knowledge only deepened my happiness. Whether Harry knew or felt what I did, I cannot say; but his hand was warm on mine and his eyes approving as we went from group to group.

Aunt Em was in her element, welcoming guests and answering questions.

"Well, no, it wasn't exactly a surprise," I could hear her saying from the bench under the copper beech-tree, "except that having Emily old enough to think about being married does come as a surprise of course. Why, it seems only yesterday it was her seventh birthday party and she and Janice and Harry and the twins were all playing hide-and-seek together and stuffing themselves on ice cream and angel cake." Then as she moved on to another group I would catch variations of the same theme. "Yes, we're delighted, and the best part is we shan't be losing her. With Harry in the mills Wallace and I needn't worry about Peace-Pipe going out of the family; and Harry being John Parker's cousin makes it all the more suitable."

Somehow it always came back to that word "suitable" as people discussed our engagement and beamed upon us while refreshments were served at the tables that dotted the lawns. I had done what was expected of me just as Father had advised me to do years ago. His words had lain long forgotten in my mind, but now they came back to me. Father had confessed that he had never learned the trick himself. Perhaps if he had he would have been beside us that afternoon. I found myself suddenly thinking of my mother, and I wondered if any of the friends and neighbours gathered there to wish me well were thinking of her too. Or had she never really counted much in their world on this side of the river?

"Well," I heard one woman say to another later as I passed, "Em must be glad about this match. No making the best of it the way she had to with the other one. Elliott certainly took a chance marrying a millgirl, but she made a good wife and mother."

"Em will certainly draw a long breath when she sees her other niece settled." A different voice chimed in. "I was saying last night Emily wouldn't have had half the show this summer with that younger sister around. She's always had the beaux, so I guess she can afford to let Emily go down the aisle first."

I couldn't help feeling relieved that I had not had to share these weeks with Janice. Not that I was jealous of her popularity, but it was pleasant to make my plans without having to consider hers. Just then I caught Harry's eyes upon me across a group of people, and I answered the secret signal of his smile.

"And don't I know I'm lucky!" I could hear his voice responding to other voices. "When I think that I almost took a job in Boston last March instead of coming here— it makes me believe in fate or whatever you want to call it."

No matter how sure I was of his love, I listened hungrily for such words as I went through the ritual of thanks.

"Oh, how nice of you to say so! Well, of course, I think he is. Yes, isn't it wonderful, he's come to work at Peace-Pipe."

Over and over my lips repeated the polite formulas; the threadbare words that somehow seem new by reason of their personal significance.

"Oh, thank you! I'm so glad you're glad about us. Why, no, we haven't made any plans yet. It's pretty soon to set a date, and Harry's busy learning the business. Maybe next summer."

People I scarcely knew suddenly kissed me and wished me well with an interest I had never guessed before, and the married women embarrassed me with attentions. I tried to be more outgoing in my response to them. I felt especially sorry that day for old maids. Maybe it wasn't so much that as relief that I felt. I saw a fate from which I had escaped. Even Aunt Em, handsome and gracious in her mauve lace, was less herself than someone I might have become in time except for this miracle. A wave of pity for all that she had missed came over me, and I stopped to squeeze her hand.

"Not getting too tired, Emily?" she asked, smiling back at my eager protests. "Oh, there's old Mrs. Norwood just coming up the path. Do run down and meet her."

I seem to be watching myself and listening these five years afterwards with the detachment of experience, as if I were looking through the wrong end of an opera glass. How small and immature I was then; how fearful that I might not fulfil all expectations! How much, I wonder, did I really feel? I had not suffered then in the flesh or in the heart. But now, because I know what such pain can be, have I the right to say that love was less than it seemed to me that afternoon?

Twilight was coming across the lawns. The golden afternoon light softened to dusky greenness, and the shadows round the tree trunks were reaching out to meet one another. Beyond the gates old Jo Kelly and another man were helping guests into their cars. Only a few latecomers lingered, and Maggie and extra hired servants were already discreetly carrying in trays and chairs. John Parker and several other men had stopped by to collect their wives and daughters, and they lingered on the steps talking to Uncle Wallace. The rich fragrance of their cigars mingled with the scent of drooping flowers. It was good to feel the presence of men after all the chatter and feminine bustle.

Harry had left to drive some friends of Aunt Em's home. Already I felt incomplete without him as I wandered uncertainly about the littered grounds. There is something a little sad about the end of a party; all the laughter and activity is over, but it has not yet taken on the perspective of memory. The paper napkins lie strewn underfoot; the glasses are warm and sticky, and plates bear remnants of the pride they once held. A dish of ice cream and cake had been upset on the grass and an army of ants were attacking it with the precision of a trained battalion. Down by the lily pool the frogs were making their familiar guttural. All sounds became intensified for me in that interval. It was as if something warned me, saying: "Listen, listen while you can."

Then I saw a figure moving by the old hemlock, and I recognised young Jo Kelly. He waved to me, but when he made no effort to come nearer I went down to him. It was weeks since I had seen him, and we had not exchanged words all that summer.

"Jo," I called, "come up and have some of my party. There's lots of food left."

But he only grinned and shook his head.

"No, thanks," he told me. "Just wanted to wish you luck on the day."

He smiled at me, and when his thin face broke into those familiar merry lines the past seemed suddenly to rise up between us. I felt it drawing us together with links we had both forgotten. Just for a moment I forgot that young Jo disapproved of our family; that he had been denounced by Aunt Em and Uncle Wallace and old Jo as a traitor to the mills and Peace-Pipe traditions. I felt only the old bonds of childhood, the memory of treats and fears and secrets we had shared together under the old hemlock where we were standing now.

"Jo"—I put out my hand and he took it—"I'm so glad you came to-day: it's like old times."

"Yes." His voice always startled me by sounding more slow and deep than I had remembered. "That's why I almost didn't come."

"But it's good to remember old times. I only wish——"

"I know," he cut me short, and his smile faded. "You wish I'd remember them oftener. Well, I've had that all out with Grandfather. He sees things your way and I see them mine. I guess it can't ever be different. Don't you tell him I was here, will you?"

"Why, no, if you ask me not to. But it would please him to know you came."

"That's why. He'd start getting his hopes up about me, and I'd just go and disappoint him again."

"Jo," I said, "I don't pretend to know what's made things different from the way they used to be. It's something you feel about the mills, I know that much, and that you think we're to blame——"

"No." He shook his head, and the hair fell over his forehead just as it used to, so that he looked once more like a stubborn pony with rough, dark forelocks. "It's not as simple as all that, and I don't blame you folks except you all think everything'll go on same's it did in your grandfather's day."

"Well, he started Peace-Pipe, didn't he? There wouldn't be any mills or work for all of you down there if he hadn't."

"Sure." Jo smiled the patient kind of smile one gives to a child. "Remember those snowballs we used to roll down the back slope when we were kids? You started with one in your fist, and then it kept rolling up more and more; and pretty soon it got bigger'n you were, and there it was pulling you along instead of the other way round. I tell you that grandfather of yours started a snowball you're going to have trouble keeping up with, one of these days."

The pupils of young Jo's blue eyes had grown enormous and dark, the way they used to get when he stood up to debate on the high-school team.

"Maybe you read what happened over in Fall River last month?" he went on.

"You mean that textile strike?" I hadn't bothered to read about it, but I had heard Uncle Wallace and Aunt Em discussing it with Harry.

"That's what I mean. If it can happen in one place, it can in another."

"Oh, but not here!" I was surprised to catch a quality in my own voice that suggested Aunt Em. "We never have trouble at Peace-Pipe, and besides conditions were terrible in that plant. Even Uncle Wallace said the workers had some justification though no strike is ever the right answer, and Harry Collins says——"

I broke off because I couldn't remember Harry's exact words and because just the mention of his name distracted my mind from other subjects. "Mr. Collins and I are going to be married, Jo," I went on, "maybe you heard?"

"No." He shook his head before he smiled and put out his hand. "Well, I guess everybody's pleased. He seems a nice fellow all right. Here's hoping you'll be happy."

"Thank you, Jo. I'm glad you came up so I could tell you about it myself. Funny, isn't it, that he came to my other party, the time you broke your leg falling out of this tree—because the hurt chipmunk bit you, remember?"

"I remember all right. It was nice being laid up here in the big house. You were all real good to me. Well, good luck, Emily. I'll have to practise calling you Mrs. Collins soon."

"Oh, there's plenty of time for that," I protested, but it pleased me to hear him say the name. "You'll be getting married yourself one of these days, and I'll be congratulating you."

His lips drew together in a thin line, and once more he shook his dark head.

"It's wonderful being in love," I persisted. "You wait and see."

"I'll wait." There was a note of bitterness in his voice as he turned away in the twilight that was all about us.

"Being in love's kind of a luxury for some of us. Can't afford to think too much about it."

Before I could reply he had turned away, leaving me feeling hurt and uncertain. Barriers not of my raising were between us once more; and I was glad when he wheeled back and returned to my side again.

"Look," he said out of the dimness. "I don't suppose you'd like a puppy for a present? It's lonesome up here since Janice's spaniel got run over, and you haven't had a dog since Bon-Bon died. That hound of mine's got a litter of six, and I have to get rid of them by to-morrow. They're not beauties, but I'll pick the least objectionable if you'll take it off my hands."

"Of course I will, Jo. You and I may disagree on a lot of things, but I'll always trust you to pick out a good dog. I suppose it's got a long tail?"

"Well, yes. There isn't much choice when it comes to that, but you can have the one with the fewest different colours."

We laughed together, and I watched him out of sight before I went back to wait for the honk of the car bringing Harry to me again.

CHAPTER NINE

NEW YEAR'S EVE, 1928, slid into 1929 while Harry smiled at me across the living-room at Peace-Pipe and the candles made little reddish glints in the sherry glass he held high. I never took my eyes from his face while the clock chimed and the bells outside rang through a cold January drizzle. I needed the reassurance of his eyes. Good as the old year had been to us, I wanted the new one to be even better and more completely our own. Janice, standing between Uncle Wallace and Dr. Weeks in her silver Paris dress that made her look like a bob-haired angel from a Christmas-tree, watched us with amused tolerance.

"Those two," she laughed, "you can see they're making

plans for 1929 before 1928 has breathed its last, and after the way Emmy's been sentimentalising all day about what happened to her in this year."

"I'm glad she's a sentimentalist," Harry championed me. "It's an old-fashioned trait, and I love it in her. Go ahead and make pets out of old junk and old years all you want to, darling, only don't neglect me."

"A likely chance of that." Janice laughed.

She had come back in November, prettier than ever and more full of life. I had dreaded her return because I had wanted nothing to change and Janice always brought change and commotion. Yet I found the readjustment less difficult than I had expected. Janice envied me my new status. I could tell that she had not thought me capable of attracting a man like Harry Collins. Then, too, the months of travelling without Maggie to keep order had given her more consideration for other people's possessions. I, for my part, was less irritated by petty pilferings and trivialities. Only what concerned Harry could touch me deeply. Looking back to it now, I wonder how long we might have stayed so if what lay ahead had been longer in coming; if it had not come at all?

The penalty of love, I suppose, must always be the fear of losing it. So old a motif, yet to each of us new with personal significance at one time or another. Love and fear, I was aware of them both that night as I had not been on other New Year's.

"There," I heard Janice sigh. "That's over for one year." She turned to Harry when the last toast had been drunk. "I hope Emily warned you about all the family rituals you'll be in for when you marry a Blair."

"She did," he whispered back, "and so far I'm doing all right."

"Well, you wait," she warned, "they have a way of piling up on you."

Our little gathering broke up soon after midnight, for Dr. Weeks had late visits to make and Harry was driving home with him because of the rain.

"Happy New Year again," the doctor said as he struggled into his overcoat. "But you youngsters listen to me. There's an epidemic going the rounds and it's no respecter of persons. I've got some pretty sick patients over there across the river."

"You mean in the Mill Infirmary?" Aunt Em was anxious.

"In the infirmary and out of it," he told her. "And it's not all plain flu either. There are a couple of cases of such high temperatures I suspect meningitis."

I didn't bother much about the word then, though now it seems incredible that there could ever have been a time that I did not know it.

"That sounds serious, Will." Aunt Em followed him to the door all concerned and full of questions. "You don't really think——"

"I'll know more by to-morrow, Em; but frankly I don't like the look of things. Keep the girls away from dances and picture shows and make them eat and rest sensibly if you can. Emily'd better stop going down to her art classes in the Recreation Centre for a bit. Just for precaution's sake, you understand, though germs don't keep to one side of the river once they get headway."

His predictions were right as it turned out. By mid-January the Mill Infirmary and the town hospital were taxed to capacity. In spite of extra medical help from Boston Dr. Weeks hardly knew what it was to snatch an hour of uninterrupted sleep. For me the only personal hardship of the epidemic was my promise not to drive to the mills to meet Harry when the five o'clock whistle blew.

A sort of gloom hung over Peace-Pipe that January which I resented because I could not always keep my own well-being clear of it.

"You know, Emmy," Harry said one night, "they've had me checking up on last year's orders and the year before that, and there's been a steady decline. I can't understand it with the stock market soaring. Why, with General

Electric and Telephone and U.S. Steel going up, the textile and cotton industries ought to be right on top too. If I only had a few thousand dollars to invest I could make a neat little turnover. Sometimes I can't help wishing——"

"Oh, darling"—I wouldn't let him finish the sentence—"don't wish you hadn't come to Peace-Pipe! I get cold all over when I think how it would have been if you hadn't. If you want to leave the mills after we're married you can try something different. But they'll be raising your salary soon, and Uncle Wallace and Mr. Parker are going to make you an assistant manager before long. I know I can talk Aunt Em into a June wedding instead of a fall one, once this epidemic gets over and done with."

"Oh, I suppose I'll stick." Harry shrugged and lit another cigarette. "Lots of the men in my class would envy me the start I've got here, but when I think what I could do with a little money and a rising market——"

"I wish I had some of my own," I told him. "It's a nuisance having it all tied up in the mills, though I never wanted more than my allowance before. Maybe when we're married they'll give me some outright, and then you can do what you want with it. You tell the market not to go any higher till after June."

"All right," he grinned and kissed me, "I'll use my influence with Wall Street, and you use yours on the family. You don't think you could fix it up for April, do you—just a year from the night we met?"

Somehow when Harry said things like that I didn't know how I could bear so much happiness. I never took being wanted for granted, then or now. There should have been something to tell me of the precipice before the earth crumbled under my feet. Why are we humans less fore-warned than the wild ducks who heed the summons of frost even though summer sun lies warm upon their feathers?

Janice had set her heart on going to a Valentine dance at the Country Club, and she begged me to persuade Aunt Em and Dr. Weeks to let us go. January had been a long,

E

cold month with little social activity in Blairstown because of the epidemic.

"It's seemed like a whole solid month of day-after-Christmases to me," Janice had sighed. "I'll have to break out some way soon or go mad."

Dr. Weeks did waive his taboos. The club dances were small and select, and the epidemic seemed definitely on the wane. We felt suddenly festive as we set off, and even Maggie fell into the spirit of the evening as she helped me on with my wraps.

"Choose a groom on a horse," she told us, "and a bride at a dance and you can't go wrong."

"Sorry about the horse, Maggie," Harry teased her from the steps. "But I think there's something in what you say."

We did seem to be a part of a special rhythm when we danced together that night. I had wakened in the morning feeling tired and heavy, and my head had ached all day. But suddenly I felt light and elated and charged with an inner current of happiness that tingled in every nerve and fibre. Somehow that night I couldn't make myself believe in death or pain or despair. Other people might know them, but not Harry Collins and Emily Blair, moving together in a close-wrapped mantle of wellbeing.

"Harry," I whispered once when the music stopped and we waited while the rest clapped for an encore. "I'm almost afraid to be so happy. You don't think——"

His arm tightened around me. "It's fatal to think about being happy. You just are, or you're not, that's all there is to that."

But he was wrong. Too much good fortune can make you smug and unaware. Happiness should be like an oasis, the greener for the desert that surrounds it.

It was three by the clock in the Square as we drove back through the deserted town. Rain was falling, and there was no sign of morning in the east.

"Good-night, my sweet." Harry kissed me and turned on the doorstep with a laugh that ended in a yawn.

The drip of cold rain in the darkness and those four

words he had spoken became one to me as I stood watching him go down the path—fond, casual words that were never meant to be weighted down with the importance I gave them. Yet all those days and weeks and months and years afterwards my heart echoed them. If they became distorted and magnified out of all proportion, the fault is mine and mine alone. For I had no right to cling to them as I did because my need of their reassurance was so great. Yet I am not the first, and I shall not be the last, to try to make a bowstring into an anchor chain.

CHAPTER TEN

"THANK you, I understand. I know you've done everything you could, and it's no use. But thanks just the same."

I was to say that so many times in the next two years that I lost count. The words would rise almost mechanically to my lips, and though they might vary, the theme was always the same. As time went on I even became confused as to whether the current specialist delivering the verdict happened to be in Boston or New York, in Baltimore or Chicago. Sometimes as I waited for my turn, the past would creep up and betray me with false reassurance. I would stare incredulously at the newspaper I might be reading and ask myself what I was doing here in a strange city, in a strange doctor's reception-room, under the impersonal cheerful eye of a starched attendant and the curious glances of other patients.

Well, I had stood it as long as I could. I was through with doctors' offices and hospital clinics. No one could say that I hadn't given them every chance. Even Aunt Em would have to admit that I had co-operated with the doctors and their treatments. In the beginning I had even hoped. This business of hoping was going to die hard with Aunt Em and with Harry. But they would have to see my side. They couldn't make me go on and on with this weary, humiliating round. I must convince them somehow, once

I got back. What had made my exit different that day was
that the doctor had not tried to be kind.

"Well," he had said, "we've given it a fair trial, and
frankly there's nothing more I can do. I might as well be
honest with you."

"I know," I said, wishing I could have been sure that my
voice kept steady. "I understand——"

He stopped me with a quick gesture and turned to speak
into the telephone beside him. I sat in the chair opposite
and stared at the coloured reproductions of French moderns
on the walls—a Renoir girl, pink and full-blown as a rose;
a Degas dancer bending to her ballet slipper; a pot of
flowers on a window-sill that would bloom forever because
van Gogh had seen it so on another morning. Someone
had chosen those paintings, I suppose, because they were
so far removed from pain and weariness of spirit and medical
paraphernalia. It was a good theory, yet one that I resented.
Somehow a blank wall was more appropriate when one
sat waiting for what one had travelled so far and been
through so much probing and pains to learn.

"Then you think it's hopeless?" I leaned across the desk
when he put back the telephone and turned to me again.

"I've learned not to use that word, Miss Blair. In the
medical profession there's always the chance one may be
wrong. I only say that I don't seem able to help you. Let's
see how long it's been." He held out a sheaf of typed reports
that the nurse had brought from the files. "H'm-m,
February, 1929, and you've been to Chase in Chicago; Mack
and Thomas in New York; Ricker in Baltimore and——"

"Do we need to go into the medical who's who?"

I had felt no surprise or resentment at his words. They
had been said to me with variations so often before, that I
could meet them almost before they had been spoken.
What I did feel was a sudden relief, a sense almost as if I
had come to the wall of a dead-end street. I need not struggle
to find a way out. I saw that he was studying me with an
expression I knew to be the usual forerunner of farewell
salvos of good advice.

"Please," I said, reaching for my things, "would you mind *not* telling me I have a lot to be thankful for, or that I must never let myself be handicapped, or that everybody has adjustments to make of some kind? I'll meet this in my own way as long as I have to, but I'd rather not be reminded that it could be worse than it is."

So there I was once more in the long bleak waiting-room of the North Station with an hour to kill before I could board the Blairstown train. The ticket windows and benches and every postcard and candy bar on display were familiar to me as the suitcase at my feet with E. B. in black letters and all the dents and scratches that two years of travelling in close companionship had put there. I had packed it in haste. A blue tassel from my dressing-gown had got left outside. I needn't have been in such a frenzy after I left the doctor's office that noon. Certainly I should have known there wasn't a train between the 12.53 and the 3.19. But somehow flight had been my only thought, not flight as I had known it before, pushing on to what lay ahead. This was to be a deliberate flight into the past where I might face what must be faced as soon as possible, without pity and without false hopes.

The coffee-stand was deserted, as I went over and sat on one of the revolving stools. I didn't really want the coffee I ordered, but I had found that time passes more quickly if one goes through the motions of eating and drinking. My own reflection stared back at me from the looking-glass above the counter. In the strong, unflattering light I studied my face critically, searching for some sign of outward change. I was still young and attractive enough at twenty-four to be noticed when I travelled alone. Only a certain tenseness and anxiety of expression betrayed me at times.

"Why, Emily Blair," the Parker twins and others were always telling me, "with your looks and brains you don't have to worry. It isn't as if anybody'd guess you had a thing wrong with you."

I knew they meant to be kind. I couldn't explain that it

was the little clumsinesses and petty irritations that hurt
my pride.

I knew that going back to Blairstown empty of hope
wasn't going to be easy. But facts had to be faced. I should
have to convince Aunt Em that I couldn't go on with this
being shunted from specialist to specialist. And Harry—I
must make him understand, too, about the loneliness and
despair that only his presence had the power to ease. When
I had been back for week-ends of late he had seemed preoccupied and constrained, and his letter of day before
yesterday had left me feeling somehow unsatisfied. I took
it out of my bag and spread the single sheet on the counter
before me, trying to find some crumb of reassurance there
that might have gone unnoticed on other readings. I was
like a child shaking an empty candy box, in hope that some
sweet may have miraculously remained.

MY DEAR [it began]—Your letters put me to shame for my
sins of omission, but honestly this week has been the worst
since the market hit bottom in '29. If you've read the papers
you know what the mills are up against. You're lucky to
be out of it with the whole place about as cheerful as the
tomb of the Capulets. Orders practically nil and the United
Textile gang cutting up—Well, maybe something can be
worked out before the next directors' meeting.

I'm sorry the treatments aren't going better. But don't
let them get you down, Emmy—I have a feeling you're on
the right track this time. So don't hurry it and have any
regrets. It's been a long pull, I know, but you've been grand,
and I needn't remind you of the sort of person you are.

I turned the page with a pang. It was one of those times
when I could have managed with a large dose of praise.

Your idea about my driving up for the Harvard-
Dartmouth game next week sounds good, but Janice has got
herself and the car all dated up. Wish I could see my way to
getting a second-hand car of my own. Funny to think we

ever talked about such a thing as a raise. Well, my sweet, it's late, and the whistle blows as usual to-morrow morning; and we pretend to be busy, with prosperity just around the corner. Sorry you won't be back for your aunt's birthday. Let me know when to expect you here if I can't get on for the game.

Love,

HARRY.

I folded the paper and put it back into the envelope. There was no reason to feel as I did about that letter. Words were not Harry's strong point, and I knew that he was genuinely worried about the mill situation. But if he had simply scrawled across the page, "Miss you like all creation, darling," or something like it, I'd have felt a good deal better. Surely he must know that it was as much for his sake as my own that I had forced myself to try one cure after another. I had fought to keep our love on the old footing. It mustn't be hurt because I had been hurt. Yet when I saw people watching us together I guessed what was in their minds.

A man had seated himself at the lunch counter, and I could see in the mirror that he was studying me curiously. I felt annoyed because his look was so frank and impersonal for all its intentness. I stared back at him in the mirror, but he continued his survey without concern. I noticed that he was on the youngish side of thirty and his clothes, while not exactly shabby, were obviously not the sort that Harry or other men I knew wore. Yet there was a kind of distinction about the man that cheap tailoring could not conceal. His head was well set, and his high cheekbones made his rather pale, dark-browed face seem broader than it really was. His eyes looked black at first because of their dark lashes and large pupils, but they were actually grey, and his hands were unusually flexible and well kept. You felt they had been scrubbed and scoured almost to the bone.

Well, I thought, there's still twenty minutes to train

time. I might as well walk up and down the platform as sit here and be Exhibit A to a total stranger!

I pushed away my cup and saucer and felt for change in my bag. My fingers must have been cold, for the dime slipped out of them and rolled along the floor like a runaway drop of quicksilver before a man's foot stopped its course.

"Oh, thank you, thanks very much," I murmured as the long, white fingers held it out to me. But I didn't allow my eyes above the range of the second coat button.

The first editions of the afternoon papers had just come in. I stopped by the news-stand and bought one, arrested by a familiar name in larger type. "Oldest Textile Plant in New England Threatened. Peace-Pipe Industries and United Textile Workers Clash on Demands. Employees in Mass Meeting To-night."

To-night. Why, that was Aunt Em's birthday. I noticed the date on the newspaper. My own preoccupation had made me forget. Now I would be there for the celebration that always took place. But it wouldn't be a very festive one with this news. Perhaps I ought to wire that I was on my way. I started towards the telegraph office before I decided that it would mean more if I surprised Aunt Em. So I went on through the gate, set down my suitcase, and stood there on the platform, reading the headlines and the finer print in the news story beneath them.

"Move to organise local union main issue in textile fight. Propose ten per cent wage cut attacked by Joseph Kelly, Jr."

Joseph Kelly, Jr. I read the name twice before I realised that this was young Jo. Young Jo Kelly with those mistaken views of his that never seemed to have anything to do with the kind and pleasant person he really was. But this was treason, throwing dynamite at Peace-Pipe, at us——

I felt a hand laid without warning on my arm, and then I was pushed so roughly that I almost lost balance. I would have fallen if I had not been held firm and fast. I turned with words of furious protest on my lips, but I never said them. At that same instant a heavily-laden station truck bore down within a few inches. The piled trunks teetered as it swerved its course, and the man steering it glared and made frantic motions at me. Only after it had passed did I turn to see who was responsible for my still being whole.

"Oh!" I knew that I was stammering because it embarrassed me to find that my rescuer was also my companion of the coffee-stand. Apparently I couldn't escape from him, whoever he was. This time I knew that explanations were in order. "Thanks again," I said. "I couldn't hear it coming. You see I'm—deaf; I don't hear a thing."

I knew that I must look at him because he would be making some sort of answer and I must follow the motions of his lips. I could feel the colour creeping over my face and neck with the effort it had been to get the words out.

He did not seem startled by what I had told him. He smiled a rather slow, grave smile as if he were acknowledging something of which he was already aware.

"I know," he said simply, touched his hat, and walked away without once looking back.

It wasn't until I was in my seat and the train just getting clear of the dingy outskirts of the city, that I found myself thinking about his answer, and wondering how he could have been so sure.

CHAPTER ELEVEN

By the time my train neared Blairstown a steady rain was blurring the window panes and the early twilight of October had set in. The station and the familiar mill sign with the Indian chief's head and legendary pipe of peace looked dingier than I remembered. The bitter tang of all mill towns was in the air as I left the stuffy car. The keenness of river damp and smoke and the faint suggestion of chemicals mingled with every breath I drew. It clung to buildings and houses and was part of every bush and tree and signpost as the smell of mice and dust, old clothes and old books belongs to an attic; as chalk and ink are part of any schoolroom since time began. Perhaps I was more aware of it than most, for ever since the deafness had come upon me my sense of smell had been sharpened. I had come to depend upon it, almost as an animal does for its very existence.

One other passenger was alighting at the station, a man from the car ahead. As he turned into the light I recognised him for my companion of the coffee-stand, the same who had rescued me from the baggage truck. He had put on his raincoat, and though his hat was over his eyes I knew him by his walk and the sharp, strongly-set jaw. I felt annoyed that he should be here in Blairstown, walking with an easy assurance as if the place and he were on familiar terms. I was further annoyed when I saw him hail the one and only station taxi, which I had been planning to take. It served me right for not wiring the house to have Janice meet me. Of course I could ask the station agent to call another cab, but that always meant explanations and talk and I felt in no mood to study moving lips and think up appropriate replies to questions.

"The walk won't do me any harm," I decided, "and I've carried heavier suitcases than this one."

There is something about falling rain that crystallises thought—at least so it is for me. It is as if seeds of emotion long dormant in my mind must stir at that moist summons even as their earthy counterparts do. So the chill drops on my face were both a goad and a caress that night as I plodded on through the grimy no-man's land which always seems to surround stations in any community. It was a good mile and a half to the house, and I had plenty of time to think. The reaction of the day's strain had already set in. I had been facing that decision so long. The past two years seemed longer, looking back upon them, than all the years that had gone before. Certain days and nights rose to mock me, more vivid because of the rain with which they must always be associated.

It had been raining the day that I first realised my plight. I had been aware of myself lying helpless on my bed in the room at the head of the stairs. My body had felt miraculously free of pain, and though I was still very weak I had been able to turn it a little. I could follow a figure in starched white who moved about my room. I had wondered vaguely why she did not speak to me, though she made me comfortable without words and smiled as she anticipated my needs. She had left the room on some errand, I remember, and I had lain quiet watching the familiar pattern of bare branches and falling rain beyond the windows. Painstakingly as only those who have emerged from illness can do, I had studied the furniture and reassured myself that every chair and picture and article on my bureau was in its place. I could find nothing amiss, and yet through the haze of my own weakness I had sensed that all was not as it should have been. It had taken the rain outside to give me the clue. A tin roof covered the porch below the western windows, and always, even in a mild summer shower, the drops had made a pleasant din that could swell to frantic volume in heavier downpours. That had been the false note in the picture—my eyes saw falling water and my ears heard nothing. Presentiment turned me cold under the warmth of the bedclothes. I had known then what I must do and I called upon every shred of strength left in me to accomplish it.

My knees buckled under me, and the effort to crawl those few yards over the carpet made me break out into a sweat. But I reached the window at last. It had been left open a little and I thrust my hand into the wetness. The water struck me with an icy chill, and I knew that my eyes had not deceived me. Rain was coming down in slanting shafts, bounding and splashing on the roof below, and yet I might have been in a padded cell for all the sound I heard.

The nurse found me there, and I don't remember how she got me back to bed. Later I knew Aunt Em was holding one of my hands, and Dr. Weeks the other. They tried to smile and act reassuringly, but they were trying so hard it was worse than if tears were running down their cheeks.

Their lips kept moving and I knew they must be speaking to each other. There they were so close I could feel their breath, and not a sound reached me. The more I strained, the more I felt a queer numbness in my ears. It was like having been turned to a wooden puppet suddenly in the midst of live actors.

I could feel my own lips beginning to move, to form words that my mind was saying over and over.

"I can't hear you," I said, and I turned to the doctor and held him fast with my eyes. "I'm deaf—that's the truth, isn't it?"

I shall always be grateful to Dr. Weeks for not hedging. His eyes held mine steadily and he gave a long, affirmative nod. After Aunt Em left us alone he went over to my desk and wrote down the answer to another question I had not asked.

"You have been very ill," I read. "The meningitis infection has affected your ears, but we hope not permanently."

I think I shall always be able to see the shape of those jerky pencilled letters, though the realisation of what had happened came slowly, in little ways. Returning to Blairstown that day brought back all the hurts and bitternesses, as if those memories were actually keeping step with me through the rain.

Especially I quickened my pace past the town hall at the edge of the Square. I could never pass it without the humiliation of a certain day when I had gone there to renew my driver's licence and returned without it. It was the summer after my illness and I was just beginning to read lips. I still missed a good many words unless people spoke slowly and remembered not to turn away as they talked. But that inspector had made me understand without any difficulty. Then there was the book of rules with the special paragraph about physical impediments. I couldn't very well ignore that. It didn't do any good to protest that I had a good driving record, and that there was nothing wrong with my eyes and other faculties. Those ten minutes are among the most painful I have ever endured. The inspector didn't relish them any more than I. He was red with embarrassment when he handed me back my old licence with an apologetic headshake.

I might have got one somewhere else. Usually there are ways of getting by rules. But I never had the heart to try again. Besides, every one in Blairstown knew what had happened to me, so what would have been the use? Yes, I thought, splashing through a deep puddle to get past the building, that was the trouble with small towns, one was too much a part of them ever to escape from oneself. Association stalked one at every corner. There was no deceiving the next-door neighbours. No matter how brave a show one might stage for their benefit.

"A little town is like a lantern," Maggie Flynn used to say. "Nothing's hid from sight."

Across the river the mill lights showed through the rain. Several of the buildings were half-dark, which I knew meant small shifts and no great rush of business. Even if I had not heard it from Harry or read it in the papers, the spacing of those lights would have told me how steadily business had slackened month by month since November, 1929. A panic in Wall Street had seemed a little thing compared to the personal calamity that had overtaken me. But now in 1931 I was beginning to realise a financial collapse could seriously affect the sort of security I had always taken for granted. Uncle Wallace and Mr. Parker discussed bank loans with Aunt Em and returned from business conferences in New York and Washington with long faces. Harry no longer spoke wistfully of dabbling in the market.

"Guess it was lucky for me I couldn't afford to buy any securities on margin," he had admitted more than once.

He had come back considerably sobered by his last college reunion. So many of his class were out of jobs, and the rest worried about the unemployment situation. He had been reckoned fortunate to be kept on at all.

"Don't think I'm fool enough not to know where I'd be

if you and I weren't going to be married," he had reminded me a little bitterly one day.

"Please, dear," I had begged, "don't say things like that. You'd got your start at Peace-Pipe before we met, and Uncle Wallace and Mr. Parker both think you have real ability once you know the business from the bottom up——"

"By that time the bottom will have dropped out and there won't be any top most likely," he had answered with a shrug. Then, seeing that his words had hurt me, he had slipped an arm round my shoulders and rubbed his cheek against mine. "Don't take what I say personally, Emmy, I've got a prize in you and I know it—only I could make good in the business if I had the chance."

He had gone on to tell me of certain innovations he was eager to see made in the mill products. There was a trend towards cheaper, less conservative merchandise, and he felt that Peace-Pipe might as well begin to meet the demand.

"Who's buying sheets and towels nowadays?" he pointed out. "It's girls your age getting married and setting up homes on a shoestring. Well, they're going to get the most goods they can for their money, and to hell with quality. Put on fancy borders and plenty of colour and do it up in smart wrappers, and the orders'll come in. It's worth trying, but get the company to see it! Peace-Pipe Mills will go on turning out the same old line, and the buying public will let them go bury themselves under their own surplus stock."

Harry's arguments made sense, but when I tried to back him up I met the same stone wall of conservatism. Uncle Wallace and Aunt Em, Mr. Parker and the directors couldn't seem to see things in any but the old terms. They were proud of their standards, and they instinctively fought against any radical changes in methods and products.

"If we can just hold out!" they always ended by saying. "Business is bound to start on the upswing soon. We've weathered other panics and depressions. Quality always wins out in the long run."

My deafness spared me much of the discussions, but no

one with eyes to see and read could fail to note the signs and portents. Other New England textile centres were becoming ghost towns, operating on skeleton shifts or shut down completely like mining towns where the vein of precious ore is dwindling, and the pulse of prosperity has slowed down. I never thought it could be so with Blairstown, yet I saw the first unmistakable signs that day. Still, I saw them as someone watching from behind the security of a window-pane sees falling snow, not as one feels who has ever been caught in a blizzard.

I was drenched through by the time I turned up our driveway. The shades were not drawn, and lamplight within shone on the wet lawn. I could see Great-grandfather Blair's portrait over the fireplace and the comb-back Windsor chairs that were more admired than sat upon silhouetted against the window-panes. Chrysanthemums in russet and copper gave back reflected brightness on the centre table. Across the hall mahogany, white damask and polished silver were as they had always been ever since I could remember, and Maggie Flynn moved from table to sideboard in her immemorial black and white. Order and comfort and tradition waited there. Once I stepped across the threshold they would take me in hand again. It is strange to look in upon the life of a household to which one has belonged when it is continuing its activity without one. I was not expected, and the household was preparing to celebrate Aunt Em's birthday as usual. I saw extra places for guests, the best china service, and the pre-prohibition sherry in readiness. My return would not alter it except by one place more, hastily set at the table. We are less indispensable than we think, even to those we love.

I wonder if soldiers feel like this, I thought, standing out there in the rain. I wonder if they feel, coming back from some unsuccessful campaign, that maybe a place and people could go on just as well without them.

Foolish to make such comparisons. What did I know about soldiers?

But at least, I kept on thinking as I reached for the

cold knob of the front door, at least if they're beaten they don't have to bring back the news of their own defeat. Their familes would have heard of that first, and I've got to tell mine that doctor number nine—or is it eleven?— has failed.

I must have frightened Maggie and Aunt Em, for they ran out and took my wet things and brought me a glass of sherry before they started to scold me for walking up from the station.

"Please, Aunt Em," I said when Maggie had hurried upstairs to draw a hot bath, "please don't ask a lot of questions. I'll tell you everything to-morrow, but just to-night I don't feel as if——"

One of the things I minded most about being deaf was never feeling sure of my voice. It would have been a comfort to know that it kept steady. I guess it didn't then because Aunt Em's expression changed to that scared, helpless one I knew so well.

"You're tired, dear," she comforted as she drew me over to the fire. "You shouldn't have walked so far and carried that heavy suitcase in all the rain."

"Don't try to be kind," I could feel my throat tightening with every word. It made me hard and curt with her as I hadn't meant to be. "We might as well face the music——" I broke off and shrugged. It helped to hide what I was really feeling. "Music that even I can hear."

I saw her wince, though she tried to act as if she hadn't understood what I meant.

"Well"—she straightened her shoulders and smiled in the encouraging way that I had come to dread—"suppose these treatments haven't helped you as much as we hoped. Dr. Lowe isn't the only ear specialist left. There are others we haven't tried."

"We're not going to try any more." Her eyes dropped before the determination she met in mine. I knew I was hurting her, but I couldn't stop. I'd been through too much in the last weeks to try to make things easy for myself or any one else. "We can't go on this way any longer, hoping like fools and catching at straws. I'm deaf—stone-deaf. I always will be and that's that."

I turned and started for the hall, but she caught my arm. I could feel her trembling under her best black taffeta dress.

"We mustn't be hasty, dear," she tried to soothe me; "and besides, there's Harry. You must give it more time for his sake as much as your own."

"It was for Harry's sake I tried this last doctor," I reminded her. "Except for him I couldn't go on. He's all I've got, and when we're together——"

I saw her face relax with relief at that.

"You'll feel different about this when you've talked everything over with Harry. He's coming for dinner tonight. It'll be a real birthday for me now you're back, even if things aren't looking very bright down at the mills. I suppose you've seen the papers?"

I nodded in sudden contrition.

"I don't know what we're heading for, and if the worst element here gets mixed up with a lot of professional trouble-makers . . . I'm worried, Emily—nothing like this ever started at Peace-Pipe before."

She had never turned to me in just that way before. I realised suddenly all she had been keeping out of the cheerful letters she had written me.

"I'm sorry," I told her. "I didn't mean to unload everything that was on my mind, but somehow—to-night——"

She turned, and I knew that Maggie had spoken to her from the hall. "Your bath's ready," she relayed the message, "and Maggie says she's laid out your dry things. Cousin Eunice is in the guest-room."

I sighed as I gathered up my wet hat and soggy purse.

"Any one else coming?" I asked.

"No, just a family party. We can play bridge afterwards. Oh, I forgot to tell you, Dr. Weeks is taking on an assistant, and he's coming too."

"What did you say?" I thought I had failed to catch her words, though I knew the motions of her lips so well I seldom had to ask her to repeat.

F

"An assistant, and I'm thankful he's got someone to take a little of the work off his shoulders. I haven't met the young man yet. He's just out of his hospital training and considered very promising. Will's been interested in him for some time now. He asked to bring him here to-night. Run along and dress now, dear, you've got nearly an hour."

CHAPTER TWELVE

I FELT anything but festive as I came downstairs in a last year's dress that Maggie had laid out for me. Janice had made use of it during my absence. The clasp of the belt was bent, and she had taken off the rhinestone shoulder-clips and forgotten to put them back. Without them it looked drab and spiritless, the way I felt. But perhaps Harry wouldn't care what I had on, so long as we need no longer be separated. I could see him standing by the fire, and I tried to make him look up and catch my eye instead of listening to Aunt Em and Cousin Eunice. Cousin Eunice was pointing to the headlines I had already seen in the evening paper, and from Harry's expression I guessed that she was giving him her opinion of the mill trouble. He seemed tired, though his face lightened in quick response when I called his name.

"Harry, Harry darling," I was clinging to him, with my lips against the sandy crispness of his hair. "I had to come back. I couldn't stand another hour of it and—Oh, dear, why can't we just be by ourselves somewhere?"

I hung back at the door, trying to prolong the moment. I saw then what I hadn't noticed at first, that he was in evening clothes, a formality that a family birthday dinner would not have rated. So, he was going somewhere after-wards. I must have shown my surprise, for he rolled his eyes at me and sighed.

"The Catons are giving a dance," he explained. "I promised to drive over with Janice and help out with some of their house guests. Of course if I'd known you were coming I wouldn't have said yes. Why don't you come along too?"

"No." I shook my head and tried not to look disappointed. "I'd just be an extra girl. It's all right, only of course I can't help wishing——"

I broke off partly because Maggie was opening the front door to Dr. Weeks and his companion. As Maggie moved away with their hats and coats the hall light shone full upon the newcomer. For the fourth time that day I was seeing the man of the coffee-stand and the railway platforms. This time there was no turning away or snubbing him.

"Emily, this is a surprise." I tried to give no sign as Dr. Weeks went through the introductions. "Well, here's one for you. My associate, Dr. Vance. Merek, this is Emily Blair, though I told you she wouldn't be here to-night."

I had expected him to make small talk of our earlier meetings, but he merely acknowledged the doctor's introduction with a handshake before he went into the other room.

"Nice fellow," Harry said as we followed them in. "Doesn't have much to say for himself the few times we've met. Guess he knows his business though. He's over at the mills a lot, taking over all that end of the practice. It was getting too much for the old man."

I kept close to Harry. The old sense of happiness in his presence flooded me once more. Everything was going to be all right, I told myself, as I sat beside him sipping the sherry that Aunt Em poured sparingly into the cut glasses that went with the decanter. Harry touched his glass to mine and smiled. I could not hear the little answering clink, but the gesture went to my heart. I didn't begrudge Janice her entrance in a new green dress the colour of spring grass. She was looking prettier than ever. Her fair bobbed head shone under the lamplight and her face had that flowerlike tenacity that always surprised me after an absence. She had matured in the last couple of months. Her eyes were less soft and childish, and there was a new set to her mouth and chin. She stood with her glass high, talking animatedly to the young doctor. Their heads were turned away so I couldn't have read their lips if I had wanted to know what they were saying. I wasn't particularly interested, but I watched to see if she could throw her usual spell over him, or if he would continue to scrutinise her as he had me earlier in the day. He appeared to be listening intently and yet, as I watched them, I saw his eyes leave her face; and though he nodded in response to some remark I knew that he was watching Harry Collins and me. There was something disturbing in his glance. I slipped my arm through Harry's, and the firelight caught the stone on the ring he had given me. I felt sure young Dr. Vance must have noticed it on the third finger of my left hand. He seemed to notice everything and to be stowing it away in some invisible filing cabinet of his mind.

I don't remember much about that meal except that it was the usual party fare, served in Maggie's best style on the best Dresden china. The evening paper had disappeared, I noticed, before we went in to the table, and all mention of the mill troubles was avoided. We had pumpkin pie made from Grandmother Blair's recipe and I knew that Aunt Em must be telling Dr. Vance all that went into its making. He sat at her right and seemed always listening, seldom speaking, whenever I glanced that way. I sat quietly between Harry and Dr. Weeks, hungry and tired and glad to be back. The despair of the day seemed to retreat to the other side of the curtains that shut out the fall night.

It was time to drink toasts in cider made from the apples on the old trees below the garden. Dr. Weeks rose and lifted his glass towards Aunt Em at her end of the table. There was that quietly fond look in his eyes that always made me feel a little sad.

"Well," he began, and I knew beforehand what the toast would be, "to you, Emily, because there's no one like you."

Aunt Em accepted it with her usual little deprecating headshake.

"I'm afraid you're prejudiced, Will," she said, as she

had said on every birthday since I could remember. Then she lifted her glass, and I saw her hand tremble a little as she held it out. "Here's to Peace-Pipe," she began, and again I didn't have to follow her lips to know the toast she was making, "To Peace-Pipe—past, present, and future."

We drank coffee before the living-room fire, and I found myself on the sofa between Cousin Eunice and Dr. Vance. It wasn't an easy position with Cousin Eunice leaning across me to make conversation with the stranger in our midst. Cousin Eunice never minded asking personal questions. I was glad that for once they were not being directed at me.

"Vance," she said, weighing his name as if it had been some commodity she was appraising. "I don't suppose by any chance you're related to the Milton branch?"

"No," he told her, and I thought I saw a faint flicker of amusement in his expression. "My family name was spelled differently."

"Really." Cousin Eunice peered at him suspiciously.

"Yes," he went on, "it used to be Vancovitch, so you see those Milton Vances wouldn't claim me."

Cousin Eunice showed her surprise. She wasn't used to people with names like that, people who were obviously unimpressed by the sort of background she admired.

"Well, I always make it a point to ask," Cousin Eunice rallied with a shrug. "It's such a small world, and somehow I never can understand people changing their names, except by marriage of course. Mine was Pratt before I married into the Blair family."

"Any relation to the Pratt smelting and iron works in Pennsylvania?" Again I thought I detected a grim amusement about his lips.

"Oh, no, we belong to the Massachusetts branch," she told him emphatically.

"Well, the world's so small I thought I'd ask." He gave no sign beyond a slightly lifted eyebrow, but I knew he was speaking for my benefit. "I was out there working last summer."

"In the iron and smelting works?" I could see that Cousin Eunice was growing more disapproving with every remark, and that it pleased him to lead her on.

"Why, yes, in a way. I was making a survey of industrial diseases."

"Oh, I see, how interesting! Do you play contract?" Already Cousin Eunice's eyes were upon the card-table being set up in the alcove.

He shook his head and watched her move over to it. I was rather sorry he didn't play because bridge was one of my accomplishments. Deafness didn't interfere with it and I had come to be a good player. I wanted to show him what I could do with cards, and now there would be no chance. The four older ones would have their table, and after Harry and Janice left for the dance I would have this strange young doctor on my hands. Aunt Em was beckoning me over to the table, but I smiled and shook my head. I wouldn't have kept her from her game, knowing how she enjoyed it.

Janice went over and tinkered the radio. I knew it must be dance music from the way her shoulders swayed in time and from the annoyed frown on Aunt Em's face. She was trying to catch Janice's eye to make her turn it off. But before she had managed that Janice had caught Harry by the arm and they had begun to dance. I watched them, indifferently at first, and then with a sudden sense of hurt. They needn't have started in so soon; they were going to have the rest of the evening for dancing.

"Come." Harry was bending over me and reaching out his hands. "Come on, dear, here's one you know: 'Two Hearts in Waltz Time.' Let's take a turn."

Yes, I remembered. They had played it that night of the Valentine party. We had danced and danced to it with big red hearts for favours. I wasn't likely to forget that tune to the end of my days.

His arms were strong about me, and though I fumbled at the start I managed to get into the swing. I was so used to following his steps that it wasn't as hard as I had expected. I thought we were doing rather well, and I stopped straining to keep the rhythm. As we passed by the sofa I looked up and saw that Dr. Vance was watching us with that frank curiosity that had annoyed me earlier in the day. What annoyed me even more was that I caught a look of pity in his eyes before he let them drop once more to the book he had picked up from the table. I turned quickly to Harry's face for reassurance. But it was not there. He was given over completely to guiding me, and I knew in that moment that all spontaneity had gone out of our motions. I lost step just then and fumbled in sudden confusion.

"Oh, I'm sorry," I apologised. "My fault."

"No, mine," Harry denied politely. "It's because we haven't tried dancing together for so long. You're not bad, Emily, really you're not."

"Well, I'm certainly not very good." I tried to laugh it off as I spoke, but couldn't have sounded very convincing. "Remember what Dr. Johnson said—at least I think it was Dr. Johnson—about the dog walking on his hind legs: the wonder wasn't that he could do it gracefully, but that he could do it at all!"

"She shouldn't say things like that, should she, Dr. Vance?" Harry turned to him after he had motioned Janice to shut the radio off. "We'll have to get you to prescribe for her when she's difficult."

It irritated me that Harry should have drawn our guest into the talk, and I must have shown it.

"You don't like to make compromises, do you, Miss Blair?"

I pretended not to have caught his words, and there was some satisfaction in making him repeat them.

"I hate compromises, if you must know!" I flashed back. "I hate them almost as much as I do doctors' office manners and their puns."

"If I promise never to make any in your hearing——" he began.

But I cut him short. "In my *hearing*, did you say?"

"Well, what if I did?" He compelled me to go on with the conversation, though any one could see that I wanted to get away. "I'm not afraid to mention your deafness the way every one else around here seems to be."

I don't remember what answer I made, but I went over to the bridge-table and stayed a long time watching the players. They didn't guess that the cards were a blur before my eyes. I felt hot inwardly at the bluntness of that remark, even more at the truth that lay behind it.

When it was time for Janice and Harry to leave for the Catons' dance I followed them into the hall, determined to seem gayer than I felt as I watched them drive off. Ridiculous to feel forlorn and left out with Harry's kiss warm on my lips and the reassurance that he would be over the next evening. Yet I could not shake myself free of my earlier mood. As I closed the front door, I turned and found Dr. Vance standing behind me.

"Good-night." He held out his hand. "I've just been thanking your aunt for letting me come to her birthday party, and it's been nice meeting you again."

"Again?" I repeated. "Oh, you mean the North Station. That wasn't exactly my idea of a meeting."

"Or mine." He shrugged and smiled before he went on. "But as a matter of fact we'd met before that."

"In some doctor's office, I suppose. I've wasted so much time in one or another these last two years I can't keep track of them all."

He let the remark pass.

"No," he said, without reaching for his hat and coat, "it happened right here in Blairstown. There was a Christmas party down at the mills and you stood on the platform holding a little muff about the size of that." He put his two fists together as he spoke. "You must have been seven or maybe eight."

"Seven," I told him. "Yes, I remember. There was—some sort of trouble, wasn't there?"

He nodded.

"My father staged a little demonstration. He'd been laid off and he wasn't in the mood to appreciate Santa Claus."

Once more he gave me one of his long, disquieting looks.

"Oh!" I said lamely. "Then your father must have been the one who——"

"Yes, he was the one. Our name was Vancovitch then. They changed it after we left Blairstown. My father's dead," he added, "he died of lead poisoning in a plant near Newark. You needn't be afraid he'll turn up with a grudge."

"I suppose you can carry it on for him," I said. "It's just the perfect time for you to come back with all this labour trouble starting."

I saw him flush and knew that my words had hit the mark I meant them to.

"I guess I deserved that," he answered. "I hadn't meant to tell you. It was an impulse, and I ought to know by this time it's a mistake to yield to them." He hesitated before he went on again. "Well, I might as well explain that I came because Dr. Weeks asked me to. We owe a lot to him from years back. He saved my mother's life, and he helped me through college and medical school. I don't know any other way of paying him back."

"Oh," I said, feeling very small, "I see."

"And there are other reasons, too . . ." Even without hearing the tones of his voice I felt the sureness go out of his manner. "This place never brought us anything but misery and hard luck. It's come to stand for everything I hated and struggled to escape from, and I knew it would stay like that always unless I came back and gave it the best I have to offer. You have to turn the tables on the past sometimes if you don't want it to play tricks on you."

He bent to pick up his things, and suddenly I found myself trying to keep him from going.

"I'm sorry I said what I did," I told him. "I've had rather a bad day, and I took some of my feelings out on you. You kept turning up, you see, and it bothered me the way you seemed to know all about me."

He scarcely seemed to notice my apology as he stood there looking in at the living-room—at the firelight on the drawn brocade curtains; at the flowers and ornaments and books and the family portraits hanging in their places. I could tell that he was taking in every detail in a special kind of way, not like the casual observer.

"It's a funny feeling"—he turned to me at last with a quick shrug—"being on this side of your front door. When I was a kid I used to pass this house and wonder what it must be like inside. Well, now I've found out."

"And is everything the way you expected it to be?"

"Why, yes!" His eyes went back to the room and the group about the card-table before they returned to me. "Yes, it's the way I expected—all except you."

I didn't want to press him, but curiosity got the better of me at last.

"Oh, so I don't run true to form?"

"No," he told me, "you 'wear your rue with a difference.'"

"My what?" I thought I must have mistaken the word.

"Rue," he repeated, "in case it matters. You know, Miss Blair, I can't help liking you in spite of my disapproval. Good-night."

He was out of the front door before I could answer. I went back to the fire and tried to go on with the piece of knitting I had begun. But I kept losing count of stitches, and at last I put down my work and went to the shelf where the dictionary was always kept. I took it down and turned to the r's. "Rue," I read, "a herb with a bitter taste; to lament, or regret."

CHAPTER THIRTEEN

It had never occurred to me that Harry and I could ever quarrel, and yet we did, the day after my return. The afternoon had been beautiful after the rain, and that somehow made the sharp, barbed words the more hard to reconcile. Everything shone in a late October brilliance that was like a coat of clear lacquer laid on the familiar hills and roadsides. The bright, washed air held a faint edge of frost, and the far smoke of bonfires and a delicate spice of fallen apples mingled with every breath I drew. It was like drinking some rare, ethereal wine, such as gods might have brewed in the days of faith and innocence. I felt renewed as I rode beside Harry in the open roadster. Yesterday's despair had fallen away like dried scales.

"Harry," I begged as we drove back along the turnpike after a trip to the cider mill, "let's turn off here and walk to the burned-out house. I haven't been there since the day we had our picnic there and you told me——"

Looking back now, I can see that he had no wish to go there; but I persuaded him against his excuses. Before we had gone far on the wheel ruts I began to notice changes. The scrub oak and elder and sumac bushes had been ruthlessly cleared, and trenches dug in the marshes on either side. I cried out in protest as I had done as a child when what I treasured lay spoiled before my eyes. A rough, unpainted shack had been set up on the foundations of the ruined house, and workmen's tools were all about.

"Oh, Harry," I cried, "it's not ours any more!"

He kept his head turned away so I couldn't tell what his response might be. I caught at his arm and made him face me.

"Just see what they've done to it, dear. And I always hoped we could own this place some day. I never thought of it being sold to someone else and changed."

But he didn't answer with the fond, reassuring look I

had expected. Instead he frowned and drew away his arm.

"Oh, don't be so dramatic about it, Emmy," he said shortly. "Things are bound to change."

His words were chilling. The brightness of the day suddenly went out for me though the sun still lay warm on the distant marshes, making broken mirrors of all the little irregular pools. There was something more than casual annoyance in his rebuke, and because I was hurt I did not let it pass as I should have done.

"And people change, too," I reminded him. "You're different, Harry. I've felt it ever since last night."

"Oh, Lord, if you're going to get edgy because I didn't know you were coming and because I'd made a date——"

I cut him short.

"I'm not getting edgy as you call it. It's only——" I saw his face grow remote and blurred through the tears I was determined not to shed. "It's only that you seem to be holding me off at arms' length. You won't let me get *to* you any more, and when two people love each other and are going to be married . . . You haven't forgotten we're going to be married, have you, dear?"

I tried to make it light and ironical, but I think my voice must have given away the desperation behind my words.

"Now, Emmy, that's not fair——"

"But you never mention it any more?"

"Well, how can I? Look what I'm making, and look at what's happening at the mills. It would be a fine time to ask for a raise so we can be married. Besides your aunt has other plans. She's been telling me about a doctor up in Montreal who's had a lot of luck with cases like yours, and——"

It came like a slap in the face, and I turned on him furiously.

"Don't you use that word about me, ever again," I said. "Whatever else you call me, I'm not a case. There aren't going to be any more doctors and treatments. I told Aunt Em that last night, and I'm telling you now, so it won't do any good to try and humour me along. I've put through two years it's going to take me the rest of my life to forget. They're over, and I've come back to marry you and be the best wife I know how to be. I have a terrible handicap, and we both know it. But I'll do everything in my power so it won't be too hard for you. It might even make us closer because it makes me even more yours. You do see how it is. Tell me you do, Harry, or I just can't go on. I can't——"

He held me close and tried to soothe me.

"You mustn't get all worked up like this. We have to be practical, you know. Calm down a little and be sensible."

"I've tried to be, Harry, but when you start talking about waiting it's like asking someone who's starving to wait while you set the table with the best linen and china——"

"Someone has to think about the dollars and cents. We can't live without them, not the way you're used to living."

That hurt me as it always hurts a woman to be told she's an expensive proposition.

"Just because I've had everything done for me doesn't mean I can't get along without lots of things I've been used to. The only thing I can't face doing without is you. We can manage with what I have. I know we can."

"Everything your father left you and Janice is tied up in the mills, and I don't suppose you know what Peace-Pipe Industries is bringing a share right now?"

"No, I don't know and I don't care. With my allowance and what you're making we'd have more than a lot of couples start on."

"Please." He pointed off behind the shack and put his finger to his lips. "I think someone's coming. Let's not stand here arguing any longer."

I followed him back along the narrow wheel-ruts, fighting off the crowding tears of hurt and humiliation. I tried to tell myself that men were stubborn about accepting financial help from a girl or her family. I had been brought up to feel that this was a trait to be admired. Perhaps I had gone too far with my plans. I had rather flung them at his head, but I had a right to discuss the future that we were going to share. It couldn't be a crime to say what one felt to the man one was going to marry. Perhaps I had been foolish and impetuous. Maggie had always warned me against rushing headlong into things.

"Least said, soonest mended," she used to tell me.

We reached the parked car, and Harry took his place beside me. But his eyes avoided mine and I knew he resented what I had said.

The sun was going down behind the broken, rough-backed line of western hills. Soon the sky would be a welter of flame above the dark chimneys of Peace-Pipe Mills. Once there had been a time when the shape of trees and hills and the molten drama of a sun's exit would have been enough to lift my heart and spirits. But that time was gone. My happiness was bound too closely to the happiness of another to be stirred in the old, impersonal way. I felt baffled and alone as we drove back through the miracle of a fall sunset over a New England mill town.

"Harry," I said as the car drew up by the steps, "don't feel annoyed with me. I've been waiting so long for this afternoon all to ourselves, and we can't let anything spoil it."

"Oh, forget it, Emmy." He reached for a cigarette and offered me one.

But I shook my head. I couldn't dismiss it as lightly as that.

"No, dear," I went on, "I meant every word I said about us and not waiting. Maybe I ought to have had more pride than to say them. I don't know what's become of my pride lately. It just seems to melt away when you love someone."

"I meant what I said, too, Emmy." He puffed hard at the cigarette and kept his eyes from meeting mine. "God knows, you're a thousand times too good for me and I know it, but——"

"Oh, Harry, please!" I cut him short. "I'm selfish and headstrong and impetuous, but I do love you so. It makes me impatient and stupid sometimes."

He put his fingers over my lips and would not let me go on.

After he had left I wandered about the garden and the path that led to the made-over stable and the apple-trees behind it. Bridget, the dog that young Jo Kelly had presented me with the day of my engagement party, came rushing out of the toolhouse to greet me. It was comforting to feel the thrash of her regrettably long tail against my legs and the wet softness of her tongue on my fingers. "That dog," Aunt Em and Maggie called her, and we had all given up hope of classifying her as to breed. But she made up for discrepancies of appearance by exuberance of spirit and a devotion to me that was almost an embarrassment at times. Everything about Bridget was at variance— her body long and rangy; her coat the silky kind that should have belonged to a lapdog; her ears drooped limply, while her tail flaunted its length like the banner of some fantastic lost cause. I smiled in spite of my own preoccupation to see her trotting before me through the dusk. Her nose pointed towards the woodyard at the foot of the orchard, but she kept looking back to make sure that I was following.

Suddenly I saw her start forward, all wagging animation. She forgot to look back at me, and I lost her for a moment in the dimness. Then I came closer and saw the reason for her excitement. A man was moving about in the woodyard, a shabby figure with a shock of dark upstanding hair. I knew it for young Jo Kelly even though our woodpile was the last place in Blairstown where I might have expected to find him. I could not see his face for the failing light, but I stood behind one of the old apple-trees and watched him leave off splitting a big log to bend and caress the dog. She leaped upon him, and even though I could not hear her whines of welcome the pantomime of her joy was deeply affecting. Watching those two, I wondered what it was that he had—this power to kindle the affections of a dog, or to stir his own kind to confidence and courage. Even those who held him an enemy had to like him. He possessed some quality one couldn't name that made difference of opinion seem unimportant. I was glad that Bridget had led me there just at that moment. I wanted to call his name and feel his thin, quick fingers in mine again. I could have taken comfort talking to young Jo there by the woodpile even though so much had happened in the last two years to send us in opposite directions.

But the dusk was too thick to make it possible for me to follow his lips. So I stood there watching him through the gap between crooked apple branches. He was lifting and piling the wood he had split, and I knew as if he had told me that this was his way of helping lighten the work that must be growing too heavy for his grandfather. I knew that Aunt Em worried about old Jo's stubborn carrying on of duties, refusing all assistance. I guessed that young Jo must also have the old man on his mind, though they were still unreconciled.

He set the last piece in place and wiped his forehead with the sleeve of his coat. Then he straightened his shoulders and stood still a moment looking up towards the house where lights shone yellow in all the familiar rooms. I wondered if he remembered the big carved bed in the spare room where he had spent those weeks of convalescence in his childhood, or if he had shed completely our side of the river.

I saw him bend to pat the dog he had given me before he swung himself over the fence and disappeared down the back road. Perhaps he was already on his way to talk to some group of workers, to urge them to organise and call a strike as he had done at the last mass meeting. Yet here was the wood he had split and piled to keep our fires burning. So ironic a situation was past my comprehension. But, whether it made sense or not, seeing young Jo Kelly there had given me back for a moment the old happy sense of confidence that used to surround my childhood. It was as if he and I shared a secret once more, the way we used to before the river had come to flow so irrevocably between us.

Bridget had returned to my side. She kept her nose pressed close to my ankles as I went up the dark driveway.

I felt grateful for her warm and living presence. Night always intensified the isolation which deafness had brought. Well I knew the truth behind the old saying: "The day has eyes, the night has ears."

CHAPTER FOURTEEN

THE Directors of Peace-Pipe Industries always met on the first day of November and the last day of April, dates which punctuated the year for Aunt Em and Uncle Wallace. I could not recall a time when they had not reckoned happenings as before or after spring or fall meeting. Of recent years my long absences from Blairstown had lessened the importance of these occasions for me. This year, however, the November meeting loomed large on the calendar, for the future of Peace-Pipe Industries hung in the balance. None of us liked to admit the seriousness of the situation. But we all knew that the strike agitation was far from idle talk; that a walk-out might be called on short notice. Warnings had been given, and the issues could hardly lie dormant much longer. We knew that representatives of the United Textile Workers would present their case to the Board. We knew the demands—dropping of the proposed 10 per cent wage cut, reinstatement of certain workers who had been laid off, and recognition of a local union to be organised by Peace-Pipe employees. We knew, too, what the directors felt about all these issues. They would never make concessions, particularly on the matter of organising.

"It's the end of Peace-Pipe if we give in an inch," Uncle Wallace had said plenty of times, and Aunt Em and Mr. Parker and the rest were in complete agreement. "When a company has operated for over half a century it doesn't have to be told how to run a business. There wouldn't be any mills to-day without the stockholders' money, and it's time some of us took a stand to see their rights protected. Who carries the losses in times like these, I'd like to know."

G

"Still, it might be wise to make a few concessions," Harry Collins sometimes ventured to remind them. "They don't want to call a strike when business is practically at a standstill. The best time to get what they want is when it's booming and they can hold you up on orders——"

"Hold us up, yes, that's exactly what they're planning to do. Bandit methods, and you needn't try to cover it up with the sort of talk they use. I'm surprised, Harry, that you'll even suggest our listening to their demands. They've got to be curbed right at the start of things."

"I'm not taking their side," Harry would argue, "but I do know we can't take care of what little business we have left without experienced millhands. We have to meet competition, and it's stiffer than ever right now. There have to be compromises on both sides——"

"There you go again!" Uncle Wallace and Mr. Parker always reacted violently to that word. "Compromise—it only means giving in by inches, and you ought to know it. Look at what happened at Danforth Mills and Still River. If they'd had any backbone it wouldn't have come to wholesale walk-outs and the disgrace of calling for the State militia. We'll never let it come to that at Peace-Pipe. The United Textile group needn't think they can frighten us by waving the big stick."

A year before, even six months ago, I would not have bothered about such discussions. I would not have strained to make out what they were saying about the mills. Now it had become important to me because the state of Peace-Pipe Industries had come to have bearing on the future I waited so impatiently to share with Harry. It was like studying a new language, the terms were so strange; and I hesitated to show my ignorance. I didn't want to keep asking what this word meant or that. Often it was difficult to follow discussions that grew heated and full of interruptions. Each person who joined in made it harder for me to follow. I had learned from past experience not to keep asking to have remarks repeated. In the days when I was first struggling to read lips I used to be reminded of the circus jugglers who could keep a number of balls going in the air at once. It seemed to me that to follow the talk of two or more people required as keen an eye and agility of mind.

So I read all I could find about the mill activities in the paper, and I questioned Harry whenever he was in the mood to be expansive. Although he came and went as usual and was with us at the dinner-table night after night, he and I were alone together less often. At any other time I might have accused him of manœuvring it so; but his interest in the business was genuine, and Aunt Em and Uncle Wallace turned to him with their problems as they had never done before. I accepted a certain tension and preoccupation, telling myself that I must be patient till after the directors' meeting. I began to live up to that date and long to have it over. Neither Harry nor I alluded to our differences of the day after my return. I regretted having been so impulsive on the subject of our marriage. He must be the first to speak of it. After all, I reasoned, lying awake in my bed, waiting for morning to show between the branches of the copper beech-tree by my eastern window, after all there were other matters as important as my own personal happiness.

"It will all come right in the night," Maggie Flynn had always assured Janice and me when we were little and in need of comfort. I had believed her implicitly then, and the habit of faith in to-morrow persisted in me as I think it must in all of us to the end of our days.

And so the first of November came round and Aunt Em and the others went down to the Wawickett House where directors' meetings had been held in the long private drawing-room where Janice and the Parker twins and I used to take dancing lessons years before. Board members from Boston would come on the ten o'clock train, and the meeting would last till mid-afternoon. It was a grey day of low-hanging clouds. Smoke from across the river mingled with the damp and lay like wet dust that could not settle to the ground.

"Ugh!" Janice shivered as we ate lunch together. "Nice cheerful weather, just the kind to put every one in good humour down there at the Wawickett House. I'm going to date up somebody and clear out."

I had half a mind to ask her to take me along, but before I knew it she had slipped away in the little car. I had never felt close to Janice, and now more than ever we seemed separated by a wall of cold glass through which we motioned to each other. For all that, I felt a new warmth in her when she was off her guard. Yet with it there was a tension I had never suspected in her. In the old days she had been gay and casual in all her relations with others. Now she took offence easily; blazed away at some unintentional slight, or grew moody and aloof for no apparent reason. Aunt Em had noticed the change and commented upon it.

"I can't make out what's come over Janice," she said. "I offered to send her to New York last month; but she said she'd rather stay here, though Heaven knows the child has always complained that Blairstown's too dull to suit her. If there were any eligible young men about I'd think she was in love."

I put on my raincoat and walked for an hour through the grey afternoon, with no objective but to kill time and avoid sodden leaves that had washed down from lawns and driveways. Even Bridget seemed affected by the atmosphere. She made no excited foragings with stiffened tail and wriggling body. She stayed at my heels, closer than a shadow.

This isn't living, I thought as I moved on aimlessly through the dampness. It's no better than doctors' waiting-rooms. I can't fit into the old ruts any more or make new ones with Harry.

I felt suddenly alien in this town where I had grown up. It was not the refuge I had thought to find in my hour of need. I felt like someone who returns to knock at the doors of the past, only to find them closed. It was in this mood that I came back to find Dr. Vance sitting by the living-room fire.

He was the last person I cared to see, and my irritation was plain. That morning I had been sorting out some sketches I had made months before with an idea of developing them into textile patterns. I wished that I had not left them spread about on the table, for I saw that Dr. Vance had been studying them while he waited. He held one in his hand as he rose to greet me.

"Aunt Em is still at the directors' meeting," I told him without cordiality. "There's no telling how long it will last."

"I know," he said; "that's the reason I came to-day. I wanted to see you, not your aunt."

If Maggie had announced him I might have had a chance to escape, but I was caught now.

"I took a look at these." He held out the sketch and indicated the others. "They seemed to be out on exhibition. I take it they're yours."

"Yes, they're mine. Am I supposed to ask you what you think of them?"

"Well, since you seem so eager for my opinion"—he squinted at the one he held and reached for the others—"I rather expected they'd be worse."

"You overwhelm me."

I rose stiffly and gathered the sheaf into the portfolio. He didn't offer to give back the one he had, so I held out my hand for it.

But he took no notice of the gesture.

"This is the only one you really pulled off," he went on. "The design's good, but it would be more effective if you reversed the dark and light."

His suggestion was right. I wondered why I hadn't realised it before. But I had no intention of letting him see that I agreed.

"You're pretty cocksure about a lot of things, aren't you, Dr. Vance?" I said.

"Maybe." He gave back the sketch as he spoke. "I never could see much point in saying what I didn't think. Now these things of yours are so good they ought to be a whole lot better. But you never bothered to work them through. That's the trouble with girls like you——"

"Just what do you mean when you say ' girls like you '?" I broke in.

He shrugged and reached for a cigarette.

"Plenty of money, plenty of talent; good looks, too much doting family and too many distractions. I think that about covers it."

Maggie appeared just then with the tea-tray. She seemed pleased that I had a caller. I noticed that she had trimmed the crusts off the sandwiches, an infallible sign of her approval. But I did not smile as she set it on a low table before me. I wished that Maggie had been less eager to offer hospitality.

"That goes to the spot." Dr. Vance held out his cup to be refilled. "I had an emergency appendix to do this morning and a couple of visits out in the country, so I skipped lunch."

I found myself looking at his hands, noticing again how strong and flexible they were, the fingers long, with slightly flattened tips. I could visualise them manipulating some sharp, delicate instrument. In my scrutiny I forgot to watch his lips.

"Look!" He was leaning across the tea-table, forcing me to follow his words. "We got off to a bad start again to-day. Let's forget it and begin all over, because the sooner we do the easier it will be for both of us. I came because I wanted to see you alone. I'm going to talk to you, and you're going to listen whether you want to or not."

My hand shook as I set down the cup. I started to rise, and I might have managed to bolt from the room if the tea-table had not hemmed me in.

"No." He went on speaking without taking his eyes from mine. "It's this way. I'm a doctor; and if I saw some-one going round dragging one foot, and I knew I could do something about it, don't you think it would be a crime if I just let him go on limping?"

"That would depend," I answered evasively, "on how the person felt."

"You know what I'm driving at—I mean you and your deafness."

"That's my trouble, isn't it? I'd rather not talk about it, if you don't mind."

"But if I can help you——"

"You can't. Please just finish your tea and go——" Once more I tried to get up, but somehow I couldn't force myself from the chair.

"You can't put me off like this." He was leaning forward, and his face had sharpened with intensity.

"Why did you have to come here?" I hoped my voice was as bitter as the feeling behind it. "Why couldn't you leave me alone? I'm not asking for pity from you or any one."

But he shook his head.

"Yes, you are," he said, "—not in words, maybe, but there are other ways. When you strain to catch what people are saying, and when you miss something and that look comes into your face, you're asking for it."

"Why do you say such things to me? Do you think I lost my hearing on purpose?"

He shook his head once more.

"Please get this straight, Miss Blair. You mustn't confuse help with pity, just because you confuse love with it."

I rose and started for the door, but I felt his strong thin hands on my arms as he pulled me back. I wanted to shake them off, yet I was too startled to free myself. He made me look at him while he went on.

"You must listen. After that it will be up to you. No, don't speak. It's this way—I've helped cure people who'd been deaf longer than you have." Once more I struggled to move away, and once more his grip tightened. "It's nothing you ever tried—it's a sort of discovery another doctor and I stumbled on. I won't try to tell you in medical terms; you wouldn't understand them, and besides we're still experimenting. But we're not quacks. We're both full-fledged doctors and we know we're on the right track."

I twisted free of him at last and began gathering up my things. I wouldn't give him the satisfaction of further argument. Better to ignore the subject, I decided. But I hadn't counted on Dr. Vance's persistence. I felt like the wedding guest who had no choice once the Ancient Mariner with his glittering eye had singled him out for victim. It didn't matter how many times I told him the specialists I'd been to and that they'd all given me up as a hopeless case. He just kept right on telling me more about this discovery of his. It seemed he and this other doctor had come on it accidentally when they were treating some steel workers for gland deficiency. Two of the men were stone-deaf, and after the treatments had been going on for some weeks they began to feel sensation in their ears.

"They showed so much improvement that we knew it couldn't have been just fool luck," he told me. "We had something, so we went on experimenting at the hospital clinic all last winter. The staff there let us work with a group of deaf patients, and I don't mind telling you we got results—three complete cures and definite response in all the other cases, even ones where the auditory nerves seemed permanently dead. We never had a chance to try it where the ears had been affected by meningitis. That's why, when I heard about you, I thought——"

"That I'd make another guinea pig to experiment on? No, thank you, Dr. Vance. I should think you'd have known how I'd feel without asking me."

I saw his face redden at that, and I was glad if I had hurt him.

"Many things are lost for want of asking," he said. "That's a proverb my father brought with him from Europe. I've found it worth remembering."

"Well, once and for all then," I told him, "my answer is ' No.' When I came back from Boston that day we met I'd made up my mind there would be no more doctors for me and no more experimenting. I've come home to make the best of things as they are, and—and I have other plans."

"That means you're going to marry Collins soon, I suppose?"

"We've been engaged for some time——"

"I know, and long engagements are apt to be risky." His eyes were uncomfortably keen in their scrutiny.

"Not when people really love each other," I said shortly.

"Maybe. I don't pretend to be an authority on that subject. Still, I've noticed that being in love isn't necessarily a permanent state."

"Just what do you mean?" I wasn't going to let a remark like that pass.

"Oh, only that marriage is the sort of business that demands all the faculties."

"You needn't have said that to me."

I felt my knees begin to shake, and I pressed my hands tight together so that he might not see how they were trembling.

"No," he admitted, "I needn't have, but you don't seem to think much of the pleasantries that successful doctors cultivate. I'll never be a successful one for that reason; apt to be on the blunt side. All right then, I'll finish what I started to say—just because you can't *hear* is no reason for you not to *see*."

He was in the hall, looking for his hat, and now it was my turn to go after him and call him back.

"I've been brought up to say 'Thank you,' even for things I don't want," I found myself telling him. "I needn't have been rude just because you were."

"It's all right by me." He smiled and took up his hat. "Call me any name you want to, only I can't understand your not being interested enough to give what I'm offering you a try. There's nothing to lose and everything to gain."

"But I tell you I can't afford to hope any more. For the last two years I've been chained to hope. Now I've broken free, you can't make me a prisoner again."

"We're all prisoners of hope some way or other, aren't we?"

"More fools then!"

"Well, maybe." He raised his shoulders once more in the expressive, half-foreign shrug. "People called Columbus a fool once, and Pasteur and a good many others I could mention. If you and I hoped a little we'd be in good company. But never mind, thanks for the tea."

"If I could be sure——" I began.

He wheeled about and cut me short.

"Who's sure of anything in this world?" Even without hearing the tones of his voice I was aware of the scorn behind his words. "I'm not a salesman. I didn't come here to give you guarantees and a lot of high-pressured talk. I don't offer you anything but a chance. Of course you needn't take it."

A car turned into our driveway as he opened the front door. I saw the nearing headlights brighten wet branches to gaunt silver in the instant of passing. They then fell into darkness again.

"Well, good-bye," he was saying. "My office hours are from two to four every afternoon except Friday, and I can always be seen by appointment."

He was gone before the car drew up at the steps. I felt grateful that I should not have to explain his presence to Aunt Em and Cousin Eunice as they came stiffly up the steps. They looked old and worn in different ways—Aunt Em peaked and grim, Cousin Eunice pouting and saggy and protesting. I was glad to busy myself replenishing the fire and pouring fresh tea.

"Aunt Em," I said, as I brought her a cup, "you look all in. Did you get anywhere at the meeting?"

"We got as far as a deadlock," she told me grimly between swallows. "Began with it and ended with it."

CHAPTER FIFTEEN

ON the desk before me as I write is a small wooden box, painted blue and patterned in quaint, bright designs. The colours are softer than they must once have been, like the eyes of those who have lived long and seen much. Many hands have left their mark upon the wood. The grain shows through in places, especially where the worn brass key fits into the little lock. That small blue box is like no other object in my room though it must be older than Grandmother Blair's pine chest, or the cherry bureau, older than the glass dolphin vases that came round the Horn by barquentine. The box, also, has crossed stormy seas. The hands that fashioned it and traced the delicate shapes of hearts and birds and flowers would have faltered, perhaps, in the laying on of those clear colours if they could have guessed how far their handiwork was to travel. Yet for me and for Merek Vance it has come to stand for all that we shared together in those months after my return.

I remember the first time I saw it incongruously set between a card index and a prescription pad on the top of a battered desk. It caught my eye because it seemed to be the one personal touch in the office Vance had fitted up for himself in a back room of Dr. Weeks's shabby old frame house just off the Square.

"I won't give in and let him experiment on me," I had vowed, resolutely turning about-face whenever I found my feet taking me in that direction. "I won't be fool enough to go through all the misery and disappointment again. He needn't think he can make me."

But all the time I knew a day would come when weakness would overtake me. Try my best, I couldn't put what he had said out of my mind.

"You mustn't confuse help with pity," he had told me, "just because you confuse love with it."

How had he dared to talk like that of love? He couldn't

mean that pity had any part in what Harry felt for me. Yet perhaps he saw what my love and need of love would not let me see.

"Just because you can't hear is no reason for you not to see."

He had said that, too, and I wished that I could forget it and the look that he had given me as he spoke.

"Being in love isn't necessarily a permanent state." I tried not to let myself remember those words and others that tormented me like thorns driven inward upon my mind and heart. "Marriage is the sort of business that demands all the faculties."

I knew that he was using my own fears as a means to break down my resistance to his plan, and I hated him for it. Yet for all my antagonism to the man himself I could not doubt his sincerity. He knew the vulnerable spot in me as surely as if his long fingers had touched a hidden spring of pain. I recoiled from his probings, though I was powerless to resist them. I hated him for having let drop those pebbles of doubt and fear into the deep pool of my consciousness. They had stirred ripples that spread and widened to engulf me as ripples will grow large long after the object that woke them has disappeared from sight. And the more I struggled against his offer of help, the more certain I became that I should find myself accepting it.

Sitting here alone at my desk, thinking back to that time and all that I felt for Harry Collins, I am shaken by the memory. For it is a memory now, not the frantic, feverish urge that goaded me then.

Love, when it comes for the first time, has the fierce and bewildering beat of spring in its pulses. Such ecstasy and despair are not to be reckoned with in terms of sanity and reason. The foolish and wise are equally at its mercy. Let no one doubt its power to exalt or betray, for it can rise renewed from bludgeonings or shrivel at a single breath. I think we were not meant to endure its rigours for more than a brief span. I am grateful to be free of its toils. Yet when I see that it has laid its bright, infallible mark upon some boy or girl, some man or woman, I feel a kind of inner comradeship. The terrible, sweet pain flows back, though the one whose presence could once inflict it is a stranger to me now.

But I must return to the small blue box. There I was, reaching out my hands to it for comfort, in that bare, plain office I had avoided so long. Across the desk I knew that Dr. Vance must be watching me with satisfaction, because I had not held out against him. It was my place to open the conversation, to explain my presence there after so emphatic a refusal. I turned the box about in my hands, tracing the design self-consciously with cold fingers while I tried to summon the words that proved to be unnecessary.

At such tense moments it often happens, as it happened to me then, that some insignificant object will become forever linked to our extremity. We must recall the exact shape of a leaf whose shadow fell across the blind of a sick-room; the scroll on the handle of a spoon our fingers gripped in the numbness of despair, the lace that edged the handkerchief we pressed to our lips to hide their trembling. I studied that little box almost without being aware of what I was doing. Yet the shape and colours of that painted design will stay with me as long as memory itself. It had been done with the same intricate, tender care that went into the fashioning of some medieval missal book, yet it also suggested a prim valentine. Two hearts held the centre of the lid, with a painted needle and a twist of thread joining them together. Stiff birds and spotted butterflies hovered at the corners, and a flowery garland encircled the whole. There were initials below the lock and fine lettering in a script I could not read. One felt the love that had gone into the making of that little box. A sense of other lives seemed to radiate from the very grain of the wood, as if one could feel the hands that had held it reaching out and touching one's own in turn.

I looked up at last, though my hands still held the box. "Well," I began lamely, "here I am."

The eyes that met mine across the desk were intent, but

kinder than I had ever seen them. To my surprise I saw that Dr. Vance was not gloating over my capitulation.

"So you like my little box," he said, as if it were the most natural thing for me to be sitting there in his make-shift office. "It happens to be my one and only family heirloom, and I'm rather attached to it."

"It's very old, isn't it?" I didn't know what else to say.

"I think so. My mother always said it had been in her family. It held the few trinkets she brought with her to America. Sometimes she'd let me play with it, or my sister, if we'd promise to be careful. I can remember seeing my mother take it in her hands, the way you did just now. I used to watch her and wonder why her eyes would look the way they did when she held it. I know now it took her back to the old days when she was young and the prettiest girl in her village, before she had to worry about winter and coal for the fire, and Father getting laid off and one or the other of us sick or needing something she couldn't give us."

"What do the letters say?" I asked. "It looks like a motto."

"It is," he told me, "in Lithuanian that I can't read. But my mother told me once what it means—that's where the needle and thread come in. It says, 'Love is like the eye of a needle.'"

"That's a queer saying."

"Yes, she had to explain it to me. The eye of a needle is a small thing, she used to say, but without it we could make nothing to keep us warm against the chills of winter."

"Why, that's beautiful!"

I found myself touching the letters that neither of us could read, in sudden recognition. It was as if a long procession of other women were speaking to me across time and space in some universal language.

"Then you believe it's true?" he asked.

"Of course. Don't you?"

"I haven't had a chance to prove it yet."

"Everything can't be proved." I was surprised that I

could talk this way to a man I hardly knew, one who had antagonised me from our first meeting. "Some things you just feel first and prove afterward."

He gave me one of his swift reassuring smiles.

"And you were the girl who wanted a guarantee that I could cure her," he reminded me.

"Yes," I admitted, "there are times when it's not easy to live up to what we believe." I was provoked that I should be giving myself and my feelings away like this. I certainly hadn't lived up to my plan of keeping the visit a cool impersonal one.

He must have felt the change in me, for before I had a chance to go on he leaned across the desk and spoke earnestly.

"I'm not asking you to believe that I can help you," he was saying, "but only that I want to do it."

"All right." I didn't trust myself to say more. "When do we start?"

For answer he rose and left the room while I waited, as I had waited in other, more handsomely-furnished offices.

"There's still time to go," I reminded myself as I measured the few feet of space between me and the hall door. I could be outside and away before the larger hand on the cheap alarm clock moved a fraction of the way to the next minute. Yet I knew that I would not go. And then he was coming towards me, carrying familiar paraphernalia.

"Oh," I said, "an injection. I've had plenty of those."

"You know," he said as he handled his instruments, "it's a funny thing, but you've never asked me whether it would hurt or not. I've been expecting you to."

It was my turn to shrug.

"Do I have to do everything you expect me to?" I asked. "Besides," I added, "pain wasn't the point, was it?"

"No, but it's a usual question."

He gave me another of his direct, searching looks.

"I'm going to ask you to give me your word that you'll see this through," he said. "It may take longer than either of us can guess, so I'd like to hear you say it."

"Don't you trust me?"

"Not altogether." I saw his eyes turn to the window that looked towards the mill chimneys and the span of the upper bridge. "I come from over there," he went on. "That's where I really belong, and I don't feel sure of myself or you or any one else on this side of the river, except of course Dr. Weeks."

"My mother came from over there, too," I found myself saying.

He nodded.

"I know," he said. "I used to hear them tell about her when I was little. She's a sort of legend, like the Cinderella story that girls who are plain and lonely and overworked have to believe in or they couldn't keep going. I never thought I'd be talking like this to her daughter."

I thought that it was even stranger that I should be there, letting him do what I had vowed I would never submit to again.

"Isn't it enough that I've come here?" I said bitterly. "Do I have to take some kind of oath on the Bible or one of your pet medical books?"

He held the needle up to the light and squinted at it before he answered.

"All right then," he said. "Let's not be melodramatic about it. You're here, and I'm ready to begin."

I reached for the little blue box, and he smiled to see me do so.

"That'll do instead of a book," he said before he went to work.

Afterwards I walked in the fall sunshine trying to forget that the old disturbing routine had begun again. Well, I had given my word, and I would keep it. I would not miss a visit, but he need not think that he could make me hope against all my doubts and prejudices.

I hardly noticed where I was walking till I found myself half-way across the bridge where I had stood so often as a child; where my mother and I had stood together all those years ago. "Don't worry," she had said. "You're safe on your side of the river. You're all Blair." But I wasn't all

Blair, and I didn't feel that I belonged anywhere in particular. Had my mother felt so sometimes, I wondered? Had old differences, old standards, and old loyalties overwhelmed her time and again as she stood where I was standing now? Surely it must have been so, though she had not had to stand here alone. A man's arm or a child's clinging fingers must make one feel more secure, I thought. Or did they twist the heartstrings into a more difficult, intricate tanglet I should never know that now.

The small blue box, for all its association with another woman, had given my mother back to me in a new image. I realised that for years I had confused her with the portrait of a beautiful woman in the ruffles and pompadour of two decades ago that an artist more famous than my father had painted. His brush had also made a legend of her even as Vance had said she was a legend to the people living over there in the crowded mill houses, to girls who tended bobbin and loom. It came to me then that I must be part of the legend, too, because I was her daughter. Perhaps they hated or envied me for that. I thought of the Christmas party for the millworkers that winter day when a man had sworn and shaken his fist; of a half-grown boy who had stared curiously at my little squirrel muff, and remembered it years later. It made me feel suddenly lonely and afraid.

"It will be different once Harry and I are married, and we will be married just as soon as this trouble at the mills is over."

It comforted me to tell myself that, even though I knew that the mill trouble had only just begun. From where I stood I could see a line of shabby figures, three or four men and a couple of women, stationed by Peace-Pipe gates. Hour after hour now they were there. They moved mechanically because it was easier than standing still on tired feet. Harry had told me that they were union supporters who had been dropped from the payroll. Other workers were being dropped each week while the deadlock between the union and the mill grew more bitter; while

H

futile negotiations went on and on without either side giving way on a single point. I could see the white placards they carried on sticks. When one or another of the picketers turned to reverse pace I could even make out a word or two: "Organised Labour," "Rights," "Unfair."

"Most of them don't like to picket," Harry had told me a few days before. "It's a protest now, but it's going to be a lot more than that if the union decides to call a walk-out."

So I turned back, but I couldn't put those distant figures with their white placards out of my mind. It ought to have been a simple, easy thing to cross over and talk with that little group. Yet I knew they would have distrusted such a gesture of camaraderie. Instinctively they would have thought there must be some motive behind my coming, and we should all have drawn back into our separate shells like cautious snails. It would only have ended in our talking about the weather, that safe conversational refuge to people who are on their guard. Even if one of them had been young Jo Kelly, I could not hope that it might have been otherwise.

Only children, I thought, can play and talk together without this self-imposed constraint. And even children's eyes are quick to note the difference between a patched sweater and a squirrel muff. They recognise the outward symbols and are more wary than we guess. I found myself wondering when I had first been made aware of the invisible barriers that are so much more formidable than those of brick and stone and barbed wire.

CHAPTER SIXTEEN

JANICE and I seldom saw each other except at meal-time, and even these meetings were apt to be occasional.

"I don't know when or where or what the child eats, most of the time," Aunt Em had sighed in the early days of my return. "I always seem to meet her going out or coming in to get ready to go somewhere else. I've given up asking questions."

"Oh," I reminded her, "Janice has always been on the go. That's nothing new."

I had given the conversation no further thought. For years now Janice and I had moved independently of each other except for occasional clashes, or when we rallied our forces to put through some mutually dreaded family gathering. So it was a surprise to find Janice alone in the living-room that afternoon when I returned from my first visit to Dr. Vance. She sat hunched in a corner of the sofa with a fashion magazine open beside her. But she was not absorbed in its pages. She looked limp and woebegone, and I saw that she had been crying.

"Janice," I said, dropping down on the sofa, "what's the matter? Has anything happened?"

She shook her head and pushed back a lock of moist, fair hair.

"Is it something I can do anything about?" I tried again.

"You can let me alone!" She frowned as she spoke. "I guess I have a right to be unhappy sometimes, haven't I? That's not just your own private privilege."

She lowered her head, and there I sat, so close that my skirt brushed hers, yet cut off completely as I always was when people turned their faces from me. I waited a moment before I touched her shoulder.

"What do you mean by that? If I've said or done anything lately—I haven't meant to be difficult, honestly I haven't."

"There you go getting personal." I could scarcely follow the words because her lips were quivering.

"But you said——" I broke off and tried again. "I'm sorry, Janice; I don't know what for, but I'm sorry anyway."

"Oh, all right, let's leave it at that, and don't start trying to cheer me up with the 'Into each life some rain must fall' line. I'm not in the mood."

"I don't feel in the mood for quoting either. But I know how it can be sometimes. I really do know, Janice."

"You can't know because you're you and I'm me. You're considered an admirable character, Emily."

"Well, you needn't throw it at me like that. I certainly don't feel admirable most of the time."

"Oh," she shrugged, "you know what I mean. You've got resources and strength of character, and people depend on you."

"And I suppose you think it's been easy." I felt suddenly bitter and hurt as if she were accusing me of being a prude. "I suppose you think I've enjoyed being cut off from everything these last two years, having to struggle to make out what people around me were saying?"

"I didn't say it had been easy, Emily, so don't get touchy the way you always do if any one mentions your deafness. I only meant that at least people give you credit for keeping your chin up. Now me—I'm supposed to be the life of the party when there *is* a party; and when there isn't one I'm expected to be happy and have fun—in a nice way, of course."

"But, Janice," I protested, "you have everything——"

"That's what *you* think!" she broke in. "But don't get the idea that I always act the way I feel, or that I like myself much. If you want to know, I hate myself."

"Well, I don't think there's anything very strange about that. Most of us do a lot of the time." I tried to comfort her because I saw that she was genuinely unhappy. "I guess we all need someone else to make us know we matter. I know I couldn't have gone on if it hadn't been for Harry; there wouldn't have been any reason to. I tell myself it must have been meant that Harry and I should meet and fall in love just when we did—before this happened to me. It frightens me sometimes to think how different it might have been——"

She gave me a long, startled look, and her eyes were dark with misery.

"Don't, Emily," she said, "don't say that."

I was touched and surprised by her solicitude.

"It's because I've been miserable and lonely, too," I went on, "that I can tell when you are. It's—it's sort of like the least common denominator in arithmetic, something shared by both. I can't explain very well, but you must know what I mean."

She did not speak, and so I went on.

"You need to fall in love," I told her. "That's all that's wrong with you."

She gave me another of those startled looks, then turned away so quickly that I only half-caught the words on her lips. I couldn't be sure, but it seemed to me that she said, "Oh, God!" before she got up and began gathering together her scattered possessions. She gave an unusual amount of care to collecting her hat and coat and bag. I remembered that long afterwards because it wasn't like Janice to be so methodical. She kept her eyes from meeting mine, but I saw that her hands shook as she folded her gloves.

After Janice had gone I stayed on in the living-room thinking of what she had said while I watched darkness swallow up the lawn and the beeches and maples. It had been disturbing to come so close to what was on Janice's mind, as if a door had been opened a chink and then shut quickly again to hide what lay behind. I thought how any one looking in at the window might well have supposed that we two were exchanging intimate confidences, yet those few broken words had left me baffled. The misery I had seen in her face was no momentary mood of boredom or futility.

I found myself remembering Janice as a child, what a nuisance she had been, always borrowing and breaking or losing my playthings, telling tales on me, and getting in the way of my plans. Still when her curved red mouth had drawn down forlornly and tears had gathered in her dark eyes I had always forgotten my annoyance and tried to make her smile again. Lightheartedness was her gift, and she wore it like a ribbon in her hair. No matter how little we shared in common or how we might disagree, I could not bear to see her wearing sackcloth and ashes.

Presently Maggie appeared in her trim black and white to switch on the lights and set the rooms in order for the evening. I watched her moving about with the same un-hurried precision that had been part of that rite ever since my childhood. She did not notice me till she came over to the sofa to pick up the magazine Janice had let fall to the floor.

"I didn't know you were in, Miss Emily," she answered my greetings, "or I'd have brought you a cup of tea. It's not too late for one now if you want it."

But I shook my head.

"Maggie," I said as I watched her putting things to rights, "what's happened to all of us in this house?"

"I don't know what you mean except some of us aren't getting any younger, and the same can be said for these sofa cushions. They're a disgrace, and I've been after Miss Blair to do something about them for months back."

"I didn't mean the sofa cushions, Maggie. It's just we all seem unhappy and pulling away from each other. Even Janice doesn't have a good time any more. She was crying when I came in a while ago."

"Oh, Miss Janice!" Maggie reached for another pillow and shook it vigorously into plumpness. "Well, I expect she's got reasons of her own."

She moved over to the table and began sorting out magazines and newspapers. Conversation with Maggie never meant suspended action. If necessary one followed her about to continue it. I had a feeling she wished to avoid more questions, but I was determined not to let the subject drop.

"Maggie," I began again as she started for the hall, "you know more about all of us in this house than we know about ourselves, but you never take advantage of what you've heard or seen the way some would. It's more than just being well trained; it's a sort of gift you have, almost like second sight."

"There's nothing to it," she protested with an uneasy glance under my scrutiny. "Nothing out of the way, I mean. I guess anybody that's worked thirty-eight years in one place gets on to signs and portents. I never listened at keyholes or read what wasn't intended for me, but I can't help knowing things. I guess it's just people don't remember I'm around, that's all. They get used to me along with the furniture. Except they need me for something I might be that sofa or chair."

"Haven't you ever wanted to go away or try another place in all these years?" I asked curiously.

"Why should I? I'd just be doing the same things somewhere else."

I looked about the familiar high-ceilinged room and beyond her to the long hall and the other rooms opening from it.

"It's a big house," I said, "as houses go. But isn't it rather a small place to make a world of?"

"Oh, I wouldn't say that, Miss Emily." She gave me one of her rare smiles, as if I were a little girl again asking her foolish questions. "World or no world, it's been plenty to tackle. All I ask is I don't live to see it break up in front of my eyes."

"You mean if this trouble at the mills gets worse——"

"Now, Miss Emily, don't take my word to mean anything. I've got to get back to the kitchen now and help with dinner."

"You'll never join a domestic workers' union, Maggie, I can see that." I laughed. "You don't believe in closed shop for kitchens, do you?"

"And don't you give me any of that union rigmarole round here," she retorted. "There's a few of us left in this town that haven't seen fit to go on strike. I should live to be told how many hours a day I'll work!"

I rose and patted her shoulder.

"I guess Uncle Wallace and Harry wish there were more like you down at Peace-Pipe," I told her. "It looks bad and getting worse all the time. I wish it hadn't come just now to delay my wedding. It's hard to be patient when you're in love, Maggie, and when things keep coming in between——"

"I expect so, Miss Emily. Not that I know much about it first hand. Love's one kind of broom that never swept me off my feet. Maybe I've missed a lot—plenty of tears anyhow. There!" She broke off and pointed to the nearest window. "Mr. Harry's been at that curtain cord again. Hardly a week goes by I don't have to pick out those knots he ties in them. If I met them in Jericho I'd know he'd been fidgeting around."

"I'll pick them out. He doesn't know when he does it, Maggie, he has so much on his mind."

She opened her mouth as if to speak, but evidently changed her mind and turned away. When Maggie disapproved of any one or anything you could tell by the set of her shoulders and the way she walked, as if she were treading on the unspoken words of criticism.

"Watch out for Maggie when she stalks," I had told Harry once, and I couldn't help thinking of that when she disappeared down the hall.

CHAPTER SEVENTEEN

I HAD not expected to meet young Jo Kelly coming down
the doctor's steps a few days later as I turned up the path.
But there he was, and there was I with Bridget leaping
between us in frantic greeting. He smiled at me across her
brown, excited body.

"Hallo, Jo," I said. "I'm glad to see you, even if Bridget
doesn't give me much chance to say so. How do you think
she looks for a lady going on five?"

He bent to pet and examine her with that reassuring
touch that made all animals his no matter who their official
owners might be.

"Pretty fair," he answered in the slow-spoken way that
was so easy for me to follow. "Better since you've been
back to give her some exercise. She was getting a bit too
fat."

"The same can't be said of you, Jo."

He had always been thin, but now his boyish slightness
had settled into gaunt maturity. His eyes were as blue and
candid as I remembered them under their dark brows; but
his cheekbones showed too prominently, and his mouth
was firmer and less merry.

"Oh, I'm all right," he assured me. "I just stopped by
the doctor's to get some medicine for a friend of mine."
He patted the sagging pocket of his shabby Mackinaw and
glanced towards the window of Vance's office. "Blairstown's lucky to get some one like him," he went on, "young
and up to the minute in his line. They mostly stay in the
big cities."

In his manner there was nothing to suggest differences of
opinion or constraint between us. He was, as he had always
been, completely without self-consciousness. Watching
him, I felt that this lack of pretence and personal importance
was what distinguished him from other people. It was a
positive rather than a negative quality that gave him the

power of which he seemed least aware. It is strange to remember now how we stood there by the doctor's steps and talked together. The November wind came up from the river with an edge on it that made one feel winter at the bones though the sun shone through bare branches of maple and elms. Change was in the air about us as it stirred behind our talk. I often think back to that day and the words that wove back and forth like shuttles carrying the frail threads of thought between us to make a pattern which it was beyond our power to alter.

"Oh, Jo," I found myself saying, "why do things have to be this way? Do you have to stir up all this trouble at the mills and work against us and talk as if we were criminals?"

He hesitated before he answered, and he kept on stroking the dog's coat with those thin, kind fingers of his.

"You've got me all wrong, Emily," he said, and I was glad that he called me by my first name in the old familiar way. "I was afraid you would. I can't work up hard feelings for any of you folks. I'm on my side of the fence and you're on yours, that's all."

"But, Jo, can't you look over the fence and see our side?"

"That goes for you, too." He gave me one of his long, slow smiles as he spoke. "Still, I guess I can't expect you to see very far."

"Why not? There's nothing wrong with my eyes."

"But you've always had this thing they call security. . You've never known what it was to wonder where your next meal was coming from, or a new pair of shoes or a place to sleep nights——"

"Maybe not, but there are other kinds of security that matter more."

"I know what you mean. Still, you try doing without a few of those things I mentioned and you'll understand better. You'll know what we're fighting for."

"There won't be much sense to higher wages and shorter hours if this strike of yours ties Peace-Pipe up all winter.

What business there is will go to other mills, if ours has to shut down."

He shrugged and straightened his thin shoulders. "Well, I don't blame you for seeing it that way. Stockholders are bound to feel differently about it."

"They take the biggest losses when times are bad." I found myself bringing out all the arguments I had heard Uncle Wallace and Mr. Perkins and Aunt Em use. But they seemed suddenly inadequate under Jo Kelly's direct gaze.

"Sure," he answered, "and they take the profits when it's the other way round. Don't forget that part."

"But, Jo, it's always been different at Peace-Pipe. You can't stand there and tell me that our family has ever profiteered. You know it's one of the best-run mills in New England and it's done everything for its workers—look at the Infirmary and Recreation Building, the night classes, and the band concerts in summer. Our family's always tried to take a personal interest. Why, Aunt Em's worrying right now about what she ought to do for Christmas. Even with this strike talk she doesn't want to give up the food baskets and presents. She says there'll be all the more need, and she won't let her own feelings stand in the way; only it's against her principles——"

"She means all right, Emily." His forehead puckered into the lines I knew so well. "Your aunt's one of the finest ever. That's why I wish she didn't have to get so hurt about this. But Christmas baskets and recreation buildings and night classes are something else again. Can't you see we don't want to be done *for*? We want to do for ourselves and those we love——"

He broke off and bent over Bridget again as if he found it difficult to get out what he was trying to say. I lost his next words and had to ask him to repeat them.

"I beg your pardon, Jo, I didn't quite catch what you said."

"No matter," he told me. "I haven't got any business talking about love."

"Why haven't you, Jo? Why shouldn't people talk about loving and being loved? This trouble at the mills hasn't made things any easier for Harry Collins and me— If any one had told me I'd have to go on waiting like this——" I broke off, not trusting myself to say more.

He turned to me with such quick sympathy in his eyes that I felt almost as if we were children again. It eased me to have spoken the words. We met once more on the old footing of our childhood, when we had shared punishments and secrets together.

"I'm sorry," he said simply, "real sorry. But don't worry about waiting. The way I figure it, you have to wait or fight for things that matter in this world."

"I guess so," I managed to answer. "It's the only world we know anything about, after all."

I tried to smile and he did too, but neither of us made much success of it. We stood there a moment without speaking; and I saw that he was looking away, over towards the mill chimneys, and his face stayed grave and set.

"No," he went on at last. "It isn't conditions we're fighting for. I guess they're fair enough as mills go, and it isn't just the pay and the hours either. But we've got a right to organise—it's our only guarantee for the future. Whatever anybody says about this union, it means a hell of a lot to most of us."

"It can't work miracles," I argued, snatching at what I had heard from this one and that. "A union can't bring prosperity back overnight or make the public want to buy what mills like ours are making. There are too many doing business, Uncle Wallace says. That's what makes all this cut-throat competition."

"That's true," he admitted. "But give us a chance and maybe we could prove a unionised mill could do better for both sides. Ever hear of collective bargaining?"

I shook my head.

"How would I hear anything?" I reminded him bitterly. "No one goes out of the way to explain things to me. It's too much trouble. See those sparrows over there picking up a crumb here and another one there? That's how it is if you're deaf. You just have to pick up what you can, and you learn not to ask too many questions. It annoys people."

"Well, at least you *try* to understand. That's more than the rest of them do over on your side of the river. Now take this collective bargaining. Suppose you got in a tight place some time and needed a lawyer. You'd want to be able to hire one, wouldn't you? Sure you would. It's the same thing, sort of—I've got a grievance, so I go to the foreman or maybe somebody higher up about it. Maybe I get listened to and maybe I don't, but it's a pretty safe bet I get laid off at the end of the week. Too many waiting to step into my shoes. Well, that's where a union comes in. I tell you we've got to stand up for the ones that are getting bad breaks, not just in Peace-Pipe. I mean the ones behind the machines all over everywhere."

"It sounds all right," I told him, "if it works. But Uncle Wallace and the rest say it's plain highway robbery the way the unions are holding them up at gun's point. He says—— Oh, well, what's the use? I'll never be able to know who's right and who's wrong. I try to understand, but even the words don't make sense. I'm not sure I know what a scab is exactly——"

"A scab." Young Jo smiled suddenly in spite of our seriousness. "Why, that's just another name for a strike-breaker—sort of polite way of saying the other fellow steals your pants while you're in swimming. Do you get me?"

I had to laugh too, and I was glad to break the tension. He could care enough to fight for something he believed in, and still joke about it. He hadn't changed his ways, and somehow that was a comfort to me.

"Thanks," I said, as I turned to go up the steps, "I'll remember."

He grinned, but before he moved away he came closer and touched my arm.

"How's Grandpa?" he asked. "I didn't like the looks of him last time I got sight. He won't speak to me any more, you know, and I kind of worry about him down there all alone."

"Oh," I explained, "he's about the same. His rheumatism's worse when it rains. But he sleeps at the big house now. He didn't want to move up, but Aunt Em and Dr. Will made him. It seems queer to have those rooms over the old stable empty after all these years."

"Thanks," he said. "I'll feel better about him nights. If he ever——" He broke off and shrugged helplessly. "But I guess it wouldn't do any good to send for me. He thinks I'm a mad dog biting the hand that's fed us. I wish he didn't have to see it that way."

"So do I," I said. "I'm glad we met. It did me good to talk to you, Jo. You make it feel like old times, and I guess we all need to remember old times no matter what happens to us."

There were no other patients waiting, so I went on through the connecting door to Dr. Vance's office.

"Your aunt's asked me for Thanksgiving dinner next week," he said, looking up from his preparations. "I thought I'd better find out if you had any objections before I accepted."

"Why should I have any?"

"I don't know, but you might. It's hard to get under this veneer of politeness of yours."

"Politeness?" I smiled. "I've been more rude to you than any one I've ever met in my life."

But he shook his head.

"Let's call it 'honest,'" he corrected. "I think you are that down here; but up at your place I'm never quite sure. You're still making your curtsies and speeches the way you've been taught. You must have had the social graces dinned into you pretty hard when you were little, or they wouldn't come so naturally to you now. You put me in mind of something I read in a book once when I was a kid. It was about Marie Antoinette going to the guillotine, and how she stepped on the executioner's foot and begged his pardon——"

"Are you comparing me to Marie Antoinette?"

He smiled at me sheepishly.

"Well, you belong to the royal family of Blairstown, don't you?"

"And just where do you come in?" I asked.

Resentment flooded me in a hot wave. I felt it brightening my cheeks, blurring my eyes. The jab of the needle brought me to my senses, and his face suddenly cleared before me. He was no longer smiling, and his eyes had that dark intentness which had first made me notice him that day in the station.

"Just where do I come in?" He was repeating my question. "Darned if I wouldn't like to know."

CHAPTER EIGHTEEN

THE Peace-Pipe Mills strike is past history now. I suppose it will never be reckoned of importance to industrial history, for it was a poor one as strikes go, ill-timed and insignificant. But for Blairstown and for us it marked the end of an era, as if a page had been turned forever on a familiar way of life. Just now I rummaged in my desk and found a sheaf of newspaper clippings neatly sorted and labelled. The print is already beginning to fade, and the paper growing brittle though the dates are so recent: December, 1931; January, February, and March, 1932. Our strike seldom made the front-page headlines of Boston or New York; only local papers carried full day-to-day accounts of its progress. I have been trying to reread the columns of print over again, but the words mean less than the scenes and faces that crowd my memory.

"You'll never get it straight, Emmy," Harry said impatiently once when I questioned him about some issue. "Can't you stay on the side of town where you belong?"

I have never quite understood all the intricacies involved; the bitter issues; the compromises that each side proposed only to be rejected by the other in the long battle that was never won—that has turned Blairstown into the ghost of a prosperous manufacturing centre. Some claim that it was already doomed and the strike mercifully shortened its slow decline. Others believe that the industry was deliberately betrayed and tricked into its own suicide. No one can say with certainty, least of all I, caught in the crosscurrents of family loyalty and sudden awareness of another way of life. Something I could not define was stirring in me in those months, feeding on my own loneliness and frustration. For the strike was somehow a symbol of my own inner conflict; as if I had become a human counterpart of the bridge which joined the two sides of our river without ever making them one.

"I don't see how this could have happened to Peace-Pipe," I said to Harry the first day I looked across and saw the stark shapes of the chimneys without a wisp of smoke curling from them. "I thought it was only talk. I didn't believe that words could do so much. They won't make the wheels of a mill go round."

"No, but they can stop them," he reminded me simply.

Harry Collins had criticised many things about the policy and product of the mills long before the strike threatened. He had argued for a compromise on the union demands at the early stages of negotiations, but when it came to the final test he sided with the directors.

"At least we haven't been disappointed in Harry," Uncle Wallace told Aunt Em. "I won't deny I was worried about his attitude a while back. From the way he talked I was afraid he might be turning radical. But he's got too much good sound sense to be taken in by that sort of talk."

"I thought we could count on Harry," she agreed. "After all, when he and Emily are married he'll be taking over more of the business. His future's tied up with Peace-Pipe, and he knows it."

"Maybe we should give the boy more chance to try some of his ideas about putting out a cheaper line of goods," Uncle Wallace went on. "Parker and I have held him back, but maybe he's right and we're in a manufacturing rut.

Once we get clear of this mess we might let him branch out a bit. How'd that suit you, Emily?"

I smiled and nodded my assent. But I couldn't let them guess that Harry seldom confided his ambitions to me, business or otherwise. I tried to let them think all was well between us because I had to believe it was. Always when we were together there was that subtle constraint, but when we were apart I could make excuses for Harry. I could convince myself that he loved and needed me as I loved and needed him.

It's different with a man, I would reason; he doesn't have to make his whole world of a single person.

Perhaps I should never have found out how wrong it was of me to do just that if the strike had not happened when it did. Against my will I was made aware of it. It dominated the town like a cloud, larger and darker than the smoke one which had always hung over Peace-Pipe. Although I was shut off from sound and the normal exchange of talk I felt the change all about me. I saw bitterness tighten men's and women's lips; I saw hunger and fear in their eyes. Even the groups of children at their games moved less freely, as if they reflected something of the grimness and dared not give themselves completely to play.

I shuffle through the clippings on my desk, and the familiar words of the headlines rise up before me: "Peace-Pipe Negotiations Fail"; "Strike Threatens"; "Mediation Hope Abandoned"; "Mill Directors, Union and A.F. of L. Representatives in Deadlock"; "No Compromise, Company Officials Reaffirm"; "Union Issues Ultimatum"; "Walk-out in 24 Hours As Truce Period Nears End"; "Strike Called for To-morrow"; "Oldest New England Textile Plant Stands Firm"; "Non-union Workers Assured Police Protection As Company Prepares to Reopen"; "United Textile Union Pledges Support at Mass Meeting"; "Eighth Day of Blairstown Strike"; "Sixteenth Day of Strike," and so on. I hardly need the words to recall those days. They will be with me always because I was part of them.

I

Even now, a year away from it all, I cannot forget the picketers by the mill gates or huddled for warmth close to the fires that burned in buckets, idle men waiting to take their turns. I cannot forget the women with shawls and empty shopping bags who stood patiently for hours where supplies were distributed; the half-grown boys and girls who haunted the railroad yards and tracks to pounce on an occasional scattered nugget of coal. I cannot forget seeing children fighting over discarded wooden crates and bits of kindling wood, dragging what they had salvaged home on sleds after the first fall of snow. I know that there were longer lines than these in other industrial centres and in the big cities that winter of 1932. I read about them in the papers between appeals to the public to spend more liberally and hasten the return to what was optimistically called "normalcy." But I did not see those jobless with my own eyes. And there was this difference—hunger and cold and resentment were new to Blairstown. There had been hard times before, but not this twilight of dogged bitterness as the days went on and on.

Janice showed more interest in the mill situation than I had expected. Indeed she was almost vehement in her senti-ments, denouncing the workers wholesale till we all lost patience. It seemed in some strange way to have become an issue of personal concern to her, though it was months later that I learned the reason why.

"Good Lord, Janice!" Harry said one night at dinner after she had finished a particularly violent outburst. "You'd better shut up and cool off."

"What do they want anyway?" Her soft lips hardened, and she tossed back her fair hair.

"I guess they want just as much out of life as you and I do." It surprised me to find myself answering her. "The trouble is," I went on, "it's so easy to say ' they.' We're ' they ' to the millhands, and they're ' they ' to us. That's when we stop being real people and turn into classes."

I broke off, having said more than I had meant to, but if I had risen up with a hammer in one hand and a sickle in the other I could not have startled the group about the table more.

"Well," Janice exclaimed, "I must say Emily sounds like a union agitator or Jo Kelly out on his soapbox!"

"And I say you girls better stop talking about what you don't know the first thing about," Harry reproved. "It's bad enough having to take the strike and the talk all day at the mills without getting it served with dinner. Isn't that so, Mr. Blair?" He appealed to Uncle Wallace, who of course agreed.

Aunt Em showed more tolerance than I had expected, but her bewilderment and concern were hard to see. She had hoped for a miracle right up to the walk-out, and she continued to pray for some impossible settlement that would satisfy both sides.

"You mustn't take the mill trouble so hard, Em," Dr. Weeks told her a week or two after it had started, when he stopped in for a cup of tea one afternoon. "Strikes seem to be the order of the day now everywhere, so you needn't feel it's a disgrace. In fact it's like an industrial epidemic breaking out all over the country. Might be a good thing in the end, I suppose, but the symptoms are pretty painful."

"It's what lies behind the symptoms, Will," she pointed out. "As a doctor you ought to know that's what matters."

She looked stricken in those days, not only for herself but for all the generations of Blairs whose lives had gone into the building of Peace-Pipe. It hurt her to feel that the long record of harmony between millowners and mill-workers had been broken.

"We always felt personally responsible for our workers," she told me over and over again. "Any family in need was free to come to us for help, and we did what we could either from the mill funds or our own pocket-books."

"I know," I would answer. "But nowadays I guess people prefer their own pocket-books. I mean"—I groped to recall what young Jo Kelly had said on the doctor's doorstep —"they don't want to be done for if they can do for them-selves."

She looked at me as if I had struck her a blow.

"Why, Emily," she said, "you don't mean to tell me you think they're in the right about this strike?"

I sighed and shook my head.

"Oh, Aunt Em," I said, "how can I know what I think? I don't know where I stand any more. I wish I'd listened more when I could; but it's more than just hearing. . . . I'm trying to find out how they feel about it, that's all. I can't help wondering how it would be if I worked down there the way some of the girls and boys I went to high school with are doing. And after all, Mother was a millhand before she married Father."

Aunt Em stiffened at that. I realised that I had made a mistake to link her name with the present. She and my father belonged to the past that had taken on the mellow haze that removed it from present-day reality and vexing problems.

"Your mother was a very unusual woman, Emily," Aunt Em reproved me gently. "If she were alive to-day I haven't a doubt she'd feel worse about this trouble at the mills than any of us."

I wished that I could feel as sure about that as Aunt Em did, but I said no more.

"I'll get Harry to talk sense to you," she went on presently as if she were distracting a child from playing with some dangerous toy. "It's hard on you both to have all this trouble on your minds when you ought to be making your wedding plans instead. I'd hoped to see you two married right after the New Year. We could do with a little festivity in the family for a change, and I'm not at all sure Harry's right about thinking it wouldn't look well at a time like this."

"You've—been talking to him about it lately?" I felt my throat tighten, and I hoped I didn't sound too eager.

"Why not, dear? I'm worried about the mills, but that's a small thing compared to your happiness. I can't change this—this terrible handicap you have to meet, but at least you needn't go on waiting. I can't see that a quiet little home wedding would be out of place, but Harry does seem to feel we shouldn't make plans till the strike's settled. . . ."

"I suppose you offered to give us enough to live on?"

"Well, why shouldn't I? There's enough for that even if most of what we have is tied up in the mills. But there's some insurance of your father's that your Uncle Wallace and I always planned to turn over to you and Janice when you married. With that and what Harry makes you two should be able to manage. I told him that, but he seems to have a lot of pride about accepting anything from us. I don't altogether agree with him, still I have to admire his attitude."

"I wouldn't care where we lived," I told her. "Those rooms over the old stable are just going to waste now old Jo's moved up here to the big house. They wouldn't be half bad with fresh paper and paint."

"Well, you and Harry talk it over. You can convince him if any one can."

She smiled at me and turned back to the letter she was writing. But her remarks had made me restless. Personal concerns forced the mill trouble into the back of my mind. I decided to go down and have a look at those rooms again before the light dwindled into December darkness.

I pulled on my old leather windbreaker and started down the path with Bridget pressing close at my ankles. It was windy and chill outdoors. Bare branches were raking dull skies and the winter sun looked like tarnished silver in the west. Yet a glow of anticipation warmed me. It took so little to set me planning in the shy, determined way that no woman can resist. As I came in sight of the stable and the windows showing square and blank above, I saw them not as they were, but as they might be, gay with curtains of flowered chintz, and yellow-paned with lamplight. I felt for the key that was always kept on a beam half-way up the stairs and let myself in at the door that opened on the small kitchen.

Everything looked mute and impersonal in its ordered bareness though the simple furniture that old Jo and his grandson had used for so many years had not been removed. Oilcloth was on the table and thick blue and white china in the cupboards, even an old almanac hung between stove and sink. The small sitting-room beyond was more cheerful because the late light slanted through the western windows. I stood in the centre of the worn carpet with Bridget beside me and studied every detail. It was a small but well-proportioned room with built-in shelves that already I saw filled with Harry's books and mine. A Franklin stove would replace the old airtight iron one. I could fairly see the firelight on my desk and favourite chairs; on Grandmother Blair's pine chest and the cherry bureau that was the colour of russet apples. Yes, I decided the place between the windows would be just wide enough to hold it. I moved over to make certain of the space, and as I did so I automatically straightened the window shades.

"Well," I said to myself, "that's funny."

There were knots in the dangling cords, and it took me a moment to realise why I had noticed them. Then I remembered how I had picked out just such knots from the curtain cords in the living-room windows only a short time before.

"Mr. Harry's been at those cords again," Maggie had said. "If I met those knots in Jericho I'd know he'd been fidgeting around."

Her words came back to me as I stood there alone in the deserted room. I told myself it was foolish to think twice about such a trivial thing, and even more foolish to take the time and trouble to pick them out. It was almost dark when I had the cords free of the last one. I hardly glanced into the small adjoining bedroom as I hurried away, locking the door behind me.

CHAPTER NINETEEN

THE strain of the mill situation was beginning to tell on Uncle Wallace. When Harry dropped in later that evening I saw that he too looked tense and tired. Peace-Pipe had been shut down for ten days though negotiations still continued in the hope that some means of reopening might be found. Every day of bickering was time lost on the orders still waiting to be filled. There were few enough of those, but contracts were contracts and business must be kept, what there was left of it.

"Harry!" I hurried over to meet him by the door, but I could tell by his look that his mind was anywhere but on me and the questions I had been wanting all day to ask him. The eagerness and joy I had felt at sight of him slipped away before his preoccupation.

"You'll have to get along without each other for a day or two, Emily." Uncle Wallace touched my arm to draw my attention to what he was saying. "Harry's going to Boston with me to-morrow."

"Oh, do you have to go?" I protested.

"Well, it's not China, Emmy!" he teased. "Your uncle needs me to go over figures with some men at the bank there, and I must say I shan't mind getting away from Blairstown for a bit. You don't know what it's like down at the mills these days with the machinery stopped and pickets everywhere you look."

"It's not very cheerful round here either," I reminded him. "I've a good mind to go to Boston myself. I might have more chance to see you there than I've had here lately."

He smiled, but shook his head emphatically at the same time.

"This is business," he told me, "and you'd better get used to the idea of not tagging along. I'm not joking," he went on; "it's serious business. Money's tight everywhere,

and we've got to convince our backers we're a good bet
for another loan."

"But Peace-Pipe doesn't have to borrow money to keep
going, does it?"

"That's about what it amounts to," he admitted. "The
banks have always controlled a certain amount of the
stock, but we're going to need more to tide us over this.
. . . Even if the mill can get under way again by January—
and it doesn't look too promising right now—we won't
break even this year, to put it mildly. Don't worry and
screw up your forehead like that. It's not becoming."

It was no use asking him more questions. He resented
having to explain what he believed I could never understand.
I felt like a child being told to look pleasant, please, and be
seen and not heard. It wasn't so much his impatience that
hurt me. I was used to trying people's patience, even
Harry's. What hurt me was that he seemed relieved to be
going away while I must get on as best I could till his
return. I sat beside him on the sofa. His arm was about
me, but that did not bring him closer.

What is it? I thought. What has come between us? I
don't matter to him any more. There's no use pretending
to myself that I do.

He must have felt me shiver, for he patted my shoulder.

"Cold?" His lips formed the word carefully, so he
would not have to repeat it.

I shook my head.

"No. I guess I'm just missing you already, dear."

"I'll be back before you know I've gone."

How could I tell him what had chilled me? I wanted
him so much, too much. Other girls, other women loved
other men, and they had not waited as I had through in-
terminable months and years. Love was never meant to be
like this, dammed up in oneself because the floodgates were
locked from the outside. The pressure was growing too
heavy for me to bear. Why couldn't I say to him simply
and honestly: "Harry, you do want me still, don't you, my
darling? You must, or I can't go on, for nothing has

meaning or reality for me except you." But I knew why I
could not say those words. I was afraid—afraid of losing
what I had by asking for more.

He shifted his position and pulled himself up.

"Well, I must be getting back," he said. "We'll be taking
the early train to-morrow, and I must pack before I turn in.
Besides, I have to pick up some things I left over at the
Parkers'."

"You'll be roped into cards," I told him. "Janice is over
there now. They wanted me to fill in, but I knew they'd
put me at a table of misfits."

"Well, I'll only look in for a minute," he said. "Glad
you warned me. Good-bye, dear. Get a good rest. You
look tired."

"That means I'm definitely not at my best." I tried to
laugh as I watched him go down the steps.

But I knew he would be up late at cards. The twins
would see to that. I wished suddenly that I had gone even
though I hated pretending to enjoy myself.

So I turned back to the living-room feeling as deserted
as it looked. The fire burned in cheerful unconcern of
empty chairs about it. Aunt Em and Uncle Wallace had
both gone to their rooms, and Bridget and I were left to
keep each other company. It was half-past nine, and I
must hunt for the detective story I had begun yesterday.
I didn't care who had killed the adventuress in the night
club; but no matter, it might make me sleepy to read
a while by the fire.

I don't know how long after that Bridget roused herself
from the rug and stood listening with lifted head. I always
knew when someone was coming by the way her ears
pointed and her throat rippled making the rumbling warnings I could not hear. She moved towards the hall, and I
rose and followed her. Peering through the narrow glass
panes by the door, I saw a man coming up the steps, and
I recognised Merek Vance. The light over the entrance
shone full on his face as I let him in.

"Sorry," he explained. "I wouldn't have bothered you

so late, but I'm having car trouble. My engine stopped dead just below your drive, and I can't get it started. If I could use your telephone——"

"Of course." I let him into the study.

When he returned presently, he shrugged and frowned. "I can't get any answer from the garage," he told me. "The man on duty must be out or asleep, and the hotel says they can't say when they can send a taxi. I wish Dr. Weeks wasn't off in his car. I've got an emergency call out on the Ridgeville Road."

"You can borrow ours," I said, "if Janice didn't drive it over to the Parkers'."

"Thanks." He didn't bother with protests or further explanations. "It would save a lot of time and sometimes minutes count."

"I'll show you the way," I said, and caught up my coat.

It was dark going down to the made-over stable, but I knew every inch of the way. He held my arm, and I could feel the firm grip of his fingers and his breath warm beside me in the cold night air.

"Here." I saw with relief that the little roadster was in its place. "The keys are probably in. She usually leaves them. Yes, she did, thank goodness."

I felt for the light-switch and turned on the ignition. I could feel the engine begin to throb and, as it started, a sudden impulse overtook me not to go back to the house. He took his place behind the wheel, but instead of getting out I turned to him.

"Let me go, too," I said. "I haven't anything else to do. I know the car better than you do even if I don't drive it any more, and I can wait while you make your visit."

"Well"—I could just make out the motion of his lips in the light from the dashboard—"I can't say how long I'll be. Your family won't worry?"

"They'll think I've gone to bed. Please don't make me go back to that book I was trying to read. I won't be a bother to you, really I won't."

He nodded and began backing the car out. He stopped

for a moment by his own to collect his bag, which he set on the floor between us. I couldn't help thinking that no matter how the times and methods changed, those limp, worn leather bags were the universal badges of the medical profession. Instinctively I would have distrusted a doctor who carried a new, shiny one. The very scratches and stains and rubbed places gave one reassurance as if each were a scar of mortal combat.

It was strange to be riding beside Merek Vance at such an hour in the little car that had taken me on so many pleasure jaunts in the past, that must always be associated with that summer of my engagement to Harry before my own personal disaster. A car, especially at night, with everything dark but the round, luminous dials and the beams of the headlights, may become a complete small world to those inside it. We take on its dimensions as if it were our larger shell. Its power seems to come from ourselves. It seemed so that night as we put the town behind us. The air rushed by, sharper for the open country that lay beyond the range of our lights on the pale cement of the road ahead. I could not see Merek Vance's face clearly. He was a shadowy shape in the overcoat that smelled faintly of wool and tobacco and other scents I could not classify. His hands held the wheel with an easy grip. If he had spoken I should have had no way of knowing what he said, and if I had spoken to him I could not have read his answer in the dimness. So for a little while there was no need to talk.

I found myself thinking back to my first meeting with Merek Vance. It was strange that I trusted him as I did in spite of my prejudices. Though I would not admit it to myself, I had come to count on those visits to his bare little office to break the monotony of days that were empty and meaningless as days have never been before or since. It was well into December by then, nearly two months since the treatments had begun. At first I had been afraid of detection, but no one took notice of my walks with Bridget. Our family intimacy with Dr. Weeks made it seem a natural thing if I happened to be seen entering or leaving his place. He, of course, knew the reason for my coming. But he asked no questions and I could trust him to deal with Aunt Em if she became suspicious. The middle-aged nurse who answered the telephone and helped with patients was equally trustworthy and closemouthed. Dr. Vance saw most of his patients in the evening or at the hospital clinics, so that I met few. I had no more faith than I had had the day of my return that he could help my hearing. He knew that and did not try to convert me. We had given our word to each other, and once the bargain was made he would keep to his end of it. He made no personal issue of the experiments, only now and then his eagerness betrayed him as he went through the routine of tests in the hope of some sign of improvement. And there was this to be said for Merek Vance: he did not put me off with excuses or avoid conversation because my deafness made it difficult. He continued to be frank, almost ruthless about my hearing.

"Deaf people strain too much," he told me once, "except for the ones who pretend they hear when they don't. After all, half the world hears what it wants to hear, and the other half doesn't bother to do anything about it."

"And what about you?" I cornered him.

"Oh," he shrugged, "I'm a doctor. I needn't remind you what you think about them, though I could, for I happen to have a good memory. But honestly, now, think back a few years: did you ever really listen?"

"Of course I did," I insisted. "And I would again if I had the chance."

"I doubt it." He shook his head. "And I'm not setting myself to be better than average when it comes to that. We none of us hear all we might."

CHAPTER TWENTY

FROM the moment we set out in the car something outside myself seemed to take me in hand. I had a sense of being in a play, given a part to act in which I had not been rehearsed. Mine was not an important role in that drama of life and death, but I have reason to remember it well.

We turned off the main road into what was hardly more than two wheel ruts. Presently I made out the shape of a house dwarfed by the larger shape of a barn behind it. Four squares of windowpane were yellow in the darkness, and someone must have heard the sound of our engine, for as we came to a stop a door opened and a man's figure showed sharply in silhouette. Merek Vance reached for his bag and got out. He came over to my side and motioned me to join him. I had expected to stay in the car; but there was no chance for argument, so I followed him to the door. After the cold night air the room in which I found myself seemed crowded and stifling. It was evidently the kitchen of a farmhouse, for a large coal stove filled one side and a sink with a primitive sort of pump the other. I remember a table covered with a red cloth, set with thick dishes, and people about it: a shrunken old man in a faded bathrobe; an old woman with a sleeping baby in her arms; a half-grown boy bent over a book, and a little girl of three or four who stared at me over the shapeless form of a rag doll.

The man who had let us in scarcely noticed me. His eyes were fixed on Merek Vance, and he talked so rapidly that I gave up trying to read his lips. I felt sure that he must be speaking in broken English, and that was almost impossible for me to follow. From his stocky strong build and his quick gesturings I guessed that he might be Italian. Vance's back was towards me, so I could not tell what he might be saying as he removed his overcoat and warmed his hands at the stove.

He must have made some explanation of my presence,

for the old woman looked up and nodded as she eyed me curiously. She motioned to the boy to give me his chair. I smiled uncertainly as I took it and beckoned the little girl to show me her doll. While I was fashioning my handkerchief into an apron for it, the two men went into another room and were gone some time. I felt as if I had been suddenly set down in a foreign country, completely cut off from communication except by gestures. Once or twice the old woman addressed remarks to the old man or boy, but I could make nothing of them. The little girl had lost her first shyness. She let me set her on my lap. She was not pretty, but neatly made and charming with her dark eyes and clear, pale skin. I had not held a child for so long that I was startled by the light firmness of her body. I could feel the delicate bones under her dress and her heart beating quick as a bird's when you hold it in your hands. She found the bright flowers on the scarf I had tied over my hair, and I marvelled at the gentle curiosity of her touch. So intent were we that I did not see the door open until she turned quickly and slid from my lap.

She ran to a woman who had come in with Vance, and tugged at her skirts, holding up the doll with my handkerchief and making shy motions in my direction. The woman did not turn at once because she was listening intently to Vance. Something about her caught my attention immediately. I could see that she was young and slight, and the droop of her shoulders showed that she was very tired. Her hair wrapped her head in smooth blackness, and the line of her throat was long and graceful. Even without seeing her face I could feel the intensity of her listening and speaking. Then she turned, and I recognised Angeletta Rossi, my old classmate, the girl who had won all the debates and played the lead in high-school plays. I hadn't thought of her in the seven years since we had marched up to receive our diplomas and the class history had predicted that I would paint pictures and she would win fame on the stage. We stared at each other across the cluttered room, and I knew that she must be remembering, too.

"Angie," I began awkwardly, "I didn't know you lived here."

"Why should you know?" I had no difficulty in understanding her as she flung the words to me over the child's upturned face. "Why should you know?" she repeated with a defiant lift of her shoulders. "We've gone an awful long ways since Blairstown High. Well——" The spirit died out of her face that had grown sharp and pale, though the features were as I remembered them—clear-cut and arresting. "Well, I can't blame you for what's happened to me."

"Mamma!" I caught the word on the little girl's lips.

"Is she yours, Angie?"

Angeletta looked down at the child and nodded.

"This one, too," she said, and pointed to the baby in the old woman's lap. "And the one in there——" She broke off, and her eyes went back to the door of the room behind the kitchen from which she and Vance and the man who must be her husband had just come. I saw her face grow peaked as she spoke, and she looked at Merek Vance in a way I can't forget.

I turned to him, too, for I couldn't go on staring at her. He met the question I did not put into words.

"Yes," he told me from the sink, where he had poured out a steaming basin of water from the kettle. "The little fellow in there's pretty sick. If I could have got him over to the hospital yesterday or even this morning——" He broke off with an expressive gesture.

"What is it?"

"Infection of the middle ear. It's spread to the mastoid bone." He was rolling up his sleeves as he spoke. "I can't take any chances with the temperature he's running."

"What are you going to do?"

"Open it. Operate."

"Here?" I glanced incredulously about the kitchen.

He nodded shortly.

"Won't be the first time I've done it, or the last. Look, have you got a flashlight out there? I left mine behind when we changed cars."

I asked no further questions but went out to fumble in the pocket of the car. Luckily I found the flashlight under a clutter of maps, driving gloves, and old letters with directions scrawled on the envelopes. As I hurried up the path I had a sense of being part of that house which I had never so much as passed till that night. The lighted windows were no longer bright, impersonal panes of glass to me. Some new and powerful force joined me to those rooms and to the people in them.

When I returned to the kitchen it was already a changed room. Merek Vance had taken it over, and the freshness of outside air blew in through an open window. Chairs had been pushed back against the walls. The old couple, the baby, and the little girl were gone; and Angeletta, too, had disappeared. The half-grown boy was busy pumping and carrying water from sink to stove while the man with the stocky body and dark face was scrubbing furiously at the bare wood of the table where the red cloth and dishes had been. Vance still stood at the sink, turning his head from one to another. I could not follow what he said, but I knew he must be giving directions from the way they moved and listened. Standing there in the doorway, like a spectator at a play, I felt suddenly useless and afraid. I looked down at my hands holding the flashlight and they seemed oddly inadequate. What good could they do in such a crisis, I thought. What had they ever done except hold pens and paintbrushes and unimportant paraphernalia?

Just then Merek Vance noticed me and came over.

"Good!" He nodded as he saw the light. "You'd better not stay around if you're the kind that faints easily; but if you're not . . . Want to help?"

"Of course, but how can I?" I touched my ears to remind him.

"You won't need anything but your hands," he reassured me. "Think you could hold the light steady for me? All right, I'd rather not ask Mrs. Gallo; it's hard on a mother —this sort of business. . . . She's keeping up well though. Funny you should know each other, but I'm glad you do.

Maybe you can talk to her while I'm in there with the boy. She's under enough strain without seeing him take the anæsthetic. Lucky I have enough to see us through."

Angeletta came back presently, bringing some aprons over her arm. Vance selected the plainest one of the lot and put it on as unconcernedly as if it had been his white surgeon's coat. He moved with unhurried precision, setting out the contents of his bag on a clean towel.

"Angie!" I reached out to take the apron she handed me, a cheap cotton print covered with incongruously gay flowers. Exactly the kind I thought that one would choose not to wear on such an occasion. "Angie," I tried again lamely, "I'm so sorry. . . ."

Her eyes met mine with a glazed, expressionless look as she reached to help me put it on. I hoped I could make her feel my sympathy, but it was hard to find words.

"You don't mind my being here, do you?"

She shook her head and bent to fasten the apron strings.

"Because if you do—I'll keep out of the way. I'd never have barged in like this if I'd known; but now I'm here I want to help. I guess there isn't any one wants to help more than I do because the doctor says the trouble's in his ears, and I'm deaf, Angie, did you know that?"

"He told me." She jerked her head towards Vance, who was standing over the stove, clouds of steam rising about him from the heating water. "I didn't know before."

I followed her into the bedroom beyond. It was untidy and badly lighted. Bedclothes and garments seemed to be everywhere, and the large sagging bed was only half-made. In a crib beside it I made out the small shape of a child whose head showed round and dark against the pillow. His face was turned away, but I saw the rapid rise and fall of his chest before Angeletta bent over him. A crucifix and rosary beads hung from a nail on the wall, and a candle in a red glass cup burned under a likeness of the Virgin and Child above the bed. Although it was a poorly-painted flimsy bit of tin the little shrine lent a kind of dignity to the room. Angeletta, bending over her child, took on the

K

ageless quality of an old master in terms of living flesh so that she seemed the personification of all women of all time.

Seven years ago last June, Angeletta and I had marched up the aisle to receive our high-school diplomas. We had been a little awed and grave because the familiar doors were closing behind us, yet flushed and eager too, because others were opening on what was going to be wonderful—maybe. Angeletta had been eager and lovely that day with a kind of glow under her skin, and her eyes big and bright as a child's on Christmas morning. I guess I must have looked that way too, though it's hard to tell about oneself. Well, we would never be like that again, that much was certain. In her shapeless house dress and with her anxious gaunt face Angeletta looked years older than I. She was poor, but she was alive as I knew I had never been in those years between. Life had stirred in her, and through her it was going on to be part of the endless procession of the future. So much had happened to her while I had stayed tight-rolled as a bulb in the security of some dusty shelf, away from the rains and the frost, from the magnetic forces of earth and sun.

I wished that I could tell Angeletta what I was feeling as we stood in that shabby room. But she wouldn't have listened or believed me. I knew, without her saying a word, that she was envying the comfort and security that mattered so little to me. The little boy's head burrowed into the hollow between her breasts. Her thin, strong arms tightened about the curve of his body. I flattened my own against my sides that I might be less aware of their emptiness as we waited there together.

But I had no more time to think or feel, once Vance summoned me to the kitchen.

"You needn't look," he told me. "Just stand here by this knothole on the floorboard and keep the light as steady as you can."

I took my place, grateful that I could become a pair of hands, nothing more.

Though I was aware of the figures about the table, I did

not look at the faces or try to follow the motions of lips. Even the child's relaxed small body wrapped in a sheet became less real to me than Merek Vance's hands in their rubber gloves reaching for this or that instrument. I marvelled that they could move without a tremor or a second's hesitancy. The cloying smell of ether grew stronger as the moments passed, and steam and more potent scents mingled with the heat from the kerosene lamps. I saw a thin line of red widen as the scalpel took its course. I had never guessed that there could be such sure precision as this that I saw with my own eyes.

The flashlight seemed to weigh more each moment. I ached from the effort of holding it steady. My hands felt numb, and I must ease now one hand, now the other. That circle of light became the only reality to me, and at last even Vance's hands were blurs. I clenched my teeth and set my feet more firmly on the reassuring hardness of the floor. Then I lost even that sensation. My whole body and mind were projected into that clear beam of light that I must keep from wavering.

I came to with a start, and the room suddenly cleared about me. The man and the boy were lifting the limp figure, and Angeletta was wheeling the crib in to receive it. The floor was strewn with soaked swabs and cotton, and the sheet that covered the table was no longer white. Merek Vance was standing by the sink peeling off the gloves he had worn. I still held the flashlight, but suddenly my hands began to shake so that it fell to the floor.

It must have made a loud noise, for Vance looked up and nodded to me across the room. Just that and nothing more, yet the gesture reassured me as no words could have done. His face, under a shining mask of sweat, looked sharpened with weariness.

I found one of the kitchen chairs and sank down in it gratefully. I was trembling by that time, not only my hands but my knees and lips as well. It amazed me to see how methodically he went on with his washing, and how he gathered up his instruments and counted and put them away according to routine. My experience with doctors had been confined to hospitals and offices with modern equipment and able assistants at hand. The sort of discipline and skill that could meet emergency alone in the kitchen of a run-down farm was something I had never encountered till that night. I had stood at the edge of a miracle, and even so I could not altogether credit what I had seen.

Vance was through with his scrubbing and sorting at last. But there were still directions to give, and he would not leave till he made sure that the child was reacting favourably. Angeletta came out from the bedroom with him when it was time to leave, and I saw him pat her shoulder reassuringly. As he turned to put on his coat she looked about the kitchen for me and then came over.

"I've got to thank you," she began, "for what you did. I won't forget it—ever."

"Oh, it wasn't anything, Angie; anybody could have held a flashlight. But I'm glad I could help, and he's going to be all right. I'm sure he is."

I saw the muscles of her throat working, and I knew that what she was trying to say came hard.

"I'm sorry I acted the way I did," she began. "But seeing you sort of brought things back. I wanted to make something of myself once and do things that count——" She broke off and looked about the kitchen before she threw out her expressive hands in a futile gesture.

"Don't feel that way about it, Angie," I told her. "Those things that we thought counted then don't seem so much to me now."

She gave me a long searching look.

"I always thought you had it easy," she said, "but I guess I was wrong. I can see you've had it tough, too, in your way. Well, good-bye."

"Good-bye." I took her hand at the door. "I'll be over again soon to see how he's getting along."

I kept thinking of what she had said, as I sat beside Vance on the drive back. I was glad that the bitterness had gone out of her face; that we were friends once more and she no longer made me the symbol of what she had missed in life. I remembered the rich clear tones of Angeletta's voice from high-school dramatics, and I wondered if the warmth and sweetness had gone out of it along with her freshness and bloom. "We've gone an awful long ways since Blairstown High," she had said, and I couldn't deny that. But it was something that we could still find each other and talk, not as two untried girls, but as one woman to another. I had Merek Vance to thank for that. It was strange that it should be so; that I must ask him to tell me more about Angeletta, who had sat beside me and shared confidences through those other years.

I felt his hand reach out and touch mine, almost as if he knew what I had been thinking. It seemed the most natural thing in the world for him to do that, and the quick, light pressure of his fingers made me know that all was well.

The hands of the clock on the dashboard pointed to a quarter-past two. The little car had no heater, and the winter air came in at every crack and crevice. It felt not only cold, but leaden as if it were weighted down with the coming day. The stars were still out, but their brilliance was dulled by early-morning damp. It was that interval before the tug of the sun begins to be felt in the east. Even though I could see nothing beyond the straight beams of our headlights I felt that we were trespassers, as if the earth were half-resentful of those who were not dead or asleep.

Just before we reached the town limits the lights of an all-night diner loomed ahead like a cheerful beacon. I felt glad when Vance turned the car into the place. My feet were numb, and my teeth chattering, as I got out and followed him inside. The crude brightness of the diner and its heavy rich smells of coffee and frying food were exactly what I needed at that moment. The glaring nickel fittings seemed actually beautiful to me as we sat down at a small table. It was empty except for the man behind the counter in his spattered white coat and two men who were hunched over another table at the far end of the narrow place.

Vance ordered coffee, and we drank it eagerly from thick white china mugs. I could see the colour coming back into his face as he relaxed over the hot drink. His hands were steadier than mine as he lighted our cigarettes.

"You've certainly got grit," he said after he had taken a long puff. "It's a little late to say 'Thank you,' but I want to, especially for not fainting."

"You said I wasn't the fainting kind. I had to prove it. But tell me—about the little boy: will he be all right?"

"Unless there are complications—yes. I'll run over at noon and see how he's coming along. He's a tough little fellow, fortunately, except for badly infected tonsils which we'll have to watch. I suspect they made the trouble, and of course if I'd been called earlier it wouldn't have been necessary to operate. But it was the only chance he had."

"Would he have been deaf if you hadn't?" I asked.

"No," he told me simply, "he'd have been dead. The infection spreads fast with children. It would have reached the brain."

"Oh," I said, "I didn't know. I could only think about his ears—because of mine, I suppose."

The coffee was thawing my chilled body and nerves. The whole excursion had been so strange that it seemed the least strange part of it all to be sitting at a quarter of three in the morning in the hot, brightly-lighted roadside diner with Merek Vance. I hadn't felt so alive and at my ease in weeks—years, it seemed; and I knew with a queer conviction over which I had no control that I should always trust Merek Vance after that night. In little ways he might irritate me; we would disagree often, of that I had no doubt; but in the essentials he would not disappoint me. His very ruthlessness was no longer something to be shunned. I recognised it now for the steel beam that keeps the whole structure of a house in place. I was at a sudden loss for words though I felt a deep inner gratitude flow out towards him across the white-topped table.

"Are you ever afraid," I asked, "when you start to operate, the way you had to to-night?"

He did not dismiss the question as foolish curiosity, but considered it thoughtfully between puffs of his cigarette.

"Well, I can't say I relish it," he admitted. "I'm not a born surgeon. I'd always rather leave the cutting to some one who is. I can do it when I have to, and it's the only way sometimes. They'll have a drug perfected soon that will check about 90 per cent of the mastoid and 'strep' infections at the start. It's going to revolutionise treatments when it's ready." His eyes took on new life and light as he spoke, and the tension and weariness was draining out of his face as he went on. "That's what really interests me: preventive medicine."

"I suppose there's a cure for everything under the sun," I said, "if it could be found."

"That's a pretty large order," he reminded me with a smile. "Back in medical school one of the professors always began his lectures on mental and nervous diseases by saying, ' Give me any plague but the plague of the heart.' I forget where the quotation came from, but that was the gist of it anyway. Of course Freud and Jung and that school think they've found the answer, and maybe they have——" He broke off and shrugged expressively.

"But you don't agree?"

"I haven't the right to express an opinion because I could never meddle with people's minds and brains. I'm mortally afraid of that, more than cutting living tissue or sawing bones. Besides, I haven't the knack of drawing people out. I get out of patience and show it; funny too, when I've got more patience than most for laboratory work and experiment. I always say," he smiled again as he put out his cigarette, "if you can talk to patients you're a doctor; if you can get patients to talk to you—you're a psychiatrist."

The food we had ordered arrived just then, and nothing ever smelled more delicious to me than those plates of crisp brown bacon and golden scrambled eggs. The pile of buttered toast melted before our hunger. We did not speak again for some moments, but Merek Vance nodded his approval of my appetite. He ordered more coffee and leaned back contentedly in his chair when our plates were cleared.

"Funny thing," he said, "your going over there with me to-night. Of course I didn't know what I was in for when we started, or I'd never have let you come along. It was queer, too, your knowing the mother back in school. I'd have thought she was years older than you; but she's had a hard time of it—the husband was laid off at the mills months ago. He told me he'd go back as a strikebreaker if he got the chance. His people own that farm, but they're likely to lose it any time, I gather. They're the kind that never get ahead somehow, like my father and mother— different race, but the same type. I can recognise it."

I found myself telling him of Angeletta and the school plays; of her striking looks and her ability. He sat there quietly opposite me, but as I talked it seemed as if he were studying me more than listening to the words I said. I broke off in the middle of a sentence and cornered him.

"Why do you look at me like that?" I asked. "What are you thinking about me?"

He shrugged, but he did not hesitate.

"I was thinking what a pity it was you weren't born poor," he said. I opened my mouth to protest, but he went on before I could stop him. "I don't mean just the money part—it's more the little comfortable rut of easy prosperity you were born into, that you'll be going on in if you marry the man you're engaged to."

"I love Harry Collins." I could feel the colour rising in my cheeks, and my heart stirred as I said his name; yet even as I said it I had to admit to myself that for the last few hours I had not given him a thought. He was not part of what had happened that night. Other people's lives had come between, and I had not missed his presence until that moment. I knew, too, that he would disapprove of this strange experience. I should not be able to share it with him as I was sharing it now with Merek Vance. So I protested more firmly because I felt I had been disloyal to Harry. "I love Harry Collins," I repeated, "and the only happiness I want is the kind of life we'll have together, whether you approve of it or not."

"All right," he nodded. "If that's what you want, I hope you'll get it; but I still think—what I think. . . . I didn't expect to like you, but I've changed my mind. You've got qualities I hate to see going to waste."

"Such as?" I faced him challengingly.

Again he shrugged and smiled.

"The trouble with you is you were meant to be a prop, and you're trying to make yourself believe you're a vine. Usually it's the other way round: the weak think they're the strong ones. Maybe that's why they get their way so often. Well, I always say a person can't be a rock and a barnacle at the same time. And who wants to be a barnacle?"

Before I could answer, the two men who had been sitting at the other end of the diner passed close to our table; and to my surprise I recognised Jo Kelly. I do not think he noticed us. If he did he gave no sign as he went out. I must have shown my surprise, for Merek Vance answered my look.

"You never know where you'll run into Jo Kelly nowadays," he said. "I couldn't place that man with him; one of the union crowd, probably."

"An agitator?" I asked.

"Well," he smiled tolerantly, "personally I think 'investigator' is a better word to use."

"Then you're with Jo Kelly on this union business?"

"I'm for unions, yes; but they're not a religion with me the way they are with him. I can't feel that they're going to solve everything, because the trouble goes deeper than that. . . . At best they're only a step in the right direction. My father was like Jo: he believed in causes too hard and in what they were going to accomplish. There have to be people like that—but you'll hardly ever find a reformer that doesn't die pretty bitter and disillusioned. I saw my father go that way, and I made up my mind then I wouldn't mix up with groups or organisations. I'd try and see things as straight as I could for myself, and stick to them

in my own way and work on my own. . . . I guess I'm
what you'd call a rank individualist."

"And yet a doctor has to follow rules and conform to
codes that are all accepted and laid out by a group," I pointed
out.

"The rules of life and death are what every one has to
conform to," he reminded me. "We just try to outwit
death, the way I had to to-night. I admit, though, it's not
as simple as I make it sound."

I did not press the discussion further. Something I had
learned in a literature class years before came knocking at
my mind. I remembered it word for word: "Eagles com-
monly fly alone; they are crows and starlings that flock
together." I found myself studying him across the table as
if I had never really seen his dark, sharp-featured face and
his keen, restless eyes before.

"I—I beg your pardon." I realised that he had been
speaking to me and I must ask him to repeat the words.
So easy had it been for me to talk with him for the past
half-hour that I had forgotten my deafness.

"I was speaking as a doctor," he told me. "The man at
the counter started the canned music just now, and I
wondered if you had any sensation yet."

I shook my head.

"Only a kind of vibration that I can feel from the floorboards under my feet and at the back of my chair; nothing
here"—I touched my ears. "You're wasting your time
with me, you know. . . . Aren't you tired of your part of
the bargain?"

It was his turn to shake his head.

"I've got faith enough for the two of us, and besides
we've only just started." He lit another cigarette before
he went on. "I'm going to cure you; only I can't guarantee
you're always going to hear the things you want to hear,
you know."

"I want to hear everything," I told him. "I can take the
bitter with the sweet."

"I can think of a lot of things a woman would just as

soon not hear," he went on, "—things like a child crying for what she can't give it, or a man's discouraged step on the stairs and his key fumbling for the lock when he's had too much to drink, and words that turn love into something pretty cheap and rotten. . . . I don't suppose you ever stopped to think it could be like that for you?"

"Why should I think of such things?"

"Sorry, I shouldn't have reminded you." He took up the bill and felt for change in his pocket. "But somehow to-night I've found myself talking to you as if you weren't one of the Blairstown Blairs."

His smile took the edge off those words. I followed him out into the chillness and once more the little car was taking us back through the unfamiliarity of early morning. The pale globes of street lamps were set at long intervals, and our house showed at last a faint, unlit shape as we turned into the driveway. I felt for the purse I had caught up when we left the house, thankful that my key was in it. I should not need to rouse the household.

We did not speak as we left the car in the old stable. Perhaps it was because I was more keyed up than I realised, or because my sense of smell had grown sharper since I had had to depend more upon it, that I felt certain we two were not alone there. There was no light anywhere in the dimness, yet the impression would not leave me as I waited for Vance to collect his bag. A faint whiff of cigarette smoke suddenly made me know that I had not been mistaken. Neither Vance nor I was smoking, and besides this scent came from above, in the rooms I had visited. As I turned to go out I passed close to the wooden stairs, and something made me reach up and feel for the key. But my fingers found only the empty nail where I had so lately hung it.

CHAPTER TWENTY-ONE

IT was mid-morning when I woke. The experience of the night before had the quality of a dream, vivid, yet unreal. Merek Vance's car was no longer in front of the house, and I could almost believe that it had never stalled there. Yet when I came downstairs to beg a belated cup of coffee from Maggie, I guessed that Aunt Em already knew something of my adventure. She looked up from a pile of mail she was sorting to eye me curiously.

"I don't wonder you slept late. From what that young doctor tells me you two certainly put through a pretty strenuous time of it."

"Oh," I said, trying to sound casual, "so Dr. Vance has been here and stolen my thunder."

"He came with a mechanic to get his car while we were having breakfast, so he had a cup of coffee with us. Janice had just been telling me about noticing that the car was gone when she came back from the Parkers', and we didn't know what to make of it."

"It's a funny thing she'd notice it was gone," I said.

"Well, she did," Aunt Em went on. "We were just trying to figure it out when Dr. Vance stopped to explain. I must say he was pleasanter than he's been the other times I've seen him. He's always seemed a morose, cold young man to me before, but he thanked me very nicely for the loan of the car and praised you and what you did to help. Whatever possessed you to go?"

Maggie brought my coffee just then, so I postponed answering for a moment.

"I don't know what made me," I told her; "it was just one of those impulses we can't account for. But I thought he might have trouble with the car, and of course we didn't know till we got to the place how serious it was. I wish you'd seen how he operated on that child, right on the kitchen table without any equipment except what he had in his bag. I'll never forget it."

"He said you turned to and helped as cool as could be."

"I was frightened, though, more frightened than I've ever been in my life. Of course I couldn't really do much. I just held the flashlight and tried to keep it steady while he worked. He was wonderful, Aunt Em; if that child pulls through, Dr. Vance deserves all the credit. But he didn't make anything of it."

"Why should he? That's all in a day's work for a doctor; but I'm glad he appreciated what you did. I'm thankful he didn't expose you to anything contagious."

I smiled and helped myself to more coffee. Aunt Em was trying so hard to overcome her prejudices. She was transparent as a child in some ways, and I knew Merek Vance must have said the right thing.

"Your uncle's left already," she went on. "He and Harry and Mr. Parker took the early train. I wish they hadn't all three gone at the same time in case anything new develops at the mills. Old Jo's laid up again. I made him go back to bed after he'd got the furnace going. I don't know what we're going to do this winter if he and the furnace give out at the same time."

Janice's door stood open half an hour later as I passed, and there she sat on the floor surrounded by a jungle of multi-coloured dresses draped over chairs, bed, and lounge— all she possessed with several of mine added to the collection.

"What's up?" I asked, pausing at the door. She started and stared at me keenly before she answered.

"I'm going to May Lowell's coming-out party in Waltham," she told me. "Florence Eaton just wrote they could put me up, and I thought I might as well go as stick the week-end out here."

"Well, why not?" I felt indifferent to her plan, though not to the clothes she evidently counted on borrowing. "But I'm not lending you the green chiffon or the Burgundy taffeta. They're going right back in my closet where they came from." I removed them firmly from the rest. "And you'd better not count on seeing Harry. He's going to be up to his ears in work."

"Who said anything about Harry?" She rose and began to fumble in a bureau drawer. "I wasn't going to sneak off with your dresses," she went on when she turned back to me again. "They can rot on their hangers for all of me. I was just trying to see if I could fix over my old blue net some way so I won't be ashamed to appear in public. You needn't always jump to conclusions, Emily; and people that go chasing all over the country with strange doctors at all hours of the night and morning needn't hand out advice!"

Her eyes narrowed and I saw that she looked tired and on edge. Her hands shook as she bent to fold the blue net and lay it in the open suitcase. Then she flung back her soft curls and faced me again.

"Oh, yes," she went on, "we heard all about your errand of mercy at the breakfast-table. It sounded almost too good to be true—like an unpublished chapter of Florence Nightingale or something."

"Don't forget," I reminded her, "that the car belongs to me as much as it does to you even if I don't use it very often. And by the way, I don't see how you happened to notice it was gone when you came back. You couldn't have seen way down to the old stable from the house."

A look of defiance sprang up in her eyes. They darkened as they always used to when she was a child facing some moment of reckoning. She mumbled something that I couldn't follow.

"What's that you say?" I persisted. "You know I can't make out a word when you turn your head away."

"Well, then"—she wheeled about and formed her words with exaggerated care—"I went down there to see if the keys were in the car. I was afraid I might have left them in. When I saw it was gone I didn't know what to think. I almost called the police."

"It's certainly something new for you to start worrying about the car keys. You know you always leave them in."

She shrugged her slim shoulders under the yellow

sweater that so exactly matched the colour of her hair. But her eyes and mouth were sullen as she turned back to her sorting and packing. I could see that the subject was closed as far as she was concerned.

I collected my windbreaker and beret and started down-stairs again. In the hall I met Maggie cleaning the carpets. Maggie was having what was alluded to in the household as "one of her off days." I could tell from the set of her head and shoulders and the way she bore down on the handle of the vacuum cleaner that her mind was even busier than her body.

"Well, Maggie," I said as she stopped to let me by, "I suppose you heard about last night."

"Yes," she nodded, "I heard, and I say good for the both of you."

I was surprised that she didn't scold me. I had expected at least one vigorous reprimand.

"And when you see him," she went on, "you'd best tell him to come by and take a look at old Jo. He's a bundle of knots this morning that'll take more than those sticky mustard plasters of his to untie."

"Why not telephone Dr. Weeks?" I suggested.

"It's not Dr. Weeks I mean." She stood with her arms about the vacuum cleaner, making something impressive and antique of its black polished handle. "No," she repeated, eyeing me shrewdly as she spoke, "it's the young doctor I'm after. No reflection on old brooms, but a new one sweeps clean."

"All right, Maggie, I can leave word at his office when I'm out walking Bridget. But why didn't you speak to him yourself when he stopped this morning?"

Again she gave me a keen look.

"I thought it would come better from you," she said, "and I reckoned you'd be seeing him same as usual."

"But, Maggie," I began, "what makes you think——"

Once more she looked at me. It was the way she used to look when we were children and all our most carefully guarded secrets turned out to be old stories to her. While

I hesitated she laid her forefinger to her lips and smiled reassuringly.

"I don't have to think, Miss Emily," she said; "I just know. You can't live with people like I've lived with all of you Blairs and not have an eye to what's going on, or a nose for what's in the air. No." She shook her head as I opened my lips to protest. "Don't say a word, then I won't have to."

I stood there without a word, watching her as she stooped and began coiling the long cord of the vacuum and fitting it into place. There was something so final and oracular about Maggie's statements that one had no need of answers or arguments. She was, as she had told me before, like a familiar piece of furniture. We flung ourselves upon her as we might on the chairs or sofa, counting on her being where we expected to find her. We took her presence for granted, and that was her hold over us. I did not know how she knew what I thought I had kept from every one. I should never know, and I was torn between scolding her and flinging myself into her arms. So I did neither, and she appeared to expect nothing more from me.

"Maggie," I said at last as if we had not spoken, "do you think we should get in touch with young Jo before we call in Dr. Vance?"

"That's up to you, Miss Emily. But old Jo won't see him, the way things are. If he could slip in and tinker with the furnace I must say it would be a help. Nobody knows how to work it like those two do. It's kind of ticklish to get him in without his grandpa or Miss Blair knowing, but I could sneak him down cellar if he came the back way. The boy's good-hearted if he is always mixed up with the wrong sides of things."

"I'll tell him if I can track him down. You don't think, do you, Maggie, that he ever comes up here to the old stable?"

"Not that I know of, Miss Emily. What makes you ask that?"

"Oh, I just wondered."

I knew it was too early to find Merek Vance at his office. He would be busy at the clinic till noon and then off on visits for another hour at least. But I would walk awhile first and perhaps find young Jo Kelly over by the union headquarters, which had been temporarily set up in a vacant building not far from the railroad station.

It was one of those raw December days when the sun has a metallic quality to its shining and even a distant red barn looks dull in the unlit distance. One feels the weight of coming snow as if it were a burden on the heart. Now and then a hard, icy flake touched my cheek or lay on my coat sleeve. The softly feathered kind would come later, and the bleakness of bare trees, stark buildings, and brown yards would be smothered in white by night. But these forerunners seemed to me like the difficult scanty tears of old, old people.

The excitement and accomplishment of the night before were gone. I no longer felt the energy that had warmed me then, and the faces of the people I met did nothing to lift my spirits. As I neared the railroad station I saw groups of children along the tracks and about the yards collecting bits of coal to carry home in dirty flour bags or boxes or toy express wagons. It was the noon period between morning and afternoon school sessions, when they should have been home eating dinner or out in the playgrounds. But there they were, as busy as the brown sparrows in the Square.

The station agent stood on the platform as I passed and, when he saw me watching them, he gave me an apologetic sidewise look.

"'Morning, Miss Blair." He came over as I paused. "Feels like we'll get snow to-night. Have to keep an eye on these kids from the mill or they'll try and root up the ties to cart home. Still, it's one way to get the place picked clean as a wishbone, and what can I do about it?" He shrugged and shifted his tobacco.

"What can anybody do?" I said, and stared severely at

L

the Indian Chief on the Peace-Pipe sign as if he might volunteer advice.

At that moment Bridget stiffened beside me, and I turned just in time to see a small, shabby boy take aim with a sling shot. The station agent ducked, and I caught the dog's collar and held her firmly. Something flew past us, and a dent appeared in the painted profile of the sign. I saw that other dents had pitted the signboard, and several letters of the legend "Peace-Pipe for Quality" were mutilated. At any other time I would have smiled over that exhibition of marksmanship, but that day I felt chilled and hurt, as if the stone or bit of coal had struck me, too.

"Fresh, that's what!" The station agent returned to me after making threatening gestures towards the little group as it scattered. "Can't trust one of them behind your back. That sign sure is a tempting target for the little rascals though. Well, kids will be kids, poor little devils."

I slipped the leash on Bridget and continued on my way. Several figures were lounging about the door of the dingy brick building where the union had set up its headquarters. They eyed me curiously as I came up to the entrance, and it seemed to me that they drew closer together as if they instinctively distrusted my coming. A woman in the little group nudged the man beside her, and I was certain that I made out the shape of my name on several lips. I had come too far to turn back, however, much as I wanted to hurry in the opposite direction. By the steps I stopped short and singled out the most familiar face, one of the workers I had often seen loading trucks in the mill grounds.

"Good-morning," I began. "I'm looking for Jo Kelly, and I thought I might find him here."

The man touched his cap and nodded a bit nervously, I thought.

"Guess Jo's inside," he said. "I'll see."

They came out of the building together presently.

"What's the matter?" Jo asked without ceremony. "Is it Grandpa?"

I nodded as he fell into step beside me. We walked away together, and it seemed to me that I could feel the curious eyes fixed on my back. I realised that it had been rash of me to go there, that Jo would be held to account later.

"I've got to talk to you," I said. "If you can spare a few moment's let's go in the station."

He followed me into the empty waiting-room, and Bridget jumped on the wooden bench between us, her head flattened against Jo's trouser leg where his knee bones pushed sharply through the worn material.

"I don't mean to worry you about it," I said, "but he's pretty badly crippled, and we think Dr. Vance ought to see him. I thought I'd tell you first, and then you can have a talk with the doctor yourself when he's made an examination."

"Why, sure," he agreed, and went on stroking the dog mechanically. "I think you couldn't do better. I don't suppose he's—changed about me any? No. Well, I guess I can't expect it, but I sure wish there was something I could do."

"Old Jo's in no shape to work with the furnace," I told him, "but he will get up and try. Maggie says it's acting up again, and no one but you knows how to handle it. She said she'd sneak you down cellar if you'd take a look at it. I hate to ask favours of you, Jo, but if you could——"

He smiled, and his teeth showed white and sharp as Bridget's.

"Why, don't mention it," he grinned. "I'll be over later —maybe I'd better make it after dark in case Grandpa had an eye out the window. Just needs a little humouring or a new grate maybe. Sure I can count on Maggie?"

"It was her idea to ask you," I said. "Maybe I shouldn't have come down here looking for you. I didn't think it might be hard for you to explain to—to your friends."

"Don't worry about that, Emily."

"I promise not to do it again, only you'd better let me know some way I can reach you if I have to."

He went over to the other side of the waiting-room,

scribbled something on a telegraph blank and brought it back to me.

"You send word down there," he explained, "and they'll know where I am. Don't forget now, if you need me."

"I won't forget."

I spoke then of Angeletta.

"Must be a couple of years since I saw her," he commented. "I'd like to help her some way if I could. But Gallo's got no use for me. He always thought I was sweet on Angie."

"I used to think you were in high school."

He shook his dark head emphatically.

"I had plenty of foolish notions then," he admitted, "but that wasn't one of them. Well, you tell Maggie to keep an eye out so's she can sneak me in. Look here, this dog's coat seems kind of poor to me. Try a spoonful of malt every day, and a lump of sulphur in her drinking water won't hurt any either. So long."

The expected snow had begun to fall in thin flakes by the time I reached the doctor's steps. I felt glad of the shabby warmth of the office while I waited for his return. The small blue box stood on top of a pile of papers and medical reports on his desk. I reached for it and touched the painted flowers and hearts and inscription with my finger-tips. Our house was crowded with old things, objects good and bad, yet none of them comforted me as this did whenever I took it in my hands.

Merek Vance came in presently, shaking snow from his collar and hair, looking more boyish than I had seen him in many visits. He stood warming his hands at the radiator and eyeing me intently.

"You look tired," he said. "Was last night too much for you?"

I shook my head.

"No, not last night—it's this town. I can't help feeling when I walk around that it's been struck by some blight."

"It's not the only place that has been," he answered. "From what I hear of the big cities, they're worse off."

"How's the Gallo boy?" I asked, glad to change the subject.

"He's coming along splendidly. We made a good clean job of it last night. The visiting nurse is going over there to change the dressing and check up on his temperature." He peered at me more closely before he went on. "You're not used to such strenuous evenings. No wonder you're tired to-day."

"Oh," I sighed, "being tired isn't what I mind. It's things you can't do anything about that get you down. It seems worth while to do what you did last night. At the time I couldn't feel anything mattered except your pulling that child through so he'd go on living and breathing. But afterwards—don't you ever say to yourself ' What for?'"

"Well, suppose I do?" he asked in turn.

"Last night it seemed wonderful to save a child's life," I persisted, "and then this morning I saw a lot of children grubbing and fighting over little lumps of coal along the railroad tracks. I suppose that was what started me thinking. . . . You know for most of them there'll never be enough coal or food or clothes or anything else to go round. I don't see how you can reconcile it—patching people up, curing them of one thing to be ready for something worse. Doesn't it seem pretty futile to you? Isn't it almost like operating on a condemned man so he'll be in good shape for hanging?"

He did not seem to mind my tirade. He went on warming his hands and watching me across the little space that divided us.

"Yes, there are times when a doctor feels like that," he said at last. "Maybe it's because you've just come round to taking notice, that it's knocked you all of a heap. I suppose I got used to the inconsistencies you mentioned and to the waste of human beings earlier than most do. I'm not reconciled to it, as you say, and I never will be. I look at it differently, that's all."

"How?" I leaned forward in my chair, and my hands still pressed the small blue box.

"You're thinking in the plural," he went on, "and a doctor like me learns to think in terms of the singular—one person at a time and do what you can for him. We have to forget mass tragedy in relieving one human being. Lucky thing it's that way, or we wouldn't be able to take it most of the time."

He was busy after that with preparations that were now a familiar routine to us both. I submitted to my part absently, hardly aware until I felt that brief prick of the needle that another treatment was over. But before I had collected my things to go he stopped me.

"Do you mind if I ask a favour," he said, and I thought he seemed hesitant, embarrassed as I had never known him to be before. "It's my birthday, and it's bad luck, I've always heard, to drink one's own health. I wasn't going to notice the day, but I seemed to feel the need of telling someone; and I hope you don't mind."

Before I could offer my congratulations he disappeared and returned with a bottle and two glasses.

"This is very old port," he explained; "but we mustn't take any chances with the law, so as your doctor I shall prescribe for you first."

He laughed and scribbled quickly on his office pad. I took the page he tore off and read what he had written there. My name came first, then some unintelligible medical shorthand and below that the familiar words: "To be taken as directed. M. Vance. December 11th, 1931." I have that bit of paper yet, though I have no need to refresh my memory.

"Now that you've prescribed," I smiled back at him as he poured the wine carefully so that not a drop should spill, "I suppose I'd better be deciding on a toast. If you were Dr. Weeks I'd say, 'Your health,' and if you were Janice I'd say, 'Happy days.' But I'm a little puzzled about you."

"I could do with health and happiness as well as any one, and I'm just entering my thirty-third year, if that's any clue." He held out the little glass as he spoke.

I took it, but still I hesitated.

"Here's to your not being sorry you came back to Blairstown," I said at last, and took the first sip.

"And here's the same to you, Emily Blair."

We drank our port without further toasts, and I thought how strange it was that I, of all people, should have been the one to wish him well on his thirty-second birthday. I went back through the years to another December afternoon. I had been seven then, so he must have been fourteen at that Christmas party when I had first felt myself the target of bitterness even as the Indian Chief's head had been earlier that day.

"You've gone a long way since then." I must have spoken my thoughts, for he looked at me questioningly with raised brows. "I was just thinking of the mill Christmas party," I explained. "You remember the one I mean?"

He nodded, and I went on.

"I don't seem to have got very far, at least not the way you have. Last night you said I was in a comfortable little rut, and you're probably right."

"Did I? Well, there are a lot of worse places to be than ruts. And I don't know how far I've gone when it comes to that. A good many people might think I'd doubled back on my tracks and landed where I started from."

I squinted at the wine in my glass before I answered.

"I think coming back to a place takes a special sort of perspective," I told him, "unless, of course, one comes back to gloat."

He followed me to the door and promised to visit old Jo Kelly as soon as office hours were over. As I turned to go he touched my arm to attract my attention.

"Maybe you're right," he said, "about my coming back to Blairstown. I thought it was all my wanting to help Dr. Weeks out; but perhaps I did want to do a little gloating, though I wouldn't admit it to myself before."

CHAPTER TWENTY-TWO

UNCLE WALLACE and Harry returned from Boston looking graver than when they had left, and Mr. Parker stayed on for more conferences with directors and bank executives.

"It's the same story everywhere," Uncle Wallace told us, "only worse in New Bedford and Fall River. Even down South they're feeling the pinch. Business isn't dull, it's just plain dead."

I tried to catch all I could, and for once Harry seemed ready to explain the situation in terms that I could grasp.

"The banks aren't going to refuse, are they?" I asked him. "They won't withdraw their backing or loans, or whatever you call it?"

"Banks are tightening up everywhere," he told me as we sat by the fire after Sunday dinner, while Uncle Wallace and Aunt Em talked and went over reports in the study. "The bankers that Peace-Pipe has always dealt with didn't exactly turn us down; but they're not taking any chances with their money."

"How do you mean, dear? Make it easy for me to understand if you can?"

He was unusually patient with me that afternoon, and I tried to ask as few questions as possible. My head ached with the strain of reading his lips, with piecing together facts when I lost words here and there and tried to follow without asking for repetitions.

The situation was simple enough when I got to the bottom of it. The banks would continue their backing and even make additional loans if they could have assurance that our mill would reopen by the first of the year.

"It's a fair enough proposition," Harry admitted; "the only trouble is we're pressed for time. The union's got us in a tight spot—just where they want to keep us till we have to come round to their terms. That's what they're counting on."

"Can't you put it up to the workers themselves? This way it's as if both sides were starving each other out. There'll be nothing left of the business if it goes on like this."

"You're right, there won't be. That's why we've got to reopen, strike or no strike. If we recognise their union, that means accepting a new wage scale. We'd be filling orders at a loss if we met their demands. They're beginning to feel the pinch down there now——"

"I know, Harry, I know. Even over here I can feel how much worse things are this week than last, and with Christmas coming and all—something's got to be done. But what?"

I searched his face, but found no optimism there.

"The banks agree with us there's only one stand to take. Millhands who want work can come back at wages we can pay; those who don't—— Well," he shrugged expressively, "they'll just have to stay outside the gates and let the union worry about them. We can get all the help we need; too many out of work in this town, and plenty of others if it comes to that."

"You mean you'll call in strikebreakers—scabs?"

I had never used the word before except to young Jo Kelly. I saw Harry's surprise at my mention of the term.

"Why, yes," he admitted, "that's about what it amounts to. I'm not saying there won't be trouble, but we've tried every other way since the walk-out."

"Trouble?" I asked. "Even more than now?"

"They may put up a fight. Still a picket line wouldn't make much show if we called in the State militia——" He broke off, seeing the horrified look on my face. "Now don't you start worrying, Emmy. Of course we hope it won't come to that. We want to keep things peaceful if we can."

I could not speak for a minute. I sat there on the sofa beside him and tried to remember all that I had ever read about strike violence and militia being called out in other plants. There was a newsreel I had seen once where officers with raised clubs bore down on men and women who retreated before them like a dark wave, and there were blurred newspaper prints of crowds being scattered by tear-gas bombs. I wondered if Harry could be thinking beyond the words he said.

"And if Peace-Pipe didn't reopen—for a while, I mean?"

I could see that he was growing tired of my questions before he answered.

"It's got to," he told me. "It's got to reopen or go under. Do you know how much we're losing every day the plant's idle? No? Well, I can get you the figures in case you're interested. The money doesn't roll in of itself, you know."

"But it's awful to talk about it like that," I protested, and I could feel tears gathering in my eyes. "I can't seem to put money first, not ahead of the people over there. Maybe I feel differently about it because I went to school with some of them. I can't just call them millhands and let it go at that. They've got their side, too, and when I see the children——"

"There you go sentimentalising." His mouth hardened as he spoke, and he turned on me accusingly. "You asked for facts, and I'm giving them to you. You've got to stop mixing up in what you don't know the first thing about, and you've got to stop middle-of-the-night errands of mercy with strange doctors."

I was so startled I had no answer ready. How could he have heard about my visit to the Gallo family so soon after his return? I had meant to tell him of it myself.

"Oh," I began lamely, "you've heard about that——"

"Yes, I heard. Things like that get around."

I felt myself growing hot, hurt by his criticism and worried because I did not wish to have him question me further about Merek Vance.

"If you ran into Janice in Boston," I said, "and she told you—well, you know how she exaggerates. . . ."

I scarcely thought what I was saying until he rose and

went to the window as if he did not want to meet my eyes. So Janice had told him. I could imagine that she had made the most of the incident.

"It wasn't anything I planned to do, Harry." I rose and went over to where he stood, toying with the shade cord in his preoccupied way. "And Dr. Vance didn't ask me to. I just went along when he borrowed the car. . . . I can't see why you should be annoyed about it."

I slipped my hand through his arm and tried to make him look at me. But he was unresponsive to my touch.

"Please, Harry," I begged foolishly because I felt so completely cut off from contact. He could put me miles away simply by keeping his face averted. "I never thought you'd mind my going. You don't really, do you?"

He turned around at last, and though he smiled I felt no reassurance behind it.

"It's not whether I mind or not, Emmy," he said, forming the words emphatically so that I could not possibly mistake them. "But you must remember you can't afford to get talked about. You're not just anybody in this town. Your family's been behind Peace-Pipe for generations. You're part of it and everything it stands for, don't forget that."

"I don't forget," I began, "but it seems to me there's a lot that none of us understand yet. What was right in the business fifty years ago, even ten years ago, may be all wrong now." I saw his eyes grow cold behind the little flecks of golden light that I loved even more than his tilted brows and humorous mouth, and I hurried on before he could turn away. "I don't pretend to know anything, but I'm honestly trying to see both sides. A business can grow too big for a family to run, like—like a snowball you roll till it gets bigger than you are." It surprised me to find myself repeating the very words young Jo had said. "That old Indian in his war feathers has seen a lot of changes since he came to be our trademark."

"And a lot of goodwill and respect are behind him, and money, too," he reminded me. "I may have criticised the kind of goods we've been turning out, and I still think we're behind the times in lots of ways; but Peace-Pipe's never let down on quality, and I'd be pretty proud of the product of the mill if I were you."

I realised that it was useless to go on with a discussion that was only drawing us farther apart. It hurt and puzzled me that he should resent my interest, that he should make such an issue of my visit to the sick child of a worker's family. He made me feel almost as disloyal as if I had joined the picket line across the river. I was relieved when he proposed going out for a drive.

Because it was Sunday afternoon the town seemed momentarily to have shed its blight. There were no shabby lines of men and women about the mill gates, and the motionless machinery and smokeless chimneys were less oppressive than in the weekday idleness. The snow which usually took on a grey film of smoke as it fell had stayed white.

The town looked its best with sharp roof lines and bare trees and lawns softened into prim beauty. We kept to the main road which had been cleared and drove north towards the dark ridges of hills. With the town behind us I breathed more freely. The little car took the miles, almost as if it had invisible wings. No one ever drove a car better than Harry. He and the engine always seemed to merge like perfectly-matched partners in some rhythm of their own. Since my deafness I had become more than ever conscious of such mechanical harmony. I felt the tension ease between us, and I relaxed beside him and gave myself to the moment. If he had reached out and taken my hand just then, I think I might have been completely happy.

Even without that I forgot to be troubled and afraid. Christmas was only ten days off, and the feel of it was in the air. Red barns were warmed to brightness on the side where the low sun struck. Apple-trees in orchards were stubbornly crooked to the clear pale sky and clumps of hemlock invading rough pastures were purple-dark against the snow. Now and then a wreath showed at some window or door, and Christmas greens and bunches of scarlet berries had been set out for sale at the roadside. Just before we turned to drive back I signalled Harry to stop at one of these stands.

"I must have a bunch," I told him; "I know Aunt Em has ordered our wreaths months ago, but these are somehow special."

He drew up obligingly while I got out to make my selection. My reason told me that the berries could not possibly be as brilliant as they seemed. It was the slantwise, winter light in that hour before sunset that laid a curious shine upon them. It was as if each and every round red ball had been dipped in glory. If only one could keep them so always, I thought, along with moments that are kindled by a look or a word or a smile from someone we love! I bought a miniature Christmas wreath, no bigger than my two fists. It would be too small to make a showing among the laurel festoons and wreaths of holly and ground pine that always filled our house. But I decided it was exactly the size to hang on a doctor's door.

Harry smiled tolerantly as I carried my purchases back to the car, and we drove home through the December sunset with the chimneys of Peace-Pipe black shapes against clouds of feathered flame.

There was a light at Dr. Weeks's house as we passed, a single oblong of brightness in the wing where Merek Vance had his office. I could picture him at his desk. It seemed right and natural to think of him there. I was startled to remember how short a time it was since he had come to Blairstown. But then it was not as if he were a stranger. Peace-Pipe was in his past, too, even as it was in mine. The shadow of those black chimneys, the bitter smoke from their throats, and the pulse of humming mill machinery had somehow marked us both long ago. We were both a part of the "product of the mill." Harry had flung that phrase at me a little while before, and I had thought little of those five familiar words; but suddenly they took on life and significance for me as the scarlet

berries had taken on strange brightness by the roadside.
Peace-pipe had made me the sort of person I was. By the
same token Merek Vance was what he was because of those
difficult years of resentment his childhood had known
across the river and its bridges.

"Peace-Pipe for Quality," another well-known phrase,
leaped to my mind. I hoped it applied to me. But I wasn't
sure of myself as I was of him. I found myself smiling to
think how vehemently the dark sharp-featured man behind
that lighted window would deny the charge.

CHAPTER TWENTY-THREE

MIRACLES are out of fashion nowadays. Or perhaps it is
only that they have been explained away from us. Radios
and newsreels and words have shorn them of their mystery.
Yet to each of us, I think, a miracle is given at some time
in our lives. We may not choose the moment it shall be
revealed or the form it shall take. We may not even realise
till long afterwards that it was our privilege to be part
of one. Our minds may betray the wonder that our hearts
accept. I fought against the miracle that was to be mine,
but there was no denying it when it came to me.

I must tell of it in my own way, though my words will
make a poor showing to those who ask for explanations in
technical phraseology. In the medical world much has
been written about the Vance treatment of deafness and
restoration of impaired nerve cells. His formula and method
of injection has been widely publicised in the last year,
hailed as one of the greatest contributions to medical science
and a boon to humanity. Already it is being put to practical
test by doctors in hospitals and clinics all over the country,
and reports of even greater uses to which it may be applied
are continually appearing. But of these I may not write
even if it were in my power to master the terms. These
seem to have no part in the visits I made to the bare, poorly

equipped office during those months which were to change the whole course of my life.

Whenever I come upon the familiar letters in print, "Merek Vance, M.D."—and I come upon them often now-adays in magazines and newspapers, I must stop and convince myself that they belong to the man whose faith and determination dominated that shabby room and all who entered it. But the printed name has less reality for me than the remembrance of an alert face that could darken to disapproval or light up in sudden sympathy. The medical journals with their impressive accounts of his discovery seem vague and impersonal compared to the makeshift rack of test tubes with their home-made labels, the long, skilful fingers that handled them, and the prick of a needle whose power I once dared to doubt. It frightens me a little to read of that doctor and his achievement. But when I remember his eyes watching me across the battered desk I am reassured. I have faltered under the directness of his look and the uncompromising words he has spoken, but they have had power over me in the past, and they will have power to hurt and strengthen me again.

That blind man in the Bible whose sight was restored to him had no explanation to offer in testimonial. He could only stand and stare and repeat, "I was blind, now I see." That is how it was with me. Whatever I am or may become, I shall never be as I was before. For I am no longer shut off from the sweet and the harsh sounds of earth. The simple, terrible impact of spoken words is mine once more, and I shall never take the gift for granted. Even though I should live to be an old, old woman I doubt that I can ever be unshaken by the first splashing of rain, by the tender clamour of bird calls in early morning, and the pulse of unseen crickets hailing frost. I shall fall silent sometimes in the midst of eager voices, knowing that the wonder of voice answering to human voice is too much for me to bear. I must listen then, not to what the voices are saying, but to the silence that once made me its prisoner. Sometimes, it may be that I shall see a look in other eyes, a listening look that I shall recognise; before which I shall be humble and kind.

I have not thanked Merek Vance for what he has done for me. We do not thank the sun for rising or the air for letting us breathe it. Besides, if I tried to thank him he would only shrug his shoulders and lift his dark brows in the way I know so well. But this much he did say once, and I have not forgotten it:

"No matter how many people the injections might have helped," he told me, "I could never have taken any satisfaction if I'd failed with you. It would have been bitter—like isolating the germ that had killed your wife or your child."

But I am far ahead of myself. What happens to people is the story. What they think about while it is happening to them is something else.

The day after my drive with Harry I woke feeling restless, weighed down with a mood of despair which I could not shake off. I felt as I used to feel in my childhood when the door of a closet closed upon me and I found myself half-smothered by the folds of heavy garments. Only when I pushed my way through them and fumbled for the doorknob would the unreasoning panic leave me. Since there was no such simple way out of my depression, I decided to go to Boston on the pretext of Christmas shopping. I must get away from the fear and futility that hung over Blairstown even if I could not get away from myself. I didn't care whether I inconvenienced Vance by missing treatments. I had never had any real faith in them. Those visits to the little office, I told myself, had merely been something to do each day, nothing more. I would put an end to them with the new year. Merek Vance couldn't hold me to a promise he had forced upon me.

So I scribbled a hurried note and left it with the little wreath on my way to the train. Vance would find it in the mailbox when he returned from the clinic, and by that time I would be gone. Harry would be working late over mill reports that night. He had told me not to expect him for supper. Aunt Em seemed glad to have me go.

"Do you good to get away, dear," she said. "A day's shopping always used to set me up when I was your age. Just enjoy yourself and forget all about mill trouble. But don't let Eunice know how worried we are about Peace-Pipe, whatever you do. You just tell her everything's going to be all right after New Year's when the mill reopens."

I promised and tried to put Blairstown behind me once I had boarded the train. But that was easier said than done. It was an express from the north, crowded with Christmas shoppers and students going home for the holidays. The stir of festivity that surged through the car had no power to lift my spirits. Bundles fell from overhead racks; skates, suitcases, and armfuls of country greens overflowed the aisles, fellow-passengers smiled and nodded and were gay and good-humoured about me. But I could not shed my own preoccupation. I stayed dull and quiet as a snail might withdraw into the narrow world of its own shell.

The exuberance was more than I could face after a while, and I closed my eyes against it. Let them think I slept. I felt too tired to strain at reading the lips of strangers. There was no need to pretend that I caught the friendly greetings of the season, especially as I was in no mood to respond in kind.

Perhaps I really did doze off for a minute or two. I shall never know. But suddenly I was aware of sound, or what seemed to be sound above the vibration of the train. I found myself sitting bolt upright on the plush seat with a queer chill at my spine. My bag fell to the floor and as I bent mechanically to recover it I lost the odd sensation in my ears.

"It's being on a train," I reasoned. "Vibration can play tricks like this sometimes."

I remembered that in the past I had once or twice been betrayed into imagining that I heard when I travelled on

M

trains. The doctors had tried to explain the affiliation between different nerve responses and the tie between sound and motion. They had even been interested enough to try other mechanical stimulation. I had spent many hours being tested with intricate machines in one office or another. I had even been taken up in an airplane on several occasions because some cases of deafness had been benefited by altitude and vibration. Knowing how these experiments had failed, I argued myself into apathy once more. There was no recurrence of the sensation I had seemed to feel, and yet I knew that something had suggested music to me—a faint thread of sound that was not part of the motion and throb of the engine.

I must have dreamed it, I decided; and yet I could not put it from my mind so lightly. In the last year I had accepted my deafness so completely that I could not remember once a dream which had given sound back to me.

And then I turned and stared down the car. There a few seats behind me a group of college boys and girls were crowded among suitcases and bags, and I saw that one of the boys was playing an accordion. It opened and shrank under his hands and he swayed to the music he must be making.

What of it? I argued inwardly. He's playing now, and you can't hear him. What makes you think you did before?

I hurried through the North Station, trying not to remember the last time I had waited there. Cousin Eunice was out for the afternoon playing bridge. I left my bag and walked away from her narrow red brick house that held no charm of pleasant association for me. The air blew strong as I crossed the Public Gardens towards the stores on Boylston Street. It felt clean and fresh on my face, though the remnants of snow beside the paths were grey with city smoke. Christmas stirred all about me; children in bright coats feeding pigeons and brown sparrows; skaters on the frozen pond, and a shivering Salvation Army Santa Claus with his tripod and kettle. I dropped a coin in it as I passed, and presently I was part of the crowd of shoppers. It was exhilarating to be in stores again, though such expeditions always taxed my power of concentration. I was more than ever aware of my handicap when customers jostled me to one side. It was difficult to make my wants known to busy salesgirls who had a way of turning their heads in another direction as I strained to catch their answers to questions. But I managed my purchases at last and completed the list of purchases Aunt Em had given me. Suddenly I found my arms full of packages and my head throbbing with the effort I had made to secure them.

I walked past my reflection in a looking-glass panel and smiled to see that I looked like all the other bundle-laden shoppers. To see me no one would have guessed how little festivity I felt. It was only mid-afternoon; but already twilight was settling over the city, and the brightness of decorated windows accentuated the early December dark. I made my way to the edge of the sidewalk and went on, letting the home-going crowd take me in the direction of Copley Square. I had no reason for returning to Cousin Eunice's house before dinner-time, and I thought a walk might help me to face the barrage of her questions. So I moved on without objective. The city sights and smells brought back associations with every block. All the futile visits to doctors' offices returned to haunt me as I recognised this landmark or that—the florist's at the corner where bunched violets kept their fragrance longer; the blind man with his magazine and newspaper stand; the pet shop window with its never-failing crop of round, lustre-eyed puppies. I did not pause to tap at that pane of plate glass as others were doing. Back in Blairstown, Bridget would be missing me, I knew, whether any one else did or not.

It seemed to me that beggars and street venders were more in evidence than usual. I tried not to notice them, shivering at the curb among their tawdry wares. The contrast from corner to corner took me by surprise: on one, stacks of spruce and fir-trees and greens making the air pungent with spice; and across the way, black headlines that newsboys held high—"Financier Commits Suicide, Bankruptcy Hinted," "Market Hits New Low for Year," "Third Largest Mass. Woollen Mill Closes." If Harry had been there walking beside me I should not have read the headlines. Or, if I had read them, their import would not have made me shiver under the warmth of my sealskin coat.

Ugh! Let me get away from headlines and people selling things I don't want to buy! I thought as I stepped off the curb and started across the street.

Usually I was timid in traffic, over cautious because of my deafness. I thought I was careful then; but I must have been more preoccupied than I realised, for suddenly I stopped short trembling from head to foot. Once more I was conscious of sound. This time there could be no doubt. A horn honked shrilly and brakes screeched at the same instant a truck shuddered to a stop so close beside me I could feel the throbbing heat of the motor. I stood there smiling foolishly into the furious, frightened face of the driver. I can see him yet, glaring at me over the wheel, while I continued to stand and smile as if he had saved my life instead of so nearly crushing it out of existence. Just as well, perhaps, that I couldn't hear the names he was calling me. His frantic gesturings finally brought me to my senses.

I don't know how I made my way across the street. I only know that I was still smiling long after I had reached safety. My knees went weak then, and my hands shook so that I could hardly keep my bundles from scattering. I found the refuge of a bench and sank down on it. I must have made a spectacle of myself, surrounded by gaily-wrapped packages, with tears streaming down my cheeks for any passerby to see. But I didn't care who saw me there. I didn't care what any one thought. It didn't seem incongruous that a strident motor horn had been the means of revealing the miracle that I could no longer deny.

I have no idea how long I sat huddled on that cold bench

in the city twilight, shaken with sobs and oblivious to the curious looks of those who passed. Maybe it feels like that to die and be lifted out of time and the infirmities of flesh and spirit. Or perhaps that realisation of well-being only comes when we who have given up hope suddenly feel its living stir within us, as Aaron's rod put out leaf and bud for a sign.

And so I walked back through the dusk with my bundles. Silhouettes of Christmas wreaths showed dark against all the lighted windowpanes in the houses I passed. My face was stiff with drying tears, and I scarcely knew how my feet took me along the streets. But I no longer felt alone. I turned once, half-expecting to see Merek Vance at my elbow. He had dragged me back from unheard danger before, and now, miles away from the congested street-crossing, he had saved me once again. He would be keeping office hours at his desk in the familiar room. I knew that, and yet it seemed to me that I could feel his hand warm and re-assuring on my arm.

I stood a moment by the flight of stone steps, bracing myself against the chill iron railing before I went in to face Cousin Eunice. My ears were dull and lifeless again. It might be days or hours before they quickened to sound once more, and I would hear it again. Yet the signal had come.

CHAPTER TWENTY-FOUR

THAT was a strange and wakeful night in Cousin Eunice's spare bedroom. I tried to read myself to sleep, but the words on the pages I turned had less reality than the pattern of the flowered wallpaper. I put out the light at last and lay, tense and wide-eyed in the darkness, my mind churning over and over all the happenings of the day. It had begun grey and tight-fisted as some knob of bud on a winter tree, and then it had changed miraculously like the tiny dried flowers we children used to watch expand to colour and beauty in a bowl of water. Yes, it had bloomed like that for me.

Although there had been no recurrence of sound since afternoon, I was certain of what I had heard. I felt certain, too, of a subtle change in my ears. Silence muffled them again, but the dullness was gone. It was as if a telephone wire, long disconnected, had suddenly become charged with a live current. It startled me, too, to realise that in spite of my stubborn refusal to believe in or hope for a cure, something secret and strong in me had managed to keep faith all along. I must have clung to it unconsciously even while my lips uttered their denials. So I drifted off to sleep at last with morning a thin grey behind the nearby chimneys; with happiness wrapping me more warm and light than Cousin Eunice's best eiderdown quilt.

"No, I can't stay," I told her at breakfast. "I must take the next train."

"Always on the go, you young people," she reproved across the silver coffee service. "No stability or sense about you. It's as if you were all too busy tracking down happiness ever to meet up with it. I always gave you credit for wanting to marry and settle down, but lately you act as flighty as Janice."

Her keen eyes scrutinised me from her puffy, well-preserved face.

"Well," she went on. "I suppose I shouldn't blame you for wanting to get back to Harry. Heaven knows, long engagements are trying enough without all you've had to put up with beside. I guess you two wish you had some of the money that's been thrown away on ear specialists these last years. It would come in handy to start house-keeping."

I lifted my coffee-cup and nodded over its gold rim.

"This is lovely china, Cousin Eunice." I touched the porcelain admiringly as I spoke. "Coffee tastes better out of these cups than any I know."

Praise of her possessions usually mollified her, but that day she couldn't be distracted.

"There's the paper," she said. "Maybe you have the courage to read it. Frankly I haven't; nothing but bank failures and mill shutdowns and suicides. With all this unfortunate business at Peace-Pipe and dividends going to be passed again—I don't know what we're coming to. Do you?"

"Harry and Uncle Wallace are too worried to talk much," I hedged. "But the mills are going to reopen—that's all I know."

"I can't see why they're not making money," she persisted. "After all, it's not as if Peace-Pipe were manufacturing luxury goods, like silk or perfumery or fancy linens. People all over this country have to sleep and wash themselves, so there's always a demand for sheets and pillowcases and towels."

I found myself thinking of the Gallo family huddled round the kitchen stove and of the gaunt, grimy faces I had seen at street curb and park the day before.

"I guess there are plenty of people nowadays who'd think a clean sheet or a towel was a luxury," I reminded her.

Without waiting for her answer I set down my cup, and rose from the table.

In my impatience to be on my way to Blairstown I reached the station nearly an hour before train-time. But that day I did not mind the bleakness of the waiting-room with all its earlier associations. The smell of varnished wood and cinders, of wet wool and rubber from overcoats and goloshes could not depress me even on so dark and moist a morning. I had felt elated as the taxi brought me through a grey drizzle that slanted in from the water front. The traffic had been hopelessly snarled in the maze of narrow, crowded streets. Sleet filmed the sidewalks and glazed the umbrellas that clustered like jungles of strange mushrooms by subway entrances and street crossings. Yet they did not seem grotesque to me that dark December morning. My heart bore up my body. I felt that curious whetting of the senses, that inner quickening that is the nearest thing to pure joy. I moved in a kind of glow of my own making. It seemed to me that people felt and responded to it. The taxi-driver smiled as he helped me out. The porter who carried my bags and the ticket-seller also relaxed their tense, pre-holiday expression and I was aware that those who waited on nearby benches eyed me with less impersonal stares. It had not been like that since the summer of my engagement when my happiness had brimmed over and flowed out in every direction.

"You don't see many happy-looking folks nowadays," Maggie had said once. "It's a treat to pass somebody that don't look down in the mouth or out-and-out sour."

Maggie would guess the truth as soon as I crossed the threshold. Her wise grey eyes would find me out though neither of us spoke a word. Yes, Maggie and Bridget would know by some common gift of insight that they possessed, and I could trust them not to betray me.

As I waited on the wooden bench with my bag and purchases I found myself thinking of Merek Vance. It occurred to me for the first time since my flight that he might well have resented my leaving town without warning. I had only missed one day, to be sure, but my note had been curt. He must have sensed the irritation behind the hastily-scribbled words. If only I might rush to one of the telephone booths and call him by long distance! Since that was still impossible I tried to think how I could make amends before I reached Blairstown. I must prepare him for the news I was bringing. So I hurried over to the telegraph stand and reached for a form. It was difficult to frame my message. Care must be taken of the wording since the local operators sometimes took far too personal an interest in the wires received and delivered.

I stared about me in search of words, and my eyes noticed a sign that recommended the season's greetings and listed a variety of hackneyed suggestions. None of these suited my particular need, but I seized the idea and began to write on the yellow blank:

DR. MEREK VANCE
COURT HOUSE SQUARE
BLAIRSTOWN, MASS.

O COME ALL YE FAITHFUL JOYFUL AND TRIUMPHANT STOP RETURNING IMMEDIATELY.

E. BLAIR.

The operator counted out the words mechanically. Her pencil hung questioningly over the "O," but I shook my head at her suggested pruning and attempt to change "ye" to "you." Whatever changes it might suffer, I told myself, Merek Vance would be able to translate the carol into medical terms.

I glanced at the clock as I crossed the waiting-room. It was seven minutes before ten. I tried to calculate the time it would take for my wire to reach its destination. I could see the messenger boy crossing the Square in his rainy-day slicker and cap, ringing the doctor's bell, and waiting with his pencil and receipt slip in hand. Perhaps Vance would be on his way out to the car. I could see him pause in his hat and overcoat while he tore the yellow envelope open. Or if he had already left on his rounds I could picture it lying among the other papers on his desk.

I thought of Harry, and my throat went dry, trying to summon words to tell him that evening when we should be alone. The station became a blur while I clung to the moment that lay ahead.

"Harry," I would say. "Harry, darling, we've had so much bad luck, you and I. Do you think you could bear something else—something wonderful for a change?"

The thought of hearing his voice once more turned me faint for an instant. It might be many more weeks or months, but I could wait for that. Everything was going to be as it had been before, only better, a thousand times better. This unacknowledged chill that had lain between us since my return to Blairstown would vanish like mist under a noonday sun. Nothing in the world, it seemed, not even the trouble at Peace-Pipe, had power to dim our happiness.

In the women's waiting-room I found a lone Gideon Bible chained to a table, and I began to turn the pages as I used to do on days when I felt the need of some sign from heaven. That was how I came upon the verse in the book of Proverbs. "Hope deferred maketh the heart sick: but when the desire cometh, it is a tree of life."

"A tree of life." . . . I could feel those very branches stirring to live green in the core of my being. I stood there shaken before the truth of those words. I tremble now as I set them down upon this sheet of paper, for they were like an echo of my own heart, of all hearts beating and hoping through time and space.

I had just settled myself by the car window when a porter passed, his arms weighed down with familiar luggage. I recognised a hatbox bearing my initials, Janice's suitcase, and a little grey overnight bag I had given her on her last birthday. She went by before I could reach out and touch her arm. Her eyes were on the porter and a seat he had found for her far down the car. But I could see her profile under a new green hat. It was tilted like a fallen leaf on the bright waves of her hair. Her cheeks were rosy from haste and moist with damp. She must have been hurrying to catch the train, and haste was always becoming to Janice. No wonder people turned to watch her. No wonder that men especially forgot subjects they were discussing when she came within range.

If I were a man, I told myself, I'd certainly be attracted to Janice—not me. I wonder she hasn't married long ago. She's had plenty of chances to. . . . Maybe she knows more than she lets on about love and men and—oh, well, she can take care of herself, I guess. But she ought to fall in love and be happy. She'd be different then. Maybe we could get to know each other if we didn't have to live under the same roof and always have to be on guard against being sisters. I want Janice to be happy. I've never wanted it as much as I do to-day.

I was tempted to rise and go to her, but already the seat beside me was filled and all my things on the overhead rack would have to be shifted. Besides, I needed to be alone for a little while longer. I needed to hold fast to my happiness that day, though I had enough and to spare for Janice and that whole carload of people. So I sat on in my place while the train sped away from the city, past towns and farms, whose streets and buildings I recognised through the December drizzle and my own sense of well-being.

Yes, I admitted, I had been overcritical of Janice lately. The habit had grown on me since my deafness. I suppose personal bitterness and anxiety had intensified petty irritations from pinpricks into deep wounds. Doubt of myself had made me resent qualities in her which under ordinary circumstances I should never have envied. Now that I could dare to look ahead and count on all my faculties again I felt a wave of affection and tenderness overwhelm me as if Janice were once more the little sister I must humour and help even when she was most trying. Memories of our childhood stirred to the rhythm of the train. Janice had been afraid of spiders, and it used to make me feel proud and protective to walk ahead when we explored wood paths and brush them away. Once we were going to be angels and wear halos and wings in a Christmas tableau; and, the day before, I had come down with bronchitis and been put to bed. Janice was all dressed and ready when suddenly she refused to go without me. I could see her still in the trailing white robe with the home-made halo slightly askew on her fair curls. There was the time she had sent me the bunch of violets when I won the high-school debating contest. That had been in midwinter, and it must have taken her allowance for two weeks to buy that little bunch. I felt contrite, remembering things like that. They mattered more than the antagonism that had followed. Suppose we had gone our separate ways and become strangers to each other—there would be time enough to change that. The next visit she made I would let her have the pick of my closet. Now that everything was going to be all right, I could afford to be generous.

Sitting there, close to the misted windowpane beyond which a wet and frosty world slid by, I gave myself up to good resolutions as I used to do in my childhood on the last day of an old year. I made mental lists to follow: I would be more tolerant of Janice; I would be less demanding of Harry while the mill trouble took so much of his time; I would not keep asking for tangible proof of his devotion; I would be more thoughtful of Aunt Em, less impatient of her set ways and unasked advice; I would try to be more sympathetic to Uncle Wallace and his blind acceptance of the business creeds of his youth; I would try harder to understand Jo Kelly and his convictions even if they didn't fit in with family loyalties, and I would show my gratefulness to Merek Vance by admitting that I had been wrong to doubt his power to help me. It is easy to be generous and forgiving when we are in danger or when we are tingling with happiness as I was in that hour and a half.

We were nearing Springwood, two stops before Blairstown, when I saw Janice reaching her bags down from the rack. It surprised me to see her doing that because usually she was anything but forehanded. As the train slowed down and the station platform came into view I was even more startled to see her moving towards the door. I half-rose in my seat to go to her, but the aisle was full of alighting passengers.

Oh, well, I thought, she'll be back again. She'll notice her mistake the minute she's off the train. It's not like Janice, though, to be so absent-minded.

I rubbed a clear place on the steam-filmed glass and stared out at the station platform where the drama of welcomes and good-byes was in full swing. Cars and buses were parked close, their tops shiny with wet. Little groups of people were hurrying to one or another, exchanging handshakes and embraces, surrendering luggage as they climbed in.

And then I saw Janice. She was standing alone with her things about her. I could tell that she was looking anxiously up and down, searching the wooden platform and the waiting cars. I pressed close to the window and pulled at my glove. I would signal to her by tapping with my ring. But just as I raised it to strike the glass something stopped me, and my hand dropped to my lap. I saw her wave, and there down at the end of the line of cars I recognised our little green roadster. The glass was filming again. I cleared it to make sure I wasn't mistaken. There might be other such cars, but not one with our licence plates, not one with Harry Collins at the wheel. He had climbed out and was coming down the platform with his long, easy strides. His hat was pulled over his eyes, but I caught the line of his chin and the familiar shape of his hand, tossing away a cigarette. He was beside her as the train began to move. I pressed my face to the cold pane and saw him stoop to pick up her bags before the station shut them out of my sight.

CHAPTER TWENTY-FIVE

I WAS at home at last and in my own room. I had come directly from the station, not stopping at the doctor's as I had planned. It seemed to me that I had not drawn a free breath since the train had pulled away from the platform at Springwood. Mechanically I had collected my things, left the car, and hailed the Blairstown station taxicab. But all the time I moved without sense of feeling. My chest felt tight as if it had been frozen over.

I won't believe it, I insisted again and again. That wasn't Janice I saw on the train; that wasn't Harry waiting for her back there in Springwood.

But I knew what I had seen. I didn't deceive myself.

I went downstairs at last, leaving the unopened packages as I had tumbled them in the hall. Maggie wanted to bring me lunch on a tray, but I told her I had eaten on the train.

"Where's Janice?" I asked her, trying to appear casual. "Isn't she back yet?"

"Not that I know of, Miss Emily. Your aunt said to-night or maybe to-morrow. She wasn't sure, and we didn't expect you back this early."

She may have said more. I do not know what, for I turned away. Bridget pushed her body against my legs and nuzzled my fingers with her moist nose. I scratched the soft place behind her ears, hardly feeling what I did. Then I reached for my raincoat and umbrella and let her follow me outside. Through the slanting drizzle I made my way down the drive to the stable. It was foolish for me to go there, but I had to see with my own eyes that the car was gone.

Old Jo Kelly was hobbling about among his tools and flowerpots under the stairs. He tried to straighten his bent back when he saw me there. I came in out of the wet and stood beside him, watching his misshapen old hands sorting out dried bulbs and seed packets. His pipe was between his lips, and the tang of the tobacco he smoked lay strong on the damp air. I inhaled it with my own difficult breaths. The scent will stay with me always whenever I recall that afternoon and my own stress.

He said something by way of greeting, but I made no effort to catch the words from his lips.

"Jo," I said, finally mustering my own as I leaned against the work bench, "where's the little car?"

"Mr. Harry come after it this morning early. I give him the keys myself."

"Mr. Harry?" I made him repeat the name to be certain. "What did he want it for?" I persisted.

"He didn't say, Miss Emily, and I didn't ask him. Maybe I'd ought to have, now you mention it. But he always makes free and easy with what he pleases round here."

"Yes," I answered, out of the chillness that had taken me, "he does that."

I started for the stairs, but as I reached for the hidden key on the beam I felt old Jo's hand on my arm. His eyes were searching mine anxiously.

"Mis Emily," he began, "you mustn't mind my asking —but those rooms up there—I've got them on my mind lately. You don't go up often, do you?"

"I've been there just once since you moved out," I told him. "That was—let me think—about two weeks ago. What makes you ask?"

The lines deepened on his face. I had not realised that there were so many. But then I had not looked at him closely for a long, long time—not really looked as I was looking now.

"Well," he admitted at last, "I haven't said nothing to the rest about it, but I've got a feeling—something's going on up there. Tell you the truth, Miss Emily, I'm afraid it's Jo. If I thought he was up to mischief there, stirring up more mill trouble with those cronies of his . . ."

He said more, but in trying to keep his lips steady I lost what followed. However, I had made out enough.

Ironical, I thought, the two of us standing there in the made-over stable, afraid to put our fear into actual words.

"I don't believe Jo would set foot up there," I told him. "He's too honest to make use of a place that doesn't belong to him. Don't doubt young Jo: he wouldn't do that to you or us."

Old Jo relaxed a little, as if he were leaning on the comfort of my words. He knocked his cold pipe on a nearby beam and watched me take out the key.

"I hope you're right," he said. "I'll try to believe the best. But someone's been up there, and who'd know where to find the key except Jo?"

"Suppose I keep this." I slipped the one I held into my pocket. "There's another one on that nail. You take that and say nothing for the present. We'll both feel easier, and it's probably nothing to worry about. We may be mistaken."

I left him and went out into the rain, feeling the hard, cold shape of the key in my pocket; feeling a still more hard, more cold inner weight. So I plodded through the wet, across the Square, trying to shake off my dread, trying to believe that there would be a reason for what I had seen. Some simple, easy explanation to make me limp with thankfulness—that was all I asked, yet more than I expected.

Merek Vance was in his office. I saw him hurry to the door as I crossed the porch. Before I knew it he had half-pushed me into the old leather chair and was standing over me. There was more colour on his cheeks than I had ever seen there, and his eyes searched and held mine before he spoke.

"I've been waiting for you," he began, pointing to the telegram which lay open on his desk. "Ever since this came I've been expecting you."

I made some foolish excuse about having had to go home first, and then I tried to collect myself to tell him about yesterday. But already it seemed remote and unreal. I might have been telling him of someone in a play that I had seen long ago from the last row of the gallery. I was glad for once that I could not hear my own voice, which must have sounded dull and lifeless. I cannot remember the words I summoned, though I tried to explain exactly what had happened without missing a detail that might prove helpful. He jotted down a note occasionally, and now and then questioned me about such things as length of sensation, the volume of sound and whether my ears had felt further stimulation from my train journey that day. He was all doctor as he listened and wrote and observed. Yet I was conscious, under his professional alertness, of pride and elation. Once I could have shared in that. It would have flowed from us to meet and flood the dingy room.

"Well"—he looked up from the paper and smiled at me —"we've done it! Of course we've got a long way to go yet; this is just the beginning. There'll have to be tests, much more thorough ones than I could give you here even if I had decent equipment. But we've proved the nerves are responding to the treatment. You feel sensation now where there was nothing before."

"Yes," I told him, and I wondered if my voice sounded as empty as I felt, "my ears are alive now. You've done that where all the other doctors failed. . . . Even when I wouldn't help you by believing you could, you did it."

"You always believed," he said, "you wouldn't have come here all these weeks if you hadn't. None of those arguments you put up ever fooled me. You talked yourself into being brave, like a scared child who makes up ghosts because he's afraid of real ones. I liked you better for that. . . ."

I let my eyes leave his face for a moment before I spoke again. His eyes were too bright and searching.

"How long," I began, deliberately shifting the subject to a more practical angle, "how long do you think it will be before I can really hear?"

"I can't make predictions," he answered. "Every case is different in response, and it may be months before we can get those nerves to function without artificial stimulus.

N

You're younger than any of those we experimented on, and I told you in the beginning I'd never worked with deafness that came as the result of meningitis. I'll need more advice and a chance to discuss this with the group in Baltimore. I want to get down there as soon as I can leave —next week, maybe. In the meantime I'll increase the injections as much as I dare and arrange with Dr. Weeks to give them to you while I'm gone. But I'm not rushing this. You'll have to go on being patient a while longer. It means too damned much to us both to take any chances now."

"All right," I said. "I haven't asked you to hurry things, have I?"

"No," he admitted, "not in words you haven't. But there's something you're not telling me. . . . That wire you sent—I've sat here with it in front of me ever since it came. You were happy when you sent it. What's come over you now?"

I shrugged and turned away. I couldn't trust myself to answer him. I would escape from the office before he forced me into admissions. As I reached the door I felt his hands on my shoulders. He wheeled me about and made me face him.

"Joyful and triumphant," he said. "Yes, you certainly look it."

I tried to twist away; but he kept his hold, and it was easier at last to look at him than to feel his eyes upon me.

"I just wrote that to fool the telegraph operator," I explained lamely. "I needed something that sounded like the season's greetings, and yet that you'd understand. It's not worth making such a fuss about."

"You were happy when you sent that wire," he persisted, "and you're anything but happy now. I think I have a right to know the reason."

"I've told you everything you have a right to know."

"'Everything' is a pretty big word—a doctor learns not to use it as often as other people do." He was leaning forward, still holding me by the shoulders, and his face was so close to mine I could feel the warmth of his breath as he spoke. "Well, I suppose I can't make you tell me if you don't want to. It might just happen that I have my own theory about what's hurt you."

"Who said anything about being hurt——" I began, but he cut me short.

"Maybe you've found out what you were bound to sooner or later. That's it, isn't it?"

I faltered under the directness of his look. I tried to keep my eyes on the floor, but again he forced me to lift them.

"I'm going now," I said. "Please don't keep me. I'm rather tired and——"

But he went on as if he had not heard me. He spoke slowly so that I should not miss a syllable.

"I've been expecting this. The wonder to me is that you didn't find out before. It would have to be now though. I'm sorry for that part."

"I don't know what you're driving at." I lied desperately, but he must have felt me trembling.

"Oh, yes, you know, Emily Blair." His hands dropped from my shoulders. "We both know. I've known ever since that first time I came to your house, the night of your aunt's birthday."

Anger rose in me like a swift and fiery tide. The room retreated in a haze, and only his face was clear in that moment. I struck at it with all the force I could summon. It was a shock to feel the hardness of his cheekbone taking the blow. We both started back and stood staring numbly at each other. The blood tingled in my hand and colour came sharp and red on the cheek that I had struck.

Somehow I was free of the place and walking across the Square with rain and tears mingling on my face. Bridget nudged at my heels in a worried way, and my hands were still shaking. It came over me then what I had done. Never since I was old enough to remember had I reached out to strike someone. And I had committed this physical violence against Merek Vance to whom I should have been more grateful than to any one in the world. I set my teeth and turned to recross the Square.

The office door was open, and he had gone back to his desk. I saw that the folder containing the record of my case was open before him and he was already adding more notes to it. He looked up and smiled as I stood there in the door. But one cheek was still undeniably redder than the other. I went straight to the desk before he had a chance to move.

"I'm sorry," I said. "I came back to tell you so. I never struck any one before. I don't know what possessed me."

He laid down his pen and closed the folder.

"That's all right," he said. "I didn't think you had it in you to forget the proprieties so completely. It's a very healthy sign. That's that, and let's forget it."

"I can't forget that easily. It makes me afraid of myself. . . . But when you said what you did—it came over me in a rush. You know too much about me. You've always known too much, and I hated you for it."

He gave the shrug that I had come to know so well.

"It's not that I know too much. It's that you insisted on knowing so little."

I felt myself flushing under the impact of his words. All my hard, frantic love for Harry was laid bare suddenly. I saw it in that moment for the pitiful, hopeless thing it had been. I had made a crutch of that love that had once been a free and ardent urge between us. My need had betrayed me into making a fool of myself. Bitterness overwhelmed me again, shutting out the momentary flash of truth that had been revealed. Before I could speak Merek Vance had come from the desk to my side.

"Don't try to think yet," he told me. "You've had a shock, two in twenty-four hours. You must give yourself time. No one can tell you what to do. I'd be the last to try, and this—this other thing is out of my line. But I'll see you through as much as any one can."

"Thank you," I said. "We seem to have forgotten what I came for. You haven't given me the injection."

He smiled, and the tension was broken by familiar routine.

"I'd like to go a little farther before we do any talking," he said when he was through. "I must have a chance to discuss it with some of the rest at the hospital, and then we'll put you through more tests. I know it's asking a lot of you to wait."

"I'll wait," I promised. "At least I won't say anything without giving you warning. When we made that bargain we didn't mention a time limit. I was a lot more certain of myself then: I wouldn't be so ready to make bargains now."

A great weariness overcame me, and I turned without a word of good-bye and started for the door. But before I reached it his arms were about me. I felt the hard muscles under the cloth of his coat, and I was too tired and shaken to protest. I was crying convulsively against him, my tears shutting out his face so that whatever he may have said I knew nothing of it. I knew only the comfort of his strength, and the surprise of his kiss, strong and compelling on my lips.

And then I was leaning against the door-frame and his face was growing clear again. He must have put his handkerchief into my hands, for I was wiping my eyes with it and drawing longer breaths. He no longer held me except with his eyes. His lips were moving, and at last I could follow their motions.

"I'm not sorry," he was saying, "not any more than you were when you struck me. So now we're even."

CHAPTER TWENTY-SIX

No hardy perennial has the enduring quality of hope. Cut it to the roots, stamp it underfoot, let frost and fire work their will, and still some valiant shoot will push, to grow again on such scanty fare as it can find. Only time and the cruel quicklime of fact can destroy that stubborn urgency.

So it was with me in the days that followed. Even as I recrossed the wet and leafless Square I let hope soften my suspicions. I struggled against my doubts, turning over a dozen possible explanations for that meeting at Springwood station, discarding them and starting all over again as a lost traveller will make frantic dashes in every direction, only to double back on his own tracks and be no better off for his effort. I could not face what I feared. I must make excuses and believe those fears would all be explained.

Vance had had no right to say what he had said. He had had no right to kiss me in that sudden disquieting way. I could still feel the warmth and pressure of his lips on mine as I hurried home through the wet. I tried to shake off the memory. Yet, there was comfort in it and a lingering glow. I had not been as angry as I should have been, I told myself. But then, he had not been angry at the blow I had struck him. Perhaps, as he had said, that made us even. When you have reason to doubt the man you love another man's kiss may seem a poor substitute, but it can bolster up a woman's pride. We may want only the love that is denied; but to know that we continued to be desirable is a prop to which we cling, and cling we must to whatever our hearts can lay hold on.

A taxi was moving out of the driveway as I came in sight of the house, and I saw Janice's coat and the new green hat flung down carelessly in the hall. Her door was open as I passed by to go to my room. She stood at the bureau, brushing her hair, and under the hanging light it

198

stood out from her face like a bright fan. In spite of all that I was feeling I had to notice that. She turned when she saw me in the mirror and waved the brush by way of greeting.

"When did you get back?" I asked, pausing in the door-way.

"Just now," she said, and turned back to the mirror again.

"On the train?" I persisted. "I thought there wasn't one at this hour."

She laid down the brush with a gesture of impatience, and even though I strained to catch the motion of her lips I could not make out what she was saying.

"I beg your pardon," I said, "I didn't quite——"

This time she wheeled about sharply and came nearer.

"I said"—she spoke with exaggerated distinctness to make me realise the trouble I was causing her—"I said the three fifty-seven was an hour late. Christmas seems to have thrown them all off schedule."

"I'm just back from Boston myself," I told her, "I went up yesterday to shop, and I came back on the ten forty-five this morning."

I kept my eyes fixed on her face, and it seemed to me that her lips tightened and the pupils of her eyes grew wider. But she gave no other sign of interest.

"Too bad I didn't know," she said, shaking the hair from her face with apparent unconcern. "We could have come back together."

"Yes," I went on, "if we'd known we might have had the car sent to meet us somewhere along the way—at Springwood station. A lot of people were being met there."

She turned abruptly and went back to the bureau. She took care that I should not see her face, but when she lifted the brush again I saw her knuckles stand out white and sharp.

"You know"—my throat was dry, and I braced myself against the door-frame, grateful for the hardness of the wood at my back—"there was someone who looked like you on the train this morning. You must have a double, Janice."

I tried to laugh, casually, but I doubt if I managed to sound convincing. She shrugged and went on brushing her hair. I did not wait for an answer, though I was certain my words had made her uneasy.

Once I had closed the door of my own room I felt suddenly limp and shaken. But I was determined to keep my doubts in check until I had given Harry a chance to explain. I wasn't naturally suspicious. I hated people who were always imagining that others were scheming and plotting behind their backs. I remembered reading somewhere that deafness did that to its victims. Perhaps this had crept upon me without my knowing; perhaps I was no exception to the rule. Love only intensified bitterness and doubt as it had the power to magnify happiness. I stood there in my wet coat and hat and pressed my hands together, palm to palm, the way I used to when I said my prayers. I found myself praying again, not so much out of belief as out of my need.

"Oh God," I prayed, "don't let this happen. Please let me be wrong in what I think. Please make it right somehow, and don't let me lose Harry."

I remember just how I stood there, making that frantic petition over and over in the dim familiarity of my room. Looking back to it now, I neither smile nor sigh. It seems as futile to me as an earlier prayer I made asking God to change the course of the Mississippi River because I had been wrong in answering a geography question back in third grade. There are things beyond the power of prayer to change. I know that now. I have learned that we can pray for ourselves alone. Whatever God we believe in, whatever name He goes by, we cannot ask that things or people be changed to suit our needs. We may ask only to have strength to do our best, no matter how often we fall short of that.

I switched on the light at last and began to take off my wet things. As I did so I caught sight of myself in the

mirror and was startled at my own reflection. Rain and
tears and all the varying emotions of the last twenty-four
hours had changed me. I saw myself in that moment as I
might look in ten, in fifteen years, as Aunt Em had appeared
to me in my childhood. The resemblance between us was
more marked than ever, and I faltered before it. Did Harry
Collins see me like that and falter too, before a future he
had given his word to share?

I won't look middle-aged yet, I vowed as I stared into
the glass. I'm young still; whether I feel young or not, I
mean to look it.

So I went to the closet and took out the blue crepe dress
that deepened the colour of my eyes. I brushed my hair
fiercely till it took on lustre again. I parted it smoothly and
let it wave back to a soft roll at the nape of my neck. Harry
had always praised my pallor. He never encouraged me
to use rouge, but that night I added a faint colour to my
cheeks and made my lips more full and red before I went
downstairs.

"Why, Emily," Aunt Em greeted me, "you certainly
put through your shopping quickly. How well you look,
dear! The trip must have done you good."

I smiled and breathed more easily. I was glad that I had
deceived her. It gave me more confidence, and I began
hurriedly delivering messages from Cousin Eunice. We sat
there by the fire, waiting for Uncle Wallace's return and
Maggie's summons to dinner. I took up a piece of knitting
I had begun, a child's sweater for Angeletta's little girl.
The yarn was Christmas red in the lamplight, and the
stitches formed with mechanical precision, like little
marching soldiers under my fingers.

Uncle Wallace was in a surprisingly bad humour that
night. He was growing more worried about the mill reopening and recent cancellations of orders. He had asked
the banks for an extension of time, and this had been refused.
He would have to make a hurried trip the next day to
New York, where a group of textile manufacturers were
meeting.

"Where's Harry?" he demanded across the dinner-table.
"A fine day he chose to be away—just when I needed him."

I could feel my heart set up a sudden hammering. I
looked at Janice, but her eyes were on her plate. I laid down
my knife and fork carefully so that my fingers would not
betray me by shaking.

"The girls are just back from Boston," Aunt Em was
explaining from her end of the table; "they wouldn't
know."

"He took the little car," I spoke up then. "It was gone
when I came back and old Jo told me Harry had been by
for it."

Janice worried a bit of bread into crumbs but gave no
other sign.

"Well," Uncle Wallace went on, "he'll be bringing it
back soon, I hope. I left a message with his landlady and
the Parkers to have him come and see me when he turns up.
I have to go over some important letters with him to-
night."

We were having our coffee by the living-room fire
when Harry walked in. I was the last to see him because
my back was to the door. He was wearing his old tweeds
and the sweater I had knitted for him long ago, the one
with the tawny flecks that matched his freckles and the lights
in his eyes. His hair curled from the dampness, and the
room seemed suddenly alive and full of his presence. Janice
set down her cup as he came in and went over to the piano.
I saw her shuffling through music sheets in apparent preoccupation.

He came over and stood behind my chair. His hands
were warm on my shoulders, and his lips brushed the back
of my neck, lightly, swiftly, just behind my ears. I twisted
my head and tried to smile up at him in easy greeting.
He was speaking above me to Uncle Wallace, and I could
not follow the motions of his lips. Aunt Em poured him a
cup of coffee, and he came round to sit on the sofa and
drink it.

I must put all my mind on what he says, I told myself.

I can't afford to miss a word, but I mustn't seem too interested. I must be as natural as I can be.

"I'm sorry, sir," he was answering some question from Uncle Wallace, "I thought they'd tell you I drove over to Biddeford to see Hawkins about those orders. Things were so quiet this week it seemed a good time to go."

Biddeford, I thought; that's a hundred miles in the opposite direction from Springwood. It doesn't make sense.

Uncle Wallace was speaking, but I dared not take my eyes from Harry's face. He sat listening, a trifle uneasily, I thought, for he reached absent-mindedly to add sugar to his cup though he had already dropped in two lumps.

"Of course, if I'd known you were leaving for New York to-morrow I wouldn't have gone," Harry went on. "I borrowed the little car. I knew you wouldn't mind with the girls both away. Good thing I did, too; the carburettor was acting up, and Janice had let the oil get low. I had it checked over so the day wasn't altogether wasted."

"Where did you have it fixed?" I found myself asking. "In Biddeford?"

Harry looked surprised at my interest. Neither he nor the others seemed to remember that the little car had originally been mine.

"Oh, some garage along the way. I can't remember just where. But it's set now for another thousand miles."

Janice came over from the piano and poured herself another cup of coffee. Her back was towards me, yet I felt, rather than saw, that she was trying to convey something to him without resorting to words. His eyes were upon her over the rim of his cup. I was aware suddenly of a current of communication between them, a tenseness that each was trying to keep in check. My hands went cold in my lap as I watched them. I knew then for certain what I had fought against believing since morning. I knew— because love is plain to those who have ever known it.

How long? I wondered with an inner numbness spreading over me. How long has it been since I—since he—since they . . .

But even in my own mind I could not finish the question.

A hand was on my arm. Aunt Em was trying to attract my attention. I forced myself to follow the motion of her lips.

"Oh, yes, Aunt Em!" I started up. "I have the things you wanted. I'll bring them down."

When I returned Harry had gone into the study with Uncle Wallace, and Janice was at the piano again. I felt the vibration of music in the room and though no tune emerged I heard for the third time a distinct sound in my ears. It was clearer than before, and I made a mental note to tell Dr. Vance on my next visit.

"Piano," I would tell him to write in his notes. "Definite response, and more sustained sensation."

I sorted out the various packages for Aunt Em and gave her the sales slips methodically.

"I'm sorry I couldn't find a better match for blanket binding," I explained, "but this was the nearest shade. I bought an extra yard just in case you ran short. If you'll excuse me, Aunt Em, I think I'll go to bed now. I won't wait till Harry's through talking business. Tell him I have a headache from shopping and trains. I'll be all right to-morrow."

I did not wait for her answer. She would only offer aspirin and sympathy, and I had no need of either. Upstairs I slipped out of my dress into my outdoor things and down the back stairs. The flashlight I felt for was in its place on the entry shelf. I followed the little circle of light it made on the steps and gravelled drive.

The rain was over; the moon struggling to clear a path among blowing clouds, an old moon toiling through space. I watched it above me and thought that it had never seemed so far, so impersonal on its timeless course.

It was dark in the old stable, but my flashlight showed me the two cars in their places. The small one was mud-splashed, the windshield still misty except for the half-circle the wiper had kept clear. I slid into the empty seat, letting the beam of light search into every corner. The dashboard pocket held the usual collection of old maps, gloves, matches, and sun glasses. I closed it wearily, hardly knowing what I had expected to find. Then, as I turned to leave, the light showed a bit of cardboard wedged between the door and running-board. It proved to be a parking ticket, damp and torn, but with printing still distinguishable. "Springwood Gar——" I made out, and a pencilled number below.

So I had not been mistaken! I stuffed the telltale fragment into my pocket and sank back on the seat. Up to that moment I had believed that I might be wrong. Now that there could be no more doubt I grew numb and hollow. Life died out of me then. I let the torch grow dark in my hands. I could not think. I could not feel. I just sat there as still as some inanimate fixture of the car.

Then I was outside once more, my hands fumbling with the fastenings of the door. A shower of icy drops from a wet low-hanging branch shocked me as they drenched my face. I stopped short on the gravelled path and stood staring up at the house with its lighted windows yellow in the darkness. There were the kitchen panes, the broad bow windows of the living-room, and the two set on either side of Uncle Wallace's desk in the study. Above it my own were bright, and Janice's also lit. I saw others grow bright and knew that Maggie must be making her evening rounds, turning down bedcovers. I could smell the tang of wood smoke from the chimney. It came strong and fragrant to meet me, and I guessed that someone had just thrown a fresh log on the living-room fire. An old Windsor chair showed its sturdy shape in silhouette against the hall window. It had stood in that exact spot ever since I could remember, and I marked it as one might mark a familiar beacon.

Yes, I thought, everything is in its place. How ordered and substantial the house and its furnishings appear to someone looking in from the outside as I am looking now! A stranger might even think that the people in those rooms moved and acted according to the same well-ordered pattern of living.

I sighed and shivered, knowing that I myself had been deceived into thinking so until a few hours ago. Well, I knew how wrong I had been. For Janice and Harry and me at least, the pattern had shifted precariously. I would open the back door and go up the stairs. I would return to those rooms and continue to put on the accustomed habits of nights and days. They must not know that I knew—not yet.

CHAPTER TWENTY-SEVEN

THE holidays stretched before me in festive mockery. They would have been difficult enough that year with the mill trouble heavy over us all. I might have been equal to that, but to put a false front on my own despair took all the strength I could muster. Christmas, like spring water, has its source in the heart, and when the heart is frozen or dried up nothing can flow out in a flood of joyous response. Yet one must not betray traditions of goodwill and joy to the world, no matter how little one may share them.

I don't know how successful a performance I gave. I only know that I ached dully from the effort I was making. My lips stayed set in a determined smile. I seemed to be carrying myself about, like the stiff wooden figures that ventriloquists manipulate into semblance of life and animation, speaking words for them as they jerk the painted jaws and head. So I went through the days with the cards to be sent and received, with presents leaving and arriving bright in seals and labels that read, "Merry Christmas," "Please do not open till December 25th."

I can recall the very pattern of the brightly-printed papers we used for our gifts that year. I can see the stars and bells, the sleigh and reindeer and red-coated figures of the designs, the snow sprinkled over the surface in large conventional dots. Janice never could wrap presents without cutting the paper too short or wrinkling it at the corners, and Aunt Em had little knack with her hands and less patience with stickers and seals. From the time I had been old enough to be trusted with scissors and ribbon, the task had fallen to me. I had taken pride in my skill, in the neat way I could fold and fit objects to paper with the least possible waste of materials. So, though I could summon no feeling for these pre-holiday rites, my hands still reached mechanically to perform them. Package after package, box after box took on perennial gaiety under my fingers; little silver bells and miniature candles and holly sprigs nestled into tinsel and ribbon as I worked at the long table in the back entry.

The Christmas-tree kept me company, waiting to be set up according to custom in the bay window on the afternoon of the 24th. It was cooler out there in the entry, and fewer needles would fall than in the heated rooms. I had to endure the bitter spiciness it shed as I worked. Sometimes if my skirt brushed a branch in passing the fragrance engulfed me, and I would lay down the scissors and ribbons because the memory of other Christmases would stir in spite of all I could do to put them from me. Happiness remembered in pain is like that, I think: we magnify it till it tricks us like a desert mirage.

So the waiting tree became a symbol of my own heart. I felt that year as if I were trimming an inner, secret tree that no one saw, working with feverish zeal to hide the bare, stark branches with a load of deceptive tinsel.

The days might have been less difficult if Merek Vance had not gone away from Blairstown. Ostensibly he left to spend the holidays with his sister in New York, but Dr. Weeks and I both knew the reason for his trip—consultations with medical associates there and in Baltimore. His brief-case bulged with pages of notes on my case history, exhaustive comments, and day-to-day observations on the treatments and my reactions to them. I was amazed and a little awed when he showed me the minute details he had so painstakingly charted. I stared at the closely-written pages, and it seemed that they must contain the records of a lifetime. Yet it was just short of three months since my first visit to his office.

"Yes," I found myself agreeing to his plans, "I will go on to Baltimore or New York, or wherever you arrange for the further tests and examinations; but I'm glad there's no need of that just yet."

That last visit was unsatisfactory, too full of exhaustive details and instructions. We met in Dr. Weeks's office, and I missed the familiar intimacy of the smaller one. Dr. Weeks's presence also made me self-conscious. He had known, of course, about the experiment, but he had had no part in it before. His close friendship with our family kept me from being entirely at my ease. He would continue the treatments during Vance's absence, and I dreaded that. I feared that I might in some way betray what was on my mind and heart. With Merek Vance it was different. I had never been able to hide anything from him, yet I knew any admission I might make was in safe keeping. He cared nothing for the Blairs and their family relationships. I think I had been aware of this from our first meeting and it had lent a kind of confidence to our friendship. Yes, I had to admit that I should miss him, that I had come to depend on him more than I realised till then.

There was so much technical discussion between the two doctors that I gave up trying to follow it. I let them talk and test and work over me as if I were a lay figure on which they experimented. All the time I sat there in bleak misery, going over the inescapable fact that I must meet and face.

· "Janice loves Harry. Harry loves Janice." Those three words beat on and on in my brain. They had the rhythm of childish ones we used to chalk on sidewalks in grade-school days: So-and-so loves So-and-so, with a crudely drawn heart encircling the names to give greater emphasis.

But now it was real, not make-believe love to tease a play-mate. In the adult world to which I suddenly realised we all belonged, I supposed a triangle would be substituted for the outline of a heart. Well, after all, what was a triangle but a heart with the grace taken out of it?

I opened my eyes, hardly realising that I had closed them. Merek Vance was touching my arm, and his eyes were kind and full of concern.

"You're tired," he was saying, "we've kept you at it too long. But there were so many directions. Dr. Weeks wants to be sure about everything."

"Yes, you'll be in my hands, Emily." The older man smiled and wiped his spectacles. "Can you put up with me for a couple of weeks?" I nodded and patted his hand. "We don't want any setbacks, you and I," he was going on. "We've got a lot to live up to now. . . . I still can't quite credit the facts, and when I think what your cure is going to mean to the profession—well, it's all I can do not to shout from the housetop."

"You'd better not let him," Vance put in quickly. "We're agreed on keeping still a while longer, aren't we?"

I nodded listlessly.

"All right, I've kept medical secrets before, and I can now," Dr. Weeks promised. "But I must say I don't see how you can do it, Emily. Think what a Christmas it would make for your aunt and for Harry. . . . You young people have a good deal more restraint than I gave you credit for."

Vance followed me out to the steps, and we both stood there without speaking. It was an awkward interval because we were thinking back to what had happened on our last meeting. I had struck him, and he had kissed me. In those seconds when we had yielded to our impulses we had been completely ourselves as we had never been before, as perhaps we should never be again. Neither of us put out a hand. I think now that we were too close in that moment for such a conventional exchange of courtesies.

"Good-bye," I said at last. "I guess I ought to try and

O

say 'Thank you.'; but that seems foolish and stupid, and I've been foolish and stupid enough already."

"Oh, we'll just say you're human in spite of being a Blairstown Blair and you haven't one speck of complacency about you. . . . That's more than I can say for myself and a lot of other people."

I flushed under his praise, tried to start down the steps, and then came back.

"Good-bye," I said, and added grimly, "I'm glad you didn't wish me a merry Christmas."

"Why should I? That's one thing you're almost certain not to have. But I hope you won't mind my thinking of you on the day, because if you ask me not to I might have to break my word."

I did not answer, and he did not seem to expect me to.

"You'll surely be back the first week in January?" I said, and he nodded his assurance. "But that's next year," I reminded him as I turned to go.

"If you count by the calendars, yes; but I never do it that way."

"How do you count time then?"

"By accomplishment, I guess, or by growth; that makes it much easier to reckon things. . . . According to that, you and I have known each other more years than we're old."

I knew he was standing there watching me go down the path between the barberry bushes. I knew he wanted me to look back, but I felt it would be easier to go without that. Then his hand was on my arm. I stopped reluctantly because I hated good-byes, and because already I felt abandoned by the one person from whom I had nothing to hide. I tried to keep my eyes from his. I knew mine would betray me, no matter what contradictory words I might summon. As I turned I saw that he held something out to me. It was the blue box that had belonged to his mother, the one I had reached for in those first difficult visits. He said nothing as he laid it in my hands.

"Oh, no!" I shook my head in vehement protest. "You

mustn't do that. . . . You said it was your one family heirloom. I couldn't take it, not after what you told me——"

But he, too, shook his head.

"You can't turn down a Christmas present," he told me. "I want you to have it. Ever since the first time I saw it in your hands I knew it belonged there. A man may have made it; but that needle and thread, and that motto, are for a woman."

I stood there not knowing how to answer him, and so he went on again, taking my silence for disapproval that I did not feel.

"Call it a present from my mother if you want to. She'd have liked you to have it. At least she would, once she'd come to know you."

Tears sprang to my eyes, so that I could not see his face. One splashed on the gay roses, and another on the hearts before I could look up again and follow what he was saying.

"I'm not a sentimentalist about my mother," he was going on. "She wasn't a saint, and I knew it. She was stubborn and proud like you. She went through hell, too— not your kind exactly. . . . Love's simpler over on that side of the river, and all mixed up with hunger and drudgery and physical pain. But hell's in the same latitude, no matter how we get there. She'd have known what to say to you now, the way I can't. That's why I want you to have this— to see you through the new year."

Still I stood there, holding his gift, too worn and miserable to speak.

"Thank you," I managed to tell him at last, and I spoke primly in words that came back from formulas of my childhood: "It's just what I needed."

He couldn't help smiling at that, and I smiled too because I must have sounded so politely incongruous.

CHAPTER TWENTY-EIGHT

I HAD written a note to young Jo Kelly asking him to drive out to Angeletta's place with presents for the children. I had no licence to drive the car, so I could not go alone; and besides I felt the need of Jo's company. He met me, as I had asked him to, at the foot of the garden, and we set off with boxes and packages piled about us. He sat with a doll carriage on his knees and a carton of groceries at his feet. Bridget had squirmed into the space between us and tucked her head into the crook of his arm. We had ordered her to go back to the house, but finally her persistence won us over.

It always comforted me to feel the wheel under my hands and the reassuring vibration of the engine. It gave me back a sense of lost confidence to be driving the car again over the familiar roads leading out of town. We left early in the afternoon, but already the light seemed thin and waning. To-morrow would be the winter solstice, and one felt the reluctance of the sun to stay even for its shortest span. Rains had washed what remained of snow into irregular patches on fields and pastures. There was a clearness to the outlines of bare trees and bushes as if their twigs had been whittled into sharp relief by wind and frost. In hollows by frozen brooks and ponds the willows showed a purplish tinge at their tips and the far hills were humped in a long procession of darker purple against the sky. The air felt keen, not windy or damp with hint of coming snow, but still and cold, so that the smoke from chimneys mounted visibly in dark smudges. Few people were out. We had the roads practically to ourselves once we were clear of town, except for an occasional truck or a half-chilled rabbit that scuttled across our way.

Neither Jo nor I made any attempt at talk. I had to keep my eyes on the road, and he seemed glad to relax in the seat beside me with the presents and Bridget his only concerns.

He had looked tired when we met, and I noticed that his old Mackinaw was still doing duty instead of the overcoat he should have worn in such bleak weather. His hands were bare, and I was glad he kept one on Bridget's warm fur. Still, there was something strong and alive about him, a driving force that seemed charged by an inner dynamo. One sees the same spirit in birds and small animals that defy winter and its rigours. One cannot pity them, for they give the illusion of having chosen their own difficult way; of preferring scanty fare and cold to comfort and easy existence.

Yes, I thought as we drove on, Jo has always been like that, going his own way, believing what he had to believe no matter how unpopular it's made him. He'll never fit into any pattern for long; but wherever he goes people take a sort of answering spark from him, the way animals do. He might have been like St. Francis in another period.

The Gallo kitchen was warm and cluttered and full of people. Garlic and strong cheese mingled with the scent of evergreen from a small tree that stood brave in popcorn and fringed-paper garlands. I was glad that I had brought some bells and brightly-wrapped candies to add to its decorations. The shy little girl with the enormous eyes had not forgotten me, and Angeletta beamed and made us welcome, shifting the baby to her other arm as she cleared two chairs by the big table. Her husband and father-in-law were out in the barn. Presently Jo went out to join them while Angeletta and the old woman helped sort and put away the things I had brought. The little girl played with the new carriage, and the boy whose operation I had witnessed sat in a wooden packing box and watched us with bright, squirrel-like eyes. His bandages were off, but he still had the peaked, bluish look of a convalescent.

"He's doing good," Angeletta assured me, "but he can't hear right yet——"

She stopped short and flushed, fearing that she had been treading on dangerous ground.

"He will though before long," I told her. "Dr. Vance

says he's made a remarkable recovery. I knitted him a cap that he can pull down over his ears when he's able to go out. You're sure to have a happy Christmas, Angeletta, when you look at him and think what might have been."

"Yes," she nodded, and reached out with her free hand to touch his round, dark head. "Yes, times are pretty bad, but I guess they could be a lot worse. You shouldn't have brought all those things, but I won't say we can't use them. It was real good of you to come, and I'm glad you brought Jo Kelly. Maybe he can make my Peter feel better. We had to sell the cow last week and we all felt awful bad."

I could think of nothing comforting to say in the face of such elemental loss.

"Thank God I can nurse the baby," she went on. "Peter talked to the union about us, and they say they'll give us some canned milk for the kids. It'll help out, but it don't taste the same; and we sure miss Bossy."

The old woman lighted the oil lamp over the sink and busied herself with the pots on the stove while I talked to Angeletta over the little girl who had climbed on my lap again.

"Angie," I said, "I know this is going to be a bad winter for you all, but it's worse for those in town. At least you don't have to go out with the children and pick up bits of coal from the tracks. You've got some wood cut, and some potatoes and winter vegetables in the cellar. That's more than they can count on."

"I know," she nodded. "If it wasn't for Peter's folks I don't know where we'd be. Do you think"—she leaned forward in her chair, and her eyes were large and anxious in her gaunt face—"do you think the mills will reopen and Peter can get on the old shift again?"

I faltered under the question, knowing what my answer must be.

"You'll have to ask Jo Kelly," I hedged. "He knows more than I do. The mills are going to reopen after New Year's, but I'm afraid there's bound to be even more trouble then. The men on strike won't be taken back on the terms they want, and you know what that may mean, Angeletta?"

"If the company put scabs in, there sure will be worse trouble." Her eyes widened and rolled expressively. "But they wouldn't do that, would they? They just want to scare the men into making terms."

I sighed and hesitated as I straightened the ribbon on the child's brown hair.

"I'm afraid it's more than talk," I said. "You know there'll be plenty ready to go back on any terms. Too many families are feeling the pinch now."

"I'd ought to know that!" Her lips tightened grimly as she spoke. "That's where they've got us, and it's where they want to keep us. I don't care what you or any one else says."

There it was, I thought, the word "they" that we all took refuge in. It would always crop up to foster hate and misunderstanding on both sides. Already I could feel Angeletta withdrawing from me, distrustful and wary.

"You know," I reminded her, "my mother worked as a millhand when she was young. I never forget that."

"That's all right to say, but you never had to stand up eight hours tending the bobbins or looms. Your folks own Peace-Pipe; I guess you don't forget that either."

"No," I admitted, "I don't. It makes a difference—that's the trouble with me: I have to see both sides and so I just seem to be caught between."

She shifted the baby to her other arm before she went on.

"It's easier to see two sides if you're not worrying about what you'll make your next meal of or if your man can weather another week of it."

"I know that—at least I'm beginning to know a little better. Don't be too hard on me, Angeletta: it's not going to be exactly a merry Christmas for us either. I needed to come and see you and the children. It can't hurt any of us to let them have fun with the things I brought. I liked knitting the sweater and the cap and finding the toys. You don't mind their having them from me?"

It was strange to be pleading my cause like that, battering against the wall of her pride and bitterness. But Angeletta and I had always liked each other, and the children's eyes turning to the packages helped more than any words of mine. The men came in presently, their breath frosty in the warm room. I was glad of their return, and we all drank a glass of home-made wine that the old man brought out from some mysterious place of hiding. I choked a little over mine, but it warmed me for the trip back in the winter twilight.

I let Jo take the wheel for the drive home. It had turned colder, and I was grateful for Bridget's warmth beside me. The car seemed empty without the oddly-shaped parcels that had crowded it on our way out. I dreaded returning to the big house and the part I must play there. Suspicion was a hateful thing to me, and I resented the need to be furtive and watchful of each move that Janice or Harry might make. Out there in the Gallo kitchen I had been able to forget for a little. At least, if I had not exactly forgotten, the dull ache and despair had retreated while I talked and entered into the problems of their existence. Now the pain sharpened once more as I turned towards Blairstown. Another family dinner must be faced, another evening must be endured.

If Harry came I would be trying to appear natural and at ease. Yet all the time I would be watching for some betrayal if he glanced towards Janice or if she brushed his hand in passing. If he did not appear, if Janice were away or left the house with some flimsy excuse, I must torture myself with fears that might or might not be well founded. I sighed and shrank deeper into my coat as I watched the minute hand of the lighted clock on the dashboard move on towards half-past five. It would have been a comfort to talk to Jo Kelly there beside me. I felt a great need of that, and though he knew so little really of my life, and I of his, yet the pull of the old associations always drew us together in spite of our differing worlds.

"Jo," I spoke as I saw the brightly-lighted windows of the roadside diner just ahead. "How about stopping here for a cup of coffee?"

He swung the car in and parked it obediently nearby. A loaded truck had stopped too. We could see two men seated at the counter, but otherwise the place was deserted. I saw young Jo notice that before he followed me in. We took the corner table, where Merek Vance and I had sat at a far later hour.

"I shouldn't have asked you to come in here with me," I said after my first sip of coffee. "I'm not exactly the company you want to be seen with nowadays, am I?"

He smiled across the table, but he did not deny the charge. It was a new sensation to feel that I must apologise for my presence; to feel that there were those who would consider me an undesirable companion.

"I guess your friends don't think very highly of me, Jo," I went on, "and I wouldn't want to get you into trouble."

"I'm used to taking care of myself," he answered shortly.

"But you don't belong just to yourself, at least not any more," I pointed out. "You seem to stand for a lot of people. You'd have some explaining to do if any of your union friends happened to walk in here now and saw us sitting like this?"

"Maybe," he admitted, and this time he did not smile.

"Jo"—I set down my half-empty cup and reached for a cigarette—"where's it going to end? One side or the other has got to give in, and it won't be the Peace-Pipe Directors. I know that much."

The tired lines of his face that had relaxed a little over the coffee and cigarettes, sharpened again as he looked up.

No one could look into young Jo Kelly's eyes without trusting him, I thought, while I waited for his answer.

"It all depends on how many of us can hold out," he told me, "and for how long."

"But, Jo, even if your union and their sympathisers help out with funds there are months of winter ahead for all those families like the Gallos. You saw what I saw over there this afternoon, and they're luckier than most. . . . How can you expect them to hold out on nothing?"

"That's what we're up against," he said. He rose then and went over to a big machine that dealt out popular music. I saw him put in some coins, and I felt the place vibrate to sound before he returned to the table. My ears were already so much more sensitive that I could make out the steady blaring of jazz though I could not yet recognise tunes as I listened. Mentally I made a note to tell Merek Vance of this and my response to the machine.

"Thought our voices might carry over to the counter," Jo explained when he returned to his place. "Can't run the chance of any one thinking I talk out of turn. The noise won't bother you any, and I can hear you through it. Go ahead."

"It's you I'm asking, Jo." He shrugged wearily and shook his head. "Well," I went on, "at least tell me this: there won't be violence when the mill reopens. Your pickets won't start that kind of trouble, will they?"

Again his face seemed to shrink into old, anxious lines, and only his eyes stayed young and eager.

"Not if I can stop it," he told me at last. "I've never believed that force and fists won anything in the long run. I'm doing all I can to keep this strike a clean one. They listen to me now, but I can't guarantee they will later——"

A spasm of coughing shook him, and I missed the rest of his words.

"You mean," I asked, "that they may get out of hand when Peace-Pipe reopens?"

He nodded.

"It'll take them one way or the other then. Plenty will turn scab and go back: half a loaf's better than nothing, they figure. I have a hunch Peter Gallo will go that way. Those that stick to their guns—well, you can't blame them for pulling the trigger, can you?"

I shook my head. Tears rose to my eyes because I felt suddenly very tired and baffled.

"I don't blame anybody for anything," I faltered across the white-topped table. "I'm very unhappy, Jo. No," I hurried on to forestall the question he might be going to ask. "No, I can't tell you why. It's nothing you could do anything about. But somehow when you're unhappy you draw other people's unhappinesses and troubles to you. I suppose it's like reaching out to like, because it used to be the other way round when I was happy. Do you know what I mean?"

I don't know what he may have answered. My eyes were too wet to see his face except as a blur. But I felt the quick response of his hand on mine, and I was grateful for that pressure. It had helped to say even so little to him. Sometimes a sudden rush of tears sharpens the sight as a quick shower clears the air of impurities. I looked straight into Jo Kelly's eyes and saw my own face mirrored in the shining darkness of those pupils. I wondered if he were seeing his face in mine, and if he felt reassured as I did by the reflection. When I forget Jo Kelly's eyes giving me back myself, I shall be past remembering anything that matters.

We talked on there under the hard, glaring lights of the roadside diner. It was always easy for me to follow him, perhaps because we had grown up together and I knew his way of speech so well. Then, too, he always listened intently and gave himself completely to the other person. I think that was one reason why people turned to him as they did. I wish I could recall word for word all that he told me. At the time I seemed to understand the issues and problems that had bewildered me for so long. He made me see Peace-Pipe strike in simple terms, not in a confusing jumble of technical phrases and abbreviations that stood for this labour organisation or that. But now only a few of his words return to me. They stir in my consciousness all these months afterward, like last year's leaves from some tree we shall never see putting out new ones in the spring.

"Men with wives and kids can't be expected to think as far ahead as someone like me," I remember he said. "To-day matters more than any to-morrow to them. It's bound to be that way when you've got a family to do for. That's why it's up to me to do more than the rest about holding on and speaking up. You're not the first to ask about the union letting us down, maybe even selling us out. It's happened before, and it might again. Still, I figure what's right stays right, no matter how many knocks it gets."

"But that's the hard part," I broke in, "to feel sure you know what's right! I get pulled in so many directions. I keep remembering what Maggie used to tell us when we were little: ' There's not the thickness of a penny between good and evil! '"

We both smiled at that, remembering the times she had quoted it to us when we used to raise childish arguments if she caught us red-handed in some misdemeanour. It seemed years since Jo and I had felt as close as we did that afternoon. It comforts me now to remember that it was so. If we had guessed all that lay ahead I think we couldn't have made better use of that half-hour together. The men left the counter and went out to their truck. We watched its tail-lights dwindle to red specks in the darkness and then go out like sparks. One or two other customers came in, but they stayed at the counter; and after quick glances at them Jo relaxed and we could go on talking.

"Whatever happens"—his words come back to me now with a queer twinge of pain—"we've made a dent that may count next time. It takes a lot of hammering to break through any wall or any system."

"If the men only didn't hate us so!" I told him. "At least that's what Uncle Wallace says. And then he says they'll come round and want to be friendly. . . . Why do they have to be so inconsistent?"

"That's because they're like a bunch of kids." He surprised me by a kind of tolerant wisdom, as if he were already years older than his cronies. "A lot of them haven't ever stopped going to grade school in their feelings: an apple for teacher one day and wanting to burn the schoolhouse down the next. That's why it's so hard to organise them and make them stay organised."

Our coffee-cups had been empty for a long time, but still we sat on, reluctant to leave and go our separate ways. I felt that he was clinging to the mood and the moment even as I was.

"Well, it's good we can still keep on being friends," I told him before I gathered up my things to leave.

"Yes," he agreed. And then he added with the nearest approach to bitterness that he ever expressed: "Plenty of people are your friends till you need them."

It was six o'clock by the big lighted timepiece above the door. I glanced at it and pushed back my chair.

"Remember I'm trying to see your side too, Jo," I said. "But it's hard being tied so fast to the other, and—and being deaf doesn't help, you know."

He leaned across the table as if he must make me feel the words that I have cherished ever since.

"I wish a lot of people who can hear would try as hard to understand," he said. "You've never been deaf to me."

CHAPTER TWENTY-NINE

I NEED not have dreaded that Christmas so, for as it turned out our household was far from festive when the day arrived. Aunt Em was the cause of this, and she never knew that her accident and suffering helped me through the holidays as nothing else could have done. It happened at dusk of Christmas Eve. She had been out, winding up a few last errands, and had walked back from the shopping district across the Square. Aunt Em always preferred to walk when distance was not too great. She prided herself on her activity and independence, and her energy and endurance had become a byword with all the family.

"Aunt Em can run me ragged in an hour," Janice used to complain.

And I would agree on that subject.

"Too bad they can't put her in the picket line," Harry had laughed during the first days of the strike. "There'd be no wearing her down if she believed in the cause."

Poor Aunt Em, it seems strange to think that we ever made such jokes about her; that so short a time ago she came and went as she pleased on legs that are helpless now under the striped afghan.

None of us will ever know exactly how it happened. The day had been one of doors opening and shutting and the confusion of arrivals and departures. Janice was off in the car, and I had been late going to Dr. Weeks for my treatment. He had been delayed and had kept me longer than usual, fussing over the latest instructions from Merek Vance. These had been to double the strength of the injections, and he had been anxious to do so with as little discomfort as possible.

"We'd better skip the treatments to-morrow," I said as I left. "It's hardly a day I can slip over here unnoticed. Besides you'll be with us for dinner."

There were lights in the church that faced the Square,

and I knew the greens must be up for the evening service. Behind the bare branches of elms and maples I could see the strong reds and yellows and blues of the stained-glass windows that had been familiar to me since childhood. There was the one of Christ blessing little children given in memory of Grandmother Blair, and the one about the parable of the loaves and fishes in memory of Grandfather Blair, and the one above the chancel given by Aunt Em and Uncle Wallace after my father's death in memory of him and the other Blairstown men who had lost their lives in France. Acting on an impulse I made Bridget's leash fast to a post and slipped into the empty church. The sexton was just finishing with the decorations at the far end of the long aisle, and the fragrance of fir and spruce boughs met me in spicy warmth as I pushed open the door. The glowing scarlet of poinsettia plants was like tongues of flame under the chancel lights. The rest of the church was dim, the organ pipes mounting tall and golden into the shadowy arches. Just so they had looked to me in the days when my head hardly showed above our pew top; just so had the Christmas greens smelled then, aromatic and rich to my nostrils. I sank down in a back pew, hoping to ease the tightness that had held me fast for days; but the old faith and assurance of childhood would not come out of the dimness to take me again.

As I rose to go I stood a moment before my father's bronze tablet with its inscription beginning, "To the glory of God, and the memory of Elliott Blair." Because I felt a great need of my father, I read and reread these words. But they only made him seem farther away. So I turned at last and tiptoed out, knowing that if he could have returned on Christmas Eve the years would have made me more of a stranger to him than he was to me.

It was almost dark when I reached our driveway, and I was annoyed by Bridget's behaviour. She kept tugging at the leash, butting her head against my legs and trying to dash off towards the garden. I did my best to discipline her, but she only grew more insistent as I tried to drag her up the steps. At last I gave in and followed her lead. That was how I came upon Aunt Em, a helpless and crumpled heap by the side doorsteps.

I have a confused memory of what happened after that: of Maggie and old Jo Kelly and myself carrying her into the entry between us; of the sharpness of spirits of ammonia and brandy spilled in the effort to get them past Aunt Em's set lips while we waited for Dr. Will; of awkward attempts to remove wraps and warm her icy hands. The Christmas-tree still stood there waiting to be set up and decorated. I saw Aunt Em's eyes turn towards it as I lifted her head to a pillow. Her face was distorted with pain, but she turned her eyes to the tree and then to me. I knew she was making wordless apology for such a catastrophe on Christmas Eve.

Catastrophe it surely was—a far more serious fall than we guessed until we saw Dr. Will's face as he worked over her. Maggie and I gave ourselves up to following directions, Maggie at the telephone and I running up and down stairs bringing blankets and robes and more pillows. It was a broken hip, Dr. Will managed to tell me when he could take me aside for a moment. He suspected it was a compound fracture that had not been helped by Aunt Em's struggles to rise and our clumsy efforts to carry her in. She must be taken to the hospital at once for X-rays before a cast could be put on. If only Merek Vance were within call. . . .

I was thinking that, too, as I did the few simple things I could before the ambulance arrived and as I sat on the little folding seat beside the stretcher. I held Aunt Em's cold hand, and tried to be reassuring though I winced in sympathy at every turn and jolt of the short journey. Aunt Em had protested feebly when Dr. Weeks had mentioned the hospital. She wasn't used to having her wishes overruled, but she had given in finally. It was touching to me to see her dependence on him. Even in the stress of those moments I realised that she counted on him as more than a doctor and more than a friend. But for myself I suddenly felt lost and alone, knowing that Merek Vance would not be waiting for us at the hospital in his white coat, with his skilful, hard-scrubbed hands ready to do their best for us.

The Blair Memorial Hospital and Clinic had been built and endowed by Grandfather Blair; yet curiously enough none of our family had ever made use of it before that night. The resident doctor and staff of nurses couldn't do enough for Aunt Em's comfort. Indeed, the whole machinery of the place was presently revolving about her. I know that pleased her even in the midst of her pain. It seemed to give her back an old assurance in family traditions. I hoped that the present and its problems would retreat for her and she could rest for a while on the old formula of the past.

"But how did she do it?" Uncle Wallace kept asking as he and I waited in the impersonal cheerfulness of the visitors' reception-room. He had returned from the mill just in time to see the ambulance leaving the driveway and had hurried on to join me at the hospital.

"She went out to do some errands," I told him, "and coming back she slipped on the side steps. You know how the eaves drip and the water freezes after the sun goes down. We don't know how long she'd been lying there."

"It would have to happen on Christmas Eve." Uncle Wallace shook his head and relighted the cigar that kept going out as we waited there together. "Em's bound to blame herself for spoiling the holiday for the rest of us. Seems to me they're taking longer than they should with those X-rays."

I looked at the clock in the hall outside and saw that it was exactly seven minutes since she had been carried into the X-ray room. I reached for a current magazine and turned the pages with determined absorption. In that next hour and a half I knew the pictures of every article and story by heart and all the products advertised on the pages. I knew the pattern of the chintz curtains as if I had designed

P

them, and I had counted over and over the coloured bulbs on a small Christmas-tree the nurses had set up in the window: nine white; six orange; six green; three blue, and eleven red bulbs—twelve if you counted the one that didn't light up.

Twice the nurses came in and called Uncle Wallace to the telephone. Once the call was from Janice, wanting to know if she should come over to the hospital. I was grateful that he told her to stay at home and take any messages that might come. The other call was from Harry, wanting to know what he could do to help. I wished that Uncle Wallace had urged him to join us. I wished that Harry had come without asking. I think if he had appeared just then I might have forgotten everything but the comfort of his presence. Perhaps I might have broken down and told him that I was going to hear again. There is no telling what I might have said to him in those moments of tension in the hospital waiting-room. But he did not come, and at last Uncle Wallace and I were relieved of our anxiety.

Aunt Em's broken hip had been set. It was a serious break, and there were complications. But everything had been done, and she was sleeping from the anæsthetic. We could see her in the morning.

"She was worrying about you all and—Christmas," Dr. Weeks told us with a tired smile. "You know how Em is—thinking of everybody and everything except herself. That tree was on her mind, Emily, so I promised to remind you. She seemed relieved, almost as if she were superstitious about it being trimmed and in the bay window where it's always stood."

I nodded my reassurance.

"It'll be up and lighted before midnight. I'll do everything right—the way she likes it to be."

We drove back with Dr. Weeks, and he came in for a glass of port. I knew when he accepted the offer of a drink that he must be worn out from the ordeal. I guessed that it was the first time he had ever been asked to attend Aunt Em, and that the strain had been greater than he would admit. He looked old and frail as I helped him into his overcoat.

"Merek Vance should have been here to-day." We were alone in the hall, and he spoke as if he were answering my thoughts. "Stone's an able doctor, but all the time we were putting on that cast I knew who would have made a better job of it. If you'd feel easier to send for him to-night to take over the case, don't consider my feelings. He'd drop everything to come. I guess you know that."

"Yes," I said, "I know."

For a moment I was tempted to accept the offer. I hesitated, then I shook my head.

"No," I told him, and laid my hand on his coat sleeve. "You've done your best for Aunt Em. I'm satisfied with that, and we haven't any right to send for him now just because it would bolster us up. He'd come if we called him. I haven't a doubt of that. But these experiments he's made that we've been part of—they matter too much. Don't mention the accident when you write or wire. You knew what he had in him before I did; but now I know. Go home now and get some rest. You look all in."

I was the last one astir in the house that Christmas Eve. As I moved about the empty rooms the despair of the morning and the tension of later hours left me. Perhaps it was not that they left me but rather they merged into one of those intervals of quiet which lie between the breaking and gathering of waves at sea. The curtains were drawn against the winter dark, the wood in the fireplace no longer burned in active flame but glowed with an incandescent rose that still kept the shape of the logs which would presently crumble to ashes. In its accustomed place on the table in the bay window another Christmas-tree had joined its green to the ghosts of other such trees that had stood there. I seemed to see them stretching back to my childhood in a long unbroken procession. There was comfort for me in the enduring sense of that continuity. I could understand why Aunt Em had remembered about it even in the midst of her own pain.

We Blairs, in common with other New England families, prided ourselves on saving possessions that might be used from year to year. Each December the familiar box with its carefully written label was brought out of the store-room, and each January it returned to wait for another holiday to come round. I knew even before I lifted the cover just how the coloured globes and gilded cones, the wax figures and neatly-wound balls of tinsel would look inside. Only the small white tapers in their tin sockets had been reluctantly discarded some years before in favour of electric lights.

"I suppose we had to come to it some time," Aunt Em had sighed over the substitution. "I'll miss the smell of the candles among the needles, even if my mind will be more at rest and I'll dare to leave the room for five minutes the way I never could before. Still, there's nothing can ever take the place of candlelight. Tapers may be dangerous, but maybe that's what makes them do whatever it is they do to us."

But nothing else had been discarded from the box of decorations. Some even dated back to Christmases when Aunt Em and Uncle Wallace and my father were children. There were cunningly-carved and painted figures of the Nativity which Grandfather Blair had brought back from a momentous journey to Oberammergau. There were tiny scarlet toadstools with painted spots, like none that grew in our woods. They were souvenirs from a walking trip my father had made in the Black Forest during his college days. There were miniature bone reindeer and sledges from Lapland and two exquisite wax angels with gilt wings and yellow hair that looked as Janice used to look when she took part in Christmas tableaux. The wax on the face of one had run, the wing of another was broken, but no tree would look complete in our living-room until they were hung high in the bristling green. Some of the tinsel had tarnished, but it still glittered as I wound it through the branches, better than the too bright artificial snow and blinding brilliance of new finery. I had to stand on a chair to set the star in its place on the topmost branch. I might have waited for Harry to put it there next day, but I was superstitious about having every ornament in place before I went upstairs. And that star meant more than all the rest, because my father had drawn and cut it from cardboard and gilded it with his own paints for my first Christmas-tree in a studio in Brussels. It was always kept wrapped in cotton, and each year as I lifted it out I felt again the poignancy of survival—the power of such frail things to survive the hands that have fashioned them.

As I unwrapped each trinket and treasure and hung them up, I felt the tightness easing in myself. Whether it was natural reaction from my long strain and the new anxiety over Aunt Em, or whether some intangible peace of the season actually did lay hold upon my tired nerves and troubled mind, I shall never know. But I felt quieted, more at rest than I had been since I had stared out of the train window at Springwood station.

There might still be a way out of what I feared. I could not doubt what I had seen. I could not dismiss it as an ugly dream or deny the blow which had struck me down at the moment when I had been most defenceless. But I had loved Harry too long not to cling to that love as those who drown at sea are found still clutching some bit of wreckage.

I must give Harry a chance, so I argued to myself. Suppose he did love Janice now: it might be a transient, fleeting urge that would pass or burn itself out. He might even come to love me more for this strange madness. I had read of such things, of women who lost a man's love temporarily only to be rewarded by a deeper bond. If my love were strong enough and I were wise enough to wait and take no immediate issue, perhaps it might be so with me. I had little knowledge of other men. Harry Collins had been my whole existence in the last years. I had been young and inexperienced when we met, and I felt even more so now. If only we had not listened to reason; if only we had dared to be reckless and happy, then perhaps the terrible gulf of my deafness would not have widened between us. Those long absences, the discouraging verdicts of doctors, the strain of reunions and partings—I realised what they had meant to us both. Harry had been lonely and restless, ready to be caught and betrayed. And Janice had been restless, too. . . . I could make allowances for Harry, but not for Janice. No, I told myself bitterly, that was something I could never reconcile.

Bridget nudged at my ankles as I went into the hall. I had forgotten her in my preoccupation with the box of ornaments and the tree. I opened the front door and let her out for a late run. But I did not follow her into the cold. I stood in the open door and waited for her to return. The porch light was on above me, and beyond the circle of warmth it made the lawn spread shadowy and dim. Winter stars shone icy-bright between the branches of the copper beeches—almost as brilliant and symmetrical, they seemed, as those I had just hung on the tree. Yet I was not thinking so much of Christmas stars as I was of that other night when Merek Vance had come to our door asking for help. Just so I had stood there on the top step, and he below me under the dome of light. My mind raced back to that night when his decisiveness and skill had saved Angeletta's little boy; when I had felt my last barrier of prejudice go down before his power. It had marked the turning point in our friendship. I knew that if he had been standing there again I should have taken strength from his presence.

Why had I fought so desperately against his help? I could find no answer as I stared out into the frost-gripped world.

Maybe it's some blind instinct, I thought, something that makes us resist what we're really reaching out to find. Or perhaps it's just nature: winter always fights the spring.

CHAPTER THIRTY

Two hours more and it would be another year—1932. All day in odd moments I had been trying to accustom myself to the change. To-morrow when I dated letters or paid bills I would substitute a new figure for the old. Yet I knew that even the simple act of shifting numerals would confound me. I would forget the change and go back laboriously to correct the mistake I had made.

"Always remember, children," a teacher whose name I had forgotten used to tell us, "every day is a new year. We needn't wait for the first of January."

But I hadn't been able to believe her, not even in third grade. As time went on it became harder to put on a new year and shuffle off the familiar habit of the old. One grew used to years, like garments. At least one knew where the holes and patched places were; one had learned not to strain threadbare folds past endurance. A new year felt stiff and semi-fitted as one tried to move in it without self-consciousness. It was like dresses that used to be made to allow for growth, too sturdy and voluminous and reaching to boot tops. Only time and hard use would accomplish the fitting, and I did not look forward to that inevitable process. A silly, feminine whim, I decided, and tried to put it from me as I turned once more to the pile of letters and telegrams on my desk to be answered.

"Thank you for your note and the flowers. I can't tell you how much it meant to Aunt Em to know that you were thinking of her. She wants me to say that she is on the road to recovery, but I am afraid she has no idea how long and painful a road it may be . . ." I found my pen writing the same sentence over and over, like the refrain of a song. "It was a serious fracture, and any such accident at her age is serious. . . ." I crossed out the first "serious" and substituted "difficult"—not that repetitions would matter to the recipient of the letter, but I must not lapse into the form-letter habit. "She is out of immediate danger now, and everything is being done for her comfort. We hope to bring her back from the hospital in an ambulance to-morrow. When she is able to have visitors I will let you know. Thanking you again for the flowers and your messages, and with best wishes for a happy new year in which Aunt Em joins me. . . ."

I laid the letter with others in addressed envelopes and gathered the sheaf to take downstairs for mailing. It was ten o'clock by the big Blair clock in the hall. I noticed the hour as I went by, and the booming of the strokes sounded in my ears, though not yet clear and sharp; but the surprise of hearing such sounds still shook me. I would find myself stopping short, trembling in sudden recognition. Human voices still eluded me, though I was beginning to catch blurred words now and again, and the radio could send its mechanical tones farther into my consciousness. I had caught myself starting up to turn off the machine several times in the last few days. But I had managed to stop the gesture before it betrayed me.

In that week between Christmas and New Year's Eve I had had little time to indulge in personal worry. My own problems retreated before the immediate concern for Aunt Em. I had been grateful for this as I was grateful for the activity that filled each hour. Down to the hospital after breakfast; mail to be sorted and read to Aunt Em; long lists of errands to be done; back to the house again; meals to be discussed with Maggie; visitors to be seen and reassured; flowers to be arranged; conferences with doctors and nurses; letters to be answered in any spare moment and late into the night—the whole ordered routine of life suddenly turned from its natural course.

"Take it easy, Aunt Em," I would beg as I sat by the hospital bed and tried to follow the accumulation of worries that had been churning in her mind through hours of wakefulness. "Things are going all right at the house, at least as right as they can be without you."

"I know," she would say, moving her head restlessly on

the pillow. "I know it's foolish to think a house and a family can't get along without you. Maybe this came to show me how vain I'd been about running things my own way."

"Now, Aunt Em," I would protest, "that's not what I meant. We just want to make things easy so you can relax and get well sooner."

The futile words would go on and on every day. But it was easier for me to cope with them than to answer her on the subject of Harry and me. She had too much time to lie and make plans. I faltered inwardly whenever she started to talk about my wedding.

"There'll be time for that when you're better," I would urge. "Let's put New Year's through first and see the mills reopened."

But it was difficult to distract her, even with the mill problems. It was almost as if, in her unaccustomed state of weakness, she sensed the panic and tension I was trying to hide.

"There's never plenty of time," she kept insisting. "Waiting, when there's no need to wait, is one of the unpardonable sins; and I'm not going to be the cause of it. Maybe we were wrong to send you from doctor to doctor: I realise that more now I've had a dose of being at their mercy. . . . Well, be that as it may, you and Harry must go ahead and make your plans. There's money in the bank deposited in your name—five thousand dollars in cash from that annuity your father left, and the same for Janice later. Wallace can tell you more about it. Harry's not making much, I know, but you'll have enough to help out till times improve—if they ever do."

It had seemed doubly ironic to me, this talk of money put at my disposal in the bank. Somehow the older generation always felt it could buy happiness for one. I had tried to sound pleased as I thanked her, but I don't know how well I succeeded. I found myself thinking of a dozen such conversations I had had with Aunt Em, as I came down the stairs with the letters.

In the hall I saw Harry's hat and his overcoat flung down on the sofa near Janice's grey fur coat. I stopped short and leaned against the newel post. My heart quickened its beating, partly because I had not expected Harry to come for another hour and partly because those two garments flung down together set an edge to the pain that stayed like a dull ache behind all my activities. Harry had stopped at the hospital that afternoon to see Aunt Em, and he had promised he would be over later in the evening.

"No, Emmy, I can't come for dinner," he had told me when he left, "but I'll be over before midnight with a bottle I've been saving. Don't ask me where I got it in these times."

I had hoped that Janice would go to the annual New Year's Eve dance at the country club. I had counted on being alone with Harry. He had been considerate and full of helpfulness to me of late. It had almost seemed that we could find our way back to each other if only we could have the chance. Yes, the seed of hope in me had dared to put out a stubborn tendril of green. I stood there irresolute by the hall-table with the letters still in my hands. Uncle Wallace was alone in his study. The door was open, and I could see him bent over his stamp album, absorbed in his cataloguing of series. Across the hall, Janice and Harry had the living-room all to themselves. How long, I wondered, since he had tossed down his coat and gone in there? An hour, perhaps, or maybe only ten minutes, and what were they saying to each other? I mustn't look suspicious when I joined them. There must be no hint of that in my manner.

I had no intention of spying on them when I peered into the hall mirror. My impulse was to make sure of my own looks. It was only when I saw the two in the living-room that I realised my opportunity to play eavesdropper for the mirror revealed them to me while I myself could keep clear of its reflection. If I had had my hearing and had stood there, unseen but deliberately listening, I should have been no more guilty than I was at that moment. For the deaf learn to listen with their eyes, and I must take my chance. I was past being honourable as I strained to catch the movements of their reflected lips.

Janice sat on the low chair by the fire. Her arms hugged her knees; her hands clasped tight together. I knew instinctively that she longed to fling them about Harry's neck. It must be taking all her will power to keep those few feet away from him.

He stood by the fireplace, looking down at her, and the lamplight was strong on his face so that I had no difficulty in following his words.

"Janice, stop going all over it again. Don't you know I hate myself for what I've let us into?"

"We couldn't help ourselves, Harry." She lifted her face to his, and I saw she was struggling against tears. "We didn't want to fall in love. God knows, we tried to fight it at first. . . ."

"Maybe we could have tried harder." I saw him stiffen as she reached out a hand to him. "No, darling, don't touch me—not here, not in this house. . . . I know what I'm putting you through."

"But we can't drift on like this. Waiting isn't going to make it easier for her or for us. It's getting too much for me—nights like this when we . . ." She let her head fall on her arms. Her curls quivered in the lamplight as sobs took her.

I saw Harry reach out and then resolutely draw back his hand. There was distress and longing on his face that I had never seen there before. I knew then that they were suffering in their way as I had suffered in mine. But they were together in their misery, and I was alone. I knew I ought to go in to them then and there without further subterfuge and spying. I was no better than they at that moment. Yet I stayed rigid, pressing my body against the table to steady my trembling.

"I was sure she guessed something," Janice was going on, her wet face lifted once more towards his, "just before Christmas. She must have seen us together, and then the

keys disappearing—but lately she's acted . . ." Her head
went down again, and I missed her muffled words.

"I can't do it," he was answering. "I can't tell her yet."

Janice faced him again, and for once tears and hopeless-
ness made her ugly.

"Harry," she said, and her lips were firm as they put
the question: "If Emily could hear, it would be different,
wouldn't it? You'd make the break?"

"But she is deaf." He shrugged helplessly before he
went on. "That's why I can't. You don't know what it's
like to be loved and not be able to return it. And I did
love her once, Janice, even if I know now I made a mistake."

"You needn't make another!" She was on her feet then,
moving towards him.

He held her off at arm's length.

"I know Emily better than you do." I could see the
muscles of his throat working. "If we take away the one
thing she feels she's got to live for—she might be desperate
enough to do something. . . ."

"How about my being desperate, Harry?"

"I know. . . . Don't think I don't, but you and I haven't
her kind of strength. Emily's like Peace-Pipe goods—a
hundred per cent quality. . . . I can't live up to her and
that's why I'm afraid. . . ."

They drew closer then. Love and fear and misery were
too much for them to resist any longer. I saw her head go
down against his tweed coat. His face was hidden in the
tumbled fairness of her hair. I moved away from the table,
and turned from the mirror that had revealed too much.
My heart still hammered frantically, but the rest of me
had gone numb. I tried to think as I stood, still clutching
the sheaf of letters in my hands. I knew that I ought to go
into that room and face them once and for all. A woman
in a book or a play would have done that, but I wasn't
behind footlights or between the pages of a book. I felt
incapable of words or actions as if I had been thrown over
some precipice and were not quite sure whether I were
alive or dead. . . .

They were seated at opposite ends of the sofa when I finally made my way to the living-room door. Janice's hair was only slightly disordered, and only the dark brightness of her eyes betrayed her recent tears. Harry sprang up a little too quickly, I thought; but except for that and a certain tension in his smile there was nothing in their manner to give them away. My hands began to shake as I stood there before them, and the letters spilled to the floor.

"Oh!" I apologised. "I'm sorry—stupid of me."

Harry was on his knees helping to pick them up. Our faces were on a level as we stooped to recover the scattered envelopes.

"Good Lord, Emmy," he said as he gathered them up, "what a lot of letters! . . . No wonder you look all in. Let's not wait for midnight to open that bottle I brought."

I nodded and made my way to the nearest chair.

"All right," I told him. "I could do with a drink now."

I held out my hands to the heat of the fire, and I did not look beyond my own fingers. Harry must have gone to the kitchen for glasses, and perhaps Janice helped him bring them in. I have no recollection of that. But presently we were all by the fire again and Uncle Wallace had joined us.

"Don't look as if you were seeing a ghost, sir," Harry was grinning as he showed the label on a bottle of champagne. "Just pretend I set the clock back to pre-Volstead days. It was a present, and there won't be enough to hurt us. If we ever needed to drink to prosperity being just round the corner, we do to-night."

"I guess you're right, my boy," Uncle Wallace agreed. "Careful how you handle that cork."

They were too absorbed to notice my silence or that I started, too, at the sudden loud pop that announced the successful uncorking. It seemed ironical that I should hear that sound distinctly above the pounding of blood in my ears.

"Well, then," Uncle Wallace held his glass high. "Here's to the New Year and better business——"

Janice tossed back her hair impatiently. "Here's to us!" she interrupted.

I could scarcely taste the champagne as I tried to keep the glass steady in both hands. I dared not trust myself to look at Janice and Harry, though I knew they must be keeping up the pretence of talk. But if they noticed my preoccupation they did nothing to rouse me from it.

I must do something, my mind seemed to be telling me from a great distance off. I must think what to say to them. I can't just sit like this from now till midnight.

I shall always be grateful to the Parker twins and their escorts for bursting in upon us as they did. They stopped on their way to the dance, stirring the atmosphere of our living-room as if by invisible brooms. We were caught up in a flurry of embraces and introductions, for the young men turned out to be holiday house guests. I remember mechanically shaking the hands they extended, and hoping that the chill of my fingers would not be commented upon. The chattering Parker twins and their young men, whose names I made no attempt to master, were certainly a god-send to me. I have been thankful ever since for the diversion they created. A group of people always made me retreat into silence. I sat in their midst making no effort to join in.

"Emily!" It was one of the Parker twins who touched my arm and appealed directly to me at last. "I think you might help us out. You haven't said a word one way or the other."

I forced my mind back to her and what she was saying —something about the dance and wanting us to go with them. Club dances were deadly unless one made sure of one's own party. It wasn't fair of Janice and Harry to desert them like this.

"And you come too," she added as an afterthought. "Even if you don't want to dance it's better than sticking around here on New Year's Eve."

"Why, of course," I told her, "Janice ought to go. I thought she was planning to, and if Harry's staying here on my account——"

He must have been listening for he came over at that.

"Now, Emily"—he laid his hand on mine, and I tried not to tremble under his touch—"don't you let yourself be persuaded. It won't kill us to see the New Year in here. I'm not backing down on a promise."

But I saw Janice's eyes on his face. I could feel their eagerness to be free of this room and of me. I knew those club dances. There were plenty of opportunities for a couple to slip away to a parked car. Even those who stayed on the crowded dance floor could be isolated by the music, severed from unwelcome talk to an outsider. I knew they were both ready to snatch at any moments together. Let them go. Let them get out of the house on any pretext while I tried to muster the remnants of my defence.

"Please go," I repeated, "both of you. I've had a pretty hard day, so count me out. You know dragging me to a dance isn't a treat to me or—or any one else."

Harry tried to protest, but I cut him short. Janice was already hurrying upstairs to change her dress, and as far as the others were concerned the matter was settled.

"Emmy"—even in his relief at the chance to escape, Harry seemed reluctant to desert me—"I hate to go off like this and leave you alone on New Year's Eve. You've had a bad week to put through at the hospital and all. You ought to have a little fun yourself——"

"Fun!" I repeated, and choked suddenly over the word.

"I can come back if you want me to," Harry insisted. "I'll go over with them now and slip off just before midnight."

But I put him off hastily. I manufactured an excuse to go upstairs as they were leaving, though I watched the cars' headlights whiten the driveway and then become indistinguishable from other hurrying specks of light on the dark road. Once they were out of sight I went downstairs again—for no reason in particular.

The house seemed empty, hollow as some discarded shell. Yet the living-room was still too full of Janice and Harry as I moved about, setting it to rights in a kind of determined frenzy. There was no need for me to straighten the hearthrug and magazines, to shake the sofa cushions into smoothness and collect scattered ash-trays. Maggie would be up to do that long before breakfast. Yet I found it necessary to keep active.

Across the hall Uncle Wallace turned off the study light and appeared in the doorway. He had a new detective novel under his arm, one that Aunt Em had rejected from the books sent to her at the hospital. He smiled sheepishly as he saw my eyes upon the title.

"Yes, I've taken to murder mysteries," he said. "Find them easier to sleep on than the newspapers nowadays. Why didn't you go with the rest? . . . Or maybe Harry's coming back for you?"

"No, Uncle Wallace," I said, "I didn't feel—exactly in the mood for—festivity."

He peered at me a little anxiously, as if he were looking through new spectacles, and seemed bewildered by the change he saw.

"But it's all wrong for a girl like you to be here alone on New Year's Eve. I'm not feeling too gay myself with Em laid up and with Peace-Pipe sitting like a ton of bricks on my mind; but I'll see the Year New in with you, if you want me to."

I was touched by his concern. Uncle Wallace liked life to flow along in the conventional pattern to which he was accustomed. I suddenly realised that I belonged to the pattern of his existence. He thought of me as young and happy and carefree, and here I was upsetting all his theories of fitness. I reached out and took his hand.

"The New Year will come in whether we sit up for it or not," I said.

"Yes," he admitted, "but you shouldn't be feeling that way about it, not at your age."

"What's age got to do with our feelings, Uncle Wallace?"

"Well, I don't know." He frowned uncertainly. "I guess I'm too old to cope with change—been used to walking on solid ground too long; now it's slipping under me, and I can't seem to keep my balance."

I had no comfort to offer him. We stood awkwardly by the fire, each of us alone with our fears and uncertainties, each of us dreading the New Year which every moment brought nearer.

When he had gone to his room, I still kept up my aimless activity. Feeling had begun to return, not only to my body, but to my mind. As the numbness lessened, a deep, inner conviction began to take form. No matter what I had seen; no matter how much I knew, I wouldn't let Harry go. Until one admitted defeat one was never really beaten. Janice had her weapons, and I had mine. She might seem to have the more powerful ones, but I would make my very handicap serve me. Harry had admitted he could not take advantage of my deafness. I had been foolish to send them off to the dance. But at least I had not given myself away. I would rally my scattered forces and accept the challenge. To-morrow I would take the offensive.

A cold rush of air made me turn just then to find Merek Vance in the doorway.

I was too startled to speak or move as he came forward in his old ulster and felt hat. He did not pause to remove either before he reached me. His hands felt icy on my shoulders as he held me off and searched my face, smiling as he did so.

"Don't look as if I were a ghost," he said. "Your front door was unlocked. I've been driving all day to get here, and I'm half-frozen; but I'll come to life in a moment. Didn't want to wire you for fear I might spoil some plan you'd made. Don't tell me you're all alone?"

When I nodded he threw off his coat and hat and went to the fire.

"That's better than I dared expect." He held out his hands to the heat of the one remaining log. I saw then that he was shaking with cold.

Q

I brought out the sherry from the sideboard.

"You look as if you could do with something stronger, but this is the best I can find. Here, I'll pour it."

It was queer to have my hands steadier than his as I filled the glass. While he drank it I put more wood on the fire and blew it into flame. It was several minutes before either of us spoke. I did not look at him while I bent to the fire, yet I knew his eyes were upon me. I could feel their probing.

"Why didn't you send for me?" he asked when I looked up at last. "Why didn't you let me know about your aunt's accident? It's a queer thing I'd have to hear of it from one of my patients across the river."

"You couldn't have come in time to set the bone," I told him, "and besides Dr. Weeks and I felt what you were doing in Baltimore was more important. We knew you'd leave everything to come."

His expression relaxed at that. The colour was coming back to his lips, though he still crouched close to the fire as if he could never thaw out. I answered his questions about Aunt Em, trying to sound as accurate and medical as I could.

"You don't look as if you'd had any dinner," I said. "Better let me see what I can find in the ice-box."

He shook his head impatiently.

"Never mind that. . . . Tell me about Emily Blair." His eyes held me with their disconcerting keenness. "You've had a tough stretch to put through alone. I had a feeling I should have come back before this—a hunch that you needed me."

"Oh, I managed all right," I told him evasively.

"Yes," he smiled as he continued to scrutinise me. "I can see you're in fine form. You look as if you'd been left out all night in a January thaw. How's the reaction to sound: clearer, less spasmodic?"

He went to the piano and played a few bars, keeping his eyes on my face as he did so.

"The Unfinished Symphony," I recognised the familiar

theme, and he nodded and let his hands drop from the keys. "I never knew you could play the piano."

"I can't, unfortunately. My childhood didn't include music lessons. But I got free tickets to concerts occasionally when I was in college. My sister and I went to one in Carnegie Hall last week. They played the Debussy ' Drowned Cathedral.' It made me think of you."

"Of me. . . . Why?"

"Indirectly, of course. It's as if you'd been engulfed by a lot of things—conventions and systems and people that were muffling you. It's only now and then that I know you're really there under it all; that I can hear the real person coming through, like those bells under water in the music——"

"Sometimes I feel like that."

I had not meant to answer him. My words came as a surprise to me.

He turned to the watch on his wrist and held it out for me to read. The hands pointed to a quarter before twelve.

"There's a lot to talk to you about between now and midnight," he went on. "Not that I can crowd it all into these few minutes, because I'll need hours of explaining when I try to tell you what the doctors think about your case. They're still checking over my notes and charts, and they'll work with us from now on. We did a lot of experimenting, too. They've even started a special clinic for research and experiments. I helped them organise it, and two doctors I know are in charge. Nothing's been made public yet, but they're convinced we're on the track of big things. And it won't stop with ears: if one set of impaired nerves can be stimulated by my formula, why not others? Think of the possibilities——"

"I wonder they let you come back here to Blairstown."

"They brought a lot of pressure to keep me there, but I said no, for the present. We'll need a couple more times before I'm ready to have you go through their tests, and I want to have you past this daily injection stage. I'm increasing the strength to-morrow and gradually working up——"

"Wait," I cut him short. "I have something to say about that."

My voice and manner must have given him some warning, for the eager excitement left his face. The anxiety in his eyes was disconcerting. I could not look at him directly and say what must be said.

"I'm through," I told him. "I'm not coming to you for any more treatments."

Once I had got those words out, I dared to face him again.

His whole body had stiffened, and the line of his jaw had grown hard.

"There's no need for staying here on my account," I went on. "You can go back to that clinic."

"You don't know what you're saying, Emily. You're not cured yet. We haven't reached a point where those nerves will go on without artificial stimulation. This is the most critical stage of all, and it would be fatal to stop the injections. I wouldn't answer for the consequences."

"You mean," I went on, "that I'd go back to where I was before you began? I'd be deaf again?"

He nodded, and I blundered on.

"I tell you I can't go on, bargain or no bargain. You proved what you wanted to prove through me. If I choose to stay deaf—well, that's my business whether you understand it or not."

"I understand all right." He turned from me and walked to the window. He stayed there, quietly staring out between the half-drawn curtains. Then he came back. Once more his hands gripped my shoulders. He forced me to look up, to follow what he was saying. "So you'd rather be weak for Harry Collins than strong for me? That's the answer, isn't it?"

I felt the scorn behind his clear, accusing eyes. I could feel myself withering under his contempt.

"Can't you ever leave me alone?" I tried to twist free

of his hold. "I'm through, I tell you. You can find plenty of other deaf people to experiment on."

"We're not talking about other people. Leave them out of this. And leave Harry Collins out, too. I thought you were over this madness. I gave you credit for having some pride!"

I was shaking now under his grip. His fingers that looked so thin and supple were strong as steel and charged with a vitality that I was powerless to resist.

"Pride doesn't stand much chance with love," I managed to falter. "But I wouldn't expect you to know about that."

"No." He bent closer, and I felt the heat of his breath on my face as he spoke. "And I hope I'll never know about that kind of love. You want to turn love into a crutch. Dead wood to lean on because you're not brave enough or honest enough to accept the truth. You love someone. All right. Maybe he loved you once, but he doesn't any more. He loves someone else. All right. Nothing so remarkable about that. Stop being a snob about your own feelings."

"It's not fair to say such things. I——"

"Are you being fair to yourself, or to me?"

"I'll do what I want with my life. It doesn't happen to concern you."

"But it does, no matter how you deny it." His hands suddenly dropped from my aching shoulders, and he pushed me away from him. "I don't know why I thought you were worth bothering about. I might have guessed you were one of the life-owes-me people. Life owes me a living, life owes me happiness, life owes me love. . . . Well, you owe life something—and you owe me something when it comes to that. And I don't mean money."

He turned away abruptly and strode over to the chair where he had laid his hat and coat. I made no move to speak or to follow him. I felt nothing except a pounding of blood at my temples, a blurring of the familiar objects in the room.

And then, suddenly, I was aware of sound: bells were

ringing outside and whistles shrilling. They were echoing
in me, in my ears that had been dead so long to the noisy
welcome of a new year. I must have cried out at the new
sensation. I must have run to the window and thrown it
open involuntarily. For there we were, side by side, leaning
out to the cold and the wild clamour.

His arm was about me, and we stood there, listening
together without moving, without speaking till the peak
of sound had passed.

He closed the window and turned to me at last.

"Well," he said, "I came to wish you a happy new year;
but there's no use in that now—you'd rather have the old
one——"

"No, no." I found myself clinging to him in frantic
appeal. Tears were pouring down my face, and I made no
effort to check their flow. "Don't say that. . . . I was a fool
to think I could give back what you've given me. It's not
that easy, is it? I'll be down again to-morrow—I mean
to-day."

CHAPTER THIRTY-ONE

STRANGE to wake to the Peace-Pipe whistle on the morning set for the mills' reopening. It was just short of three years*since I had heard that long shrill blast, for it had been silent in the weeks after my hearing began to return. I started up in bed, shivering under the covers at the challenge of that distant summons. Never again, I knew, would I take the sound for granted.

I thought of all those who must be listening to it at that moment under the roofs of Blairstown: women looking anxiously at their men who started fires of broken crates and salvaged coal; women who put coffee on to boil and sliced bread as thin as they dared for a noon dinner pail; children huddled close under old quilts, watching with bright, curious eyes while they whispered together.

"There's the whistle. . . . Hear it?"

"Papa going back to work, you think?"

"He told Mamma ' *No* ' last night, but he's putting on his pants and shoes. What you bet we get stew for supper?"

"There's going to be men with guns by the mill gates, real honest-to-gosh guns, and things they throw that make you cough and cry. Ma says we got to go the long way round to school. We might get hurt if the picket line starts to rush 'em. She says there's no telling what to expect. Come on, let's get up."

I thought of Uncle Wallace dressing in his room at the end of the hall, slipping the folds of his tie into a careful knot, trying to look as if this were any day and not one to be reckoned with in Peace-Pipe history. I thought of Aunt Em lying helpless in her cast, straining her ears at every real or imagined sound. Whatever happened or did not happen, she would believe we were keeping important facts from her. She would lie there rigid and uncompromising, feeling that somehow she had helped to betray Peace-

Pipe Mills by falling and breaking her hip. I thought of old Jo Kelly wrestling with the furnace in the cellar, his crippled hands and stiff knees stubbornly responding to his will while he tried not to remember a boy's small alert figure following him about on other winter mornings. I thought of young Jo, too, rousing himself in some room across the river, his eyes more dark than blue, his shoulders defiant under the old Mackinaw. I thought of Merek Vance in his makeshift office, quietly sorting and filling his doctor's bag with extra bandages and antidotes that might be needed if a hurry call came. I thought of Harry Collins—but no, I would try not to think of him, not once all day.

Uncle Wallace had begun his second cup of coffee when I reached the dining-room. The morning paper was open beside him, but I made no reference to the headlines in heavy type, "Mill Reopens To-day Under Armed Guard."

"Aunt Em had a fair night," I reported as I took my place. "Of course she's beginning to worry. She wants the paper as soon as you're through with it."

"I'll take it up before I leave. We must keep her reassured, Emily. I know I can count on you for that."

"Yes, Uncle Wallace. How—how much in the way of trouble do you expect?"

"That's hard to say, but we're not taking chances. If there should be any attempt at violence we're prepared to meet it."

"With more violence?"

He evaded my question and went on after a moment.

"I want you and Janice to keep away from that part of town for the present. Better stay on this side of the river till we have things well in hand. The weather prediction is for snow to-day. That's to our advantage."

"Yes," I said, "snow's hard on a picket line, especially if shoes happen to need mending."

Uncle Wallace looked grim as he folded his napkin.

"Emily," he reproved, "I don't doubt your good intentions, but your sympathies are running away with you.

You've had too little experience to take a long view of the situation."

"I've never worked behind a loom or tended the bobbin machinery," I reminded him. "I've never tried to live on a millhand's wages."

"You've never tried to run a mill so that wages could be paid—remember that too." He rose from the table and pushed back his chair. "You don't realise we're obligated all round, to our stockholders as well as our workers. We have to take a firm hand now, or else . . ."

His shoulders sagged expressively.

"Or else what?" I persisted.

"Close down—be taken over by a receivership. . . . It would amount to the same thing as far as we're concerned. God knows, Peace-Pipe's never compromised with its product or its principles, and we won't be bullied into it by a bunch of paid organisers that have shut down bigger mills than ours. There are plenty of workers to fill the shifts, and we mean to see they're protected. Well, don't worry, and don't let Em get worked up about it. By the way, this house is freezing again. Old Jo must be having more trouble with the furnace. Better get someone in to help him."

Maggie was in anything but a good humour when I approached her on the subject. Yes, she admitted, the house was cold, upstairs and down, but that was no reason for a trained nurse to go round sniffling and wearing a sweater over her uniform and demanding hot tea or coffee every hour. She'd be warm if she kept as busy as she was paid to be. Old Jo was doing his best. He wasn't fit to be up and tinkering with the furnace. He'd be the next to take to his bed, and then it would be even worse. That substitute boy always managed to do the wrong things with dampers and drafts. We'd have to worry along somehow while the cold snap lasted.

So that first week in January began—a week that grew more tense as each day passed. Snow fell intermittently, but brought no relief from the cold. The hard, tight flakes took on a greyish tinge before they reached the ground. After the recent smokeless weeks I had half-forgotten that familiar heaviness on the air. Once more the chimneys of Peace-Pipe dominated the town with clouds of their own making. Wherever I went, whatever I did, I was conscious of that; and though I did not cross the bridges I felt the distant throb of machinery. Morning, noon, and night, I found myself straining to catch the sound of the mill whistle. Those were the times to be dreaded, I knew, when gates opened or closed on arriving and departing workers; when the line of picketers pressed closer and the armed guard left off lounging about the millyard.

"We're satisfied with the way order is being kept." That was all I could find out from Uncle Wallace, and Harry was uncommunicative on the hurried visits he made to the house. Both were nervous and on edge through those days. Neither could be drawn into talk.

Except for Merek Vance I should have known less of the situation than if I had been with Cousin Eunice in Boston. He did not evade my questions as he increased his injections and made daily notes on my improvement. I was glad to avoid references to my outburst of New Year's Eve, and he tactfully made no mention of it. It was good to reach his office each afternoon when I left Aunt Em and the big house on a pretext of errands or a breath of fresh air. I relaxed in the worn leather chair whose broken springs and resulting hollows I knew so well. The weight of fear and uncertainty that kept me tense, even when I slept, would lift gradually as we talked across the desk.

"The weather and Jo Kelly are keeping things reasonably quiet so far," he told me by Wednesday. "But I've been through a couple of strikes before this, and I'm not making any predictions."

He had had an emergency call or two. A few flying bricks had found their marks. There had been bruises to be treated, some stitches taken, a broken wrist to be set, but nothing serious yet.

"Dr. Weeks and I are more afraid of another flu epidemic," he admitted. "A lot of the picketers are home with chills and fever, and every other family's been scrimping on food. No wonder a good half of the strikers couldn't hold out and turned scab. That makes the ones that stick more bitter."

"Bitter about—us, you mean?"

"Yes, of course, but there's plenty being lavished on the union, too. They feel they could have made a stronger stand with more financial help. Claim they're taking the brunt of the strike and the union hasn't lived up to its promises of backing. I guess there's more than a little truth in it. The United Textile Workers group is pretty well involved right now with Fall River and New Bedford and some of the bigger plants. It's going to take all the organisation's funds to win those, and they naturally count more than a small family-owned mill like Peace-Pipe."

"I see. . . . Then you think the strikers will be squeezed out or just have to accept the old terms."

He shrugged.

"Looks that way now, but things can change overnight in situations like this. The strike should never have been called to my way of thinking, not with business lagging the way it is and banks withdrawing funds all over the country. Well, I'm no prophet and I'm no industrialist; I'll have to stick to patching up broken heads."

"What about Jo Kelly?"

"So far he's the spokesman and keeping things clean. But I suspect there's an element that would like to see him out and put on a show of their own. He's done a good job, but this feeling that the union may be up to some double-crossing is bound to react on him."

"Jo Kelly hasn't a mean streak in him," I said. "I've never known him to bear a personal grudge to any one. People must feel that and trust him the way animals do."

"Yes, he's one of the finest. I only hope he'll watch his step. . . . I saw him last night, and he was asking for you. He seemed worried about your aunt."

By Thursday Uncle Wallace looked more cheerful, and

the Blairstown newspaper ran an editorial complimenting
the Directors of Peace-Pipe Industries on their firm stand.
"The traditions of quality and integrity have not been
sacrificed," it read. "When all efforts at negotiations failed
the company did not stoop to compromise. ' We will continue to give work to those who want it,' Mr. W. J. Perkins
was quoted as saying in an interview to the Press yesterday,
' and we have taken measures to protect our returning
workers. We never have been, and we never will be, dictated
to by an element which must eventually defeat its own ends
by exorbitant demands and high-handed methods.' Other
industrial plants may well watch and benefit by the stand
which Peace-Pipe directors have taken."

That night Maggie told me that old Jo Kelly had given
out. Dr. Weeks had ordered him to bed that afternoon and
had personally seen to the order being carried out. It
was a heavy cold, and the doctor was taking no chances of
pneumonia. He had given the old man a sleeping powder
to keep him quiet, and Maggie had promised to keep an
eye on him.

"The nurse won't, that's one sure thing," Maggie had
remarked grimly. "Said she couldn't run the risk of any
contagion for your aunt. Now all we need is for the furnace
to act up."

She came to me later that evening with a queer expression
on her face.

"I've got an idea young Jo's been down cellar," she told
me. "About half an hour ago I thought I heard coal being
shovelled. Then the heat started coming up good in the
registers. When I got a chance to go down just now the
ashes was taken out and the fire fixed to last through the
night. There was something chalked on the floor. It said:
' Back in morning. Don't worry.' I don't know who else
could have done that but him. He's got a good heart, I'll
say that for the boy."

"Yes," I agreed, "he always manages to find out if we're
sick or in trouble. But I hope he'll be careful——"

I broke off, remembering the precautions he had taken

when we stopped at the roadside diner. I was tempted to leave a note for him by the furnace, but decided against that. He probably wanted no notice taken of his visits. Later there would be a chance to thank him.

Harry had not appeared at the house for several days, and I had seen almost nothing of Janice except for hurried glimpses of her figure flitting through the hall or at the wheel of the car. The mill situation had reassured me somewhat about their chances of meeting. Ever since New Year's Eve I had tried not to think of what must be said when the moment came for me to speak out. By day I could take refuge in activity. It was at night in my own room that I was at the mercy of my own emotions. Bitterness would overwhelm me as I lay wakeful through the long hours of darkness and chill half-light. I no longer deluded myself with hope. At least I fought it in my consciousness. But during brief snatches of sleep it would lay insidious hold upon me once more. Then I would believe that the reality had been the dream; that Harry Collins and I had never been separated. So I came to dread sleep and its treachery.

By Friday of that week the strain was growing more than I could hide. My nerves were like fiddlestrings taut to the point of breaking. The muscles of my face stayed stiffly set, and my eyes were glazed with sleeplessness. In spite of my efforts at cheerfulness Aunt Em noticed the change in me and worried each time I came into her room. Even Uncle Wallace commented upon the dark circles under my eyes.

"Don't take things so hard, Emily," he cautioned. "Your aunt's getting along as well as we can expect. A few days more, and we'll feel we've turned the corner with this mill trouble. There was only a little demonstration yesterday when we opened the gates; a few pickets tried to rush the lines, nothing really serious. Of course we'll keep the guard on a while longer, but there's no cause for you to worry so."

Merek Vance alone made no remarks about my appearance. He seemed to take the outward signs of my feeling as a natural reaction. Indeed we talked little together on my visits, which were briefer than usual and devoted entirely to the routine of injections, sound tests, and note-taking. He knew when to speak and when to keep silence. I was grateful for that and asked nothing more of him.

I had come in out of the cold that Friday afternoon to find Janice moving restlessly about the living-room, and the radio giving out such a blare of sound that even I recoiled from it. I flung down my wraps and hurried in, words of involuntary protest rising to my lips.

"Janice," I cried, "tune that thing down or stop it!"

I hardly realised what I had said until I caught the expression on Janice's face; her start of incredulous surprise.

"Well!" She gave me a long, curious look. "You're certainly the last person in this house I'd expect to complain about a little music!"

"Oh, never mind me—but you might remember there's sickness in this house."

She hunched her shoulders and moved to turn off the radio switch.

"Oh, all right then, have it your way, only stop staring at me like that. You can have the whole place to yourself. I don't want it."

"Janice, wait, you've got to listen to me."

I found myself moving across the room to her. She stopped reluctantly in the act of gathering up some scattered possessions. The colour went out of her face though she tried to appear unconcerned.

"What's come over you anyhow, Emily?"

My throat felt dry, and my head throbbed. I knew I could not keep hold of myself any longer.

"How do you think I knew the radio was on?" I asked her.

"I'm sure I don't know." She shrugged again. "But it doesn't matter, does it?"

"It happens to matter a lot to me," I went on without taking my eyes from her face. "I could *hear* it—that's why. You can ask Dr. Vance if you don't believe me."

"What's he got to do with it?"

"He's cured me. At least I'm on the way to being cured."

"But—that doesn't seem possible . . ." Her eyes grew wider, and I saw sudden fear start up in them. "I mean, we'd—we'd have noticed it."

"I took pains you shouldn't. I had reasons—and I wanted to be sure first. I'd been disappointed so many times before, I was afraid to hope, and now"—I knew my voice must have broken before I forced myself to go on—"now there isn't any point to that."

Either she missed my meaning or she was determined not to show that she sensed it.

"Why, it's wonderful, Emily!" she began. "You certainly ought to feel happy."

She reached out her hands to me, but I drew back.

"How can you stand there and say that to me, after—after——"

I could not trust myself to go on for a moment. We stood there facing each other, alert and wary.

"What did you expect me to say? I can't make you out."

"Can't you? I shouldn't have thought that would be hard to do, especially for you and Harry. You thought you were playing safe, I suppose. Perhaps you thought I didn't see and feel other things just because I couldn't hear what you said."

Janice's hair had loosened and tumbled into her eyes. She pushed it back with a little defiant gesture before she answered.

"All right," she said. "Why didn't you speak up instead of spying on us? I was all for telling you. God knows I was. But Harry was so afraid of his job and Aunt Em feeling the way she does about you two marrying; and then you came back and made him feel you couldn't go on living without him. What could I do? I didn't want to love him, Emily, and he didn't want to love me. We tried not to—at first. It's the truth, whether you believe it or not."

"That's going to be a great comfort." I was beginning to tremble in spite of my effort to keep calm. The room was retreating in a haze about us. Such a fierce rush of words struggled in me that I felt I should go down under their weight.

It was then that I felt a hand on my arm. I turned to find Maggie at my side. Her face was crumpled with excitement and fear. Her breath came short under her black dress.

"Miss Emily! Miss Janice! Come quick: there's trouble —right at our back door. Some kind of a fight, I think. A brick went through the pantry window, and there's a lot of noise. You'd better call the police."

Janice started for the telephone as I followed Maggie down the hall. I could hear sounds now. Voices were shouting, and there were thuds at the back door. I reached out to unbolt it, but Maggie tried to hold me back.

"Miss Emily, please! Wait till the police get here. Whatever it is, they sound awful rough to me."

"I'm going to find out." I pushed her aside.

"It's all right to talk brave," she protested, "but this isn't any time for fool's courage."

I don't remember how I got the door open. I must have switched on the light that illuminated the steps and the path that led from the cellar entrance. I seemed to be part of some drama thrown on the black and white of a motion picture screen. Three men retreated before me down the steps, moving towards two other men bent over another figure stretched out on the frost-whitened driveway. They were only a few yards away, but before I could reach them I felt Bridget brush by me, her ears stiff, her body flattened to the ground. The men tried to push her away, but she stood over the sprawled shape, quivering and sniffing and giving long, shrill howls that even I could hear.

The men were speaking to me, but I could not follow them. One tried to stop me as I came close to the little group. I shook him off and went on. I think I knew even before I recognised the familiar Mackinaw jacket that Jo Kelly lay limp at my feet.

"Jo! Jo!" I could feel myself repeating his name incoherently over and over as I gathered his head into my lap.

"Careful, Miss Blair," one of the men was cautioning, his face so close to mine that I could not miss the warning. "He's hurt. . . . A brick must have caught him right there —you can see."

He pointed to the spot where the bone showed white under the soaked hair. Already I could feel a sticky warmth on my hands and the smell of blood from an open wound. I could not look at the place. I kept my eyes on the mouth whose lines I knew so well; on the thin sensitive hands that Bridget was licking in frantic appeal. I took one of his wrists in my hands and tried to find the reassuring beat of his pulse before I turned once more to the man who had spoken to me.

"Get Dr. Vance," I told him. "Take the little car. The keys will be in it. Bring him back with you as fast as you can. Hurry!"

Maggie had come out with a blanket and pillows. We eased them under him and made him as comfortable as we could, crouching there in the cold. I managed to make out fragments of what the men were saying. I even put in a question or two of my own.

"He sure got an awful slug from the looks . . ."

"We told him to keep away from here. Just this morning I says to him, ' Jo, we know you're on the level, we don't ask questions, but you better stay on your own side of the river if you want to keep out of trouble.' And then he had to come up here again to-night."

"But he was only helping us out," I faltered, "with the furnace. See, there's the ashes he must have been carrying out when they——"

"Yes." Another man came closer and joined in. "And there's his flashlight. They must of got him when he come out. Wisht we'd got here in time to head him off."

"But every one trusted Jo Kelly." I turned from one to another of the faces about me. "You did, didn't you? Who could have wanted to hurt him?"

R

"Well," one of the men hesitated before he answered, "you see there's been feeling lately. Some said he was trying to double-cross us. Might even turn scab himself next. They been watching him pretty close, so when he started to sneak up here they didn't wait to ask questions. But I guess they didn't mean to do more'n put a scare in him."

"He always did have one foot in trouble from the day he was born." Maggie had returned with a bottle of brandy and a spoon. She was trying to get a few drops between his lips. Her hands kept steady, but her face was distorted with tears. It was the one and only time I had ever seen Maggie cry. "You wait till the police get here," she was saying. "They'll get to the bottom of this."

The five men drew together then and began to whisper. They hesitated and pulled their caps over their eyes.

"Look!" One of them touched me on the shoulder and glanced furtively down the drive. "We'd better scram, or they might pin this on us. The police won't worry about who done it if they can find someone to lock up. It don't seem right to clear out this way, but he'd be the first to tell us to. There's a car now."

I dared not shift my position to stop them as they disappeared into the back garden. Jo's head felt so heavy on the pillow that I ached from the effort to keep it steady. Maggie had forced a little more brandy between his lips. The air was full of that strong, sharp smell. His eyelids quivered faintly, but he gave no other sign. I wondered, as we waited there beside him, if Maggie were remembering my seventh birthday party and young Jo lying as limp and white under the old hemlock-tree.

CHAPTER THIRTY-TWO

THE bare, shedlike hall where rallies, revival meetings, and occasional dances were held was already crowded when I reached it through the dripping greyness of a January thaw. I hesitated for a moment, searching the group of men, young and old, who stood by the open doors. They stared at me and then uneasily at one another. Evidently, I had not been expected, for no one seemed ready to take the initiative about seating me. At last a young man came forward. He nodded awkwardly, and I recognised him as the one who had been chief spokesman when we worked over Jo Kelly's limp body two nights ago.

Only two nights ago, that's all it was. I had to stop and tell myself that all over again, before I answered his nod with one of guarded recognition.

He turned and beckoned me up the long aisle, signalling to someone many rows in front. I followed him, keeping my eyes on the floorboards, wishing that I might have stayed inconspicuously near the doors. People moved closer together on one of the benches; a woman lifted a child to her lap, and I crowded past knees to reach the vacant place. I could feel eyes regarding me, especially women's eyes under hatbrims and woollen shawls. Even though I could not hear it, I felt the ripple of curious interest my presence had created. The man beside me sat stiffly, staring straight before him. I could feel the hard muscular strength of his body under the cheap material of his suit. His thick, blunt-fingered hands looked out of place in idleness on his knees. On my other side a girl in a checked coat and tilted beret dabbed more powder on her nose from a ten-cent-store compact. Her hair was as black and shining as the flimsy patent leather shoes she wore. I saw her eyeing my wrist-watch appraisingly when I pushed back my glove to see the time.

Ten minutes before three. I sighed and hoped that they

would begin on time. I must force myself to look up at the platform. The sooner I did that, the easier it would be. There were several rows of heads between, but I could find gaps to peer through. Yes, there were the simple uncompromising lines of the box whose shape I had dreaded to see. I was glad they had covered it with an American flag. Maybe some people might object. Jo Kelly had never served in the army or navy. The battle he had fought would never earn him a patriotic memorial. But I couldn't help thinking of the little printed labels pasted on articles one bought: "Made in America." It seemed to me that young Jo had a right to those words and to the flag that he used to help old Jo raise and lower on our pole each Fourth of July and Memorial Day.

There were only a few floral tributes. But then it was January. Flowers were scarce and prices high. A big, gaudy wreath, reminiscent of those that heralded the opening of some new store, minus the gold streamer with the legend "Success," had been prominently placed. I guessed that it had been sent by the local chapter of the Textile Workers Union. There were several other less spectacular offerings that I knew must represent collections of quarters and dime contributions. That was all except for the red roses I had sent, standing in an ugly tin container on a wooden table.

A group of twelve men mounted the platform steps. They moved self-consciously, and I guessed that they must be trying to keep their shoes from squeaking. Yet there was a kind of clumsy dignity in their bearing that made up for the varied suits they wore. I noticed that they had all managed to put on white shirts and dark ties out of respect to the occasion. They seated themselves on folding chairs at one side of the platform. Those on the other side, closer to the coffin, were soon filled. I recognised a young priest, Father Fergus, from the Catholic church across the river and the Methodist minister, old Dr. Ellis, whose service to the mill families had included all denominations for the last twenty years. It was going to be an unorthodox service,

I gathered. Evidently there would be eulogies from others too, for there were three strangers, who must be officials from the union or the labour organisations. A woman whose face I could not see had taken her place at an upright piano flanked by two anæmic-looking potted palms. The figures on the platform rose, and we all struggled to our feet.

"Mine eyes have seen the glory of the coming of the
    Lord:
He is trampling out the vintage where the grapes of
    wrath are stored."

The whole place was pulsating with the sound of many voices. The strong, stirring rhythm beat all about me in waves, so that I hardly knew how much of it I was hearing, how much of it I was feeling. I clutched the seat in front to steady myself against the torrent of music; against the familiar words that were returning in me with a new significance. I had learned them years ago when we used to march into the high-school auditorium. Some of those men and women about me must have marched to them then, as young Jo Kelly and I had done. And now we were singing for him. No, I thought, not for him but for ourselves, gathered there bewildered and unreconciled to his death.

"He has sounded forth the trumpet that shall never
    call retreat;
He is sifting out the hearts of men before his judg-
    ment seat."

Terrible words and true, whether one believed in an Old Testament judgment seat or not. "Sifting out the hearts of men": I trembled at these words, remembering the shortcomings of my own heart taking the easy way of least resistance through all those past weeks and months of testing. But I had no doubts about Jo's heart. His had been whole and honest and free of compromise. He had given the best he had always—and for what? For a Cause that already seemed lost; for personal loyalties that had brought about his betrayal. I could see his slumped body lying on our gravel path, defenceless against the assault of those he had counted as his friends; his life snuffed out in bitterness and humiliation.

We slid back into our cramped places, and the service went on. I did not try to follow what they were saying up there on the platform, beyond bowing my head with the others when prayers were being said. It was too difficult to fix my eyes on the moving lips, and my mind was too full of the past to focus on the reality of this present scene. I had never realised fully how close the ties were between us. We had shared so much, without ever demanding anything of each other. It was a kind of love, I thought, that one didn't recognise as love till one suddenly found oneself without it. Jo and I had argued and disagreed. We had taken our different ways and still counted each upon the other. Something was gone out of my life now. I should have to rely on the memory of it.

The eulogies were being spoken. One of the strange men had taken his place beside the table. My roses quivered in the vase beside him when he pounded with heavy emphasis. Women were crying all around me. The faces of nearby men looked grim and set as they listened. Already, I felt, they were beginning to make a symbol of Jo Kelly. I could imagine that union orator charging them not to forget what he had stood for. But I couldn't bring myself to think of him that way, perhaps because I had never seen him in the picket line or addressing some group of workers from a soapbox.

It was over at last. Men and women began to mount the steps to the platform and move on in a long, quiet line. I had no wish to join them and turned to make my way out of the building. Now and again a familiar face passed, and I acknowledged it with recognition. The hall was stifling with close-packed bodies and damp clothing. I thought I should never make my escape; but I was free at last. The moist coolness of the outside air was good to breathe as I reached the doors. It was then that I felt a touch on my arm, and looked up to find Merek Vance beside me. I was glad to let him lead me out to his car.

"I thought you must be there," he said, "though I couldn't see you for the crowd. They hadn't figured on so many coming, not even on a Sunday. I'll drive you back after I've stopped at the hospital."

The streets were almost deserted as we drove on. The suspended activity of Sunday was over Blairstown. Across the river the sky was clearing behind Peace-Pipe chimneys. I was glad that they had chosen a Sunday for Jo's service. It meant that men and women who had returned to work could pay their last respects.

"I can't go back to the house, not yet," I said when Vance rejoined me after his errand at the hospital. "I'll have to get myself in hand first. Aunt Em's upset enough over all this without her finding out I went to the funeral."

"Then they didn't know you were there?"

Merek Vance sat back in the seat beside me, his hands resting laxly on the wheel. I had never seen those supple, strong hands of his so still. His face looked drawn, and there was a tired sag to his mouth.

"No," I explained. "No one knew I was going, but I had to be there. After all, Jo would be alive now except for trying to help us out with the furnace. Old Jo was too sick to leave his bed, and Uncle Wallace said he couldn't go—not in his position and with the union taking charge instead of having a service at the church. Well, Jo won't know I went, but at least I'll know one of us was there. I'm glad you went too." Again I searched his face, struck by a defeated weariness I had not seen there before. "You look so tired," I added, "as if you hadn't slept since the accident."

"A doctor grows used to losing sleep," he reminded me. "But he never grows used to losing a patient."

"You did everything you could."

"It wasn't enough. Perhaps if we could have sent for a brain surgeon from Boston . . . But there wasn't time for that. The only chance he had was an emergency operation, and we lost."

"You tried. I know you'd have given everything you had to save him."

He gave me a wry smile and spread his hands in a futile gesture.

"That's a great comfort, knowing that all the study and skill it's taken years to learn can't cope with what a well-aimed brick or club can do. Makes a doctor feel like giving up the human system and mending boilers or cracked cylinders."

I stared back at him incredulously. It was my turn to speak out in sudden protest.

"You can't say a thing like that! You haven't any right to, after what you've done for me!"

"And look how happy it's made you! Why, only the other night you were begging me to give up the treatments. You wanted to be deaf again."

"Forget what I said then, and I'll try to forget what you said just now. Besides, you told me once you couldn't guarantee to make me happy."

"I had my nerve going on to you about happiness."

"Maybe happiness isn't as important as we think," I said. "Most of us talk too much about it. I don't remember Jo Kelly mentioning happiness often. I guess he managed to get along without it, or maybe what he believed in made up for that. We'll never know now."

Impulsively I reached out my hand to his—partly to comfort him and partly because I also needed comfort.

"I'll never be reconciled to Jo's going out like that," I found myself saying. "I'll never be able to look at Bridget without wishing he'd stuck to animals and left human beings and their troubles alone. He had so little to call his own, not even a place where he could keep one of the dogs he was always picking up and having to give away."

Merek Vance did not smile at my words.

"You know," he said presently, "there's a sort of greatness about being as inconsistent as Jo Kelly was."

We were silent after that, sitting there together in the car, each of us thinking his own thoughts. The afternoon was slipping into twilight, and a low mist was coming up from the river, chill and faintly bitter with a hint of chemicals and smoke. Nothing new or strange in that. Time and again Jo Kelly must have felt it as he crossed one bridge or another at this hour.

CHAPTER THIRTY-THREE

WE sat together on the sofa with the fire burning before us and the curtains drawn for the night. Somehow we had put through the ordeal of Sunday night supper, with Harry making desperate efforts to appear interested in food and what Uncle Wallace was saying; with Janice restless and furtive over her untouched plate. Harry must have insisted on her going upstairs, for she had seemed reluctant to leave us alone. There had been a frantic, defiant appeal in her eyes as she turned away.

It had to come some time, I told myself, watching Harry put out one cigarette and then nervously light another at his end of the sofa. I suppose it might as well be to-night; only Jo Kelly's funeral was enough to go through for one day.

He leaned towards me in the firelight, and I saw the fear and misery in his eyes. His mouth that I had loved for its full-lipped, easy laughter had fallen into ineffectual lines. All the humour and charm of his face seemed to have been lost. Or perhaps I was seeing what I had determined not to see there before.

"Emmy," he began, "there isn't any name you could call me that I haven't called myself. You've got to believe that, even if I can't expect you to understand. . . ."

He broke off and waited for me to help him out.

"Then Janice has told you? That makes it easier for me."

"It's wonderful about your hearing. I can't believe it yet. You deserve that—only why couldn't you have let us in on it? Why all this secrecy?"

"I didn't trust myself or Dr. Vance at first. You know what I'd been through with doctors."

"Yes, I know. How long has this taken?"

"I've been having the injections ever since I came back last fall, but it's been so gradual I could hardly feel the change till lately. Then I really began to hear sounds. Dr. Vance can't promise how long it will be before I'm cured; before I can hear voices clearly and all that people are saying, without reading lips too. I thought I couldn't wait for that, but now I'm not—so impatient, Harry. There doesn't seem to be the same reason to hurry."

He turned away at that. I could see him struggling to find words for what he was trying to say.

"Love's a hell of a thing, Emmy. You don't need me to tell you that."

"There's no good in trying to find the reason for its going," I said, "or in going back to set the exact moment when it went. Let's say as little as we can about it."

"But you must believe that I still care about you. It's just that I didn't know till—till a few months ago what it was to feel this other way."

The muscles in his throat were working quickly. I could have no doubts as to his genuine distress. I looked away for a moment before I could bring myself to answer.

"There's only one kind of love I want, Harry, and you can't give it to me. I was stupid and stubborn not to realise how it was, long ago. But you see I'd come to depend on it so. It's a pity two people can't fall out of love at the same time, the way they fall into it."

"Oh, God, Emmy, don't! I've made such a mess of everything. I wanted not to hurt you, and I've only made things worse for us all."

His head dropped to his hands. I longed to reach out

and touch his thick, springy hair. But it was too late for that now. After a while he straightened his shoulders and went on.

"If I'd had any sense or spirit I'd have cleared out long ago."

"With or without Janice?" I put the question to him bluntly.

"Don't ask me." He spread his hands in a hopeless gesture. "I don't know where I'm going or what I'm doing, between the mills and the strike and my job and wanting to love you and loving Janice. I'm not blaming any one but myself. That's the hardest part."

I twisted the ring he had given me, watching the firelight bring little flecks of brightness into the stone. It was going to seem queer to take it off, almost like losing the finger that had worn it so long.

"We're all to blame in different ways," I told him at last. "You and Janice didn't play fair with me, and I didn't with you when I found I was going to hear again. We all thought it was easier to be a little dishonest than to hurt someone a lot.

"Harry," I began after another long pause, "we might as well be practical. You and Janice want to be married as soon as possible, don't you?" He started to speak, but once more the pulse in his throat beat visibly; and I did not wait for his words. "All right then. How are you going to do it?"

The lines in his forehead deepened. His face grew bleak.

"If I could find another job—— But it's the same story everywhere: mills shutting down all over the country and business just about paralysed. I've been around. I've seen the fellows behind desks, going through the motions and scared stiff the axe is going to catch them next. I tell you, Emmy, I'd be up against it to find a file clerk's job at twenty a week right now. And Hoover has the nerve to start a ' Don't Hoard—Spend Now ' campaign right in the middle of a depression."

"I know. . . . Well, how about your going away for a while?"

He shook his head forlornly.

"It's no time for me to leave the mills. Besides, if I did there probably wouldn't be a job for me to come back to. If your family didn't fire me—and they'd have a right to— Peace-Pipe may not come through these next months."

"That's a chance we'll all be taking," I reminded him. "There'll be a lot of explaining to do. Aunt Em is going to take this hard. But she'll have to accept it, once you two are married. I'll handle her the best way I can, if you'll only go away."

"Don't be noble, Emmy! I can't take that too."

"I'm not being noble. It's not nobility to accept facts. The way things are now, we're all three miserable. Well, subtract one person, and that leaves two who might be happy if they had a chance. I mean you and Janice. But you can't stay in Blairstown, not for a while anyway. People will talk too much, and I couldn't bear it seeing you here together every day."

"And what could we go away on? You know how I'm fixed for money, and Janice hasn't any of her own."

"There'll be some money in the bank in her name if you go there to-morrow. Don't ask any questions. It's not enough to last forever, but it will see you through for a while."

"But we can't do that, not on your money! I've got some pride left."

"Don't you think it's a little late in the day to talk about pride?" He winced under the bitterness behind my words. I hurried on before he could make further protests. "Besides, Janice has as much right to that money as I. It came from my father and she'd be having her share in a few years anyway."

"But, Emmy, I tell you we can't do it. I'd borrow the money—it isn't that: it's you, making this possible——"

I felt suddenly very tired, as if my strength and determination were about to desert me. I had lived up to this so long that there was a sense of relief in knowing it was almost over.

"Please, Harry," I went on, "please listen. Don't make things harder than they are already. Money's the least part of this. It came from Peace-Pipe Mills, and I don't want any share of them now. I've seen too much lately, and I've felt too much. A few days ago I wouldn't have lifted a finger to help you and Janice. I was willing to play dog-in-the-manger to keep you two from having what I couldn't have for myself."

"You had a right to feel that way, Emily."

"After you've seen someone die—someone eager and alive like Jo Kelly—it shakes the spitefulness out of you and the self-pity. I'm beginning to learn that feeling sorry for yourself is a pretty expensive luxury."

"No one could accuse you of that. You've taken more than your share of jolts without a whimper."

"Maybe I didn't whimper in public, but I had ways of my own." I rose, and he rose too. His arms reached out, but I stiffened myself against the impulse to lean against him once more. "Here," I said, and I laid the ring in his palm. "Don't tell me to keep it. I'd feel better if you turned it in for old gold, though. I'd rather not think of someone else wearing it. And, Harry, you tell Janice whatever you want to about the money. Make up any excuse, but don't tell her it was mine. It mustn't be one more hurdle between us. I'd rather not see her now. She'll understand that."

I know he followed me to the hall. I think he called to me as I started up the stairs. But I didn't look back. I didn't pause to draw a long breath till I had reached my room. Maggie was there, going through her evening routine of turning down bedcovers.

"Miss Emily," she began, "that dog of yours has been pawing at the spread again. She's too smart, that one, for comfort."

"Oh, now, Maggie," I protested, "you know she never jumps on furniture. She's been trained not to."

"She's trained herself to twist her claws in the fringe

and drag it down where she can make a fine soft nest. If you don't believe me, look at the hairs on it."

I refused to take an interest in Bridget's accomplishments, and Maggie went on with her folding and straightening. I slumped down at my desk and shuffled through a pile of letters. I had no wish for conversation just then, but still Maggie lingered, obviously manufacturing unnecessary tasks.

"Miss Emily," she began again, touching my arm to draw my attention. "I took the liberty of telling old Jo you went to the funeral. I was sure that's where you were going. It isn't often I break out about what I'm not supposed to know. But I was sitting with him this afternoon while it was going on, and I couldn't think of no other way to give him comfort. I think you'd ought to tell him about it to-morrow. It's taken him hard—his mind feeling one way about young Jo and his heart another."

"All right, Maggie, I'll see him to-morrow. I wish he wouldn't take it this way."

"I've tried to talk him out of it. 'Jo,' I says, ' you stop calling that grandson of yours stubborn. Maybe we're the stubborn ones, you and me. Maybe our minds have got stiff along with our knees, and we won't give in to it.' But he just lays there and says nothing makes sense any more."

I laid down the letters and sat looking up into that plain face, whose blunt features had been familiar to me for longer than I could remember. Looking at Maggie Flynn always made me feel young and inexperienced. That was strange, I thought, remembering that for nearly forty years her life had been lived vicariously through ours. Yet she possessed some secret formula, like that of the ancient alchemists, for turning our little triumphs, our weaknesses, and our shortcomings into wisdom.

"Lots of things don't make sense to me any more," I told her. "Right and wrong and tragedy and happiness—I can't seem to tell where one begins and the other ends nowadays."

"Maybe we're not supposed to," she said, folding her

arms over the bedspread she held. "'Tisn't as easy as sorting out linen from cotton or real silver from plated."

I had no answer for that, though there was much that I could have found to say to her that night. She made no move to go, and I saw she was looking at my hands. Her eyes were on the finger that looked bare now without Harry's ring.

"You're tired, Miss Emily," she said at last, "and no wonder. I've known a long time how things were and how they'd have to end. It wasn't for me to speak out, and it wouldn't have done the least good if I had. But I keep right on seeing what I see, and I tell you you're alive now —like no one else around here is."

"What—what do you mean, Maggie? Haven't I always been alive?"

Her forehead puckered into deeper grooves above the rims of her spectacles.

"Oh, yes, in a way, I guess," she admitted, "but just middling. You put me in mind of that climbing rose used to be by the front porch. Just kind of held its own there, nothing more. Soil was too rich for it, not enough grit and sand to make it take hold. Once it got moved over where it had to turn to and do for itself, it started to pick up and bloom. You remember what it's like now every summer?"

"Yes," I said, "I remember. Good-night, Maggie."

CHAPTER THIRTY-FOUR

I DID not know that my visit to the ell storeroom would take me so far into the past. I did not guess how painful I should find some of the going. But I have doubled back on my tracks at last and caught up with the present. When I have set the last word on paper I shall have no need to open that door again upon the accumulated souvenirs and possessions. I shall no longer be haunted by what lies dusty and discarded behind it.

It has not been easy, these months since I returned from the silent shore where deafness had kept me so long. Once I thought that regaining my hearing would solve all my problems, but now I know it has only made me more aware of them.

"He that hath ears to hear, let him hear." I say that over and over to myself each day. For it is not enough to listen with restored ears. I must listen with a restored mind and heart as well. That is my particular obligation; the only payment I can make for a gift that was lost and returned to me. I must listen to the sounds of earth and to the voices of men and women as if I were hearing them for the first and the last time.

I had to come back to Blairstown to rid myself of its hold. It may be different for those who live in big cities, yet even there one cannot escape the pangs of recognition. Landmarks are everywhere under the sun. Here, it seemed to me, I could not find a house or a tree or a postbox without some personal association. Each was like a tombstone marking some memory I wanted to forget: here he kissed me; here we met by chance; here we were happy; here I stumbled crying past that fence-post. Walking the streets of Blairstown was a daily penance for me when I first returned after the six months I spent working and undergoing further treatments in the hospital in New York.

Just now I have been in to settle Aunt Em for the night. We have played our evening game of double Canfield on the table by her couch, and I have blessed for the thousandth time the human ingenuity that went into the evolution of a pack of playing cards. Just so we sat the afternoon when I told her of my break with Harry Collins. It came as the second shock to her that day, for Dr. Weeks had been the one to tell her of my cure. A shock of joy; a shock of pain. I was glad that I had let him bring her the good news first. I needed all my strength to meet her questions and protests. I can see her pale, dry fingers now with the familiar rings as she shuffled the cards and laid them out in formation.

"Emily dear," she had said across the table and the black and red of the suits her hands were sorting, "if anything could make me rise up from this bed and go down on my knees it would be what I've heard to-day. There's nothing that young Dr. Vance could ask that I wouldn't give him for what he's given you and all of us. I can't get over it yet, that he should have been the one when all the rest failed. But there must be some queer kind of pattern behind it: his coming from across the river; his father that crazy troublemaker at the mills. It's—it's shaken me."

I tried to explain about Merek Vance and his discovery, and all that it might mean to the world of medicine. But she had not been able to think beyond what it had done for me. Her gratitude and relief must keep turning back to that and to her plans for my future.

"I don't question your keeping these treatments secret, dear," she said, and there had been the shadow of reproach in her eyes. "You've been through so much strain and disappointment I can understand how you might feel you couldn't take me into your confidence. But Dr. Weeks says no one but you three knew—not even Harry. I don't see how you could have helped telling him, the man you're going to marry."

The moment had come. I swallowed hard and kept my eyes fixed on the cards spread out on the table. I remember

s

I even reached out and moved a black seven to a red eight before I answered.

"I'm not going to marry Harry Collins," I said before I could trust myself to look up. "That's what I came to tell you."

It was easier once the words were spoken. One thing I have learned in all these months. What we dread to face is always simpler than we expect. It may be more painful, more bitter, but always simpler.

The hardest part was that she blamed herself as much as she blamed Harry and Janice. For days she brooded on it, and I could do nothing to ease her. Even now, though she is beginning to be reconciled to the inevitable, I think she still believes she might have prevented what happened if she had been farsighted enough. Aunt Em has never learned to accept compromise in any form. The code she has laid down for herself is inflexible. She cannot understand any deviation from it in those she loves.

"I should have known," she said over and over in those days after the first shock of revelation; "I should have sensed trouble ahead. I ought to have seen that you and Harry were married as soon as you recovered from that terrible illness. Instead I urged you from one doctor to another. It doesn't excuse me that I thought I was doing it for the best. I should have known somehow——"

"But, Aunt Em," I would protest wearily. "How could you possibly have known? How could any of us know? Love isn't predictable. It's an unknown quantity. I counted on it too much. Maybe that's why this had to happen. But at least we don't have to keep saying, 'If only we'd done this or hadn't done that!'"

"Oh, Emily, if you weren't so brave about it all!"

"Please, I'm not brave, Aunt Em. I'm just trying to be practical. It's worse to go over and over things. I don't believe love can ever be patched together again, once it's broken, and I'm not going to spend the rest of my life torturing myself by fitting the pieces together."

"I can't help thinking how different it might have been

if your father and mother had lived. They would have known what to do. They wouldn't have failed you the way I have."

"I'm not so sure of that," I had to remind her. "You always did the best you could for Janice and me when we were little. When we grew up we had to go our separate ways. It wasn't any fault of yours if we didn't do what you expected of us."

I remember thinking, as I said those words, of the words my father had spoken years ago on the boat that brought us back from France.

"Always do what's expected of you, little Emily. I never did."

Certainly I had not lived up to his advice. I wondered if he could have guessed, holding my small, untried hand in his, how difficult it would be for me to benefit by his warning.

I remembered how he had also charged me to be happy for Aunt Em's sake; to make up to her for what she had missed in her life. Unconsciously I realised that obligation had stayed with me through the years. I had tried to live for her satisfaction as well as for my own. At first it had been natural and easy. The pattern of our lives had followed much the same course. I had acted and reacted as she might have done. She had approved of my engagement to Harry Collins because he was the suitable sort of young man she might have married in her own youth. Yet, subtly, imperceptibly our patterns had begun to vary. Against my will I had broken through mine and left her hurt and baffled. Perhaps, I thought, Janice's particular brand of ruthlessness was kinder in the end.

I found it almost impossible to speak of Janice in the days immediately following that hurried marriage in a nearby city. I had thought that we were strangers, but I could have met losing Harry to a stranger with more fortitude. Old associations, old grudges, and old jealousies were always rising up to confound me. Yet family condemnation of her was so fierce that I was forced to defend her sometimes. The intensity of Aunt Em's bitterness centred on Janice. Harry had been weak and faithless, but Janice had deliberately preyed upon his weaknesses and set out to steal him from me. Aunt Em's vocabulary failed her when she tried to give full vent to her feelings about Janice's betrayal.

"It was bad enough for Harry," she kept insisting, "after all we've done for him, here and at the mills, to let himself be swept off his feet while you were away trying to get back your hearing. But he wouldn't have fallen into the trap if it hadn't been deliberately set. There's no getting round that. I thought Janice was just young and careless and on the flighty side, and all the time she was bad—bad through and through. There's no other name for it."

"Please, let's leave Janice out of this," I would plead. "I'm beginning to understand that we can't fight against our feelings sometimes. It only makes them grow stronger than we are in the end. And let's be honest about one thing—love isn't something that can be trapped and caught. You can't steal it from someone unless that person has lost it already. I didn't want to believe that. But I've had to."

Merek Vance was the only one I could turn to without having to be constantly on my guard. With him I could talk without restraint or say nothing as I might feel inclined. My reactions to sound were steadily increasing with each treatment. I was beginning to hear voices more or less clearly now, though I missed many words unless I depended upon the motion of lips.

"We'll have to give you daily blindfold tests," he used to say with a smile. "You were always so clever at lip reading you fooled most people into thinking you could hear, and now you'll be fooling yourself."

I remember the day of the big demonstration down by the mill gates and how we were together in his office when the police-car sirens shrilled and the distant crackle of gun-fire came in sharp staccato from across the river. We looked at each other, knowing that what we had feared was happening. He laid down the needle and syringe and reached for his bag. He did not speak, but I saw him quickly slipping in extra paraphernalia before he started away.

"You're going down there?" I asked. "Let me go, too." But I had to obey when he shook his head. I watched him run down the path to his car and drive away leaving me more alone and useless than I had ever felt in my life before.

I must have waited hours in his office, moving restlessly from chair to window, only to repeat the process a few moments later. Twilight came, the street lamps went on outside, but still I made no move to go or to turn on the light by the desk. The firing had stopped across the river. I strained my ears against the stillness. But the emergency searchlight in the millyard had begun to sweep the dark like some ominous white finger.

"What! Still here!" Vance stumbled against me in the dimness.

He snapped the lights on quickly and I saw that his face was grave. One cheek showed a large bluish bruise.

"That's nothing," he answered my look. "I took a couple of cracks intended for someone else. I should have worn my white coat and looked more like a doctor." He tried to smile without much success before he went on. "Scab trouble again, and a pretty general free-for-all. Picket line charged the shift coming out, and the guard tried to scare them. They fired in the air mostly, but a few picketers were hit and plenty of others beaten up and gassed. It's a bad business, and we haven't seen the end of it."

I knew he was speaking the truth then, and I know even more surely now with Peace-Pipe Industries shut down for the last six months and the workers' houses clustered about it half-empty of occupants. The mill whistle no longer punctuates the day into ordered periods of morning, noon, and night. The chimneys rise gaunt against smokeless skies, and no pulse of machinery beats behind brick walls and windows. The Wawickett River flows on unhindered below the bridges, its dams open now since there is no need of its power. I have read of ghost towns, and I am reminded of such as I take my daily walks across the river. But it seems less like that to me than like some deserted beehive that once swarmed and hummed with activity.

I do not pretend to understand all that has gone into the failure of Peace-Pipe Mills. Uncle Wallace and the directors blame the strike for paralysing production at a critical time. Those more sympathetic to union demands insist that recognition by the company would have saved the mills from discord and disintegration. Others merely shrug and lay the whole collapse to business conditions which are slowly but surely shutting down other industries all over the country. All I know is that something living and vital went out of the mills after those last bitter spurts of spirit by the strikers and the harsh violence that went into curbing them. I only know that business dwindled, diverted to larger companies, and that the banks finally withdrew their backing. Peace-Pipe has gone into receivership, and there are rumours that it will soon be consolidated with one of the great cotton and textile companies that control a score of smaller units.

The trademark of the Indian in his proud feathers with his legend of "Peace-Pipe for Quality," if he survives at all, will no longer stand for the ideals of a family-dominated industry. Already that painted image on the board by the railroad station is beginning to show signs of the times. His paint is peeling and dented, and he seems, in more ways than one, the symbol of a vanishing race. I want no part of him or what he has stood for, and yet I am glad I shall not be here to see his final humiliation. For to me he will always belong to the years that changed my life and the lives of all of us who lived through them in Blairs-town. Hardly any one mentions young Jo Kelly now. But down there in the dingy frame houses where women hang out their lines of washing and stand patiently for donations of food and coal, where men pick up any chance at an odd job and wait grimly for something to turn up, down there I think he is remembered for what he was and what he tried to be. I know that for me he will always be there, a solitary, unseen picket keeping faith by the mill gates.

Merek Vance and I talked of Jo Kelly and of Blairstown on our last meeting many months ago. It was late spring in New York, and we sat together in a little park near the hospital where I had gone at his urging. There must be further tests and examinations by a group of specialists who were organising a clinic to develop and perfect the Vance method of stimulating impaired nerve cells. He had persuaded me to go there after a long session of arguments. I had wanted to stay at home. It had seemed like running away from my own problems and associations just when I had begun to meet their challenge. But once more his firm insistence had overcome my prejudices. I know now that he was wiser than I.

"You need more help than I could give you even if I stayed on to see you through," he had said, handing me a sheaf of wires all urgently summoning him to work with his associates at important medical centres. "I can't very well refuse to accept such offers, now we've proved the cure is effective. You helped me to prove that, and it's up to you to go on contributing yourself—so, don't start that argument about not wanting to act the guinea pig. We've had that all out before. Besides, you can work with other deaf patients. The clinic will keep you so busy you won't have time to think, and that's what you need right now, whether you know it or not."

So I gave in and let Merek Vance arrange for my stay at the hospital when he left to take up his new duties. I had to fortify myself against wistful looks and disapproval at home. Aunt Em was well enough for Dr. Weeks and Maggie to care for her, though it was evident that she would not regain full use of her legs. The fracture had mended, but she would never again move without stiffness or pain, and her heart must be guarded against the strain of exertion. She would be a semi-invalid for the rest of her life. We all knew it, and so we all avoided acknowledging the fact.

Uncle Wallace had been against my leaving, but he accepted it finally. Peace-Pipe Mills and the shadow of failure that was gradually engulfing them were the only realities for him in those days before the final shutdown. It was Maggie Flynn who stood by me in the decision to go. I think if I had weakened at the last moment she would have taken her broom in hand and swept me out of the front door.

"You've had trouble enough here," she had said as she helped me with my packing. "I don't mean there can't be plenty of it for anybody anywhere, but you're too young to go into storage yet. Time enough for that when you're old like me and used to the smell of camphor and moth balls."

She had smiled grimly as she spoke, but I noticed that she kept her eyes lowered.

"It's not that I want to run away from what has to be faced, Maggie," I tried to explain. "I'm past minding the gossip or the looks or knowing that people know—about Harry Collins and me. That's over and done with now. I'll come back when I've done all I can to help at the hospital. Blairstown hasn't seen the last of me yet."

Maggie had listened, her long arms continuing to smooth and fold a dress of mine to fit my trunk. I can see her now, standing stiff and unyielding on the worn roses of my bedroom carpet. She seemed, as she had told me herself, like a part of the furniture. When she spoke, it was almost as if a familiar table or chair had passed judgment upon me after years of silence.

"You'll be back maybe, but not to stay. This town doesn't fit people same's it used to. You and Dr. Vance now—you're both grown too big for it, and folks can't squeeze back into clothes they've outgrown, no matter how hard they may try to."

So I had gone away to plunge into the experience of work that was new and often difficult for me to accomplish. I was to be a volunteer worker in the clinic in ex-

change for the care I was to receive. It wasn't easy for me
to adjust to long hours or to taking orders like any other
unskilled probationer. I was clumsy and stupid at first, un-
used to the routine and the following of even simple rules.
But the doctors and nurses were patient with my ineptitudes,
and after the early weeks of adjustment I began to improve.
For the first time in my life I was paying my own way
with hard work.

Looking back to that period in the hospital clinic, I
realise that my services must have been far more on the
debit than the credit side of the ledger. I think that only
medical curiosity in my case and Vance's influence kept
me on. But I tried as I had never tried to succeed at anything before. I was interviewed for hours by visiting
doctors and put through long and exhausting tests. I helped
with case histories and filing reports, and I made myself
useful with the deaf patients who came for the injections.
I was best at that, especially with timid children or the
confused older people who had not learned to read lips.
Perhaps the fact that I was myself still a little dazed and
bewildered made a bond between us. In time the staff came
to recognise that and to let me deal with patients in my own
way. They accepted me after a fashion, though I never
achieved skill or efficiency.

In those months I saw Merek Vance whenever he came
to the hospital for consultations. But these were infre-
quent, for he was dividing his services between several
medical units. Once he asked me to appear before a large
group of doctors at a conference where he was to deliver a
lecture. I dreaded the ordeal and the questions which I
must meet.

"It's the penalty for being my prize patient," he smiled
when he came to take me to the meeting. "But we'll celebrate when it's over. We'll have dinner afterwards and a
whole evening to ourselves. You're working too hard, I'm
afraid, but it's becoming to you. No, I don't mean your
hat and dress, though I approve of them. I'm glad you
wore blue. I've always liked you in it."

It pleased and surprised me to have him say that. I hadn't thought he noticed what I put on.

When Merek Vance rose to speak I felt as I had felt on that winter night in Angeletta's kitchen. Once more he was in command, and once more he carried assurance with him. Seeing him there among others of his profession I was more than ever conscious of his quiet authority. He looked young, almost boyish, beside the doctors who crowded the auditorium. The light from the reading-desk where he had spread out his notes edged his thin face, making the features stand out in sharp relief: the dark brows and wide-set eyes; the high cheekbones, the full, expressive lips and prominent chin. He seemed charged with vigour and intelligence that brought a quiver of response from his listeners the moment he began to speak.

There were no easy words of introduction. He plunged headlong into his subject with a kind of impatient exuberance that had no time to waste on trivialities. Sometimes he paused to elaborate on his notes with quick, lucid explanations and concrete examples. Unknown phrases and medical terms confused me again and again, but always the sense of the words and the power of the voice that carried them swept me along.

Sitting there in my seat below the platform, I felt awed and alone. It was as if I had lost Merek Vance and the bare little Blairstown office forever. Once we had shared it, but now he had gone on—it frightened me to think how far. He could not escape from the dignity of accomplishment which would be recognised wherever he went. Once, long ago, I had stood on another platform, a little girl holding a squirrel muff, and he had been a shabby, long-legged boy looking up from the crowd below in the mill-yard.

Queer, I thought, the way things work out. But Aunt Em was right. There's a sort of pattern behind it all.

I was glad that I had remembered. It didn't seem to matter that our positions had been reversed in the years between.

After the meeting was over and I had been through my part of the questions and open discussion that followed, Merek Vance and I drove to a small Italian restaurant near the Medical School where he had studied. We sat outside under a striped awning, our table a part of the sidewalk so that we could have reached out and touched passersby without moving from our places.

"Thanks for this afternoon," he said. "You did me proud. I hope you didn't mind too much."

I watched his strong hands breaking one of the chunks of crisp bread, and I must have smiled, for he turned to me with a curious tilt to his brows.

"What are you thinking to make you look like that?"

"Oh, only that you've done about everything except box my ears, and you must have wanted to do that a good many times. I guess you'll never have a more difficult patient than I've been."

"I'm not making any predictions," he laughed. "Here comes the soup. If it's not as good as it used to be I'll know for certain I'm growing old and critical."

We had progressed to coffee before he showed me the telegram with the offer from the Pacific Coast. I knew he was watching me intently as I read and reread the words. Here was recognition and opportunity that come to few: his own laboratory and assistants for further research; financial endowment for the future if he would join the staff of a great western medical centre.

"Well," he asked when I handed back the slip of paper, "what do you think I should do about it?"

I started at his words.

"You're asking me?" I stammered. "Why should you when you've always seemed so sure where you were going?"

"But I am asking you," he persisted. "I think I've earned the right to know how you feel."

"I don't see how you could refuse. It means everything for your future and a chance to go on without worrying over a practice." I smiled as I pushed back my coffee-cup, and went on: "Speaking from personal experience, I doubt

if you'd be very successful at that. You're apt to forget to
send your patients their bills."

That had come to be a joke between us. He acknowledged
it with his lips, but his eyes stayed grave. We said little
as we jolted uptown on a lumbering green bus. We did
not return at once to the apartment house near the hospital
where I had taken a room. The night stayed warm and
soft with spring and river mist. We found an empty bench
under a plane-tree that was just putting out new leaves.

"It feels like Blairstown to-night," I said when we had
settled ourselves. "I mean there's the same smoke and grit
mixed with river damp."

"Yes," he agreed, "and across the Hudson there are
plenty of factories full of workers wondering what's ahead
for them. It's like that everywhere. I've seen a lot of mill
towns since I've been travelling around. You'll find they're
all pretty much alike, whatever they produce: same chimneys, same smoke, same whistles, same river, mostly,
dividing the two sides of town."

I have remembered his words. I have thought of them
often as I crossed the bridges over the Wawickett since my
return.

"Peace-Pipe Mills are closing soon," I told him. "I suppose you heard. That means Aunt Em and Uncle Wallace
are going to need me till they grow more used to the change.
It won't be easy to fit into their ways again, but I'm going
back. Not just for them—there are things I have to see
through for myself. No one can do it for me."

This time he did not question my decision.

"All right," he said, "go back. You'll have to lay the
ghosts in your own way. I know all about that. You
helped me get rid of mine. You didn't know that day in
the North Station when the baggage truck nearly ran you
down how close I was to turning tail. Seeing you put me
on my mettle; made me want to lick the town and what it
had done to me and my family. I hated you that day, and
yet your deafness was a challenge I couldn't resist."

After that we were silent. Perhaps because there was so

much I wanted to say I found that words were difficult to summon. I think, too, that unconsciously we were both missing the familiar boundaries of the little Blairstown office. Always before, even when we had talked most intimately, most honestly together, we had not been alone. Harry Collins had been there with us. His presence had dominated my life for so long, and now suddenly it was gone. The knowledge made me shy and constrained as I had never been with Merek Vance before.

"It seems queer," he spoke as if he knew my thoughts, "not to be jotting notes down on that folder marked ' Emily Blair.' I——" His arm pressed closer between my shoulder and the wooden bench rail. "I can't help missing that even though I'm glad you're well over the bad stretch. It'll be easier going from now on."

I knew what he was trying to say and that it was for me to speak first on a subject I had avoided.

"I suppose you know that Harry—that they're living in Pennsylvania," I said. "He got work in some smelting and iron company."

Vance nodded.

"As a matter of fact I saw them both when I was out that way a month ago. They had a pretty tough time of it for a while. But they've stuck together and they're happy . . . because they're right for each other."

"Yes," I answered. "I don't resent that the way I used to. It's as if I were someone else who felt like that once."

"You can't keep scar tissue from growing over," he reminded me; "inside or outside, it's the same."

"I'm glad they went away from Blairstown," I said. "Janice never fitted in. Her roots aren't there the way mine will always be."

His shoulders jerked in the familiar shrug of impatience. Once more he turned on me with the old ruthlessness.

"There you go!" he burst out. "As if roots were all that mattered!"

"Well," I protested, "you'll have to admit they're rather important."

"Of course they are, but so are branches. I'd say the farther a tree grew away from its roots the more life it had in it. And that goes for people too."

"Meaning . . . me?"

"Yes, meaning you." His arm tightened about me. "It's been a fight all the way for both of us and I'm not letting you settle back now. I know what you've been up against . . . half-smothered with comfort and conventionality . . . too much background and not enough room to turn round in and face the present or the future. Any millworker's daughter had a better chance to come through alive than you had. I have to give you credit for that. Maybe it was your deafness that kept you from being completely caught. If you hadn't had that to meet and if you'd married the man you loved when you wanted to——"

"Please," I begged, "let's not talk about that."

But he cut me short.

"I've earned the right to talk about love or anything else to you. I'm through keeping hands off your life and your feelings. I had to keep still about a lot of things before. It wasn't easy to sit back and see you dominated by a shadow. Yes, you were clinging to a shadow though you wouldn't admit it."

"I know, now," I told him. "But it's harder to shake off shadows than realities sometimes. That's one reason why I know I must go back to Blairstown. You're right about roots and branches. I'll do my best to grow in the right direction."

"And I'll make sure that you do." I could not see his face in the darkness, yet I knew the expression that would be on his lips and behind his eyes. "Go on back to that old house and those old people," he urged. "I want you to. I can wait while you prove to yourself that you're no longer part of them. We'll know, both of us, when you're free for to-morrow."

We must have spoken other words after that, but I do not recall them. I remember rather the lights on the Jersey shore as I saw them over his shoulder; the moisture of river mist turning to rain; the strong swift pressure of his lips on mine as he left me at my doorstep and strode away down the lengths of wet asphalt.

Even then I did not know as I watched him out of sight how great was to be my need of him at every turn. I did not dare to believe that he might also come to have such need of me. But these months have made me know that he does and that we must go on together.

To-night, sitting in a room that seems suddenly to belong to someone else, I shall lay away these pages, for they have answered their purpose. Perhaps it was foolish to imagine that the first quarter of one's life should be recorded. Memories will withdraw into their right perspective if we let them have their way. On the desk before me is a long railroad ticket stamped with the names of many places. These are strange to me, all but the last one which I know from the familiar postmark on the letters I have watched for week after week. Once I might have faltered before such a transplanting. But that was yesterday. Now I am ready for to-morrow.

THE END